# THE BLIGHT

**by Lee Morrow**

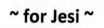

~ for Jesi ~

# THE BLIGHT

Lee Morrow

# TABLE OF CONTENTS

Chorma is a magnificent nation, a modern workers' paradise, and its citizens are all very happy to live there. The Chormans lucky enough to live in the city of Khostok are especially proud of the Lubukov Agricultural Laboratories, where researchers work tirelessly to develop the most cutting-edge scientific techniques for feeding their Motherland.

Of course there are malcontents who claim that the research done by the Labs is not exactly of the agricultural sort -- but it is very unpatriotic to say these sorts of things aloud, and the Department of Internal Observation keeps a close eye on those who spread such baseless rumors.

The true nature of the Labs is revealed on the day that an experimental biochemical weapon leaks into the city's water supply, and the quarantining of Khostok begins. For those who drink the tainted water develop a syndrome known as the blight, which stains their skin and drives them insane. The military can not control them; science can not comprehend them. And the madness that spreads through Khostok is only the beginning...

# A NOTE ON RUSSIAN NAMING CONVENTIONS

Though Chorma is not in Russia, as a part of the Soviet Union they are certainly under Russian influence. For this reason I have tried to maintain Russian naming conventions for the characters wherever possible.

Russian names include a person's given name (Alexei), the patronymic taken from the father's name (Nikolaevich, "son of Nikolai"), and the surname (Raikov). For women, the patronymic usually ends in -evna (as in Yuryevna, "daughter of Yuri") and the surname often takes an -a ending (SokolovA instead of Sokolov.)

In polite company the given name + patronymic (Alexei Nikolaevich) are often used together. In addition, a nickname (Lyosha) is used by friends and family. For convenience here is a reference table for the characters' nicknames:

Alexei - Lyosha

Elena - Lena

Grigori - Grisha

Ivan - Vanya

Nikita - Nixa

Tatyana - Tanya

Veronika - Nika

Vadim - Vadik

Vasili - Vasya

Yuri - Yura

# CHAPTER ONE

Gun in hand, Dmitri stood facing the breaker box. The fuses were all helpfully labeled by room and floor -- L2 ADMIN OFC, L1 LAB A, G REC DESK, U1 LAB B, U2 STORAGE, etc. -- but he wasn't reading the labels; in fact he wasn't seeing the breaker box at all.

No, Dmitri was seeing cars. Big, beautiful American cars. Cars with dazzling chrome details and enameled paint as bright and shining as candy. Those were the cars he was dreaming of. And if it was unpatriotic to want an American car or two, then so be it. What he was about to do was not so terribly patriotic either; his capitalist fantasies were just another thing to add to the pile.

Dmitri raised his gun and fired three rounds into the breaker box. It blew outward at once, vomiting sparks onto his lab coat as it died. In that same instant the facility known as Lubukov Agricultural Laboratories, also known to government officials as the Lubukov Bureau of Bioweapon Research, lost power. Darkness fell like a hammer.

On the ground floor, one level above the breaker box Dmitri had just destroyed, a group of researchers were just sitting down in the Labs' cafeteria for their dinner. The sudden blackness caught them in mid-stride. One or two people swore aloud, someone tripped over the leg of their chair, and a junior researcher named Alexei was so badly startled he dropped his dinner tray. There was a crash and a wet splattering, and someone yelped in surprise.

"What's this? what's going on?"

"The lights went out!"

"No, the power's out...listen, listen," someone shouted. The brief silence that followed was deafening. "Nothing's running at all. The whole building's lost power."

There was a groan. "Wonderful, simply wonderful."

"But -- what about our project? We need to keep the compounds refrigerated...we've spent months on the synthesis, this is going to destroy all that work!"

Multiple voices began commiserating loudly about the soon-to-be-ruined project. Alexei took a hesitant step forward, and his shoe came down in something that squished.

"Aren't we supposed to have backup generators?"

"Yes, and they're probably broken! Just like everything else in this miserable place."

"But the inspector was just here last month!"

"Of course! and I'm sure he walked out with a nice present from the Security Chief too! Twice your monthly salary, just to overlook the little details like those generators."

"Ah, I've had enough of this. I'm going out for a cigarette. If any of you -- "

From somewhere below them came a dull, muffled boom, like a distant cannon. The floor quivered beneath their feet.

" -- what was *that*?" someone shrilled.

"Maybe something fell over?"

"That was an explosion!"

"Nonsense, this isn't a munitions factory!"

"...something in refrigeration, maybe," whispered a voice, nearly at Alexei's elbow. "When the power failed..."

His heart had leapt into his throat and Alexei swallowed hard, trying to force it back down. Telling himself not to think about that noise -- and it had certainly sounded like an explosion to him -- Alexei shuffled backwards, away from his spilled dinner. He accidentally kicked his empty bowl and it rolled away, metal clattering on the tile. He froze again.

"Well, if the whole building is going to blow up -- " someone began, and at that moment the lights came back on.

There were multiple sighs of relief. Blinking against the light, which was dazzling after those few minutes in total darkness, Alexei looked around and saw the researchers getting back into their seats, grumbling and muttering. He discovered that he'd splashed both his shoes when he'd dropped his dinner and a generous puddle had gathered around his feet.

"Need any help?"

The offer came from someone seated a few chairs away, a tall lanky fellow with overlong brown hair and oversized glasses. Alexei had seen him in the hallway a few times and thought he might have been one of the senior researchers, but couldn't be sure. "I'm fine," Alexei mumbled, and went off in search of paper towels.

"Guess you were wrong about those generators, eh?"

"If the power failure ruined those compounds -- "

"Did something explode?"

"I'll bet it did -- and you can be sure they'll blame us for it too."

As a matter of fact, something had exploded. The fault, however, lay not with the researchers but with a previously insignificant lab assistant named Dmitri. He was the sole party responsible for the events that followed, though it must be said that his incredible good luck played a part in the disaster that would come to the Lubukov "Agricultural Labs", and to the city of Khostok that surrounded it.

Dmitri had the good -- or bad -- fortune to be just arriving outside the door of Cold Storage #5 when the volatile compounds within, kept under refrigeration that had failed some minutes ago, reached their critical temperature and detonated. Their insulated containers turned into shrapnel grenades and shards of glass and metal were blasted throughout the cold storage compartment, shattering multiple other containers in the process. Had he been a minute too early Dmitri would have been inside the storage room when the blast occurred, and the sequence of events that led to what would later be known as the Khostok Disaster might never have happened at all.

The door of Cold Storage #5 shuddered in its frame from the force of the explosion. Dmitri froze with his hand on the door handle, nearly dropping his flashlight onto the floor of the darkened room. He knew at once what had happened -- the chemicals in cold storage were kept refrigerated for a reason -- and only the urgency of the situation pressed him onward.

The generators would be up and running any minute now. And once the power was restored the electronic ID-badge readers, like the one mounted outside the door of Cold Storage #5, would resume normal functioning. When that happened the manual override keys he'd gone to so much trouble to steal would become useless bits of metal again.

With trembling fingers Dmitri inserted his key in the lock and turned it. A blast of cold air hit his face as the door swung open, reeking sharply of a half-dozen spilled chemical compounds. Dmitri held his breath and stepped into storage, swinging the flashlight beam around the rows of shelves. Broken glass glittered like diamonds in the dim light.

It seemed like nearly all of the storage containers had fractured, and for a moment the anxiety was like a hand clenching around his insides. He spun around, glass crunching underfoot...and then he spotted it.

The stuff was on the third shelf from the top, all the way over on the right-hand side of the storage room, near the door. It was the color that gave it away: the liquid in the sealed glass tubes was a purplish-black, thick and opaque. Its technical designation was UEC-571, but those researching it had quickly dropped the multi-syllable title in favor of a shorter nickname. Around the lab UEC-571 was known simply as "ink".

There were five bottles there, mercifully intact, and Dmitri grabbed the lot of them and crammed them into the pocket of his lab coat. Adrenaline surged through his veins, making him feel lightheaded, almost giddy. He had the stuff, the ink, five little bottles worth thousands upon thousands of American dollars. It meant any place he wanted to go, any pleasure he could fathom...any car he wanted. He would have a whole garageful of them once this was all over.

Now all he had to do was escape from the Labs with the stuff.

When the ancient and ill-maintained generators finally brought the lights flickering back on, Dmitri's heart sank. He hastily switched the flashlight off and tucked it into his pants pocket, near the gun that nestled under his belt. Then he forced himself to slow from a jog to a brisk walk, gritting his teeth against the desire to sprint down the hallway. The bottles clinked together merrily in his lab coat pocket and he put a hand on them.

Dmitri was still on U2, the second underground floor, where the cold storage rooms were located. He desperately needed to reach the ground floor and get out into parking lot before anybody traced that explosion down to Cold Storage #5. Preferably he would be well out of Khostok before they noticed the ink was missing. He was pretty certain that the destruction wrought by the exploding containers would distract them from noticing the theft right away, but now he could no longer rely on the power outage for a diversion.

The door that led into the stairwell lay directly before him, and Dmitri couldn't resist the urge to start jogging again. He was reaching out for the handle when the door swung open of its own accord, and he leapt backward in surprise as a man emerged from the stairwell.

"Dmitri Arkadievich! Hey, how are you?"

And of all the people who might have intercepted Dmitri on his flight from the Labs, it would have to be Yevgeny. Red-faced and full of unwanted goodwill, Yevgeny slapped his fellow lab assistant on the shoulder. "What're you doing down here? you felt that earthquake too, eh?"

Dmitri swayed, his mind swimming with money and cars and ink and wildly ringing alarms. He'd started to mumble something about washing up some glassware when Yevgeny looked down. "Ah, what's that?"

Dmitri looked too. There was a dark purplish-black stain on his lab coat, starting from the bottom of one pocket and spreading across the white fabric like the bloom of a dark flower. It was growing larger even as he watched it, horrified. Clearly not all of the bottles had survived the explosion intact; or perhaps they'd struck one another and cracked while he was running.

"I think your pen is leaking, comrade." Yevgeny chuckled and reached for the pocket, leaning close enough for Dmitri to practically taste the vodka on his breath. "Your coat -- "

The gunshot echoed in the empty hallway, startling them both. Dmitri had barely given himself enough time to draw it before pulling the trigger, and the shot buried itself in Yevgeny's sagging paunch. The drunk man took a step back, blinking at his stomach, then looked up at Dmitri. Then the second bullet struck him in the forehead, and the light went out of Yevgeny's eyes.

Dmitri pelted up the stairs, taking the steps two at a time and half-sobbing as he gasped for air. There was no time to think about it now; time was a luxury he didn't have. Maybe later, much later, when he was sitting on the cream-colored calfskin of the driver's seat in his enormous, gleaming American car, he would give himself a chance to think about what he'd done. He could curse himself as a fool and a murderer then, and feel sorry for poor Yevgeny. But now he simply hadn't the time for it.

He was on the ground floor now, shoes slapping the tiled floor of the hallway. The bottles of ink were jingling together again and he clapped his hand over them, then swiftly yanked it away when he felt the slick, oily wetness there. He'd almost forgotten that the ink was soaking through the fabric of his lab coat pocket. Still running, he took one look at his black-smeared hand and swept it along the wall, scrubbing the stain away. He left a broad streak behind on the wall, a glistening black comet trail against the white plaster.

Dmitri almost paused to wonder what, exactly, the ink was supposed to do, or if it was a Very Bad Idea to get any of the stuff onto your exposed skin. But there was no time for that either.

It felt as if it had taken centuries to get from cold storage up to the ground floor, but in reality it had been no more than five minutes since the lights had been restored, even if you counted that tragic interlude with Yevgeny down on U2. Now Dmitri had dropped all pretense of hurrying to the bathroom or rushing to get back from his dinner break -- now he was racing madly down the hall, bursting through the doors into the reception desk area, darting past the other lab employees as they shouted in indignation.

Because there was something else closing in on him now. To discover the missing bottles of ink in cold storage might take hours, and someone was certain to stumble across Yevgeny's body in a matter of minutes...but now these were trivial concerns. The black streak on the white wall had reminded him of something, something far closer on his heels than some hapless intern's discovery of a dead body. Now that the power was back on in the Lubukov Agricultural Labs, all the electrical equipment would be functioning again --

-- including the biohazard sensors.

Dmitri was five steps away from the front doors when the alarms began blaring. He screamed aloud, and several employees who'd been struck motionless by the alarm turned curiously towards him. But today luck was on Dmitri's side, or more correctly, luck was against Khostok. The lab assistant collided with the front door, knocking it open, and he spilled out onto the pavement with a cry of triumph. Ignoring the shocked looks from the smokers loitering outside, Dmitri bounded down the front steps and away from the Labs, making a beeline for his car.

He could scarcely believe he'd escaped. And indeed Dmitri had just barely escaped; not thirty seconds after his shrieking exit from the building the biohazard alarm system remotely locked every single door in the Lubukov Agricultural Labs. The loiterers outside, finished with smoking their cigarettes and laughing about the crazy fellow in the stained lab coat, found themselves unable to get back into the building.

Worried about returning late from their breaks, the ones stuck outside banged on the front doors. It wasn't that they couldn't see the flashing red lights above the door, directly below the plaque that read LUBUKOV AGRICULTURAL LABORATORIES. And they weren't deaf either, so they certainly heard the loud, repetitive blatting of the alarm that accompanied the light. They just failed to register it, or failed to realize that this was not an unplanned drill.

The employees trapped inside the building, who had just become prisoners of the biohazard alarm system, understood the reality of their situation much sooner.

~~~~~

Alexei had just finished cleaning out the last bits of carrot and celery from his shoelaces when the alarm began to sound. His head snapped up.

"What now?!" someone demanded.

A series of muffled *klunk!-klunk!-klunk!* noises rang out, barely audible beneath the wailing of the alarm. Only one or two of the employees present in the cafeteria identified the sound for what it was: the bolts slamming home inside the door locks, all over the facility. The senior researcher with the oversized glasses was one of these people, and he rose slowly to his feet.

As if the lot of them had been mesmerized, all attention was turned to the flashing light mounted on the wall beside the clock. The red glow washed over the silent, upturned faces in waves. There was a sign mounted just beneath the light, clearly legible even from across the room, that read 'BIOLOGICAL HAZARD ALERT'. Tacked up beneath that was a sheet of paper with the correct procedures to follow.

"Maybe's there's a fire," one of the researchers said aloud, in a tone that begged other people to agree with him.

"It's not a fire," the senior researcher said. "That's the biohazard alarm."

Someone in the cafeteria dropped their spoon.

"Biohazard?! why? what's leaking?"

"Something exploded earlier! I knew it!"

"Keep your heads, comrades -- I'm sure it's only a drill!"

*Of course it's only a drill*, Alexei said to himself. *That's all this is, just a practice run. They're testing the alarm system to make sure it's functioning, that's all. And any minute now they'll be through with the test and shut the thing off. Any minute now they'll --*

-- he bolted.

Alexei was across the room before anyone else could react. He threw his weight against the panic bar on the cafeteria door, and when the door refused to give way he rebounded hard enough to go sprawling onto his rear on the tile floor. Dazed, he stared up at the door for a moment, then got to his feet and deliberately shoved down on the bar. It sank back into its socket, but the door didn't budge. He shoved it again, harder this time.

Under the constant, incessant wailing of the alarm Alexei heard something like a human voice, but garbled and distorted so that he couldn't make sense of it. He lunged against the panic bar for the eighth time and that was when the hands fell on him, dragged him back from the door. Someone spun him around and shook him, quite hard, and as if by a miracle the garbled voice snapped back into normal human speech.

" -- until someone comes to deactivate it!"

" -- what?!" Alexei squeaked. Now he could see who was shaking him: it was that long-haired senior researcher, holding him by both shoulders. Alexei moved as if to go back to the door and the fellow gripped him harder.

"The doors are all locked!" The man spoke very slowly and clearly, half-shouting over the noise. "They lock automatically when the alarm is triggered! They're not going to open until someone comes to deactivate it!"

"What?!" Alexei said again, and at that moment the alarm stopped. The sudden stillness was jarring. Everyone in the cafeteria was on their feet, looking around like awakened sleepwalkers.

"It stopped!" someone cried out, their voice tremulous with relief. But the red light on the wall continued to flash, off and on, as steady as a heartbeat.

"The siren -- " began the senior researcher, and Alexei twisted out of his grip, lunging against the door again. It might as well have been a stone wall. Then the taller man was dragging him away from it, a hand under each arm. pulling him back over to the lunch tables.

"It's only a drill -- I told you so!" declared another employee. Someone else was at the door keypad, trying combination after combination, heedless of the blinking 'LOCKED OUT' that flashed on the tiny screen.

"This isn't a drill." The senior researcher pushed Alexei into a chair and stooped down in front of him, bringing the two of them face to face. "Comrade..."

"Huh?" Alexei said, blinking.

"What's your name?"

"...Alexei Nikolaevich." He was coming back into himself by gradual degrees. The adrenaline was draining away too, leaving him shaky and weak. It was the alarm, he decided...now that the awful blaring was gone, he could hear himself thinking again. He began to realize that everyone in the cafeteria was staring at them.

"Good, good. Nice to meet you, Alexei Nikolaevich." The senior researcher patted his shoulder. "My name's Yuri Ivanovich."

"H'lo," Alexei muttered, his face starting to burn.

"Are you alright now, comrade?"

"Yeah."

"Good to hear." Yuri straightened up again. "This isn't a drill," he repeated, addressing the little crowd of employees. "The siren is supposed to cut off after five minutes -- the procedures say so. This is a real alarm."

"But why did the alarm go off?!" someone was asking. "There's nothing toxic in here!"

"Well, nothing except for the soup of the day," Yuri said lightly. Nobody so much as cracked a smile. "But for the alarm to go off, it means there's been biohazardous material detected somewhere in the building," he explained, adopting a more sober tone. "The sensors catch it, the lights and sirens come on, and all the doors are locked remotely. We can't have whatever-it-is leaking out into Khostok."

" -- but what about us?!"

Yuri, who was apparently the only Lubukov Agricultural Labs employee who had bothered to read the Disaster Procedures manual, had fallen into the role of a teacher with a classful of frightened students. "Well, since the danger's not in the lunchroom, and all the doors are sealed tight, we're safe here." He pointed up at the ceiling, and heads turned in that direction. "There's a special ventilation system going right now, just in case whatever-it-is is airborne. Can't you hear it?"

The crowd nodded in assent. Now that the alarm had stopped, the whirring of the fans was quite audible. "It's vacuuming up all the atmospheric particles in all the rooms, sending them down into a special containment chamber."

More eager nodding. A rotund older man with graying hair spoke up. "So once it's through with the vacuuming, the doors unlock?"

"Ah...no." Yuri looked guilty. "When the sensors were triggered it alerted the Security Chief; his role is to notify the authorities to summon a cleanup crew. They'll get a special code from the authorities and the system will make them enter it on every keypad in the building; that's how they'll get us out."

There were various sounds of disbelief. "We have to wait for the cleanup crew to let us out?" "How long will that take?" "What if the Chief doesn't contact anyone?" "We could be in here for days!" "Who's going to tell my wife?", and so on.

In the midst of these complaints, someone knocked loudly on the outside of the cafeteria door. The effect on the lunchroom crowd was instantaneous. "It's the cleanup crew!" a man shouted, and several people went hurrying over to answer it.

"...that can't be the crew," Alexei murmured. Yuri looked down at him, canting his head to one side like a puzzled dog. "Eh?"

"It's been less than ten minutes since the alarm started." Alexei still looked pale, but his voice was steady. "They couldn't have gotten here so quickly."

Yuri nodded. "I suspect you're right," he said gravely. Meanwhile, the crowd gathered at the door were unable to open it. "It's still locked from in here!" they yelled. "You've got to unlock it from the outside!"

"But I'm locked out too!" came the response.

"What? who are you?"

"My name's Vadim Simonovich!" said the voice from outside. "I'm just a lab assistant -- I ran out in the hall when the alarm went off, and now I'm stuck out here!"

"What? Vadik?" The portly older researcher wriggled his way through the crowd, pressing in closer to the door. "Vadik, this is Boris! Can you hear me? You say you're out in the hallway?"

"Yes -- yes, I can hear you!" Vadim replied eagerly. "Yes, I'm stuck out here! all the doors are locked!"

"The stairs, Vadik! Get to the stairs -- try to get up to the first floor! Maybe they can get a window open up there!"

"I've tried it. The stairwell's locked down too."

Groans of disappointment followed the news. "Ah, then we're all stuck waiting on the cleanup crews," Boris sighed. "Anyone else out there with you?"

"No," Vadim answered in a tiny voice. "I've been up and down the hallway and it's just me out here. But I guess someone must've been here a minute ago, because there's this...stuff, all over the wall. Dunno what it is, but it wasn't here this morning."

"...'Stuff'?" Boris echoed. "What stuff?"

"Not sure...some kind of black oily stuff. Someone smudged it all along the wall out here."

The crowd at the door exchanged looks, puzzled. Alexei looked up at Yuri, but Yuri was facing the door now, his eyes widening behind his glasses.

"Maybe this is some guy's idea of vandalism?" Vadim remarked. "It looks like old engine grease, but it doesn't smell like it." He paused. "Nope, it's not engine grease. Maybe -- "

" -- Hey!" Yuri shouted suddenly, rushing toward the door. "Comrade! don't touch it!"

"What?!"

Alarmed by his outburst, the other employees moved aside for Yuri to get past them. "That black stuff -- don't touch it!"

"Why not? what is it? do you know?" Vadim's voice had gone up by an octave or two.

"Nevermind -- did any of it get on you?!"

The man outside hesitated for a long minute. "I - I got it on my fingers," Vadim confessed. "And I...I tasted it."

Yuri swore under his breath. "What's wrong? what is it?!" Boris was asking, and everyone else seemed to be wondering the same.

"I just wanted to see what it was!" Vadim protested. "I only tasted a little bit! Do you know what it is? is it poisonous? tell me!"

All eyes in the room were on Yuri now. "...I don't know what it is," he said finally. "I don't think it's poisonous though. Just...just stay away from it, comrade. There's cleanup crews on the way to the Labs; we'll make sure they have a look at it when they get here." He turned and wandered away from the cafeteria door.

Out in the hallway Vadim continued to panic. "Tell me! tell me what it is! it's going to kill me, isn't it? isn't it?!..."

"Calm down, calm down!" Boris shouted back at him. "You're not going to help yourself by losing your head! Lie down on the floor, take some deep breaths -- "

Boris was still trying to console the young man when Yuri got back to where Alexei was sitting. He sank into the cafeteria chair beside Alexei. Then all in one motion Yuri swept off his glasses and sat forward, putting his head in his hands.

"You know what that stuff is, don't you?" Alexei whispered.

"Not really."

"But you have an idea."

Yuri shrugged, and a knot tightened in Alexei's stomach. "It's bad, isn't it?"

No response.

"...Comrade?"

Nothing.

"Are you alright?"

Yuri stirred. "I'm praying," he mumbled through his fingers.

"You're what?"

"Praying," Yuri said, and then amended, "I'm praying that I'm mistaken about the stuff in the hallway."

~~~~

"You're kidding."

"No sir."

"...the entire facility? all five levels? every single sensor?"

"I'm afraid so, sir. We're lit up all across the board."

There was a longer pause. "You said there was a power outage just before the alert, correct?"

"Correct."

"Now, I'm not telling you how to do your job, but...isn't there a chance that the power failure caused those sensors to throw out false positives?"

"I considered that, sir." The speaker hesitated, and Regional Defense Secretary Glukhovsky could hear the *chink* of glass-on-glass and the sound of gurgling liquid on the other end of the phone connection. "But the sensors triggered one after the other, not all at once."

Anton Fyodorovich Strugatsky, the Chief Security Officer at the Lubukov Bureau of Bioweapons Research, known commonly as the Lubukov Agricultural Labs, could not communicate this in mere words. Language was inadequate to convey the sheer mindless horror of sitting at his desk in his office, watching the little red lights on the indicator panel flicker to life, one by one.

The bulb labeled 'Cold Storage #5' had been the first to glow, accompanied by the polite electronic pinging that had initially caught his attention. Then a second sensor on U1 had triggered, and a third followed moments later. That was when the alarms had begun to blare, coming in faintly through the heavy wooden door. But inside Strugatsky's private office there were no loud alarms -- in here was only the ping, ping, ping of the indicator panel and the gradual opening of those countless little red eyes.

CSO Strugatsky had watched them all light up, row by row, floor after floor, until the entire panel was lit. Then he had gotten those three things, the three most critical things, from the locked drawer in his gorgeous oaken desk. Then he had placed the call to Regional Defense Secretary Glukhovsky, to give him the bad news.

"Any idea what it is?"

"None, sir." Strugatsky admitted. "There's twenty or more different compounds in Cold Storage #5. We've fairly sure which one of them caused the explosion, but that shouldn't have triggered any biohazard alarms."

"How many of the compounds would have tripped that alarm?"

"Only seven of them." There was a pause, and Glukhovsky heard a gulping sound. "One of the seven was UEC-571."

Glukhovsky hissed through his teeth. "That's not good."

"I agree, sir."

"Well, you've done your job admirably, regardless." Glukhovsky's tone was brisk. "I'll get in touch with the Chorman Special Forces immediately. Of course we'll have to stop traffic from crossing the Volgin River bridge, but Khostok shouldn't be under quarantine for any longer than a few days."

"Understood."

"Colonel Akimov himself might be coming down in person, you know. I'm sure he'll be pleased to meet you."

"Likewise, sir."

"You've done your nation a great service by raising the alert, comrade. I'm sure you know this."

"Thank you, sir." Strugatsky let the receiver slip back into its cradle. He considered the three important things he'd laid out on his desk, then picked up the first two -- the glass and the bottle -- and helped himself to another shot of vodka.

He would have liked very much to meet Colonel Akimov, in fact. He'd heard stories, of course, but Strugatsky had never met the man, or for that matter anyone else with the Chorman Special Forces.

But the fact that he was never going to meet Akimov was a distant concern to him. More than that, Strugatsky would have given his right arm to know what comically unlikely circumstances could have set off every single biohazard sensor in the Labs.

The answer to this very valid question would not be found until much later, after Colonel Akimov and the rest of the Chorman Special Forces had arrived. Some time after arrival the CSF investigators would discover that the biohazard ventilation system Yuri had talked about, the one that vacuumed up potentially contaminated air from every room in the facility, had been compromised. It was doing an admirable job in sucking up the contaminants, including a large amount of ink vapor from Cold Storage #5...but it was not routing this air into the special containment chamber he had mentioned.

An engineer had incautiously installed the biohazard ventilation ductwork right beside the ones for the central air and heating. And the explosion in Cold Storage #5 had been strong enough to jolt the pipes loose from their fittings, allowing them to cross-contaminate. The ventilation system was, in effect, picking up biohazardous vapor from Cold Storage #5 and routing it throughout the entire central air system.

The employees of the Lubukov Agricultural Labs were blissfully unaware of the aerosolized ink filtering down from every single air duct in the building. They sat patiently under the invisible downpour, waiting for the cleanup crews to release them. Only Strugatsky, alone in his office, understood the true scope of the contamination at the Lubukov Agricultural Labs. And he did not intend to stick around for the Chorman Special Forces to tell him how doomed he was.

He picked up the third important thing from his desk, pulled back on the slide, and inserted a round into the open chamber.

~~~~~

To understand the significance of the Volgin River bridge you would first need to understand the geography of Khostok itself. The city had been founded in an era when inaccessibility was a boon to a town's defenses, rather than an impediment to interstate commerce. For this reason Khostok was one of the earliest human settlements in Chorma. It was established on what its founders considered to be an ideal site: fringed by steep and jagged mountains to the north, west and east, and hemmed in by the Volgin River to the south. Prior to the building of the Volgin River bridge the only access to Khostok had been by boat, or a long and arduous hike across the mountains.

Of course the original founders could not have anticipated how inconvenient this would someday become. There had long been talk of building a second bridge across the Volgin River, as traffic had an increasing tendency to bottleneck on either side of the existing bridge. But then the Lubukov Agricultural Labs had been built, and talks of additional bridges had ceased. Those who built the Labs had chosen Khostok precisely because there was only one access point to the city, and they wanted it to stay that way.

It was only fair to admit that the Labs had brought employment to the city, boosting its status and population along with its economy. And of course the citizens were encouraged to enjoy the prestige of having one of the State's most modern research laboratories in their own hometown. The research conducted there went toward feeding the nation, and what could be more inspiring than that?

The facility itself was a white concrete building three stories tall, its sides gaily painted with murals: honest, rugged-looking farm folk harvesting fruits and vegetables as large as the harvesters themselves. Here were three peasant women, fat and smiling, rolling along a potato the size of a car. Here was a farmer with three-meter-long stalks of wheat slung over one shoulder. There was a team of four children bearing a monstrous cucumber. And here was a young couple with a logging saw, slicing into an apple that must have weighed better than two hundred pounds.

If the citizens of Khostok wondered why a laboratory dedicated to breeding better food crops needed a six-foot-tall chain-link fence around it, or armed guards, or watchtowers, they did not ask. The Department of Internal Observation was everywhere in those days, lurking unseen, and such questions were distinctly unpatriotic. Likewise they did not ask why a sliding steel gate with guard posts beside it had been installed on the Khostok side of the Volgin River Bridge. They acknowledged that the gate must surely be there for safety's sake, and did not go inquiring about who was being protected, or from what danger.

But in spite of its imposing appearance the gate at the Volgin River bridge saw little use. The technicians stationed there dutifully kept up maintenance on the gate, and the guards stood at their posts, but they were seldom called upon to do anything more than that.

So when the call came in to the guard post late that night, ordering them to close the gate, Sgt. Kirilov could scarcely believe it. He took the phone from the boy who'd answered it, and only after he heard Regional Defense Secretary Glukhovsky's voice on the other end did Kirilov conclude this was not a prank call.

Not once in the three years he'd been stationed there had there ever been a request to actually use the gate for its intended function, and Kirilov was eager to comply with the order. Especially with the way the Regional Defense Secretary had phrased it -- as "a matter of national importance, both for Khostok and for the whole of Chorma." It wasn't every day that a glorified security guard such as Sgt. Kirilov was involved in matters of such significance.

"What d'you suppose is coming?"

"Eh?" Kirilov glanced over at Lt. Bekinsky, his second-in-command. After the gate had been closed -- with such a resounding, satisfying *CLANG* -- Kirilov had hurried out to stand on the road before the closed gate, and had chosen Bekinsky to stand beside him. Both men were wearing their holsters, automatic handguns prominently displayed on their hips. This wasn't strictly procedure, of course...in fact, nowhere in the procedures did it mention guards standing out in front of the gate after it had been closed. Kirilov just felt it made a better impression this way.

"You know...something's gotta be heading this way." Bekinsky jerked his thumb over his shoulder, back toward the river. "Otherwise we wouldn't be closing the gate."

Kirilov considered this. Obviously Khostok needed the protection offered by the gate, or it would never have been installed. Perhaps there were dissidents targeting their Agricultural Labs, and closing the gate would halt the would-be terrorists before they arrived in the city?

But that didn't make a whole lot of sense...anti-State activists were usually dealt with quietly by the DIO. And wouldn't the terrorists merely turn back at the bridge, to return another day after the gate had been opened? They couldn't keep the gate closed indefinitely, after all.

While Kirilov was pondering this a pair of headlights winked into view on the road leading up to the bridge. He snapped to attention and Bekinsky did the same. Carrying out orders of national importance was much more satisfying when you had an audience.

For a tense moment it didn't look as if the antiquated little car was going to stop -- it was doing sixty or more -- but at the last minute the driver put on his brakes and came to a shrieking halt in the yellow pool of light that lay before the gate's barrier. The smell of burnt rubber filled the air.

Kirilov marched over to the driver's side window. "The bridge is closed, comrade!" he barked, relishing the authoritative sound of his own voice. "Matters of national security! You'll have to turn back!"

Peering in through the window, Kirilov saw that the man behind the wheel was a squirrely-looking young fellow, one hand resting on a bundle of black-stained white fabric that lay in the passenger's seat. He looked out through the glass at Kirilov, then down at Kirilov's pistol holster, then over at Bekinsky, then at the guard post. At last he rolled the window down.

"I'm sorry sir, but I absolutely have to get across the bridge," he explained, then rolled on before Kirilov could raise an objection. "My grandfather's in the hospital in Byatin, he's critically ill, all of my relatives are there, this is my only chance to say goodbye to him -- it'll just take a minute, less than a minute, to open the gate enough for me to get by, and if you stop me here -- "

"Sorry, comrade! I have my orders!"

The young man's face darkened. "You're going to prevent me from going to my grandfather's deathbed? On whose authority?" He flapped a hand in the direction of the gate. "I know my rights; I haven't been accused of anything! I can't be held here like a criminal! My father's cousin is the Minister of Commerce, and I'll see to it that he hears about this incident! For you to be -- "

Bekinsky had come up on the passenger's side of the car, his palm resting on the holster of his gun. "Well, you can tell your father's cousin to take it up with Regional Defense Secretary Glukhovsky; the gate's been closed on his orders."

For a moment the driver was dumbstruck. "I -- I'll do just that, then!" he snarled, but he was already rolling the window back up. "Both of you just lost your jobs! And if you're not talking to the DIO a week from now, I'd be very surprised!"

Kirilov stepped back as the young man swung his car in a sharp U-turn and sped off into the night, back the way he'd come. He scowled to himself. 'Tell your father's cousin to take it up with the Regional Defense Secretary'...now why hadn't he come up with that one? That should have been him, not Bekinsky. Nonetheless they'd done their duty, and that was something to be proud of. They went back to their posts in front of the gate.

"Next time we get another one of those clowns -- " Kirilov started, but Bekinsky's shout of alarm cut him off.

"Look out -- he's coming back!"

Kirilov turned to find those headlights bearing down on him again, much faster this time. In an instant he realized the driver had merely gone out just far enough to get the distance he needed to pick up speed, and now --

" -- the bastard's ramming the gate! Look out, look out!"

Briefly regretting his decision to stand in front of the gate, Kirilov dove into the ditch beside the road. Weeds slapped him in the face, and a rock caught him neatly beneath the ribs as he tumbled into the dirt. But when he looked back up he found that Lt. Bekinsky had somehow gotten the idea that he should stand his ground, and had drawn his gun on the onrushing metal juggernaut.

The first two shots had no apparent effect, but the third struck the windshield, which spiderwebbed and fell inward with a tinkling sound. At this the driver must have jerked on the wheel, for it lurched suddenly to the right, careening off the road and missing the gate entirely. It met the fence that bordered the Volgin River and passed straight through it, uprooting two of the wooden fenceposts and snapping the nylon cables that had been strung between them.

For a moment the vehicle seemed to hang in the air, frozen, and then it plunged down the steep, overgrown bank toward the river and was lost from view. Seconds later there came a horrific crash, the scream of wrenching metal mingling with the musical notes of shattering glass.

Kirilov swore fluently and scrambled back to his feet, wading out of the weeds with one hand clutching the bruised spot beneath his rib cage. Bekinsky was running towards the spot where the car had disappeared, still holding his firearm. The two men halted at the gap in the torn fencing, looking down the grassy riverbank that sloped down into the Volgin River. The bridge's floodlights shone dimly on the twin tracks of churned-up grass and earth and the mangled remains of the rusted little car that lay at the end of those tracks, half-submerged in the eddying water. Wisps of steam rose up from the wreck.

"See if you can get the Secretary on the phone again," Bekinsky whispered. Kirilov nodded, mouth dry.

Down in the river, Dmitri sat in repose behind the wheel of the last car he was ever to own. It was not one of the big, beautiful American cars he had dreamed of, but at this point he was beyond caring. Water gurgled through the cabin, flowing around the young man's chest where the steering column had entered it, lifting the bundled lab coat from the passenger seat.

The water, already stained pinkly with blood, took on a darker color as it found the crushed glass tubes that contained the Unidentified Experimental Compound 571, known familiarly as 'ink'. Oily black streaks uncoiled from the lab coat, drifting down the Volgin River toward the pumping station and treatment plant that provided the water supply for the entire city of Khostok.

And so the disaster began.

## CHAPTER TWO

It was happening again. Alexei was twelve years old and his mother was crying in the kitchen. And he knew, with all the suffocating certainty of a nightmare, that she was crying over his father.

He hesitated in the hallway, just out of his mother's line of sight, listening to the disembodied sobs and scuffing the toe of his sneaker against the fraying carpet. His mother was frequently upset, even what the adults would have called "hysterical", but she cried so rarely that her current outburst was downright unnerving.

Twelve-year-old Alexei wondered what was wrong with his father. Maybe his parents had had another of their frequent arguments, a bad one this time. Maybe his father was sick or had been injured at work. Or maybe -- and this seemed the most likely -- his father had finally been fired for being too drunk to run the lathe at the factory. Yes, that was probably the case.

Adult Alexei, who knew exactly what had happened to his father, screamed inaudibly in negation. *No, no -- don't go in there. Not again.*

The boy didn't listen. His battered sneakers carried him over the threshold and into the kitchen, across the yellowing linoleum. Now he could see his mother, her robust frame covered by a floral-printed house-dress, her head crowned with a wiry cloud of gray-and-black hair. He must have made some sound to alert her, for those pink-rimmed eyes found him and in an instant she was flying across the kitchen, faster than he would have imagined, seizing him by the arms.

"Alyoshka!! are you alright?!"

Alexei nodded, and at last he began to feel afraid. "What's wrong?"

"What's *wrong*?!" She shook him back and forth. "It's your father! The DIO's taken your father!"

Alexei couldn't understand, and the face that loomed closer and closer was making it difficult to think. "What?"

"The DIO's taken your father!" his mother wailed, her flushed, contorted face filling his field of vision, blotting out everything else. And then, inevitably, in a tone that held inconceivable horrors: "Do you know what they're going to *do* to him?!"

-- "Hey! Guys, wake up! everyone, wake up!"

Alexei jolted back into consciousness to the sound of a steady, monotonous thumping.

*Drums*, he thought groggily, trying to connect the noise to the flashing red light he was seeing. And why was he on the floor, of all things? Wincing at the stiffness in his back, he worked his way up into a sitting position, waiting for the bizarre light and noise to fade away with the rest of his dreams.

Only it didn't. Near as he could tell from the strobing flashes of light, Alexei was, in fact, sitting on the floor in the lunchroom at the Lubukov Agricultural Labs where he worked.

As his memories came filtering back he spotted the silhouettes of the other employees as they roused themselves out of sleep. A number of them had folded their lab coats under their heads as makeshift pillows, and not a few looked as puzzled as Alexei felt. He was beginning to remember now. There had been a biohazard alert --

"Hey! guys!" the muffled voice shouted again, and the thumping increased in volume.

"That's Vadim!" someone exclaimed, and the researcher named Boris grunted loudly as he climbed to his feet. "We hear you, Vadik!" he shouted, moving towards the door. "What's wrong?"

"We're rescued!" Vadim called out from the other side of the lunchroom door. "They're here!"

Nearly everyone was awake now, and several people leapt upright at the news. They had shut off the lunchroom lights earlier that evening, thinking they should sleep a little while awaiting someone to override the door locks, and now someone flicked the switch to bring the room back to its former fluorescent glare. Alexei screwed his eyes shut briefly.

"Excellent!" Boris shouted back. "Who's here to save us?"

"It's the DIO!"

Smiles faded. Boris glanced at the people gathered behind him, his expression blank, then back at the locked door. " -- what's that now?"

"The DIO's here! I can see them -- there's three guys standing down by the stairs!" Vadim's voice drew away from the door momentarily. "Comrades, we're down here! We've got people locked in the lunchroom!"

"The Department of Internal Observation doesn't deal with these things," somebody whispered. Alexei turned to find Yuri sitting up next to him, his long hair ruffled and glasses askew from sleeping. The biohazard warning light glinted redly on the lenses. "They might send the Special Forces...but not the DIO."

Alexei's mouth had gone dry and he swallowed reflexively.

"I don't think they can hear me -- hold on!" Vadim called out, and then his footsteps pattered rapidly away from the door. "Hey! down here!" His shouts came echoing back from further and further away. "Hello! Comrades! they're down this way!"

The listeners at the door held their breath. "What's wrong?" they heard Vadim asking, very faintly. "Why aren't you -- "

And then there was silence.

" -- Vadik!" Boris shouted into the door. "Vadik! are you still there? What's happening?"

The silence remained.

"Vadik!!" Boris hammered on the door with a closed fist. "Answer us!"

"Sssh!" someone hissed, and they all froze. Now they could hear it: slow, shuffling footsteps, advancing on the lunchroom door.

For a long minute nobody so much as breathed, and then Boris whispered, "Vadik?"

"...they're gone."

Vadim's tone had changed so dramatically that they almost didn't recognize him. Boris stared into the door. "What? the DIO's gone? why? are they going to bring back help?"

Something whumped against the door from the outside -- Vadim, sitting down in front of it. "They weren't there."

The dismay in the lunchroom was tangible. "The DIO's left us, you mean?"

"...I don't think they were...really there." They had to strain to catch Vadim's words. "When I got up close, they just...disappeared."

Stunned, the crowd at the door started to mutter amongst themselves. A few broke away from the larger group and started to lie back down again, but the majority remained with Boris, still trying to make sense out of what had happened.

"Stress-induced hallucinations," Yuri murmured, almost to himself. Alexei turned to him. "It's not uncommon in a situation like this, especially if he was just waking up. Sleep deprivation can also make them happen. Even just wishing for rescuers can make someone think they see them, if they want it very badly."

It all sounded reasonable enough. And Alexei would have eagerly bought it if he hadn't seen the senior researcher's face, and realized that Yuri didn't believe a single word of his own explanation.

~~~~~

"Sergeant! Sergeant, wake up!"

"Eh?"

"Sir, they're here! wake UP!"

"Mmm." Sgt. Kirilov was sleeping someplace far more comfortable than the lunchroom floor at the Lubukov Agricultural Labs, and was disinclined to leave his nap for whoever-it-was that was bothering him.

"*Sir!*" the annoyance shouted, and Kirilov received a sharp kick to the shins. This brought him awake in a hurry, and he was half-out of his padded desk chair before he recognized Lt. Bekinsky. "Hmmmrff...wha?" Kirilov remarked, scrubbing a hand over his face. The clock on the wall said 7 a.m., a full hour after his shift should have ended -- why had he gone to sleep here, in his office at the gate outpost, rather than heading home?

"Sir," Bekinsky panted, "the Chorman Special Forces have arrived, and they need to get into Khostok right away. We've got to open the gate for them."

This information had a galvanizing effect on Sgt. Kirilov, who sprang to his feet and flew out of his office with Bekinsky on his heels. That was right -- he and Bekinsky had elected to stay behind after their shift was over, to meet the CSF when they came. Glukhovsky had told him they'd be arriving by midmorning at the latest, and Kirilov's strongly patriotic spirit insisted on giving the CSF an account of the night's events: the prompt closing of the gate, the squirrely young man who'd attempted to run them down, the heroic shots Kirilov had fired -- at no small risk to himself --  that had sent the potential gate-destroyer sailing into the Volgin River.

A quick glance at the gate cameras showed a queue of four massive black military vehicles, the armored sort used for personnel carrying, sitting patiently on the bridge behind the gate. Kirilov punched the codes into the keypad and slapped the button. Once the steel gate panels had fully opened the first of the vehicles trundled forward into Khostok with a belch of diesel exhaust.

Kirilov felt a brief stab of concern when it looked like the convoy was simply going to pass by without stopping, but once all four vehicles had pulled inside the gate the lead car rumbled to a leisurely halt, and the rest followed suit. Clumsy with haste, Kirilov entered the code and hit the "CLOSE GATE" button, then stepped out onto the road as the gate began to slide shut.

Confronted with the line of military vehicles, Kirilov and Bekinsky hesitated. Then the passenger door on the leading vehicle swung open and Kirilov rushed down the line towards it. He was nearly there when he caught sight of what was disembarking, and Kirilov halted so fast that Bekinsky almost collided with him.

His first, panicked impression was of something inhuman, some sort of long-snouted, hairless subterranean monster. Then Kirilov realized he was looking at a man in a full-body chemical protection suit, albeit a very tall man in a needlessly scary-looking suit, and he felt silly.

Perhaps his reaction was understandable. The nuclear-biological-chemical protection suits worn by the Chorman Special Forces were entirely black, to start with. The gas mask that shielded the wearer's face was black rubber, made after the Soviet style, which featured a long downward-pointing muzzle that terminated in a cylindrical air filter. The mask's eyeholes were circles of mirrored glass. Cinched behind the gas mask was the hood of a long, belted overcoat made of rubber-coated fabric, which descended to just above the knees and closed with a zipper in the front. The pants beneath the overcoat were rubberized as well, as were the black gloves and the heavy steel-toed calf-height boots.

"Greetings, comrades!" the apparition croaked at Kirilov. The muffling effect of the mask gave its voice a hollow, almost robotic quality.

Still quite openly gaping, Kirilov's eye fell on the visor cap that was perched atop the creature's hooded head, vacuum-sealed in clear plastic. He also noted the insignia that decorated the left breast of the overcoat. Then it hit him that this rubber thing was actually a colonel, quite likely the leader of the convoy, and he snapped into a salute with such force that he nearly struck himself in the head.

"-- Greetings, sir! Sergeant Oleg Kirilov of the Volgin River Gate Patrol!" Kirilov found that he was shaking. Beside him Bekinsky made a similar introduction.

"At ease." The colonel waved at them. "Comrades, I am Colonel Akimov of the Chorman Special Forces, here under orders from Regional Defense Secretary Glukhovsky. Now, Secretary Glukhovsky tells me there was an incident at this gate last night -- one involving a car?"

Bekinsky waited for his superior, but when Kirilov proved to be too intimidated to answer, he stepped in. "Yes, sir! there was a car! He was turned back and attempted to ram the gate, we fired on him, and he lost control and went off the road and into the Volgin River."

"Mmm. When was this?"

"Around seven -- I mean, around 1900 hours, sir."

"And where did the vehicle enter the river?"

Bekinsky pointed to the gap that the car had punched into the fence. The tire tracks were visible as twin lines of crushed grass, disappearing over the high point in the riverbank.

"I see." Col. Akimov turned back to the car and depressed a button on the side of his mask. "Vulture, Parrot, Egret -- front and center."

Doors banged open and three similarly-suited soldiers leapt down from the second vehicle in the convoy. They saluted the colonel, who nodded and gestured for them to follow him as he headed off toward the fence. Kirilov trailed along after the colonel, with Bekinsky bringing up the rear.

From the high point of the riverbank, with the splintered fenceposts lying in the grass around them, the group looked down into the river. The early-morning sunlight shimmered in the thin blanket of fog that had gathered down along the waterside, pooling around the wreck and drifting over the surface of the water, blurring the details. Nonetheless they could still see the crashed car where it lay half-in and half-out of the river, its nose submerged in the water like an animal that had died while going to drink.

Akimov turned sharply to the two guards. "Did either of you go down to the river after the car crashed?"

Kirilov looked panicked. "We only went halfway down the bank, sir," Bekinsky admitted. "Just to see if the driver was still alive. We didn't touch anything."

"Mmm," said Akimov. "Vulture -- take them."

One of the three soldiers broke away from Akimov's group and came back toward Kirilov and Bekinsky. "Let's go now comrades," he rasped through the mask, and made a shooing gesture with both arms. The two guards retreated before him, back toward the vehicles. "We've got seats for you in the carrier. The colonel's going to handle it from here."

"W-where are we going?" Kirilov demanded, finding his voice at last. "We were just -- we can't abandon our post!"

"Oh, no worries about that." The soldier codenamed Vulture opened the door of the personnel carrier, revealing a blackness inside. "The CSF is here now. Everything's under control."

Whimpering under his breath, Kirilov stepped up into the vehicle. Bekinsky took a long look at the soldier's gas-masked face before he stepped up as well. His unease had started with the unprecedented order to close the gate, and everything else that had happened -- the desperate young man, the crashed car, and now the CSF -- had only made him more and more uneasy. Now his unformed fears had finally begun to crystallize.

They hadn't closed the gate to keep the danger *out* of Khostok, after all. No, the heavy protective suits made it quite clear: the danger was already here, in the city. They had closed the gate to keep it inside.

~~~~~

"Shit!!" Veronika yelped.

Grigori overheard her from all the way in the kitchen, and he laughed out loud. "That's so ladylike."

Veronika snorted. "You're a lady, eh? or how would you know?!"

No answer, but she heard the telltale squeak of floorboards as Grigori settled into the chair at the dining room table. The house was easily three times as old as either of them, and some nights it seemed like every single board creaked or groaned or otherwise announced itself.

The downstairs boarders, the Popovs, had repeatedly complained, but Veronika didn't mind. She had lived here since she was born, and the noises were comfortingly familiar. Besides, nobody could take a so much as a step in the house without her overhearing them; it was almost like having sonar.

Turning down the hot water and turning up the cold, Veronika started rinsing her hand again, cleaning out the shallow gash she'd received the day before. She was hissing through her teeth, but this time she managed to bite down on the impulse to start cursing. Once the water in the bathroom sink ran clear she shut it off, blotted her hand dry and wrapped it in gauze, leaving the fingers free so she could work.

When Veronika reached the kitchen she found Grigori munching on a piece of toast. A battered metal carafe bubbled away on the stove. "Coffee?" she asked. "That's just the thing your ulcer needs."

Her brother smiled around a mouthful of bread. "My ulcer only needs one thing." Grigori inclined his head toward the half-empty bottle on the handmade wooden shelf above the table.

"Even worse -- that stuff'll kill you."

"Ah, but I'll die happy."

Veronika managed to locate the loaf of bread and took out two slices, then poured herself a cup of black coffee. "What happened to you?" Grigori asked as soon as she'd seated herself.

"Oh, I was working on a carpet stain yesterday and there was this nail sticking out of the baseboard." She waved her gauze-wrapped hand at him. "I just didn't see it."

"Ugh." Grigori frowned. "This happened at the Kravchenkos', right? You should quit."

Veronika merely laughed. "Of course not. I know where the nail is now. Besides, I like working for the Kravchenkos."

"What? everyone at the shop says they're all beasts. Especially their son."

"I didn't say I liked *them*, just working for them." She snickered. "They're never home. I'm there all day by myself in that mansion, just keeping the dust off the furniture. It's like being a museum curator."

Grigori shrugged, flicking his shaggy black hair out of his eyes. "Besides," Veronika went on, "you're not getting all that much at the shop, are you? if I quit, we won't be able to keep the house on the rent the Popovs are paying. We'll have to sell it."

It was a cheap way to end the argument, and Veronika knew it. "I'm getting promoted to head mechanic soon," Grigori said, his spine straightening. The creaking old house had been their parents' and neither of them would ever have given it up willingly.

"Of course you are," Veronika agreed, and then with more conviction she added, "You know more about cars than the rest of them put together. I'm surprised the others can tell a tractor from a donkey."

Grigori let out a bark of laughter. "True, true." Still chuckling, he took a sip of coffee and suddenly made a face.

"Your ulcer again?"

"No, no...it's the coffee." Grigori scowled into his cup. "Tastes strange."

"Strange how?"

"It's..." He took another sip, looking contemplative. "It's weird. Maybe a bit like the flavor of honey, but not all that sweet."

Curious now, Veronika tried her own coffee. She hadn't noticed it before, but there was a bit of a honeylike aftertaste there. It was so subtle, though -- she couldn't be sure the taste hadn't been there last week.

"Could be a new coffee we're getting," Grigori mused.

"Nope -- I've been buying the same brand."

"Well, then, maybe we're just lucky and some kind soul has spiked our tap water with honey. We won't have to buy sugar again, eh?"

Veronika rolled her eyes. "Just eat your breakfast, Grigori," she said, smiling in spite of herself.

~~~~~

Nikita faced off against the stove. He eyeballed the lone pot as it bubbled away atop the range, waiting for it to explode or catch on fire. When it did neither he let out a slow sigh. "Okay," he said aloud, pointing at the pot with the wooden spoon he held. "Grain cereal. Milk. Some water. Sugar. Vanilla...and something else."

He was drawing a blank. The pot burbled innocently and Nikita took a peek inside, but the appearance gave him no clues as to what he was missing. At least it didn't smell like it was burning yet, and that was something to his credit.

"Cereal, milk, water, sugar, vanilla..." A bead of sweat rolled down the side of his face and he turned, scanning the kitchen. It was a wholly alien place to him, a stranger's kitchen with blue window curtains and loudly yellow sunflowers in the wallpaper. Nikita supposed that his sister-in-law had decorated it this way, but his brother must have been the one to maintain the look after his wife had died.

"Water, sugar, vanilla..." The pantry caught his eye. " -- cinnamon!" Nikita exclaimed. He dropped the spoon onto the countertop and threw open the cabinet, only to be greeted by seemingly hundreds of different bottles, cans and jars. He groaned.

Ten minutes later Nikita was still fumbling through the pantry's contents, picking things up and squinting at labels in the light of the single bulb overhead. "Clove...no. Dill...no. Thyme...not that either. Parsley, oregano, basil, no no no..."

"Uncle Nikita?"

Nikita leapt up, knocked his head into the underside of a shelf, and bit his lip to keep from cursing. "Elena?" He poked his head out of the pantry and found his ten-year-old niece standing there in the kitchen, already dressed in her school-clothes and still blinking the sleep out of her eyes.

"You've dressed yourself! Good!" he said, then immediately felt like a fool. Elena was ten years old now, not four. Of course she could dress herself.

Elena rubbed her eyes. "I turned the stove off," she said, pointing. "The cereal was boiling over."

Nikita gasped and bolted to the stove, but the crisis had been avoided. "Thank you," he said sheepishly, hunting for bowls in the overhead cabinets. "Just take a seat -- breakfast's coming up."

Obediently Elena climbed up into her chair and began drumming her heels against the wooden chair-legs. She seemed so much quieter than the way he remembered her...but then again she'd only been five years old when he'd last seen her. Ten-year-olds were quieter than five-year-olds, weren't they?

Nikita laid two bowls onto the countertop and began ladling the steaming cereal into each one. Great God, had it really been five years since he'd moved to Byatin for that all-important engineering position? Five years spent tinkering with motherboards and transistors and completely forgetting that he still had family that wasn't dead and buried yet. He'd been over to visit his brother constantly in the years right after Ekaterina's death; he had practically done half the work in raising Elena. And now five years had passed with barely a telephone call, and his niece was almost a stranger to him.

"Here we are, breakfast for two." Nikita whisked both bowls over to the table and dropped a spoon into each. Once he'd set out the napkins and the mugs of hot tea he took a step back, surveying his work. Not bad for someone who typically had cold leftovers for breakfast.

Elena murmured a thank-you and started to dig in. "I thought this might be easy to eat, since you just lost that tooth," Nikita explained as he slid into his own chair. "Plus I remember this was your favorite."

She nodded, smiling. "You even remembered that I don't like the cinnamon."

"Ah...that's right, of course."

The two ate in silence for several minutes. "Papa didn't come home last night, did he?"

"Mm?" Nikita gulped reflexively. "No, he didn't. I imagine they've kept him behind at the Labs...your papa's doing some very important work, you know."

Elena knew. "How long will he have to stay?"

"Oh, I have no idea. They've at least got to let him come home to change clothes though, eh?" Nikita knew they had cafeterias and little dormitories at the Lubukov Agricultural Labs, but he couldn't see them keeping their employees away from their families for any more than a few days. The management had to have families of their own, after all...surely they would understand.

"But that's why Papa asked you to come visit, right?" Elena stirred her cereal absently. "Because he knew he wouldn't be here."

Nikita felt very briefly insulted -- and then he was just immensely sorry. "Elena, I *wanted* to come visit. I missed you and your papa, that's why."

"Oh!" But she seemed to believe him, for she broke into another sunny smile, showing the empty gap her baby tooth had just recently occupied. "How long are you staying?"

"A good long while," he promised. And he was being sincere about it; though it hadn't been stated in so many words, Nikita's boss had given him to understand that his 'leave of absence' from work could be extended to much longer than two weeks, if he wished. Possibly even if he didn't wish it. What with the computer industry failing and all. There were just so many new companies out there these days...and now that importers were beginning to crowd into the Chorman market...you understand, Nikita, we have to stay competitive or soon we'll all be begging on the street-corner.

But he had told the truth about missing his niece and his brother. Nikita's financial situation was secondary to his fondness for his extended family. He willed himself to believe this was true.

"You even put honey in the tea!"

"Eh?" Now this was one thing Nikita couldn't take credit for. "No, I didn't -- I, uh, couldn't find the honey."

Elena looked puzzled. "But it does have honey in it! just taste it!"

He took a sip from his mug, and now it was Nikita's turn to look puzzled. "It's not sweet enough to be honey..." he said slowly, and glanced back at the samovar. "Maybe the tea just tastes like that?"

"But we always drink that tea for breakfast and it never tastes like this." Elena was adamant.

"Something must have changed, then." Nikita took another bite of his cereal. "You know, your grandmother lived during the Great Patriotic War, and she always told your papa and me that the tea companies used to put all kinds of different plants into the teabags, to keep the real tea for the soldiers."

"The Great War is over though," Elena observed. "We were learning about it in history class last month."

"Ah, yes, but it's still a good way to save costs, right? Lots of other plants are cheaper than tea leaves."

He could see that she wasn't fully convinced, but Elena let the matter drop. "At least it tastes nice," she remarked, and Nikita took another sip of it. Actually, he was inclined to agree with her on that.

~~~~~

But the Great War was not over. To be sure, the battlefields were abandoned now, the draft was over, and the soldiers had returned home to their native land. But for some of them, the war would never be over. The fight continued, unseen and unsung, in the hearts of those who had been the most deeply wronged, those whom the nation was too ashamed to acknowledge.

Mikhail knew this better than anyone.

Alone in his tiny apartment above the train station, Mikhail was busy compiling his evidence. The process was a painstaking one, but his sense of violated justice sustained him through the long sleepless nights.

This morning his object of interest was an old newspaper article, yellowed and brittle as a dry leaf, that he'd culled from the local dump. People used newspapers for wrapping and packing all sorts of things that subsequently found their way into the landfill, and from there into Mikhail's hands. This particular paper had once been used to hold an order of fish from some deli counter -- though they had vanished their smell remained behind, like a pungent ghost.

LOCAL PARK DEDICATED TO SCIENTIST KONSTANTIN DRAGOVICH, the headline declared. The photo depicted a bronze statue with an upraised arm, and a small knot of Khostok citizens standing around it. Above and slightly left of the statue was an indistinct blob. Though the untrained eye would have mistaken the blot for a discoloration on the paper, likely caused by wrapping it around a raw fish, Mikhail identified the dark blur as one of the DIO's aerial stealth cameras, caught on film at a moment when its invisibility camouflage was compromised. Likely running low on batteries, he imagined.

With infinite delicacy he snipped the picture away from its accompanying article, careful lest he crumble the ancient paper. Dropping it into a clear plastic bag, he sealed the bag with tape and laid this newest piece of evidence into the open folder on his desk.

Mikhail had three hundred and forty-two of such folders, all of them uncategorized except for the word EVIDENCE scrawled across the front. The true gems of his massive collection, which had taken several years to compile, were those he had pinned to the walls of his apartment. Aside from newspaper articles the walls were also crowded with magazine covers, commercial flyers, printed ads of all sorts and numerous pieces of mail, both his own and that of others.

These incriminating exhibits were frequently notated, Mikhail's comments scribbled onto the paper or, when the piece of evidence was not large enough, written directly onto the wallpaper itself. He had resorted to the folder system quite early in his investigations; it had taken only a few months for the walls to become completely filled. If not for the landlord's faith in Mikhail's paltry monthly stipend from the Veterans Welfare Board, Mikhail imagined he might have been evicted long ago.

Hanging in a glass frame above his bed was the rejection letter Mikhail had received from the same Welfare Board, denying his claim for greater benefits. Not that he felt the rejection deserved any such honor, but looking at it each day reminded him of the grievous trespasses his country had made against him.

He had read and reread the letter perhaps a thousand times or more, and knew it practically by heart. *We regret to inform you*, it read, *that your application for expanded benefits has been declined. Our records indicate that you already receive Tier 5 benefits, which is the appropriate compensation for the services you have rendered to the nation of Chorma.*

*We find several claims made in your application to be entirely fabricated, including the following: that you were "subjected to extensive torture via implantation of mind-control devices", "incarcerated without trial for several months in subhuman conditions", "programmed by the Department of Internal Observation via said mind-controlling implants to assassinate* several key political figures", and that you are "continually subjected to a harassment program orchestrated by the DIO which includes wiretapping, poisoning of your tap water, filling your apartment with intoxicating gases in order to prevent you from compiling evidence against them, and surveillance by alleged invisible flying cameras."

The rejection letter went on to assert the Welfare Board's official cover story, one it had maintained since Mikhail's discharge from the Chorman Defenders Army all those years ago. *Our records indicate*, the letter said, *that after you were drafted you served only two months of your mandatory three years' assignment. In your first combat mission you were struck in the head by a piece of shrapnel and thereafter committed to a field hospital.*

*Though you made a full recovery from your wounds, the hospital staff afterward observed you to exhibit a profound degree of mental disturbance, and in light of your repeated accusations of torture and surveillance by the Chorman Defenders Army and the Department of Internal Observation we were forced to terminate your assigment and discharge you from the CDA. In light of your minor injuries and the circumstances surrounding your discharge, your continued receipt of Tier 5 benefits is not only appropriate but rather generous.*

So they had decided to accuse him of lies rather than own up to the terrible truth. It mattered little. Mikhail had lost the battle but not the war. The evidence contined to pile up, repeatedly astonishing him with the scope and breadth of the DIO's crimes against Chorma. And once he'd amassed enough of it he wouldn't content himself with simply petitioning the VWB to increase his benefits. Oh no -- every newspaper, news program and radio station was going to hear about the horrors that were being perpetrated right under their noses. They would --

-- the dull roar of a diesel engine broke into his thoughts. Passing cars and trains he was familiar with, but this was the sound of an altogether different vehicle. Carefully closing his EVIDENCE folder on the photo of the uncloaked aerial stealth camera, Mikhail crept over to the window. The window-curtain was a taped-together patchwork of multicolored plastic bags, most of them from the local corner store, which permitted light to enter while filtering out the infrared gaze of the DIO's omnipresent stealth cameras. He peeled this curtain away at the corner and pressed his eye to the window, scanning the street below.

And that was when he saw them. A convoy was passing by beneath him, four black armored military vehicles jolting along the ill-repaired pavement. Hardly daring to breathe, Mikhail watched them roll on past, headed for the police station.

These weren't Defenders Army vehicles, or they would have been forest-green. And the DIO didn't use military vehicles at all, preferring to disguise themselves as ordinary citizens while they went about their dirty work. That meant these diesel monsters could only be the Chorman Special Forces.

Adrenaline thrilled in Mikhail's veins. Was it a coup? Had the Chorman government finally tired of the DIO's program of covert suppression and decided to establish the dictatorial police state it had always dreamed of creating? Or was there some other, more chilling reason for this open display of military power on a public street during what the government claimed was peacetime?

Could it -- could it even be that the DIO had decided to take more drastic measures against those thorns in its side, those undefeated freedom-fighters who dared to amass evidence against its sinister empire?

Without looking, he reached toward the stockpile of bottled water beside his desk, plucked out one bottle and cracked open the safety seal. Well, whatever their reason, let them come for him. By God, let them come. He was ready.

Oh yes, the war was not over at all. In fact, it was just beginning.

~~~~~

Police Chief Petrenko was having one of those sorts of days which seem a specific sort of punishment for disobeying the impulse to stay in bed. He had been at his position for eight years and as a consequence his instinct on these matters was rather good. He had known exactly what sort of day it would be when his assistant had poked her head into his office to inform him that Regional Defense Secretary Glukhovsky was on the line, and it was for him.

He had listened to the Secretary's assessment of the situation, agreed wholeheartedly with his suggested line of action, praised the excellent forethought and careful consideration evident in such a plan, and promised the enthusiastic compliance of the Khostok Police Department. All this he had done automatically, with the honest and fervent hope that none of it would be necessary. Not because he had no desire to comply with the inbound Special Forces unit, but because if the Secretary was correct about the threat, the consequences to Khostok could be cataclysmic.

But now his assistant was informing him that the Chorman Special Forces had arrived and were awaiting him downstairs at the police station's reception desk. On the elevator ride down from the administrative offices to the ground floor Petrenko stole a moment to light himself a cigarette. *Like a man going to his execution*, he thought to himself.

The police chief felt he was more than prepared to meet the Special Forces, but the sight of the five soldiers who awaited him at the reception desk was still a little unsettling. It was the masks, he decided. Sure, perhaps they needed the breathing protection, but clear glass eyepieces would have functioned just as well as tinted ones. And was it necessary for the *entire* protective suit to be black? Adding a little color would not have decreased its protectiveness in the slightest.

A number of police officers and other station employees were making a show of busy absorption in their duties while watching the soldiers from the corners of their eyes. In spite of their pretense at ignoring them the officers still hung back from the CSF at a safe distance, like a herd of prey animals with predators in their midst. As Petrenko crossed the lobby he saw several people eyeing the AKS-47s that hung from the soldiers' backs.

"Police Chief Petrenko," rasped the tallest soldier, the one in the plastic-wrapped visor cap, as he stepped towards the chief. Petrenko winced inwardly at that voice. Completely unnecessary for them to sound like that, too. "I am Colonel Akimov of the Chorman Special Forces."

The two men shook. Petrenko's sweaty hand squeaked against Akimov's rubber-gloved one.

"Comrade...I do apologize for the short notice, but we will need your police station."

Petrenko swallowed his cigarette smoke and began violently coughing. Akimov waited patiently for him to finish.

" -- *all* of it?" Petrenko managed at last.

"No, no, of course not." Akimov waved. "But you do have a public broadcast system here at the station, for emergencies and such...am I right?"

Petrenko confirmed it, and asked what it was needed for.

"I will be making an announcement to the citizens of Khostok. They will need information, and an assurance that we are here to help them -- above all, to help them." He nodded firmly. "You've been informed of the situation?"

"I spoke to the Regional Secretary," Petrenko admitted. "He didn't have much information though. Something about a leak at -- "

Col. Akimov raised a hand to cut him off, then glanced over his shoulder. The half-dozen officers who'd been eavesdropping the hardest all jumped as if stung, then buried themselves in their tasks again.

"If you'd direct us to the place we can make our broadcast, there might be more privacy there," Akimov suggested.

"Of course," Petrenko sighed. He led Col. Akimov and his men to the elevator. Petrenko looked back just in time to see the mixture of pitying and wildly curious looks from the station employees before the elevator door slid shut, closing the six of them into the car.

"There *was* a chemical leak at the Lubukov Agricultural Labs," Akimov explained as they ascended skyward. "That in itself is not the problem."

Petrenko waited, his cigarette twitching in the corner of his mouth.

"It seems that a lab employee was attempting to steal a weaponable biologically hazardous substance. He escaped the facility in advance of the lockdown, but was stopped at the Volgin River gate."

"Oh, that's good."

"No, it's not. As a matter of fact it's very bad."

"How so?" asked Petrenko, feeling his shirt starting to adhere itself to his back.

"The employee ran off the road and ended up in the Volgin River, along with the bioweapon. The weapon's containers were damaged in the crash, permitting the substance to leak into the water."

"Shit."

"Precisely."

"But...that means..." Petrenko's mind flew ahead. "The bridge's upstream from the water pumping station. Everyone in Khostok gets their water from that station."

"And now you see the true danger we face in this situation." Col. Akimov half-turned to the chief, and the elevator lights flashed white fire on the eyepieces in his gas mask. "And the necessity for making this announcement." The elevator dinged and opened onto the fourth floor, and Akimov allowed Petrenko to disembark first.

Numb with the implications of what he'd just been told, Petrenko led the soldiers down the hall to a door whose brass plaque read EMERGENCY PUBLIC BROADCAST SYSTEM. "Right in here," Petrenko said, unlocking the door with quaking hands. "It's a bit dusty, we don't really use it much...mainly we play music through it during parades and festival days and stuff like that...early warnings when a blizzard's coming, you know, that kind of thing...we can also make recordings here if you need to put the announcement out on the radio or the TV stations too...but I'll get a technician to set everything up for you, shouldn't take too long, we have several people on staff who can run the system, it's just..." He realized he was babbling and cut himself off.

Col. Akimov stood in the center of the broadcast room, scanning the equipment that lay shrouded under dust covers, the microphone jutting up from the speaker's desk. "This will be excellent. Also, I will need a favor from you while the announcement is being made."

"S-Sure."

"The water in Khostok must be shut off," Akimov said, looking back over his shoulder. "As soon as possible. This is the only way to begin managing the contamination risk. The broadcast, of course, will mention this to the people, and clean water will be brought in for their needs. The CSF will see to everything."

There were a few failed attempts before Petrenko managed a "yes, sir" and ducked out of the broadcast office to look for that technician. And after that, he had a very difficult phone call to make to the fellow in charge of the Khostok Water Pumping and Treatment Plant.

This was definitely turning out to be one of those days.

## CHAPTER THREE

At noon the sirens began.

The sound oscillated back and forth between a low wail and a high-pitched shriek, rising and falling. Most of the Khostok citizenry barely recalled the existence of the public announcement system, or if they did recall it they were unaware it could do anything more than play parade music. Those few who were old enough to remember the system's original use were also old enough to recognize the sound of the air-raid siren for what it was, which threw them into confusion.

But the desired effect was achieved -- whether puzzled or alarmed, a large number of people were out on the sidewalk or leaning out of open windows when the sirens cut off some minutes later, and the sound of a human voice came crackling out of the hundreds of citywide speakers.

"CITIZENS OF KHOSTOK," the announcement began.

People who'd been murmuring together suddenly stopped, looking around for the source of the voice.

"THIS IS COLONEL AKIMOV WITH THE CHORMAN SPECIAL FORCES. WE HAVE AN IMPORTANT MESSAGE TO GIVE YOU, AND WE ENCOURAGE YOU TO STAY CALM AND LISTEN WELL.

"THERE HAS BEEN AN ACCIDENT AT THE LUBUKOV AGRICULTURAL LABS. WE HAVE REASONS TO BELIEVE THERE WAS A CHEMICAL LEAK, AND THAT THIS CHEMICAL MAY BE DANGEROUS. ALL NECESSARY MEASURES ARE BEING TAKEN TO PROTECT THE HEALTH OF ALL CITIZENS. YOUR PROMPT COMPLIANCE WITH THESE MEASURES WILL HELP ENSURE YOUR SAFETY."

There were several exclamations of alarm which were quickly shushed by those straining to hear every word of the message.

"KHOSTOK IS NOW UNDER QUARANTINE. REPEAT -- THE CITY OF KHOSTOK IS NOW UNDER QUARANTINE. ALL TRAVEL IN AND OUT OF THE CITY HAS BEEN SUSPENDED UNTIL FURTHER NOTICE. WE ALSO HAVE REASONS TO BELIEVE THE MUNICIPAL WATER SYSTEM HAS BEEN CONTAMINATED. THE WATER SUPPLY WILL BE SHUT OFF MOMENTARILY, BUT IN THE MEANTIME CITIZENS ARE STRONGLY DISCOURAGED FROM DRINKING ANY NON-BOTTLED SOURCES OF WATER."

More windows were opening, people calling down from upstairs apartments to the spellbound audience on the street, trying to verify what they'd heard. Housewives with dishrags in their hands wandered out onto the sidewalk; late sleepers stumbled out of doors half-dressed or with their hair still dripping wet from the shower.

"WE ARE IN THE PROCESS OF IMPLEMENTING AN EVACUATION PROGRAM FOR THE RESIDENTS OF KHOSTOK. AN UPCOMING ANNOUNCEMENT WILL GIVE THE LOCATION OF EVACUATION CENTERS FOR EACH NEIGHBORHOOD. ONCE THE ANNOUNCEMENT IS MADE, PLEASE PROCEED TO YOUR EVACUATION CENTER IN AN ORDERLY FASHION. BRING YOUR IDENTIFICATION DOCUMENTS WITH YOU, LOCK YOUR HOMES AND TAKE ONLY ONE ITEM OF LUGGAGE -- YOU WILL BE RETURNED TO KHOSTOK ONCE THE CONTAMINATION HAS BEEN CLEARED. REPEAT -- CITIZENS WILL BE ALLOWED TO RETURN TO THEIR HOMES ONCE THE CONTAMINATION HAS BEEN CLEARED.

"PLEASE STAY ALERT FOR FURTHER ANNOUNCEMENTS. MESSAGE ENDS."

The broadcast system crackled and went dead. Shocked silence settled on the listeners. Children too young to understand began querying their parents, who either hushed them or ignored them completely. A few people laughed, others began to loudly explain to each-other why it was impossible to leave. They had jobs to do, bills to pay, pets to look after -- who would water their houseplants? What about all the food in the fridge? The children were in school right now! This was ridiculous! and other observations in a similarly pointless vein.

~~~~~

"Shit," Veronika said again, under her breath. Grigori, standing beside her, said nothing, and neither did any of the other commuters sheltering under the bus-station awning. The nearest broadcast speakers were mounted on the side of a brick warehouse that stood behind the bus stop: a cluster of three plastic trumpets, like a bunch of khaki-colored flowers. People were staring up at the speakers as if expecting something else to issue forth -- a retraction, a clarification, more information, anything at all.

"Well, at least we get a day off from work, eh?" Grigori remarked at last, elbowing his sister in the ribs. Veronika just frowned.

"Hey." Grigori elbowed her again.

"What?"

"Hey, you remember..." His voice had dropped to nearly a whisper, all joking gone out of him now. "...the coffee this morning tasted funny. Remember that?"

Veronika did remember. Maybe it was related and maybe it wasn't, but that wasn't her concern right now. At the moment all of her thoughts revolved around her hand, the one she'd gashed on a nail while working at the Kravchenkos' last night. The one she'd washed off in the sink this morning.

Underneath the sterile gauze, the cut in her hand was tingling.

~~~~~

Meanwhile, in a sunflower-wallpapered kitchen, blue curtains stirred in the breeze that came through the open window. Nikita had already dumped the tea down the drain and sent the hot cereal after it. He started to turn on the water to rinse the food away, then realized his error and snatched his hand away from the knob.

"I'm sure it's nothing," he said aloud, sweeping the cereal remnants into the sink disposal with the serving spoon. "They might even call off the evacuation if they test the water and find out there's nothing in there. It's just a precaution, I'm sure of it. There's just too much risk if someone *does* get sick -- there's always a scandal, an inquiry has to be made, people get paid compensation not to talk about it, all that nonsense -- so whenever there's a chance of people getting ill they have to go through this whole process until they know exactly what..."

Trailing off, Nikita turned back to Elena. She was still sitting in her chair, staring down at the table. Tears rolled silently off her cheeks to patter onto the wood grain of the tabletop.

"Oh, Lena." Nikita went to her chair, hesitated for a second and then bent over to embrace her. When she responded by hugging him back he let out his breath in a sigh. So she hadn't changed that much, after all.

"You're going to be okay!" he repeated, stroking her honey-colored hair. "Trust me, you're going to be okay. I won't let anything happen to you. If they make us evacuate -- "

" -- they said there was an accident at the Labs!" she cut him off with a wail. "Papa works at the Labs! what about him? They're going to evacuate him too, right?"

Nikita could have kicked himself. Elena wasn't worrying about the evacuation or the tainted water or anything of the sort. She was grappling with the very real fear that the accident might have made her an orphan.

"Of course, of course." Nikita fumbled for something reassuring. "After all...if there was an accident at the Labs...they'll have to get them out first, right? that'll be the safest thing."

He could feel that her little shoulders were still tense -- she wasn't buying it. "They might even have evacuated him already," Nikita added, and winced at how hollow that sounded. "But I'm going to be right here with you, whatever happens."

Elena nodded against his shirt. "But I still want my papa," she insisted.

Even though he expected that, it still panged him to hear it. But it was alright, really. Nikita felt much the same way about finding his brother.

~~~~~

Mikhail shut the window and let the patchwork plastic-bag curtain fall back into place. His seamed face fairly glowed with exultation beneath the grey stubble. It was even worse than he'd expected; it was an outright declaration of war.

He had to give the DIO credit for the intricacy of their plan. Sabotaging the Labs in order to create a convenient accident was certainly not beyond them, for who would accuse the government of attacking a government-owned research lab? It also let them make claims of poisoned water; Mikhail found this an especially nice touch. The "poison" threat conveniently justified them cutting off Khostok's water supply. There would be no need to sweep the city streets after that: the very real danger of death by dehydration would drive even the most reluctant evacuees from their homes and into the arms of the DIO's trained attack hounds, the Chorman Special Forces.

And quite naturally the so-called "evacuation centers" would demand identification papers from everyone who queued up to escape the waterless, contaminated city. After distributing enough drug-laced bottled water to render the herds complacent, undesirables could easily be culled from among those citizens sheeplike enough to be spared. Aerial stealth cameras would sail invisibly up and down the queues, scanning the citizens with their infrared eyes, looking for those not tagged with tracking implants or mind-controlling hardware.

It went without saying that Mikhail would not be among the evacuees. But he was no stubborn old man teetering on the brink of dementia -- no, Mikhail Litvinenko was a soldier, with a soldier's training and iron resolve. Moreover he had anticipated just such a citywide cleansing operation as this one since long ago. And this soldier was prepared.

Mikhail began bustling around his little apartment, stacking his evidence folders, stashing the more incriminating documents under the mattress. There was much to do now. Provisions to pack, boobytraps to set, arrangements to be made. He was not a bit sorry to leave his old apartment -- the traps would protect the evidence he had compiled if the landlord tried to poke around in here before heading down to the evacuation center. And Mikhail was exchanging this place for much more comfortable surroundings, those with their own drug-free water supply.

Within an hour or two, he would be checking in as the sole guest of the Hotel Litvinenko.

~~~~~

Col. Akimov tore his eyes away from the map of Khostok that decorated the wall of the public broadcast system's office. An anemic-looking intern was fishing a series of tapes out of the broadcast equipment: recordings of Akimov's speech, intended for distribution to the radio stations and TV stations of Khostok. Akimov pointed the muzzle of his gas mask at the intern, who noticed the attention and scuttled hastily out of the office with a double-armful of recordings. The door clicked shut behind him.

"Permission to speak, Colonel?"

"Permission granted, Hawk."

"Excellent announcement, sir."

"Thank you." Akimov allowed himself a rare smile, since his face was hidden by his mask anyway. He turned to the four CSF soldiers who had accompanied him up to make the broadcast.

"Comrades," he began, drawing himself up to his full height. "You four are my elites. You will be the first to hear our strategy in managing the Khostok quarantine. I will be dispensing special duties to each of you as the situation becomes clearer.

"Our objectives are as follows: Secretary Glukhovsky has indicated that it is absolutely essential for us to both maintain the quarantine as well as sanitize Khostok itself. There will be several steps involved in meeting these two goals.

"First and foremost, we must obtain and control the Lubukov Agricultural Labs. We will need to know exactly which chemical has leaked, and to gather all of the data they can offer on that substance. The Secretary was only able to provide so much official documentation; those at the Labs will have been studying this chemical, and their knowledge is indispensable.

"Second, we must press the employees of the Labs into study of the bioweapon -- its effects, its transmission methods, its antidotes if any exist, its lethality to human and nonhuman life. To formulate a test for detecting this bioweapon's presence in the human body will be their highest initial priority.

"Third, we must establish processing centers. Citizens will be directed to the nearest center for 'evacuation', and will undergo a screening that detects whether or not they have been contaminated by the leaked bioweapon.

"Fourth, we must establish holding camps to separate the population after they have been processed. These will be of two types: clean camps, to hold uncontaminated citizens, and quarantine camps to contain those who test positive for the chemical.

"In our fifth step, once we have seen all citizens of Khostok accounted for we must evacuate the clean camp populations to nearby Byatin.

"And in our sixth and final step, we must deal with the contaminated populations of the quarantine camps. Those contaminated must be sanitized by any means necessary; the findings of the Labs will assist us here. Is this all understood?"

"Understood, sir!" the soldiers chorused, saluting, and Akimov found himself holding back another smile. Such crisply mechanical responses for organic creatures. These elites were a credit to their entire species.

"Then let's get back to the vehicles."

~~~~~

"We've been abandoned."

"Hush, lad."

"They've left us to die in here! They have!"

"Now cut that out; you're scaring people with that nonsense."

" -- or they're going to wait until we're good and weak from starvation and then send the liquidators in! They'll come marching in here with their jackboots and automatic rifles and -- "

"Vadik!!" Boris slammed a fist against the locked lunchroom door. "Shut up!"

Vadim, mercifully, did consent to shut up for a minute or two. A couple of the lunchroom prisoners sighed in relief, though most had already grown accustomed to the noise and were scarcely aware that he'd stopped crying.

Alexei was likewise unaware that Vadim had fallen silent. In his case, it was because he'd crammed himself into the corner of the lunchroom furthest from the door and put his hands over his ears. In truth he felt Vadim's dire predictions were completely accurate, and Alexei had anticipated the same outcome himself: slow starvation or the business end of a gun. It would be the only way for them to cover up the accident. Alexei didn't share this with anyone, but it made listening to Vadim nearly intolerable.

Something nudged the toe of his shoe, and Alexei opened his eyes. Yuri was standing over him with a paper plate in one hand and a mug in the other.

"Hungry?"

Alexei shook his head, letting his hands fall by his sides. Yuri tilted his head to one side, considering, then sat down next to him anyway. "Some of the guys decided to cook up some breakfast...eggs and toast, nothing fancy. Coffee if you want it. Lucky we've still got power in the building," he remarked. "The refrigerator's still cold, the air's still running..." he gestured with his fork up towards the vents overhead. "Could be worse. At least we got trapped in the lunchroom...imagine those guys who got stuck in the labs, eh? Nothing to eat but mold cultures."

Alexei stared at the floor.

Chewing on a piece of toast, Yuri glanced at the clock. "...Feels like we've been in here much longer than twelve hours, huh?"

"Yeah," Alexei said.

"You know, they can't just leave us in here." Yuri reasoned. "It'd be a big scandal if we all vanished. We've got families -- in Khostok, in other cities."

Alexei shrugged his shoulders.

"Got a wife? girlfriend?"

"Um, no," Alexei admitted.

"Ah, well, you're young. You've got time."

Alexei realized he was doing nothing to keep the limping conversation on its feet, but the way his stomach was knotting up made it difficult to talk. "So you, uh, do you have a family?"

"Yep. I've got a daughter." Yuri beamed at him. "Brightest child you've ever seen. Gets top marks in her Science class. Hey, you should meet her -- after we get out of here I'll invite you over to dinner, how's that?"

Alexei blinked at him. "Oh...uh, sure, of course. Thank you."

"Don't mention it. But don't get any funny ideas about Elena -- she's only ten years old." Yuri leveled his fork at Alexei.

Alexei blushed and stammered, but Yuri was already chuckling at his reaction. "Kidding, I'm kidding."

"Heh, of course." Alexei smiled faintly. He was feeling more and more like having some breakfast after all.

"Hey, look at that!"

"Huh?"

Yuri had half-turned to look back over his shoulder. "The biohazard light! look!"

Alexei looked for a good several seconds before it hit him: the flashing red light had gone off.

Before he could react a gurgling scream ripped through the lunchroom, killing all the conversations, and Alexei's heart surged up into his throat. A moment later Boris pounded on the lunchroom door, harder this time. "Vadim!" he bawled. "Stop that!"

Vadim shrieked again, the sound of a man in agonizing terror. "They're here!" he shouted, and it sounded like he was clawing at his side of the door. "They're here! oh God, the liquidators are here for us!!"

Boris lifted his hand to beat on the door again, and one of the other employees held him back. "Listen!"

"Huh?"

"Ssh, listen! listen!"

They listened. At first there was nothing but Vadim's quiet sobbing and the whir of the ventilation system.

"...what -- "

" -- ssh! Can't you hear it?"

Alexei sat forward, holding his breath. And then it came to him, a low rhythmic thumping, like distant machinery. It grew in volume, swelling louder, and the floor began to quiver.

"Those are boots," Yuri whispered.

From somewhere out in the hallway there came the sound of the stairwell door being unlocked. Vadim gave a positively inhuman howl and flung himself against the other side of the door.

"Help me!! help me!!"

The lunchroom captives were on their feet, inching away from the door. Now they could hear another voice, deep and raspy, shouting out commands over the tromping of heavy rubber-soled boots.

Alexei ducked behind Yuri, who was brandishing his coffee cup as if to bash someone with it. His hand was shaking so that coffee was slopping out onto the floor, but he seemed not to notice. Even Boris was backing away from the door, his normally florid face white with contagious fear.

"No! NO!" Vadim screamed. "Don't shoot!! don't -- "

There was the noise of an impact, and then all was still.

Nobody dared breathe. And then, with chilling clarity, they heard sound of keys clicking on the external door keypad. The locks clunked open and the door swung outward, revealing an inhuman silhouette looming in the doorway.

Alexei choked back a scream.

The thing stepped into the room, its black skin shining like a frog's, the muzzle of its gas mask swinging left and right as it took in the petrified employees. It gripped an AKS-47 in its gloved hands, not aimed but held at the ready. Light flashed from the glass eyepieces in its mask.

"Is anyone sick?" it croaked.

No response. The thing took another step towards them, and the employees shrank away from it. "Is anyone in here sick?" it asked again, more slowly.

Yuri cleared his throat. "No, no, nobody sick in here."

"Mm." The soldier -- for that's what the thing was, only a soldier in an imposing-looking protective suit -- lifted a hand and depressed a button on the side of his gas mask. "Colonel. Eagle here. More employees in the lunchroom. About fifteen or so." He paused. "No, they say they're clean." Another pause. "We've got one down in the hallway. Potentially contaminated. "

"...Vadim!" Boris exclaimed. He moved as if to leave and the soldier's rifle snapped up. "Stop!"

Boris stopped.

"Back against the wall," the soldier ordered, sweeping the sights across the rest of the crowd. Everyone stumbled backwards, pressing themselves against the tacked-up announcements and notifications that littered the wall of the lunchroom. Alexei could feel his bladder threatening to betray him and prayed that wouldn't happen.

"Sorry, sir. Please repeat." With a hand on the side of his mask, the soldier stood in silence for several minutes, nodding occasionally. "Copy that, sir. Over."

The soldier looked up at the captives again, dropping his hand. "Your attention please," he asked, rather unnecessarily. "The Chorman Special Forces, under the leadership of Colonel Akimov and by direction of Regional Defense Secretary Glukhovsky, have taken control of the Lubukov Agricultural Labs in response to the recent biohazard alert. At this time we believe some of the hazardous material that triggered the alerts may also have made it into Khostok. The city is now under quarantine."

Nobody spoke a word, but their expressions were eloquent enough. "We will require your cooperation in working to manage the potential threat resulting from this leak. Your facility and your knowledge represent valuable resources needed by your fellow citizens. For the time being, you will all be conducted to the overnight dormitories on Level U2 of this facility. You will be given food and clean clothing, and more information as necessary.

"Any questions?" the soldier asked, fingering the trigger guard of his AKS-47 in a significant manner.

"...what did you do to Vadik?" Boris asked.

"Who?"

"The young man out in the hallway," Yuri explained.

"Oh. Your comrade will be taken care of," the CSF soldier said vaguely. Shards of ice crystallized in Alexei's veins. "Any other questions? No? good. Now, we are going to go out this door, down the hall to the stairs, and straight down to U2. I will be following you. Do not attempt to leave the group, or to deviate from this course. Understood?"

Several people nodded. Stepping back out through the doorway, the soldier swung his rifle in a wide arc. "Then let's go."

Stumbling and crowding one-another like sheep, the employees filed out the door, past the soldier. Boris was one of the first out in the hallway, and Alexei heard him shouting Vadim's name in a way that was pitiful to hear. "Keep moving!" barked their new captor, and the line jolted forward again.

Alexei's whole body was buzzing with anxiety, clouding his thoughts. In a kind of fog he shuffled forward after Yuri, passing out through the door under the soldier's expressionless gaze. Glancing back, he found what Boris had seen -- Vadim lay motionless on the floor in the hallway, arms and legs flung out in all directions, dried blood matting along his hairline, a blackish stain -- a bruise, most likely -- discoloring his nose and mouth. The soldier had put himself between Vadim and the door, preventing anyone from reaching the young man as they filed out of the breakroom, but that didn't stop the employees from seeing him.

Yuri halted in front of the soldier. "We need to get medical attention for him," he said, pointing to Vadim. Alexei ducked his head and quickly scooted away, desperate not to get involved. Obviously the man had no compunctions about beating down unarmed civilians; Yuri had to be insane to draw attention like that.

"We will handle it," the soldier rasped. "You just -- *hey! Keep away from that*!" he bellowed suddenly, and Alexei felt a warm trickle along the inside of one pants leg. He flattened himself against the wall as the soldier charged forward, pushing the employees away from the left-hand side of the hallway. Some small part of his mind was grateful that he'd chosen to wear black pants to work.

"Keep right! keep right! stay away from that wall!"

Everyone cowered away from the wall in question, looking up with wide eyes. Alexei saw nothing but an inky streak running along the plaster, as if someone's pen had broken in their hand and they'd wiped the stains off onto the wall.

Then it struck him -- that was the "graffiti" Vadim had talked about, thinking it was engine oil. He'd tasted some of it...

Alexei hesitated, looking back, and someone blundered into him. "Keep moving!" the soldier shouted again, and Alexei was carried forward with the rest of the crowd.

They reached the stairs without incident, their footsteps resounding hollowly in the uninsulated stairwell as they descended. At the door for U2, the second underground level, the soldier stepped forward to type the override code into the keypad and open the door for them, letting the employees file through ahead of him.

But they'd barely gotten through the door when the group suddenly came to a dead halt.

There were a half-dozen cries of alarm and disgust, and someone coming down the stairs behind him bumped into Alexei again, sending him staggering out of the stairwell door and into someone else. They sprawled onto the tile floor to the sound of the soldier shouting for them to keep moving and demanding to know why they had stopped.

On his hands and knees, Alexei's arm brushed something cold. He turned and found himself looking into the face of a stranger.

His first impression was that this curiously cold and grey person was someone who'd been in the lunchroom with them, though the face was unfamiliar. Yes, he must've fallen with the rest of them while coming down the stairs, and now he was lying on his back with his eyes open because he was stunned by the fall. His skin was the color of wet clay because...well, because it was. And the small round hole in his forehead was...was...was...

"Move away, move away!" barked the soldier, elbowing his way through the crowd. When he reached the corpse he paused, swore loudly, and reached for the button on his gas mask. "Colonel sir!" he said. "We've got a situation here. Dead body on U2." The soldier waited, listening. "I don't -- *hey*!!"

"Comrade!!" Yuri shouted, but all too late. Alexei was gone.

He'd never run so fast in his life; he practically flew. In his defense, it wasn't the dead body as much as the conviction that they were being taken to meet the same fate as the grotesquely staring thing on the floor. They'd all be lined up against the bathroom wall and shot in the head, one by one. That, his mother had assured him, was how they did things in this country.

Over the sound of his gasping breaths Alexei could hear soldier's boots pounding against the tile, but he was much faster than his heavily-equipped pursuer. Alexei skidded around a bend in the hallway, lab coat flapping around his knees, and sighted the door leading into the second staircase. He was practically there already, and in his mind's eye it all unrolled before him with perfect clarity. He would reach that door, sprint up the stairs, emerge onto the ground floor and flee through the main entrance. Nobody up there would be expecting him; the only person who knew he was trying to escape was the soldier behind him, and there was no way that one could catch --

There was a sharp little explosion. At first he mistook the noise for a firecracker; he only recognized the sound of gunfire when the second and third bullet hit their intended target. It was like being punched by a giant, and to Alexei's point of view the floor whisked itself out from under his feet and slapped up against the side of his body.

*I've been shot*, Alexei said to himself, and then his brain settled into neutral. His arm and side were pulsing with a steady burning heat. He tasted dust.

The floor quivered as the soldier closed the gap between them, muttering under his breath. *I've been shot*, Alexei remarked again, and vaguely wondered if the soldier was coming to put a bullet in the back of his head and finish what had been started. He supposed that being executed first was better than being the last, after all.

"*Eagle*!" someone bellowed.

"Hawk!" the soldier responded. "I was just -- "

"Stand down, soldier!" The first voice also had that curious gas-mask-distortion to it, but it was louder than Eagle's and even more terrifying. Alexei managed to turn his head to one side, looking back the way he'd come. From his skewed perspective as he lay on the hallway floor he saw two CSF soldiers now: the one who'd shot him, who was still holding his AKS, and an even taller one with different insignia on the left breast of their protective suit.

Eagle switched on the safety and let his rifle drop against the carrying sling, putting up both hands in a supplicating gesture. "Hawk, I was just -- "

" -- We need these people to *help* us! shooting them is *not* going to accomplish that!"

" -- but he was escaping!" Eagle protested, pointing down the hall at the stairwell door that Alexei would never reach.

The soldier known as Hawk turned and wordlessly clomped their way down the hall, stepping over Alexei's prone body, all the way to the stairwell door in question. They pressed down on the handle and pushed into the door with their shoulder. After several tries Hawk came clomping back again, stepping over Alexei a second time.

"That door?"

Eagle did not respond.

"This civilian was trying to escape through that door?"

Eagle's voice was tiny. "Yes, sir."

"The stairwell door? the one that is locked? the one he couldn't possibly have opened since he did not know the goddamn keycode that unlocks the doors?"

"Yes, s -- aagh!" Eagle squawked as his superior grabbed hold of the respirator on his gas mask, shaking it back and forth.

"You knew you were the only one down here, and each and every door has to be manually unlocked." Hawk tugged the soldier's mask right and left and Eagle clapped both hands over the respirator, trying to prevent it being twisted off. "And yet your only solution to preventing an escape -- the escape of a valuable asset, whom we want to keep alive -- is to *shoot him in the back*?!"

"Sir, look! look!" Eagle cried out, pointing again.

Alexei looked as well. Yuri, who was creeping down the hall toward the two soldiers, froze in his tracks.

"What are you doing here, comrade?" Hawk asked, still holding his subordinate's mask.

" -- I...just trying to...get to him," Yuri said. His face was chalk-white. It dawned on Alexei that Yuri was trying, of all things, to rescue him.

Hawk made an offhanded gesture and Yuri scuttled over to Alexei. Up close, Alexei could see that he was sweating. "You're okay, you're okay..." Yuri whispered, almost to himself, as he probed around the burning areas on Alexei's back. "It's just your shoulder and your arm. You're okay. C'mon, get up and let's go before they change their minds, eh?"

Alexei made the mistake of looking down at himself, and found that his formerly white lab coat was dyed a deep crimson all along one sleeve. The bottom fell out of his stomach. "I'm dying," he whimpered.

"No, it only looks bad. You'll be fine." Yuri was pulling Alexei to his feet, a hand hooked under his good arm. Alexei's shoe skidded in the blood that had pooled on the tile beneath him. His own blood, bright red on the white tiles. "Oh god..."

"Ah, come on. I think my daughter's got more guts than you." Yuri gave another tug and Alexei lurched up onto his feet, his good arm slung across Yuri's shoulders.

"That's right...you're okay, you're okay..." The two of them stumbled off down the hall together, back toward the rest of their group. Meanwhile Hawk had just finished berating Eagle and had send the soldier hurrying in the same direction. Arms folded, Hawk watched as Yuri and Alexei made their way down the hall.

"Thank you, young man," Yuri whispered as they passed alongside Hawk.

The soldier paused, then snorted through their mask. "I'm not a man," Hawk said, and stalked off toward the group as well.

# CHAPTER FOUR

In the days following the chemical leak at the Lubukov Agricultural Labs, the Chorman Special Forces spread through Khostok like a virus. On the morning after the leak there were twenty CSF soldiers in the city; that night there were fifty. At the end of the first week there were well over two hundred soldiers in Khostok, establishing camps and distributing clean water, bustling about like humanoid ants in their glossy protective suits. The sound of their croaking voices carried over the rooftops and echoed in the repurposed gymnasiums and auditoriums that now served as camps to hold the city's displaced citizens.

Curfew hours had been declared on the first day. Necessary personnel had been ordered in to work; all other civilians had been ordered to stay home and await the announcement summoning their neighborhood to the local processing center. The public broadcasting system spoke almost hourly during daylight hours, encouraging, reminding, promising, occasionally threatening.

Meanwhile, down by the waterside along the banks of the Volgin River, a different kind of invasion was occurring. The taking of the river was much slower and quieter than the CSF's conquest of Khostok but it was no less efficient. In the week since Dmitri's ancient little car had plunged through the fence and into the river, the Volgin River valley had changed.

As it so happened the least of these changes was the most visible one: a blanket of fog hung over the river, concealing it from view.

The fog had been rising daily since the car crash, as if the near-opaque whiteness was the river itself, swollen with rain and preparing to overrun its banks and flood the city. Thus far the mist had not yet reached the fence, though it crept incrementally closer with every hour. The CSF soldiers stationed at the reinforced Volgin River Gate certainly noticed the expanding fog in the valley beneath the bridge, but maintaining the quarantine occupied a far larger place in their thoughts than an unseasonal and unusually persistent weather phenomenon.

Below the ghostly veil that lay over the valley the alteration of the Volgin River continued unabated. Plants sprouted and flowers bloomed in the weak sunlight that filtered down through the fog, and living creatures crept about in the undergrowth. But as yet nobody had ventured down into the valley, so the nature of the blooming and creeping things that now lived there was unknown.

And still they continued to change.

~~~~~

Veronika considered herself one of the sanest people she knew. In high school and those brief months she'd spent at college she had been known for her stability; her classmates thought her a bit abrasive, or maybe even a little callous, but ultimately a very practical person. Not the sort to lose her head over boys, or drink herself stupid at parties, or jump from the roof after failing a final exam.

Privately she took courage from the idea that she could depend on herself, if nobody else. She'd been given the perfect chance to lose her mind four years ago, but she hadn't taken it, and now that the opportunity had passed she was more unflappable than ever. Veronika was not, nor had she ever been, the sort of person to go into hysterics over the possibility that she might be ill, even seriously ill. Certainly not the sort of person to disintegrate into childish blubbering over something so simple as changing out a bandage.

Gritting her teeth, Veronika unwound the last spirals of gauze and let them drop into the wastebasket. She gasped at the sight of her arm, then held the breath and forced herself to let it go in a slow, measured hiss.

Eight days had passed since she'd cut herself on the nail at the Kravchenkos' place, putting a good-sized gash into the side of her left hand. And it had been seven days since she'd washed the hand at the bathroom sink.

The cut she'd received had completely healed, but Veronika barely noticed. At first glance her entire arm looked gangrenous, diseased. Not only that, but the dark discoloration was growing -- at first it had been the side of her hand, near the healed gash. Then the color had spread to the entire hand, and then it had crossed her wrist and begun working its way up her arm, staining the healthy tissue.

The fact that it *wasn't* gangrene did little to reassure her. As horrible as it was, necrosis was something that could be understood, could be found in the dictionary and could be combatted. The thing currently eating her arm was an enigma, and the horrible possibilities were nearly unlimited.

In the simplest terms, it was turning her skin black. Not the black of an infected limb, but a patchy blue-black like oddly-colored bruises, appearing just beneath the surface of the skin and darkening as they spread. She had no pain or swelling, though the affected area was more sensitive and the skin perhaps a bit warmer than normal. And from time to time the whole area would tingle all over, pins and needles, as if she'd fallen asleep on the arm. But if Veronika had been blind she might have remained unaware of the black discoloration creeping up toward her shoulder.

She had wasted some of the precious clean water the CSF soldiers had distributed in the neighborhoods, boiling it and washing her arm with generous amounts of soap. After that had failed Veronika had spent one painful night in the bathroom with a wire brush, the door locked, trying to scrub the stains away. When Grigori had found her a half-hour later he had nearly broken down the door in an effort to get her to come out. "It won't come off," she had said, fighting with him for the brush without realizing she was doing it. "It's under my skin. It's inside me."

When the self-inflicted abrasions had healed over the next day they were replaced with skin of a smooth and shiny jet-black, like latex rubber. That was when Veronika had begun to doubt what she was seeing. Now she simply kept the arm covered in gauze, but the lack of pain or stiffness would make her start to doubt that anything was the matter with it, that it was all in her head. Then she would unwrap her arm and the sight would make her nauseous all over again.

There were times that she felt her screws were coming loose, a half-turn at a time. Little things, mostly. Her mind had begun to take strange, sudden detours into places she didn't recognize.

She'd catch herself wondering what would happen to her tomato garden when they evacuated, or who would watch her pet dog, or how her sister and her husband were getting by. Then it would dawn on her that she had no tomato garden, no dog and certainly no sister. Usually the tingling of her arm would distract her shortly afterward, and she'd try to forget about it. She could have told Grigori, of course, but she didn't want to worry him.

And that was really the reason why Veronika kept her arm wrapped in gauze. It was partly so she didn't have to see it, but really it was Grigori she wanted hide it from. Sighing, she flexed her hand one more time and held the strip of clean gauze between her first and second finger, starting to wrap herself again.

She had been so nearly positive that the thing in the sink was, like the nonexistent tomato garden, purely in her head. When she had spotted the dark patch in the bowl of the sink, down near the drain, her first thought had been mold -- after all, the two of them hadn't used the sink since the announcement about the water supply. It was only when she got closer that she began to suspect it was not mold in there, but a hallucination.

There was a tiny, tiny plant in the sink, growing on the metal grate of the drain. In truth it did look rather fungoid: it was fuzzy, like a patch of black fur, with little tendrils reaching up towards the faucet. It only began to seem unreal when Veronika leaned in closer and realized that there were tiny dots scattered throughout the black fuzz, minuscule orbs in shades of indigo and violet and royal blue. The size of and shape of pinheads, the orbs had a strange translucence to them, making them look almost gemlike.

Thinking of the gas bubbles in sea-kelp, Veronika had unthinkingly reached into the sink. She didn't touch the fuzzy patch, but when her gauze-wrapped fingers had come close enough the black stuff seemed to move, very slightly. And just as she was thinking she was seeing things, the little orbs began to change shape.

Veronika had bent so close her head was in the sink, and there could be no mistaking it -- the "orbs" had been flower buds, and now they were opening, petals unfolding like tiny mouths to reveal blossoms that glowed, literally glowed, with a faint undersea luminescence. And then just as her arm had started tingling, Grigori had walked into the bathroom.

He had screamed and dragged her away and gone on to douse the thing with alcohol and light it on fire, which got rid of it at the expense of a horrific stench, like burnt sugar. This had pretty well resolved the question of whether she'd dreamed up the little plant, unless it were somehow possible for two people to share a hallucination, and that Veronika doubted.

But recently Grigori had not seemed too incredibly stable himself. His overreaction regarding the plant had been one thing, but there were many other things she had noticed recently, and it was starting to scare her. Thank god the announcement this morning had cleared their neighborhood to report to the local processing center for evacuation. Veronika might have started the week as one of the sanest people she could think of, but she wouldn't be ending it that way.

Somewhere off in the house the floorboards creaked. Veronika lifted her head, listening, and then there was another squeaking thump. Grigori was getting out of bed.

A pang of premature homesickness struck her. She wouldn't be hearing the old house again, she knew. The announcements had promised they would be returned to their homes after the quarantine of Khostok had been lifted, but between the two of them neither brother nor sister really believed this was true. Wherever they ended up -- likely in some cheap government-sponsored housing project -- it'd be an alien environment, with quiet doors and noiseless floors, and strangers moving around above and below her as silent as ghosts.

"Mom!"

Veronika's skin prickled. She hoped she'd misheard him, but then Grigori shouted again, louder this time.

"Mom!"

The bedroom floorboards sang out as Grigori wandered into the hallway. She heard a soft impact, as if he'd blundered into the wall. "Mama!" he called, his voice cracking.

Veronika tucked the end of her bandage into place and rushed to find him. Sure enough Grigori was in the bedroom hallway, fumbling against the wallpaper as if trying to find an invisible doorknob. "Grigori!"

He turned in her direction and looked straight through her, and Veronika's words stuck in her throat. His pupils were enormously dilated, the irises swallowed up by twin pools of ink.

" -- Ilsa?" Grigori said uncertainly. "Where's Mom? she's left the laundry out on the line and it looks like it's gonna rain today."

Veronika stared back at him. In one corner of his mouth was a dark stain, like coal dust smudged on the skin.

"She's got that new dress out there; we'll have to take the laundry in ourselves if she doesn't." Grigori moved as if to go past her and Veronika put a hand on his shoulder.

"Grisha..."

"...who?" He squinted down at her bandaged arm, then up at her face. "Where's Mom?"

"She's dead, Grisha."

"Huh?"

"She died four years ago. With Dad." Some small part of her wanted not to tell him -- if Grigori had forgotten about the accident, so much the better -- but she wanted him to be here with her. Too much was falling apart for Grigori's brain to take a vacation right now. "The car crash, remember?"

"...the car..." Now Veronika could see his irises again; the pupils were shrinking back to their normal size. He blinked several times rapidly, like someone coming out of a deep sleep. "Nika?" He looked surprised to see her there. "What's happening?"

She shrugged and let her hand fall. Really, she had no clue what was happening.

Grigori was turning left and right, discovering the hallway. "I...think I was sleepwalking," he said.

Sleepwalking. Veronika liked the sound of that. To think that Grigori had been "sleepwalking" was about as plausible as thinking her arm was just bruised, but at the moment she would take any explanation she could get.

"C'mon, let's get to the processing center," she said softly. "We don't want to be the last ones on the bus."

~~~~~

Perhaps it was for the better that Nikita had never married. If he couldn't look after a child for a week without accidentally poisoning her, he clearly wasn't cut out for family life.

"Feeling okay?" he asked for perhaps the fiftieth time. Elena was leaning her head against his side and he felt it when she nodded in reply. If she was tired of being asked she gave no sign of it. The nightmares she'd been having seemed to have taken all the spirit out of the girl, and she huddled against Nikita without speaking.

The processing center was no more than a series of tents erected in Dragovich Park -- they had sprung up overnight, like blue plastic mushrooms emblazoned with the Chorman Special Forces logo. The plastic sheeting rippled in the morning breeze that swept through the grass. Beyond the tents, somewhere, buses sat waiting to receive the Khostok citizenry.

Nikita had never given it consideration before, but to individually examine and evacuate forty thousand human beings was no weekend task. The queue leading up to the main tent was seemingly endless, sectioned off with stakes strung with plastic chain, folded back on itself like a gigantic intestine.

The two of them were buried somewhere in the middle of the colon, surrounded by people on all sides. Claustrophobic as it was, the bodies around them were at least keeping them insulated from the chill of the early morning. Nikita had lost sight of the end of the line and so he presumed they were getting closer to the processing tent, but at the moment it seemed miles away. They crept forward by inches, with nothing to do but listen to the murmurs and cries that rippled through the crowd.

"My aunt was evacuated last week and she still hasn't contacted me. Where d'you suppose they're sending them?"

"...for hours and hours! they should have more than *one* person up there processing us!"

"They're just checking papers, right? I've only got temporary citizenship, but it's current...do you think..."

"...you should see him! his entire foot, all blackened! It looks like the potato blight, that's what I said to him, just like a potato. He says it doesn't hurt him any, but you know..."

Tucked underneath Nikita's arm, Elena stirred and muttered something. Nikita bent down to her. "What's that?"

"...just like this," Elena repeated.

"What? just like what?"

"They lined us up just like this." Elena's voice was low, almost a monotone. "Out in the snow, the rain, for hours, just to get a spoonful of that pigshit they were calling soup. Not that anyone cared about how the prisoners were getting by; we were 'enemy combatants', after all. They'd have ground us up and fed us to each-other if the didn't need us to build their damned railroads and -- "

"Elena!" Nikita grabbed her shoulders and twisted her around to face him. His heart skipped a beat when he saw her eyes: the blue was gone, replaced with a bottomless black. He dropped to his knees, still holding onto her. After a panicked second he found the thin ring of blue iris and realized that her pupils were just severely dilated.

"Elena!" Nikita cried, shaking her. She blinked, not seeing him, her face contorting as she swore again.

He slapped her then, and the wave of guilt that washed through him was sickening. "...Lena," he whispered, but he could already see her pupils shrinking, the blue coming back to her eyes. She started a little when she focused on his face, as if she'd forgotten he was here. "Uncle Nikita?" she quavered, holding her cheek.

Still kneeling in the grass, Nikita pulled her into a hug. His eyes were burning. Elena oof'ed and hugged him back.

"Are you alright? are you alright?"

Elena nodded for perhaps the fiftieth time. "When are we gonna get processed?" she asked, and Nikita shook his head. "I don't know, Lena, I don't know. Hopefully soon."

The line was not moving all that quickly and so Nikita stayed on his knees for awhile, holding his niece and wondering how on earth things had gone so wrong so quickly. When he looked up he realized that the man and woman in line ahead of him were watching them.

"She's not feeling well," Nikita explained.

The man, a big broad fellow with wild black hair and a bruise in the corner of his mouth, nodded in understanding. The girlishly skinny woman who stood beside him had the same eyes and the same dark hair, though hers was long enough to reach below her shoulder-blades "We're not feeling too well either," she admitted.

Nikita could see that -- the woman's left arm was swathed in bandages halfway up to the shoulder. He didn't ask.

"How old's your girl?"

"Oh...she's ten. But she's not mine," Nikita said, still patting Elena's back. "She's my brother's daughter. I'm just watching her." And doing a terrible job of it, he added.

The woman was considering Elena. "She was probably sleepwalking," she said gently.

Nikita wondered if Elena could have fallen asleep in the middle of the day, while standing up. Then he decided that yes, she could indeed have done that...you had to consider that she was under stress, and sleep-deprived from the nightmares she'd been having ever since they'd announced the accident at the Labs.

Yes, sleepwalking. That sounded good. Easy to understand, not at all dangerous or frightening. Nodding to himself, Nikita rose to his feet again, letting Elena settle back against his side.

"I'll make sure you get some sleep on the bus," he promised. Elena looked up at him -- her eyes were still blue, thank God -- and gave a little smile, wide enough to show the gap where her tooth was missing.

~~~~~

As far as such establishments went, the Hotel Litvinenko left much to be desired. Most amenities a guest would take for granted were missing -- electricity, for one, and running water was another. Though lavishly decorated, the opulence of the hotel's interior was dulled under a fuzzy coat of dust, blurring the carven details on the gold-painted furniture and fading the carpet to a washed-out gray. Pigeons nested in the topmost floor, painting the eaves white with their droppings. The mice had thoroughly claimed the rest of the building, leaving their tiny footprints in the dust that lay on glass-topped tables and silk bedsheets.

The lack of water and power further diminished any charm the hotel might once have possessed, back when it was known as the Hotel Komarov. The fountain in the lobby was dry, its marble basin littered with tarnished coins. The lamps, with stained-glass lampshades made to resemble drooping flower blossoms, were unlit. The elevator was stuck forever at the first floor, its door open to receive the vanished hotel guests.

The sole occupant, also the de facto owner of the hotel, did not mind. Lighting could be provided with oil lamps. Heating and cooking were both accomplished with small military camping stoves, and there was a generous supply of fuel for these. Bringing the water up to the seventh floor had been the most challenging task, what with the elevator being inoperable, but the guest had managed.

Even the staircase was useless at a certain point. The stairs leading from the second to the third floor were completely crammed with furniture: coffee tables, dining chairs, brocaded lounge recliners, sofas...even a great armoire lay on its side on the staircase, its glass doors shattered. It looked as if a moving crew had given up halfway through their assignment. And throughout this jungle of broken wood and ripped fabric someone had strung a series of ropes, tying the biggest pieces together and binding the whole mess into an impenetrable blockade.

All this was intended, of course, to deter unwanted visitors. The stopped elevator and blocked stairs were not enough to prevent the hotel's only guest from ascending to his penthouse on the seventh floor, to the suite reserved for visiting officials and other dignitaries. He simply walked up the stairs to the second floor, then stepped into the open elevator shaft and stood atop the roof of the stalled elevator car.

Looking up into the shaft from this angle, one could locate a rope-ladder made from broken chair legs and lashed together with satin drapery cords. After climbing this up through the shaft from the second to the third floor -- thus cleverly avoiding the blockade -- one could take the staircase the rest of the way from the third to the seventh floor, where the Hotel Litvinenko's sole guest had made his home.

The penthouse was resplendent with ruined luxury, an eulogy for the hotel's wealthier days. Classical paintings in gilt frames hung on the cobwebbed walls, the carpet's faded pile was deep and soft as spring grass, and beneath the veneer of grime one could still see the formerly milk-white marble of the bathroom floor. The bath would comfortably have accepted four people, and the taps were gold with mother-of-pearl knobs. The four-poster king-size bed was covered with finest silk sheets and a heavy quilt, both of them grey with the dust of years, but in former times the sheets had been white and the comforter a deep crimson embellished with silver and gold thread.

All of this splendor was lost on the guest, who appreciated the hotel mainly for its security and its view. He had left his cookstove in a circle of scorched carpet in the middle of the bedroom, and his military surplus sleeping bag lay just beside it. A backpack brimming with bottles of water had been flung beneath the marble-topped dining table. Beside it were four precious boxes of ammunition, brought up to the penthouse with much strain and toil.

The guest himself lay stretched out on his stomach on the patio deck outside, peering down through the railing at the ground seven stories below. From his vantage point he could see for miles up and down the street, all the way down to the Victor Kurylenko Concert Hall. From this distance the CSF vehicles parked outside the concert hall were small as black beetles; the buses themselves were green caterpillars of larger size, and the people that swarmed in and out of the vehicles were tiny black-and-white ants.

Setting his binoculars down beside his face, the guest reached out with his right hand. His fingers danced across the barrel of his Mosin-Nagant rifle, lying beside him on the concrete deck, and closed around the bottle of water. He took a drink, relishing the taste of clean water unadulterated by brain-scrambling chemical agents, and set the bottle back down again, picking up his binoculars once more.

And Mikhail resumed watching.

~~~~~

Several miles away, at a slightly lower elevation, Colonel Akimov of the Chorman Special Forces reclined in the leather desk chair at his provisional command post on the top floor of the Khostok Police Station. The seventh floor had been mostly dedicated to administrative functions, but Police Chief Petrenko had assured him that the people performing those functions would be only too grateful to surrender their offices to the Special Forces in the event of a crisis such as this.

The station had been an ideal spot for his command post for many reasons: its central location in the city, its fortified structure, the availability of surplus manpower in the form of the local police officers, the radio signal boosters it possessed. From his post at the station Akimov could tap into police communications and make hourly broadcasts of his own, letting the citizens of Khostok hear that the situation was under control.

And it *was* under control; he felt it in his bones. At present everything was running smoothly, moving parts fitting neatly into place. Like a well-oiled machine.

Petrenko had cordially provided a large map of Khostok for Akimov to keep in his provisional command post; this was spread across the oaken desk in the former human resources office. Akimov went to the desk and bent over the map, throwing his shadow onto the colorful gridwork of roads and city blocks.

Akimov was particularly gifted with mechanical systems -- had he not joined the Forces, he might have become an engineer. To visualize a system in motion, seeing in his mind's eye the action of each individual part upon the others, was second nature to him. With the map before him he called upon this ability now, charting the progress of the evacuation.

As he watched the map became filled with tiny gray dots, like ball bearings: the unprocessed citizens. They flowed through the network of streets which channeled each of them into their designated processing center. From the centers emerged two different colors of ball bearings: red and blue. The blue dots cascaded through the mapped-out streets to the boxes marked EVAC CAMP, and from there the dots were loaded into tiny green rectangles which drained out of Khostok via the Volgin River Bridge. The red dots were diverted into their own camps, which were indicated on the map by boxes labeled QC CAMP -- Quarantined Citizens.

It was, Akimov reflected, like a giant sorting machine at a factory. You could consider the blue dots to be products which met quality standards, and the buses were shipping them out to the consumers. The red dots, those defective ones which had failed to meet tolerance, were being funneled into reject boxes.

Thus far this system was running as predicted, and all of his calculations had proven accurate. The evacuation camps had been erected and were already receiving the clean citizenry. Establishing these had been easy -- they were tent cities like the processing centers, quick and cheap to build, meant to hold each citizen for a day or two at most. Beside the evac camps the buses sat waiting to transport the uninfected to Byatin.

The QC camps, of course, were different. Thus far the CSF had appropriated an auditorium, a large gymnasium, a hospital and a middle school for use as semipermanent camps for holding the citizens who would remain in the quarantined city, at least for the time being. For these luckless ones, who at current numbered only a few thousand, work was being done at the repurposed Lubukov Agricultural Labs.

Identifying the leaked bioweapon and developing a test for its presence in the human body had been, of course, the easiest part of the Lab's duties. Now they were dedicating themselves to the task of curing the infected.

The fate of the little red ball bearings in the reject boxes would depend on the Lab's research. And speaking of the Labs, Akimov had a status report to receive. He rose from his desk to reach for the phone.

~~~~~

"Thank you all for coming," Yuri said wearily.

One of the soldiers -- Alexei thought his codename might have been Kestrel -- half-rose from his chair. "Don't get smart with us!"

Hawk, still seated, cuffed Kestrel on the back of the head. "Put your ass back where it belongs, soldier."

Kestrel reseated himself, grumbling and rubbing the base of his skull. Hawk gestured to Yuri. "Please continue."

Yuri sighed and nodded. Of the three researchers up at the front of the presentation room Yuri had been unanimously nominated to speak on their behalf. And Alexei, who would rather have been almost anywhere else at the moment, had been chosen to run the overhead projector while they gave their hastily-prepared report on the bioweapon. He had tried to ask off on the grounds that he was still wounded; he had even opened his shirt collar to show the bandages around his shoulder. But it had done no good -- the senior researchers had pointed out that he still had both arms and therefore enough mobility to operate a projector.

The dust that lay thickly on the chairs and floor testified to how rarely the presentation room at the Lubukov Agricultural Labs had been used. Alexei found the cord for the projector was still wrapped in its plastic sleeve, never before opened. Those who'd furnished the room had certainly never anticipated giving a presentation to such an audience, either.

Still fiddling with the cord, Alexei stole a glance at the handful of CSF officers who sat facing the projector screen. Fluorescent lighting gleamed on their protective suits as they waited for the requested briefing to start, looking comically out of place in the padded office chairs.

Alexei supposed the occupation of the Lubukov Agricultural Labs had been hard on the soldiers as well as the lab employees, but since they never removed their masks they were very difficult to read. The toll on the researchers was much clearer, and not without reason: they were living in the Labs twenty four hours a day, seven days a week, working ten-hour shifts day after day, showering and sleeping in the narrow underground dormitories on U2, eating the military rations the CSF brought them.

Not one of them had left the building since the biohazard alarm had sounded on that afternoon. Such conditions were enough to make them feel like prisoners already, and to have soldiers marching through the halls and barking orders at them only solidified the impression.

But even that would not have been enough to turn them all into mental wrecks, not in such a short span of time.

Standing to one side of the projector screen, Yuri waited as Alexei plugged in the projector and flicked the switches on. The hum of its fan sounded loud in the awkward stillness of the room. Alexei straightened up and found Yuri watching him -- the senior researcher pointed to his own shoulder and tipped his head to one side.

Alexei flashed him a thumbs-up. *(I'm fine.)* He felt his cheeks starting to burn and grabbed one of the folders full of transparencies, flipping through the pages. He knew Yuri meant well, but remembering the incident always made him feel about six years old. It seemed like the entire staff of the Labs had been on hand to witness his spectacular breakdown.

Getting shot during his ill-fated escape attempt was one thing. Being dragged back to his comrades while sobbing about bleeding to death was another thing entirely. At least he'd managed to keep from crying outright until they'd put him on his stomach on one of the dormitory beds and Yuri had begun swabbing the wounds with alcohol.

Alexei was given to understand that they had heard him throughout the entire building. Thank god he didn't remember too much of that. And thank god a hundred times over for having created morphine.

"I'll try to keep this short," Yuri was saying. "As you may already be aware, we've identified the leaked chemical that triggered the alert -- a substance coded Unidentified Experimental Compound 571. We call it 'ink', for short." He took a deep breath. "Of all the weaponable compounds stored here, this was probably the worst thing that could have escaped the Labs. The ink -- "

A long, wavering scream tore through the air, rising up from somewhere else in the Labs. Alexei jumped, Yuri flinched as if stabbed, Kestrel lifted his head to look around, and Hawk did not budge at all. The researcher named Boris slurred something unintelligible and staggered away from the front of the room, ran headlong into a chair, wobbled away from it, reached the door of the presentation room and struggled with the knob for several seconds before getting the door open and disappearing into the hallway.

Kestrel had turned around to watch Boris' departure. "He's got to be getting into the medical alcohol. There shouldn't be anything else for him to drink here."

Yuri cleared his throat and tried again. "...as I was saying, the ink was easily the most dangerous thing we were storing here at the Labs. Most of our documentation on it is outdated, simply because it was considered too risky to handle." Yuri tapped on a pile of yellowed folders that lay on the desk beside the projector, and Alexei saw that his hand was shaking. "The official data tells us only so much, but from it we do have some useful information."

Yuri motioned to Alexei, who placed the first transparency sheet onto the projector. A molecular model appeared on the screen, outlined in black against a glowing background.

"For one: the ink is alive. It is a multicellular microorganism of unknown nature, far more complex than a simple virus. It seems to have some effect on plant and animal life but shows a strong preference for attacking humans, where it grows on them as a parasite. Next page, please."

The molecular drawing was replaced with a photo of a blurry dark patch on the back of a human hand, like the skin had been rubbed with charcoal. "The second thing these reports tell us is that the ink is very infectious and very contagious. It is able to exist outside the human body, but once it gains access to the bloodstream it will begin reproducing within the host as well. It can accomplish this via inhalation into the lungs or through an open wound.

"Like a virus, the ink will reproduce itself rapidly once it has access to the bloodstream, multiplying until it infects all organ systems in the host's body. After a certain point the infection will be visible as grayish or blackish patches on or under the skin, caused by high dermal concentrations of ink. The infection itself has been referred to as a 'blight' from time to time, as in this state it seems to resemble the fungal infections common to potatoes."

Alexei went to pick up the next transparency and blanched. Nonetheless he stuck it up on the projector, turning away from the screen. One of the CSF officers gulped and coughed into his mask.

"This image shows a cross-section of the brain from an individual with a late-stage infection by the ink. The black streaks you see here, the ones that look like tree roots, are the result of the ink growing into the brain itself. We theorize that these roots cause brain damage or release chemicals that are responsible for the psychological symptoms that characterize all cases of infection.

"Once the blight has progressed to this state, mental derangement is guaranteed. Victims will present with psychotic episodes, visual and auditory hallucinations and delusions, coupled with sleep disturbances. Intense pain often accompanies these episodes, which are intermittent at first, though they increase in duration and frequency as the infection progresses. By the final stage, the victim is completely psychotic and entirely unable to sleep."

Yuri paused, and in the silence there was a general shuffling of feet in the room. "Simply put, you go insane." He turned to the officers. "And then you die. Everyone dies from this. According to the archived data we've found, there is a 100% mortality rate among the victims. Typical cause of death is heart attack, but many of them appear to die from simple exhaustion." He switched off the projector and stood in front of the darkened screen, hands hanging at his sides. "Any questions?"

Hawk straightened up. "How was the UEC-571 synthesized? what materials were used in making it?"

Yuri only shrugged. "I'm not sure it *was* synthesized," he admitted.

"You're not sure?" Hawk sounded incredulous. "Where did it come from, then?"

"I'm afraid that's above my pay grade." Yuri pushed his glasses up into place, and they promptly slid back down his nose again. "Only the Chief Security Officer knew where the ink came from. It's been in cold storage for quite some time, you know."

Kestrel sat forward in his chair. "And why haven't you asked him? we need this information to -- "

" -- because CSO Strugatsky blew his brains out the day the biohazard alarms went off," Yuri snapped.

Hawk cuffed Kestrel even more firmly this time. "One more word out of you..."

Growling, Kestrel fell silent. Yuri heaved a sigh. "Any other questions?"

"Yes," Hawk said. "What's being done to cure this thing?"

"Well...lots." Yuri suddenly looked tired. "We've tried over two dozen different therapies; nothing is working. We can't even provide palliative care to these poor souls...narcotics and sedatives have no effect on the victims whatsoever. In fact they seem immune to most of the drugs we have on hand."

"But what have you tried?"

"Oh, plenty of things. Antifungal treatments, a wide array of topical sterilization agents, broad-spectrum antibiotics, antivirals..." Yuri started ticking these off on his fingers. "Heat and cold therapy, radiation therapy...you name it. At the moment -- "

That faraway scream sliced through the room again. It wasn't as loud as the first one, but somehow that was worse; instead of terror, this was a cry of anguished despair. After it trailed off there were a series of short exclamations. Just two syllables, repeated over and over.

(oh god, oh god, oh god...)

The cries faded back into silence once again.

Alexei tasted bile. Yuri had sunk down into a chair beside the projector, his glasses off and his face in his hands.

The room waited. Nobody spoke.

At length Yuri got back to his feet, wiped his forehead with the back of one hand and donned his glasses again.

"...at the moment we're attempting treatment using acidic agents," he finished. "It's not working. In fact, all of our efforts to treat the victims seem to be *accelerating* the course of the blight syndrome. Under normal circumstances there's about a month's duration between initial infection and terminal psychosis. But when you attack the ink with chemical agents, trying to burn it away or poison it...it seems to cause a rebound effect that speeds up the progress toward the final stage. Trying to cure the blight has only shortened the victim's lifespan." He gave a chuckle that was entirely lacking in humor. "We're killing our patients. Perhaps that's not a bad thing though."

Hawk made an impatient sound through their gas mask. "Colonel Akimov is asking if you've tried dermabrasion on the test subjects yet."

"...what?"

"Since the infections are on the skin or just under it, he thinks it might be worth trying. They use that kind of thing on burn victims, he says."

"He thinks we need to start debridement on the victims," Yuri echoed in disbelief. "Or 'test subjects', as he calls them. Does know what he's asking? does he even know what that means? Do *you* know what that word means?"

Kestrel moved to stand up and Hawk held him back.

"He's asking us to start flaying the skin off these people while they're alive. While they're conscious." Yuri swept a hand through his hair, leaving it in disarray. "Did you miss the part where I said that painkillers don't work on them?"

"I'm only relaying a suggestion from my superior," Hawk said tonelessly.

"Well obviously your superior has got all the medical training of a box turtle."

Kestrel leapt to his feet and Alexei reacted without thinking, shoving the projector cart in between Yuri and the CSF officer. Kestrel hesitated and all at once Hawk was standing, grabbing the hood of Kestrel's protective suit to pull him back. "This briefing is over!" Hawk shouted. "Back to your stations!"

The other officers were up from their chairs and out of the presentation room in moments, and the two other researchers slunk out after them. Hawk swung Kestrel bodily toward the door and released their grip on his suit. "You too."

Grumbling into his mask, Kestrel followed after the rest. Alexei began sweeping the transparencies back into their ancient folders, stacking them into piles.

"Did you have any questions for us?" Hawk asked, in a different tone of voice.

Yuri was shaking all over. He took off his glasses and attempted to polish them on his lab coat, then returned them to his face where they sat askew, one side higher than the other.

"We don't have anyone else left to study," he said weakly. "Of the ten patients you've brought us, we've killed six of them trying to cure their blight. The rest are like Vadim Simonovich and he's..." Yuri made a hopeless gesture. "That was him you were hearing."

"We'll get you more...patients. Is that all?"

"No. There's also..." Yuri swallowed visibly. "...my daughter is in Khostok. I want to see her."

"Impossible. Nobody in the facility is allowed to leave, and we certainly can't have outsiders entering the building. The possibility for cross-contamination -- "

" -- do you have any children, sir?"

Hawk paused. "No."

Alexei made a show of shuffling the old transparencies around in their folders, watching Yuri with a kind of sick fascination. Whatever made him think he could talk to their captors -- and that's what the CSF were, their captors -- in this way? or maybe he'd just stopped caring if they shot him. Looking at his slumped shoulders, Alexei began to think this might be the case.

"My daughter's named Elena. Elena Yuryevna Sokolova. She's only ten years old."

"You don't under -- "

" -- Her mother's dead. I'm the only one left for her."

Hawk stared down at Yuri in silence. The room was so quiet Alexei could hear the air whistling in and out of the gas mask's respirator.

"Listen to me," said the soldier. "I have very little authority here. My orders are to supervise the CSF's occupation of the Labs and make reports to the Colonel. That's all."

Yuri made an attempt to straighten out his glasses. "Will you at least mention it to the Colonel, then? I'm sure he's got the authority to approve something like that."

"He won't," Hawk said. "...but I'll bring it up anyway."

"Thank you."

Hawk grunted in reply, then abruptly swung around to face Alexei. "How are you feeling?" they demanded.

Alexei immediately spilled the folder's contents out onto the floor. "Huh? I feel fine!" he insisted. Why were they asking? did they suspect Alexei had contracted the blight? was he about to become the Lab's next patient?

"Yeah? what about your shoulder?"

When it dawned on him that Hawk was asking about his gunshot wounds Alexei felt very foolish indeed. "It's fine," he said, and bent down to gather the fallen documents.

Hawk nodded. "Then keep up the good work, comrades."

The two researchers watched the soldier go stalking out of the room. Yuri half-smiled and bent down to help Alexei pick up the transparencies.

"I think she likes you."

"Eh?" Alexei said, blinking. "...that one's a woman?!"

"Well, I assume so. She said she wasn't a man, anyway."

Alexei had to admit that there were only so many ways to interpret that sort of statement. "Lucky me," he muttered, and picked up another sheet.

~~~~~

"Are they gonna make us take off our clothes, uncle?"

"I'm not sure," Nikita admitted. Aware that he was violating some unwritten code that stated adults should always know everything, he added: "If we look sick, they might ask us to. Let's just do what the soldiers tell us, okay?"

"I'm not sick." Elena wrinkled up her brow.

Nikita looked down into her still-blue eyes. "Of course not," he said.

After the grinding boredom of standing in line, Nikita was nowhere near as happy to reach the processing tent as he'd anticipated. The atmosphere in the tent was hushed, like a hospital, and the people queued up inside the tent had the moon-eyed look of cows at a slaughterhouse. Fluorescent bulbs had been strung up from the tent's roof supports, buzzing and lighting the interior with a merciless glare.

Signs hung everywhere:

HAVE YOUR IDENTIFICATION PAPERS READY

COMPLY WITH ALL ORDERS FROM CSF PERSONNEL

FORGING STATE DOCUMENTS IS A CRIMINAL OFFENSE

ONE CITIZEN AT A TIME IN EACH STATION - NO EXCEPTIONS

NO TALKING IN LINE

A CSF soldier, nightmarishly inhuman in the protective suit and gas mask they all wore, stood at the head of the line. "Station fourteen," he called out, and the first citizen in line moved to the designated station. "Station three. Station twenty-one. Station eight...that's station *seven*, comrade, you belong in station *eight*! eight! yes, that one!...next citizen, station twenty!"

The "stations" themselves were a long row of numbered booths, partitioned off from one another with temporary dividers. Each booth was screened off with a plastic curtain hanging in the front. Nikita saw plenty of citizens entering the booths but nobody exiting; it was like a magic trick. He supposed the processed civilians were being sent through a second curtain at the rear of the booth.

The bandaged woman ahead of them in line had turned back to Elena. "What's your name, little one?"

"Elena," said Elena, clutching at Nikita's hand.

"That's a nice name," the woman said. "Tell you what...if you run into any trouble while they're checking you, just give us a yell, okay? I'll come in and knock some sense into 'em."

Elena giggled.

"Station sixteen," the soldier droned. The woman stepped out of line and gave Elena a little wave before vanishing behind the plastic curtain in front of the sixteenth booth.

A cold little snake curled up in Nikita's stomach; it was nearly their turn in the booths. If they were just checking papers, he realized, the line would be moving faster. And they wouldn't need to screen themselves off from view. Clearly the chemical leak had sickened a few people already, or the CSF thought it had, otherwise they wouldn't waste time and resources with this processing routine during the evacuation.

The big fellow ahead of Nikita was muttering to himself. "This is the worst possible time for this to happen," he whined. The soldier who was calling out the stations ignored him.

"I can't be standing in line for hours like this; my feet are killing me," he went on. "These government types have got no human heart, not at all. They can see me standing here, six months pregnant, and nobody so much as offers me a chair." The man put a hand on his very flat stomach and sighed dramatically. "All this stress is going to affect the baby, I just know it will...oh, if only Anatoly were here..."

"Don't say anything," Nikita whispered, edging away from the man. Elena's eyes were huge and round, her expression puzzled. If the stuff from the Labs had gotten into the water supply it might be causing people to fall asleep spontaneously; it was certainly possible that that's what was happening.

"Station twenty-five," the soldier said. The big fellow kept on muttering, seeming not to hear. "Twenty-five!" barked the soldier, giving the man a whack on the shoulder. The man pitched forward, caught himself before he fell and looked around wildly. "What? what?"

Clearly the soldier was at the end of his tether. "Station twenty-five!" he shouted again, reaching for his truncheon. Nikita breathed a sigh of relief when the big fellow finally came to his senses and went hurrying off to the correct booth.

Stepping up to the head of the line, Nikita coughed. "...Can I go into the booth with my niece?" he asked timidly. Without turning, the soldier pointed up at the sign overhead:

ONE CITIZEN AT A TIME IN EACH STATION - NO EXCEPTIONS

"But she's -- "

" -- I'll be okay, uncle."

Nikita looked down at her and Elena squeezed his hand. "I promise."

"Station eleven," the soldier called out. Before he could stop her Elena disengaged herself from him and ran up to the booth, slipping in behind the curtain. Nikita couldn't even go after her on the pretense that he had her identification papers: Elena had already tucked these into the bookbag she was carrying.

He felt helplessly, absurdly positive that he'd never see his niece again. Then the soldier called out for station two and Nikita left the line, moving robotically to the second booth and lifting the curtain to let himself inside.

Inside the booth was a table, and beside it sat a CSF soldier. A lone bulb shone down into the booth, spotlighting them. There were no other chairs.

"Papers please," said the soldier, in the weary tone of someone repeating something for the thousandth time. Behind the soldier, in the back of the booth, there fluttered a second curtain -- the exit.

Nikita laid his identification papers down on the little table and the soldier scanned them over.

"Name?"

"Sokolov Nikita Ivanovich."

"Age?"

"Thirty-five."

"Occupation?"

"Computer engineer."

The soldier examined the seal on his papers and handed them back to Nikita. "Please remove your clothes."

"Huh?"

"Remove your clothes. All of them, including your underwear."

Nervously Nikita did as ordered. There was noplace to put the discarded clothing and so he dropped everything in a pile on the ground, his jacket on the bottom and underwear on top. All at once he became aware that they were technically outdoors, with only thin plastic sheets shielding them from the elements. The CSF soldier rose from his chair, pulling a pair of thin latex gloves on over the protection suit's rubber ones.

"Hold still please."

If nothing else, the physical examination was remarkably brisk and impersonal. The soldier merely inspected his skin and looked into all of his orifices, then ordered him to put his clothes back on. Once he was dressed again Nikita felt a little less like a farm animal and more like a human.

"Stick out your arm."

Nikita obeyed. The soldier grasped his elbow, swabbed out his inner arm and stuck a disposable syringe into the skin.

"Ow!"

"Blood sample," the soldier explained. He drew the syringe back with a half-ounce of blood in the chamber and pasted a bandage over the injection site. Reaching into the box beside his desk, the soldier drew out a tiny liquid-filled bottle with a foil-covered top. He stuck the needle into the foil and depressed the plunger, squirting Nikita's blood into the bottle. Nikita watched without comprehending as the soldier shook the bottle and held it up to the eyepiece in his gas mask, examining the contents.

Apparently satisfied, he dropped the bottle into a wastebin beside the box. From the stack on his desk the soldier drew out a printed ticket bearing the logo of the Chorman Special Forces. Picking up one of the two rubber stamps on his desk, the soldier stamped the paper and handed it over to Nikita. "You may go," he said, stripping off the latex gloves and dropping them into the wastebin.

Nikita looked at his ticket. "The citizen bearing this ticket has been processed through the Dragovich Park Provisional Processing Center," it read, along with other words that meant essentially the same thing. Stamped on his paper in glistening blue ink was a large letter 'E'.

"What does this mean?"

"It means you're done." The soldier jerked his thumb at the plastic curtain in back of the booth. "Get going."

Nikita pushed past the second curtain and found himself in back of the processing tent, behind the row of examination booths. Sunlight poured in through the open tent flap that served as the exit. Four soldiers stationed at the tent's exit were checking tickets and shouting out to those exiting the booths, trying to keep people flowing out of the tent. "This way, comrades, this way! Your families are outside! Keep moving, keep moving! Don't keep the buses waiting!"

Elena was nowhere to be found.

Like a box on a conveyor belt, Nikita fell into line at the exit. One of the CSF soldiers took his ticket from his outstretched hand, looked at it, and pointed him off to the right. "Camp Blue!" he said, handing the paper back. "Next!"

Nikita wandered out of the tent, and the sunlight all but blinded him.

All in all, he had been in Dragovich Park for six hours today. He had waited in line until it seemed like the ennui would kill him, had eaten nothing all day, had been stripped and stabbed and generally treated like cattle. But it was only when Nikita emerged from the processing tent and into the sunlight once again that he really, truly began to feel afraid.

Behind the processing tent there were people -- human beings -- in stockyard pens. Or at least that was his first impression. Chain-link fencing topped with barbed wire bordered the grassy yard behind the tent, separating it from the rest of the park. Within the yard were two smaller fenced-in pens, each filled with crowds of Khostok citizens anxiously clutching their tickets. CSF soldiers at the entrance to each pen were double-checking tickets and admitting people into the fenced areas, or turning them back with gestures indicating they were at the wrong one. Beyond the pens and the fenced-in yard sat the green buses, waiting to be filled.

His niece seemed to have evaporated completely. "Elena!!" Nikita shouted, feeling the first stirrings of panic. He would have asked one of the soldiers bustling about in the yard but he had the impression they would just stick him into one of the pens and forget about him. "*Elena*!!"

" -- Look, there he is!"

" -- uncle!"

His heart leapt. The shout came from the pen on the left-hand side of the yard, the one identified with a hand-lettered sign reading CAMP RED. A crowd of people were pressed up against the chain-links from the inside, some calling out for water, some demanding to know where their families were, all of them watching the CSF soldiers as they hurried back and forth through the fenced area.

In one corner of the pen Nikita spotted the dark-haired woman, waving to him. The other people in the pen seemed to be giving her a wide berth, and he was halfway to the pen before he realized why.

The woman's bandages were gone; they must have taken them during her processing. Her left arm was blotched with indigo and black all the way up past her elbow, like the skin of a corpse. She was holding Elena's shoulders with her unblemished hand, keeping her from being jostled by the crowd.

"Lena!" Nikita broke into a sprint, Elena reached out for him through the chain links and Nikita took her hand. "Are you okay?"

"I'm fine!" she insisted. "Auntie Veronika's been looking after me!"

The woman smiled at Nikita. He wanted to smile back, but that arm...it was all he could do not to reach through the fence and push her away from his niece. It looked so diseased, so contaminated. Was that what the CSF had been looking for?

"Just wait right there," Nikita told Elena. "I'm going to come in there with you. Don't move, understand? I'll be right there in a minute."

"I'll watch her," Veronika assured him, patting Elena's shoulder. "We're not going anywhere."

"Thank you," Nikita managed, squeezing Elena's fingers one last time, and darted away from the fence. When he reached the gated entrance there were only a few people in line ahead of him, presenting their stamped tickets to the soldiers at the gate. Nikita fell in behind the last of them, and as he did so he noticed something.

Everyone in this line had a ticket stamped with a red letter 'Q'. His was the only 'E' in the line, at least that he could see.

So those with red Q stamps went to 'Camp Red', wherever it might be. They had told him at the exit to get in line for Camp Blue, so likely that's where all the E's were headed. But why decide that during the examination? They couldn't be splitting them up between camps at random; there had to be using some kind of criteria.

He scanned the rows upon rows of strained faces peering out through the links of the Camp Red enclosure. Sure enough, several of them -- nearly a third, it looked like -- had the same dark stains that Veronika did, somewhere on their exposed skin. And there was no telling how many were concealing such marks under their clothes. Nikita was too far away from the Blue pen to verify that those people were the ones who'd been cleared as free from the stains, but he was beginning to suspect they were.

"Ticket, please," the soldier at the gate prompted him. Nikita handed it over and was completely unsurprised when the soldier hesitated at the stamped letter. "You're in the wrong place, comrade. You go to Blue." He waved toward the other pen, handing the ticket back.

"My niece is going to this camp," Nikita said calmly. "I've got to go with her. She's just a child."

"We'll look after her. And you're all going to Byatin anyway, so you'll see her there."

"If we're all headed to the same place, why can't I go with her? This camp can't be full to capacity or you wouldn't still be sending people to this gate." He indicated the small knot of people who'd gathered in line behind him, all holding Q-stamped tickets and looking bewildered by the holdup.

The soldier heaved a sigh. "Because Q tickets go to Red and E tickets go to Blue. That's why."

Now Nikita could feel the anger welling up, amplifying the panic. He squelched both of them and leaned toward the soldier, dropping his voice. "No, that's not why. But I'll tell you why...it's because the people in here aren't going to Byatin. They aren't getting evacuated at all. They're being quarantined -- that's what the 'Q' means," he growled. "Only the Es will get to evacuate. But I don't care if I do get quarantined. I'm just saying that you had just better let me through this gate or I'm going to let everyone in this pen know that they're all infected with that blight thing and aren't going to be evacuated."

The masked face swung in his direction, and Nikita looked into the mirrored circles that were its eyes.

"And if you try to stop me with force, there's too many witnesses -- people will panic," he added. He was starting to get a bit dizzy from all the adrenaline; really, he wasn't so sure that the CSF were all that reluctant to hurt him. But there were so many people watching, the consequences of something like that...

" -- piss off," said the soldier, and reached out to shove him -- through the gate, into the Red enclosure. Nikita tripped over his own feet and nearly fell, barely able to believe his bluff had worked. He was in!

"Uncle!" Elena came running to him, darting through the crowd of adults. Nikita swept her up into his arms just as Veronika caught up to them. "Sorry, she got away from me."

"Calm down, you're okay." He petted Elena's head and allowed the tension to drain back out of him. The way his knees were wobbling he might have just dashed across a busy highway. "Calm down," he repeated, partly to himself.

Elena looked up at him, clutching at his waist. "When are we gonna get 'vacuated?"

That was really the question, wasn't it? when were they getting evacuated? *Were* they getting evacuated at all? The supposed omniscience of adulthood was no help to Nikita here...he had no clue what the CSF meant to do with all the people in the Red enclosure, stained from exposure to some unknown chemical agent. And now Nikita was stuck in here with the rest of the contaminated citizens. And so was his brother's daughter.

"...Lena," he started to say.

" -- *Grisha*!"

Veronika's shout carried over the hubbub inside the enclosure. Nikita looked up. The big fellow who'd come with Veronika was out of the processing tent, standing in the yard outside the two pens. He was shuffling slowly toward them, his face contorted, groping at the air in front of him like a blind man. His eyes were open but unseeing, and even at this distance Nikita could see that their irises were swallowed up in black.

The small hairs pricked up on the back of Nikita's neck. Suddenly he was sure -- this was what the CSF were screening for. And these people weren't sleepwalking.

The big man, Grigori, came to a sudden stop. Lucidity flashed across his face. Nikita looked into his fathomless eyes and realized that the man was terrified.

All at once Grigori cupped his hands around his mouth. "Everyone! Listen to me!!" He bellowed. A hush fell on the crowd in the Red enclosure. Even the soldiers lifted their heads, distracted.

"Listen! everyone, listen!" Now he was shouting into the silence; the man had a voice like a megaphone. He paused, looking into the crowd, and Nikita could see him fighting back tears.

"You're all going to die," Grigori said. "They're going to kill you all."

"Grisha!" Veronika hissed. Nobody else made a sound.

"I've seen it," said the big man, and took another step toward the pen. Tears overspilled his eyes and ran down over the black smudge in the corner of his mouth. "They're going to poison-gas the city once they've evacuated everyone who didn't catch the blight. You're all going to be murdered."

Like a switch had been thrown, the CSF soldiers all came alive suddenly. "Grab that man!!" someone barked, and within seconds there were four black-suited soldiers on Grigori. He vanished for a moment, and then the pile of bodies seemed to heave upward and two of the soldiers went flying into the grass. Nikita saw Grigori brush the third soldier away as casually as swatting a fly, and the fourth one seemed to run headlong into the big man's fist.

"Get him, get him, get him!"

The yard was inundated with CSF soldiers now, unholstering their rifles, brandishing truncheons. Everyone was shouting. Barely aware of what he was doing, Nikita snatched his niece up into his arms and pelted towards the far corner of the yard, narrowly dodging a citizen who was running headlong in the opposite direction. The people in the enclosure had begun to panic, some of them fighting their way up to the fence to see what was happening, others trying to get as far away from the conflict as possible.

Nikita could not reach the corner itself -- it was too packed with people -- and so he dropped Elena down beside the chain-link fence, bracing himself against it with both hands so he could shield her from the impending chaos.

Through the metal links of the fence Nikita could still see Grigori flailing away at the soldiers, a giant among mere mortal men. He broke away from the three who were trying to hold him back and charged the gate of the Red enclosure, roaring like a bear. Nikita had the brief vision of Grigori simply plowing headlong through the gated entrance like a runaway train, ripping apart the metal fencing and sending the soldiers tumbling like bowling pins.

He never reached the gate. There was a loud rattling noise and Grigori pitched forward, landing facefirst in the grass. Red flowers bloomed on the back of his white shirt.

Somewhere in the enclosure, Veronika screamed.

Pandemonium erupted. The people who'd been struggling to see the action suddenly surged in the opposite direction, away from the gunfire. Shrieking filled the air as the weaker were trampled under the wave of panicked humanity. Nikita crouched down over Elena, clutching at the gate as people stampeded past. Someone's knee struck his head a glancing blow and the world spun off-course, tilting crazily. Elena was bawling, an animal sound of terror.

There was a terrific crash as something struck the chain-link fence. For an instant Nikita thought a car had rammed it, and then he looked up and saw what it was. Veronika -- there was no mistaking that stained arm -- had flung herself onto the fence and was climbing, six feet straight up and into the barbed wire.

"God," Nikita whispered, though he couldn't hear himself over the screaming of the crowd. Two soldiers were hastily dragging Grigori's body from the yard while several more stood between the corpse and the pens, shouting for order. The guards at the entrance to the Red enclosure were waving back the people who were trying to flee through the gate. One of the gate guards fired into the air and the mass of bodies lurched backwards again.

That was when Veronika reached the barbed wire strung along the top of the fence. Her scream was inhuman, and Nikita saw her plunge to the ground outside the pen, dragging the coils of wire after her. Veronika rolled about in the grass, thrashing and kicking like a rabbit in a snare, the barbed wire tangled about her legs.

"One's gotten out!" shouted a soldier, running towards the pen. Veronika had struggled free and was on her feet just as the soldier reached her, his AKS aimed at her chest.

Possibly he didn't mean to shoot her, but Nikita would never know. Almost in slow motion he saw the muzzle of the rifle drawing closer, Veronika's hand coming up to wrap around the barrel. She wrenched the rifle out of the soldier's grip, seized the barrel in both hands and swung it like a club. The rifle butt struck home and the soldier's head snapped sideways in a spray of glass, his eyepieces shattered.

"There's another one!"

"Quiet, everyone, quiet!"

"Grab her!"

"Get back from that fence!"

Veronika sidestepped the fallen soldier and brought the rifle butt crashing down on the head of another. His knees buckled, and then a wall of soldiers seemed to close in on her, cutting her off from view.

"Hold her, damnit!"

"I've got her!"

The knot of soldiers sank down to the ground, taking Veronika with them. Over the din of the frightened crowd and the sound of shouted commands Nikita could hear Veronika screaming, over and over again. One of the soldiers rose up out of the struggling mass of bodies, hefting his truncheon over his head.

He brought it down, and the screaming stopped.

"Cease fire! that's a direct order from the Colonel! everyone, cease fire!" An artificially-amplified voice cut through the roar of the general confusion. A tall soldier with differently-colored insignia on the breast of his protection suit had emerged from the processing tent, megaphone in one hand, calling for order. The soldiers guarding the gate stopped firing into the air, and those who had tackled Veronika to the ground got back to their feet. The young woman was a low silhouette, lying motionless in the crushed grass.

Something stirred against Nikita's chest. His ears ringing, he looked down to find that Elena had buried her face in the front of his shirt, arms around his middle. Her whole body shuddered with sobs. He discovered that he was holding her in his lap, sitting on the trampled ground of the Red enclosure, and as the fog lifted he heard himself and realized that he was saying something to her.

"Don't look, Lena. Don't look."

## CHAPTER FIVE

Sharik's luck was finally running out.

He supposed it was only a matter of time until it happened. Fate had thrown so many prizes his way in the past few weeks; it seemed only fair that the good luck should be followed with bad. The Lord giveth and the Lord taketh away, or something like that.

Wandering down the silent street, as vacant of cars at 3 p.m. as it had been at 3 a.m., he thought back to the dawning of his good fortune. It had all started with the store...no, no, it had begun even before that. He simply hadn't noticed it right away.

It had been the little things at first. The police had stopped harassing Sharik during his naps in the park, or under the overpass. He could relax unmolested in the humble home he'd made in the alleyway between the furniture warehouse and the canning factory -- nobody dragged him out onto the street to scold him for being a public nuisance or to chuck his bottle into the gutter.

That was right around the time that all the public water fountains had stopped working -- the ones in the mall and the bus station as well as those in the library. Even the big fountain in the park had stopped flowing, though there was still plenty of drinkable water left in the basin.

Bigger concerns had preoccupied him, of course, and he hadn't noticed the absence of police or citizens until that day at the store. Awakening early one morning with a powerful thirst, Sharik had gone to the corner gas station in hopes of finding something to cool his throat. He had found the door inexplicably closed and locked, in violation of the business hours posted on the door.

After nobody came to answer his knocking, Sharik had looked around and realized that the entire street was empty. No early commuters, no idling police officers, nobody killing time at the bus stop. So rather than wait for someone to come along and unlock the door for him, Sharik had grabbed a brick and done what any other thirsty citizen would have done.

After bashing in the glass of the shop's front door, Sharik had let himself into the store and gone on a quick shopping spree, stuffing cans and bottles into the ragged backpack he wore. Once he was loaded down like a pack mule everything his bag could possibly carry, Sharik had stolen a peek outside and found that the coast was clear: no police, no bystanders, nobody coming to find out why the door to the shop was smashed in. It was as if Sharik was the only living soul in Khostok.

He had gone skipping back to his alley home, or would have gone skipping if he hadn't been carrying ten liters of finest vodka on his back, along with a multitude of cans and boxes. At home Sharik had thrown himself a private party, and slept so soundly that he hardly stirred when the public broadcasting speakers began to blather their nonsense again. Evacuation this, processing that, all citizens should do such and such. Thankfully the announcement was short, and he had gotten back to sleep right afterward.

When the store remained untouched three days later Sharik had begun to suspect something. Nobody had come to patch the broken door or even to sweep up the glass. Come to think of it, no opportunistic soul had come along to help himself to the bounty inside, either. Sharik supposed that the proprietor of the store might have run into some misfortune and abandoned his business, but that didn't explain why Sharik was the only one looting.

Nonetheless, it wasn't his concern. Grateful that the store was his alone, Sharik had gone back inside for several more bottles, and a few cans for good measure. On the way out he'd paused to pick up a tube of antibacterial ointment and some anti-itch cream. In spite of all the care he'd taken -- even going so far as to wash it off in the basin of the park fountain -- the cut on his foot was getting worse instead of better.

On the way out of the store Sharik had been badly startled by the sound of a woman's voice, so close it was almost in his ear: "*Vanya*! Vanya! Come in out of the rain! you're getting your new shoes all muddy!"

Sharik had known at once that it was his mother calling him, and felt it was terribly unfair for her to be pestering him just as he'd found the biggest, shiniest frog he'd ever seen, there under the ferns down by the river. He'd just opened his mouth to ask if he could keep the frog when the dream popped like a soap bubble, and Sharik found himself standing there in the broken glass by the shop door, holding a tin of herring and wondering what had happened.

It wasn't all that unlike him to drift off in the middle of the day, though dreaming of frogs was a pleasant change from the spiders and scorpions he frequently encountered in his waking dreams. Still, though his memories of his mother were blurred and indistinct, he was pretty sure that she had named him Nikolai, not Ivan.

Back in his cardboard-walled home, Sharik had peeled away his threadbare sock to inspect the foot. The cut he'd received was no longer hurting, but the foot was beginning to look quite ugly, blotched all over with black stains. It tingled and itched from time to time and there was a shiny black patch on the sole of his foot, where the cut had been, that puzzled Sharik to no end.

He recalled one of his old comrades who had died of such a thing; a rusty nail had gone up through his boot, and the foot had swelled and turned black and stunk to heaven. That's what he assumed this was, though his foot hadn't swollen at all, and though it did stink he was fairly sure that was only from his shoe, not from the wound itself.

Still, he had rubbed liberal amounts of both ointments into his foot and donned his sock again. That had been last week, and though nothing had swollen or fallen off the blackness continued to spread, climbing its way up towards his knee. One or two of those dark patches had popped up on his chest, and there was a baseball-sized one under his right eye. Bruises, they looked like, though they weren't painful. They weren't especially pretty, but other than the tingling he barely noticed them anymore. Other things were more important.

The drink, which had always been so kind to him when the rest of the world was so cruel, had begun to play tricks on his mind. Sharik caught himself flying awake in the middle of the night, positive that he'd left the stove on, or shouting for someone to give back the candy bar they'd taken from him. Just last night, in fact, Sharik had spent two hours arguing with his lawyer about the divorce settlement only to snap back to his senses with the realization that he'd never been married in the first place.

There were loud debates and long monologues taking place in his head, too, ones that didn't involve him. Sharik remembered another of his departed friends, poor old Kolya, who had complained about a similar phenomenon. Kolya had always claimed that it was the mouthwash that made the people start talking, and had begged Sharik to stick to vodka in order to avoid the same fate. Sharik had kept to his promise almost completely, and so was bewildered that his head should become a multi-party telephone line.

That was the reason for his walk this afternoon. Roundabout noon Sharik had been struck with horror: his husband had found the letter meant for Sergei! had he read it? did he know? should he tell Igor he was breaking it off with Sergei, confess everything?

With a strenuous effort Sharik had come up halfway out of the dream -- he had never been married, after all, and certainly not to anyone named Igor. But though he no longer had any illusions about that, he was still stuck listening to a long and tearful monologue courtesy of Igor's wife, whoever she was. The voice in his head dithered back and forth between telling Igor and not telling him, between leaving Sergei and just telling Igor she was going to leave him.

After two hours of this the unseen woman had moved on to debating the merits of leaving Igor and moving in with Sergei, and Sharik was about ready to scream. He had gone for a walk in the city to clear his head. The streets were echoingly empty, the shops all closed, the windows shuttered and blind, but Sharik could not appreciate the solitude. There was no peace inside his head.

His whole leg tingling and burning, Sharik stumbled along the sidewalk, heading nowhere in particular. He had spent so long listening to the woman's voice that he had almost begun to agree with her when she started to compare Sergei's lovemaking to Igor's and found Sergei to excel in all the evaluation categories. It was a brutal shock when a man's voice suddenly interrupted the woman, growling in Sharik's head --

*-- disgusting, just disgusting what they've been doing to these poor fools, without even*

*enough sense to rise against their masters. All the years I've been saying it, trying to help them, trying to make them understand, and not a soul has listened to me. And now on the government's orders they've all gone and snuffed themselves like this poor simpleton here, drinking the poison the DIO's put into their tapwater, going to their deaths as tamely as dogs. Fare thee well, comrade, fare thee well, and know in your heart that Mikhail Litvinenko will avenge your suffering, will bring justice --*

There was a sort of popping sound, like a child's firework. And Sharik dropped away into blessed, merciful silence.

Seven stories above, on the balcony of his penthouse at the Hotel Litvinenko, Mikhail drew back on the bolt of his Mosin Nagant rifle. A gleaming brass casing flew out and tinkled musically on the floor of the patio, still smoking from the gunpowder.

Reaching out for his binoculars, Mikhail inched forward on his stomach to the edge of the balcony. Down on the street below, the remains of the vagrant -- God rest his soul! -- were stretched across the sidewalk. The black stain under his eye had vanished along with the right side of his face, but Mikhail knew what he had seen. And he wasn't the sort to sit idly by while a fellow Chorman died an agonizing death from the DIO's contaminated water.

But here was something else. Mikhail adjusted the binoculars, zooming in on the body below. The usual splash of red and white and pink and grey was there, as it always was, but there was something off about it this time. And then he saw it.

Black. There were black tendrils mixed into the spilled grey, like thin black worms.

Mikhail bared his teeth. What fresh atrocity was this? Obviously the DIO had changed the recipe; this new poison was doing something altogether strange to those incautious enough to drink the city's water.

Muttering a prayer for the departed soul, Mikhail rose to go and dispose of the body.

~~~~~

All in all, the dreams weren't so bad. Sometimes they were quite nice. They could be dull as dirt, of course, but even that was okay. And then sometimes she would dream she was someone happy, in a pleasant place, and then the world seemed alright.

Like the dream where she was on the beach with the other children, building sandcastles, listening to the roar of the surf. After playing in the ocean they retired to a blanket in the sand, eating handmade sandwiches from a real wicker basket. She could feel the warmth of the sand between her toes, smell the salty air. The experience thrilled her; she had never been to the ocean before, and was always sad when the beach vanished away like all the other dreams.

Of course sometimes -- quite a lot of the time, in fact -- she dreamt she was someplace boring, doing something mundane. Washing out glass beakers, for instance. Arguing with her landlord. Shopping for groceries. Fixing a flat tire.

And then sometimes there were nightmares. The sand and the ocean would evaporate and suddenly she was in a car, flying out of control across the rain-slicked asphalt, directly into the path of an oncoming truck. She would hear the shriek of metal as the truck's bumper crashed into her passenger-side door, feel her body wrenched to the side from the force of the impact, the crunching sensation followed by a brilliant starburst of pain as her right arm struck the gearshift and broke.

But the nightmares weren't all physically painful, either. She was tormented by a recurring one where she was a child, standing in the kitchen, and the woman she believed to be her mother was screaming at her, shaking her. Her mother claimed the DIO had taken her father away, had made him disappear, for crimes against the government too numerous to mention. They would make him confess, her mother said, and once he confessed the DIO would come for his wife and child as well. They always confessed once the DIO took hold of them; the DIO's methods were merciless.

Clutching her arms so she couldn't flee, her mother told her everything. About the red-hot pokers, the buckets of ice water. About the knives. About what they did to your legs, your fingers, your eyes. About the little rooms too narrow to lie down in. About how they wouldn't let you sleep for days and days and days on end, wearing you down until in the end you were less than human, less than a worm, squirming in your own filth on the floor in some underground dungeon. And then, only then, would they let you die.

The dreams came one after another, in a ceaseless parade, and plenty of them were nightmares as godawful as this one. She dreamt she was attacked, beaten, shot, stabbed. Or she would be the one in the DIO's clutches, and everything that crazy woman had warned her about was coming true.

Every now and then she would wonder if these dreams were really dreams at all. For one, they were too vivid: they swamped all of her senses, brighter and more colorful than waking life. These dreams were as real as breathing, and when they were good dreams this was a wonderful thing.

But when they were nightmares, it was a taste of purest Hell. Because the other undreamlike feature of these dreams was her total helplessness. She was not under her own control; she was a puppet on invisible strings, jerked back and forth by an unseen hand. She couldn't so much as lift a finger of her own volition.

When the dreams were good ones, her lack of autonomy was no great concern. She was content to drift along with the current, soaking in bliss. But when she was in the kitchen with her insane dream-mother, or flying out of control toward the truck, or quaking and bleeding on the cold cement floor in the DIO's interrogation chamber, her immobility was a torture in and of itself. Sometimes she would have given anything just to make a sound; to be unable to scream held a special horror all its own.

And sometimes it was even worse than that. Because sometimes she herself was the DIO.

Hers was the hand holding the chain, the poker, the knife. Then she would panic, mentally thrashing and flailing, fighting for control of the body that was not her own.

Her powerlessness aside, the good dreams almost made her forget about the bad ones. There were birthday parties, festivals, ice cream, popcorn. There were movies and games, times spent drinking with friends, mountain climbing, sailing. A good many of these things she had never done before, and at these times she was almost grateful that the body she'd fallen into knew what it was doing, knew how to rig a climbing harness or how to handle the tiller of a sailboat without her help. In her moments of clarity she would watch the hands before her face with a distant fascination, admiring their skill.

Such clarity was rare. It was easier to ride along with the dreams like a boat on a wave, carried along, forgetting everything else. The painful moments were less painful that way. But sometimes a little voice whispered in the back of her head, reminding her that this was not who she was, these bodies were not hers, these memories belonged to strangers.

She flew through a host of people, all ages, all sexes. She might be an elderly woman one moment, her joints all aching and bones as brittle as sugar candy, and then a helpless infant the next. In quite a lot of the dreams she was male, though this did not bother her until she dreamt she was in bed with her wife.

At first the experience was terribly bizarre to her, even embarrassing. She felt like a voyeur. But the guilty feeling faded away and left something strange in its place. She came to appreciate the dream-wife's undeniable charm, her soft and curvaceous body, her smoldering eyes. There was nothing wrong with admiring such sensuous beauty, especially not when one did so through the eyes of the woman's husband. By the end of the dream she was receiving the dream-wife's kisses and caresses and soft whispered words as if they were meant for her.

This particular dream stirred her in ways she couldn't quite place. In those rare lucid moments she would catch herself thinking back to it, trying to recall the dream-wife's face, her breasts, her legs, the scent of her skin.

And then there was the last dream, the one she always came back to, which never varied that much. She would always open her eyes to find herself on a bundle of blankets on the floor, shivering, disoriented.

In this dream she was in a room about ten feet by ten feet square, with walls of brushed aluminum and a grated metal floor. A big steel door was set into one wall and bare metal shelves surrounded her. There was the bucket on the floor for the obvious reasons, and frequently there were bottles of water or reheated military rations waiting on a nearby shelf. There were no windows.

This dream, however, was different -- in this one, she could control her body. Not that it mattered much; there was nothing to do in her cell. At one point there must have been a handle on the inside of the door, but this had long been removed, and now there was no way to escape the metal room. As in the rest of her dreams, she was helpless -- a prisoner.

Standing up, she would wobble to the shelf for her food, or to the bucket to relieve herself. If she looked down she could see that she was wearing some sort of shapeless white hospital gown, and beneath the gown her arm and both legs were grotesquely discolored, like she'd been splashed with black paint. She could feel her flesh crawling and prickling, like ants under her skin.

Occasionally there were interruptions, annoying but inconsequential. People in white lab coats would come into the room to stab her with needles, or to force her to swallow pills, or hook her up to machines that chirped and beeped, or to argue about the discoloration on her legs and her arm. The doctors -- she assumed they were doctors -- brought a CSF soldier along with them each time they visited, and looking at the masked soldier brought muddy fragments of memory drifting up from the lake of her thoughts.

Two of the doctors were different from the others. They asked how she was feeling, were careful when the injecting her, and always came as a pair. The older of the two was tall and lanky, with overlarge glasses and caramel-colored hair grown out halfway to his shoulders. The younger had shaggy black hair and pale grey eyes that darted around restlessly when he wasn't speaking.

As nice as they were, she would rather they hadn't visited her at all. The two insisted on calling her by name, reminding her that she had once been a woman named Veronika. And remembering her name brought back a host of memories, attached to other names. Then she would recall the processing center, and Elena and her uncle Nikita -- Nikita, who looked so much like the doctor in the oversized glasses that she almost brought it up to him once or twice.

But then the name Grigori would come back to her, as it always did, and despair would settle like an anvil on her chest. When it came to that, the only thing to do was lie back down and pull the blankets up over her head. If Veronika was patient, the dream of the metal room and the doctors would also fade away, and if she were lucky, she might find her way back to the beach again.

~~~~~

"Have you seen my mama?"

Nikita was busy, and ignored the question. It wasn't directed at him so much as everyone in the communal bathroom.

"Have you seen my mama?"

And he would be damned if he would lose his place at the urinal. Not after having waited for twenty minutes for his chance to relieve himself. Nikita gave it three days before people's inhibitions broke down and all they started using the same urinals at the same time. He felt even sorrier for the guys in line for the toilets -- without running water, they were reduced to using the portable closets the CSF had lined up in the hallway outside.

"I can't find my mama!" the voice quavered.

"Grandma, you're in the wrong bathroom," someone replied.

Zipping himself up, Nikita turned. The man in line behind him stepped up to the urinal. nudging him away as he did so.

Standing in the middle of the restroom was an elderly woman, her white hair falling in wisps down over her face, her dress stained and wrinkled. A large black stain stretched across her cheek, like an inky birthmark. Her pupils had nearly eclipsed the irises of her eyes.

Most of the men gathered in the restroom were deliberately looking away from her. Some were naturally shy about having a woman in the men's room, especially an old one, but there was more to their downcast eyes and hunched shoulders than that. Nikita saw them shooting furtive glances at the old woman, wondering, fearing. How many of them had the same black marks somewhere on their bodies? How many of them knew what the stains meant?

He moved toward the exit, past her, and the old woman reached out to him. Instinctively he twitched away -- it was automatic, like dodging a snake.

Outside the restroom he turned down a hallway, passing the long row of portable toilets and two flights of stairs before coming to the opened double doors. Here on the threshold Nikita hesitated, looking out into the vastness of the auditorium.

The CSF had taken away as many chairs as possible, leaving the floor of the cavernous amphitheater clear for the beds to be assembled. By his estimate there were five hundred military-issue folding cots packed onto the polished hardwood floor, arranged in regular columns and rows like the houses in a city. If his guess of five hundred beds was correct, considering that some were sharing a cot with their small children, then there were six hundred or more evacuees sheltering here in what the CSF called Red Camp Three.

"Don't block the doorway," croaked a soldier who stood guarding the double doors. Nikita jumped and skittered away into the rows of beds, glancing back over his shoulder.

He was starting to piece things together. To the CSF, "red" meant "quarantine" or "infected". The fact that they were interred in Camp Three meant that there were at least two more camps like this one, established in different locations throughout Khostok. If they all held the same populations as this one, and there were no more than three camps, that still meant nearly two thousand souls were being held back in Khostok while the "blue" -- uninfected -- citizens were bussed away to Chorma's capitol city.

There was a sort of soup kitchen assembled in the auditorium, running along one wall. Other evacuees were ladling out bowls of steaming liquid from giant metal pots the size of bisected trash barrels. A soldier slouched against one wall behind the kitchen workers, supervising. The sour odor of pork and cabbage greeted Nikita as he slipped past the waiting queue.

Two thousand of them or more. Two thousand citizens sickened by something the Lubukov Agricultural Labs had been working on. Officially it might be something like a pesticide, or some sort of growth hormone meant for cattle, or an experimental food additive.

Unofficially, Yuri had always confided that none of their work had the slightest thing to do with crops or livestock. And that made the situation at hand so much more delicate. If the leak meant the risk of exposing the government's biological weapon research program to the people of Chorma, or to the world at large, there was a massive incentive to make sure the situation in Khostok was kept under a tight lid.

They obviously couldn't let the blighted citizens leave the city and appear in Byatin hospitals. Even if the infection wasn't contagious -- and Nikita suspected it was -- the last thing the government would want was an inquiry into the nature of the blight. Oh, these are the sick refugees from Khostok? let's see, what do they have? they've gotten something that stains the skin black and turns them into schizophrenic nutcases? now, what sort of food additive would have side-effects like that?

So the CSF would have to cure them here, in Khostok, before releasing them. And if they couldn't?

Nikita broke out in goosebumps. Well, then it came down to the question of which would create a bigger scandal: two thousand people sick from a leak at a secret bioweapons lab, or two thousand people dead from tragic but accidental pesticide exposure.

"Uncle!"

He'd been so wrapped up he had walked right by their cot without seeing his niece. He doubled back. "I thought you were napping?"

"I woke up," Elena said. She was bundled up in the scratchy little blanket they'd been given, squinting around the auditorium. Her eyes were pink-rimmed but for the moment she was no longer crying, and that was a good sign.

"Well, since you're awake I've got a surprise for you."

"You do?" She perked up. "What is it?"

He brought out the candy bar with a little flourish. It felt half-melted from having been in his pocket for so long, but he supposed it would still taste the same.

"Ooh!"

The look on her face made all his trouble worthwhile. Nikita handed the treat over and sat on the cot beside her as Elena tore off the paper.

"Thank you," she said, smiling around a mouthful of chocolate. "How'd you get this though?"

"Ah...I found it." Or, more accurately, he'd found a woman selling them out of her purse, among other snacks. At first he had been incensed that anyone had the nerve to ask such a ridiculous price something so small, but then he understood that the law of supply and demand was in effect here. And besides, he wasn't so sure that his cash was going to be good for much else in the near future.

The candy bar was halfway devoured already. "Whoa, slow down! You're getting it all over your face."

Elena giggled. Feeling more parental than ever, Nikita took her chin in one hand and started rubbing away the bits of chocolate with his thumb. One smudge refused to come clean, and his heart stilled when he realized why.

It wasn't from the candy. The spot next to her mouth, no larger than his pinky nail, was black as ink.

"What? what is it?" she asked, seeing his face.

Nikita drew back his hand. "Nothing."

She shrugged. "You want some too?" Elena asked, offering him the candy bar.

He took a good long look at his niece's face, his stomach sinking lower and lower. "No thanks," he said. "I'm not hungry."

~~~~~

"...Kingfisher here."

"Kingfisher, this is Colonel Akimov. Is your report ready?"

"Yes, sir."

"Then proceed."

"Yes, sir." Akimov heard a rustling of papers coming through the line -- Kingfisher was sifting through the reports his men had brought him. "As of 0800 hours today, the evacuation of District Four is at ninety-six percent completion. All the neighborhoods in the district have been called up to the processing centers. Five percent of the processed population have been found infection-positive and were quarantined in Camp Red Three. The infection-negative populations were referred to Camps Blue Nine and Blue Ten pending their evacuation date."

"Good, good," Akimov replied. "State your plans for the remaining unevacuated citizens in District Four."

"Yes, sir. Local announcements are being broadcast to direct late evacuees into water aid centers where they can be detained and processed. I have several squads doing house-by-house sweeps of the evacuated neighborhoods looking for squatters and other non-evacuated civilians."

"Good approach." The thought of the CSF squads roving from block to block, sifting through the houses like the teeth of an enormous black harrow, sent a little thrill down Akimov's spine. "What results are we getting from the sweeps?"

"Since their implementation, twenty civilians have already been evacuated and processed."

"Excellent work. Keep it up, comrade."

"Thank you, sir. But..." Kingfisher cleared his throat, and papers rustled in the background. "...there's one more thing."

"Go ahead."

"Well, some of the sweep squads are reporting unusual findings in the evacuated houses." More rustling sounds. "Here's this one -- 'cleared residence, no inhabitants found. Evacuation notice given two weeks ago. Bathroom and kitchen show heavy mold growth inconsistent with length of time residence has been abandoned'. That's not the only one, sir...here's another. 'Cleared residence, no inhabitants found. Sink and shower covered with black/blue fungus of some sort. Possibly toxic. Recommend sending in cleanup crew'. And this one is similar -- 'residence clear, no inhabitants. One of the men reported seeing an inhabitant from the street, but after a thorough search there were no civilians found in the house. Black fuzzy plant growth all over the bathroom'. Sir, I've got several reports like this one, all from different houses in District Four."

Akimov scowled. So the squads were turning up some sort of fungal infestations. Perhaps these were linked to the ink, given their presence in previously water-saturated rooms like kitchens and bathrooms.

"What actions have your men taken against this growth?"

"We assumed it to be hazardous, sir," Kingfisher replied. "We've been avoiding contact with it as per safety protocols."

"Understood. Have the sweep squads continue to avoid these infestations, but make sure they don't fail to report them."

"Copy that."

"Otherwise, the sweeps are to proceed as normal. That is all."

"Copy, comrade Colonel. Kingfisher out."

The line clicked in his ear and went dead. Akimov settled back into his desk chair. No, he didn't like this at all. Now the black teeth of the harrow were sifting through the houses and coming up covered in this moldy stuff, this black organic fuzz. This was one area where his data was lacking, an unknown variable to solve for. It complicated the equation.

Akimov sighed in spite of himself. Compared to mechanical ones, biological systems were so much less predictable, and so much messier to deal with.

~~~~~

It was late afternoon at the Lubukov Agricultural Labs, and Hawk was tidying up her office.

The office was a comfortable one, with soft carpeting and a desk made of genuine oak. Hawk ran a dustcloth over the desktop, appreciating its shine. Whatever solvents they had used for cleaning it had completely removed all evidence of the late Security Chief Strugatsky. Getting the last traces of the Security Chief from the carpet and the wall behind the desk had been even greater tasks, but now not even a stain was left to mark his passing.

But she hadn't chosen Strugatsky's old office for its material comforts. Rather, its location in the building made it ideal for her needs. Phone lines ran down from the office to all the other major departments in the Labs, letting her subordinates contact her quickly in the event of an emergency. And she wanted the Lab's civilian employees to see that she'd taken over the office of their former boss -- it would give her a psychological advantage when it came to keeping them in line.

Nonetheless she couldn't let her subordinates suspect her of growing soft in the luxury of her position. She knew they would, if given half the chance; the other soldiers feared her now, but they were always ready to doubt her. Of them all, only the Colonel had judged her on her achievements alone.

After giving the desktop a final pass Hawk folded the cloth and tucked it away in the desk drawer. She took a quick survey of the office, found everything in its place, and smiled inside her mask. Letting herself out of the office, she nearly tripped over the legs of a small fat man who had inexplicably chosen to take a nap in the hallway just outside the door.

"Guh!" said the man, starting awake and struggling to his feet. Hawk watched him rise. He was one of the employees, identified by his lab coat as a researcher. A fringe of fuzzy gray hair ringed his balding head. Standing, he was at least a foot shorter than Hawk, perhaps more.

"You're the one in charge of the Labs now?" he confronted her, frowning. Hawk nodded.

"They said you weren't in your office."

Well, this was the first Hawk had heard of anyone asking to see her today. Perhaps her subordinates had chosen not to bother her with the little man's request, but that wasn't their call to make; petty annoyances like this could still yield useful information.

"Who told you that?"

"Oh, I don't know their names. One of them was called Eagle, I think."

Completely unsurprising. She would take this up with Eagle tomorrow. "Why were you asking for me?"

He squared off his shoulders. "I needed to talk to you," he said importantly, "about the deplorable situation here in the Labs."

Hawk considered the man, weighing the potential benefit of the conversation against her appetite for dinner. She decided that dinner could wait -- it was what the Colonel would have done, she thought. Stepping back, she held the office door open for the little man.

She saw him glance up at the door as he came into the office, finding the lighter patch of wood where the brass nameplate reading CHIEF SECURITY OFFICER ANTON STRUGATSKY had once been mounted. So he had noticed it -- that was good.

Hawk closed the door behind her visitor. "Take a seat, comrade."

Unsurprisingly, he remained standing. Hawk smiled as she took her own seat behind the lovely oaken desk that had belonged to her predecessor.

"My name is Boris Grigorievich Orlov," said the man, drawing himself up to his full height. "I am here to inform you that the CSF's treatment of the Lab employees is intolerable, and can not continue."

"I see." This little toy bulldog was proving unexpectedly amusing. "Please elaborate."

"How old are you, lad?"

She let the error slide. "Twenty-eight."

"I thought so. You were born after the Great War ended."

"My father was in the war," she said.

He ignored her. "So you know nothing about the enemies' prisoner-of-war camps."

Hawk waited patiently. She doubted that this fellow, age notwithstanding, had seen any combat himself, but there was no sense in going on the offensive so soon.

"Well, my uncle was in the war," the man declared, and Hawk suppressed the urge to laugh out loud. "He saw the camps. He knew what the enemy was capable of. But even they, who were responsible for the loss of so many Chorman lives, did not treat their captives the way you CSF have been treating us."

Hawk maintained a receptive silence, propping her elbows on the desk and tenting her fingers together. The man took a deep breath.

"First of all, you have incarcerated us in the Labs for no good reason, separating us from our families. Second, you have forced us to labor unpaid, and render medical assistance to these blighted civilians when none of us are doctors and few have any medical training. And third, you have harassed and in many cases assaulted us without cause."

Now that he had spoken his piece the little man seemed to deflate, growing suddenly older. "Is that all?" Hawk asked.

"That's enough," he said wearily. "These conditions have already driven one young man to a violent and pointless death by his own hands. Consider that."

Hawk nodded to show how well she was considering it. "You're referring to Vadim Simonovich Zinetsky, of course."

Hearing the name from her caught Boris off-guard. "Yes, him."

"I was sorry to hear about the death of your comrade." She paused respectfully. "Though I think his terminal blight rather than unpleasant working conditions may have led to his suicide."

A little spark kindled in the man's eyes, and Hawk went on before he could interrupt. "Regardless, I thank you for your opinion, even though you are wrong on all counts." She tried to keep her tone casual. "For one, we have a very valid reason for keeping the Lab's employees here. It was the bioweapon being developed by *your* lab that leaked, meaning that *your* specialists and *your* facilities are the only logical choice for researching its effects. It goes without saying that thousands of lives depend on the research conducted here.

"Furthermore, you are hardly laboring unpaid, unless you think your food, supplies and other necessities are materializing out of thin air. And you misunderstand your duties if you think you are meant to be 'rendering aid' to the thousands of blight victims rather than researching a treatment for the weapon your lab developed.

"And third, if any of you have been harassed or assaulted..." Hawk paused for emphasis, "...it was not without cause."

Little Boris looked a full decade older than before she had spoken. "You're still forcing us to work," he protested. "Even if you say we're being 'paid' for it, it's still forced labor."

"It's nothing of the sort."

"Then I quit."

Hawk made an openhanded gesture. "You're free to do so. But don't expect us to donate food and water to you out of charity."

He hadn't grown any younger, but a flush of anger was blooming in the man's cheeks. "Don't bother. I'm leaving the Labs."

"No, you are not."

Boris slammed his fist down on Hawk's desk. She did not flinch. "The CSF can't keep us here! You've got no right to do that!"

"In fact, we do."

"On whose authority?!"

"Regional Secretary Glukhovsky, of course."

"He authorized the CSF to -- to abuse and incarcerate innocent civilians, to -- "

"The Secretary has authorized the Chorman Special Forces to implement and enforce the quarantine of Khostok." Hawk laid both gloved hands flat on the desktop. "And we are doing precisely that."

"But -- but -- the quarantine only applies to blight victims," Boris sputtered. "Uninfected civilians aren't...they can't be..."

To launch an all-out attack against this self-important little man wasn't necessary; she could bring down his balloon with a single well-placed dart. She'd be enjoying her dinner in fifteen minutes at the most. "You may want to sit down for this, comrade."

Boris ignored her again, or he was too distracted to understand.

"Now," Hawk lifted a finger, "I want you to listen."

They stared at each other in silence. "I don't hear anything," he whispered.

"Keep listening."

The seconds stretched into minutes.

"...the air conditioner?" Boris asked.

"Precisely."

"...What about it?"

"Well, you have a ventilation system here at the Labs, don't you? The one that's supposed to vacuum up dangerous gases and send them to a special chamber to be neutralized?"

The man nodded.

"It may interest you to know that this ventilation system was damaged by the explosion in Cold Storage #5."

"It wasn't venting?!" the man exclaimed.

"No, that wasn't the case. The part of the system responsible for vacuuming up the gases was running fine."

"Then what?"

"Mmm." Hawk ran a finger along the raised edge of her respirator filter. "Tell me...have you ever wondered why the CSF wear their protection suits at all times, even inside the Labs?"

No answer, but Hawk didn't expect one. Slow horror was creeping into Boris's features.

"I'll tell you why. As near as the CSF had been able to determine, the explosion ruptured some of the pipes that lead from the venting ducts into the neutralization chamber. This breakdown allowed the contaminated gases to escape into the ductwork that supplies the central air and heating for the Labs. Until the CSF arrived to patch the leak, all of the employees here at the Lubukov Agricultural Labs were receiving steady round-the-clock doses of ink-contaminated air."

Boris was sinking into that chair now, ever so slowly. Hawk rose from her own seat, leaning across the desk, pushing the muzzle of the gas mask right up underneath his nose.

"You -- all of you -- are infected," she whispered. "You may not show symptoms until later, but you've all got the blight, no mistake. And until you find a cure for it...none of you are leaving this building."

~~~~~

Hot showers and hot baths. If there was one thing the dead envied the living, it was hot showers and hot baths. What Alexei was having right now was not exactly either one, but it was blessedly close enough.

He'd gone to the trouble of saving the daily water ration the CSF had given them, lugging that water all the way up to the lunchroom kitchen, heating it in one of their soup pots, and dragging the heated water back down to the shower room. It had been an undertaking, but the moment the water touched his skin he found that all the effort had been worthwhile. Kneeling on the tiled shower room floor with a metal cup borrowed from the lunchroom, Alexei dipped the hot water out of the tub and poured it down over his head and shoulders, washing away the traces of soap.

He knew he'd find the shower room vacant -- it was practically abandoned now that the water had been shut off. Alexei hadn't bathed in four days, but it seemed like some of the other employees had not bathed since the quarantine began -- even if they didn't admit it, you could smell the truth. How they were supposed to maintain sterile research environments under such living conditions was anyone's guess.

And speaking of research, Yuri had mentioned something at dinner that had caught Alexei's attention. Something about a new experiment he was undertaking, with fresh materials. The other researchers had been indifferent; after several weeks of the CSF's occupation they had begun to care as much about experiments as they did about bathing. But Alexei had noticed Yuri's enthusiasm, and wondered about it. Yuri hadn't talked like that since Vadim's death, and anything that could fire him up to that degree was probably worth hearing about.

Rinsing the last of the soap from his hair, Alexei reached for a discarded shirt to dry himself with. After the quarantine was over, he promised, he was not going to take showers or towels or comfortable beds for granted. Or real food -- once he got out of the Labs and back into a real house, he was never going to eat another military-issue meal ration again.

Once he got out.

Goosebumps prickled across Alexei's skin, and he rubbed them away with the shirt.

The dormitories down on the second underground level of the Labs were a shabby affair, better suited for penniless college students. There were four cots in each room, four undecorated walls, and a bare bulb overhead. A rickety card table in one corner held a dented coffee pot and a hotplate. Behind a curtain sat a now-useless sink and toilet, gathering dust.

As Alexei might have predicted, he found the room empty. Of his three roommates, he knew Anatoly was still in the lunchroom having his dinner, and Boris had gone to speak to the CSF officer in charge of the Labs' occupation. And if his instincts were correct, Yuri was up in the lab with his new experiment.

Well, this was as good a time as any to see what he was working on. Slipping into the clean pants and shirt the CSF had brought them, Alexei left the dorm and headed for the lab.

It was after-hours, and most of the lights in the building were off. Alexei found Yuri sitting in a pool of halogen lighting in an otherwise darkened lab, bent over the lab table with a look of frozen intensity. Alexei cleared his throat and Yuri snapped out of his trance.

"Lyosha!" He looked pleased. "Didn't hear you come in! had your shower already?"

Alexei nodded. "What're you working on?" he asked, craning his neck.

It was as if Yuri had been waiting for someone to ask. "Look, look at this," he said, bubbling over with excitement. When he stepped out of the way Alexei looked down on the table and found nothing more impressive than a sealed glass tank, about the size and shape of a child's fishbowl. The bottom was covered thickly in dark mold, as if something had rotted in the tank, and the air inside was cloudy with a sort of thin white fog.

"Someone leave their pets behind?" he asked, wrinkling up his nose.

"No, it's -- take a closer look!" Yuri all but pushed Alexei down to eye-level with the black fuzz. Dutifully Alexei looked at it, squinting through the clouded glass.

If it was mold, the stuff growing in the tank was unusually plentiful. It was nearly two inches deep on the bottom of the tank, and streaks of it had grown up along the glass sides of their prison, reaching for the top of the tank. It had a hairy sort of look to it, though the individual strands were thicker than hairs; some of the tendrils were almost the width of spaghetti noodles.

Its color was unusual too...up close, it wasn't precisely the same black as the penicillin mold it resembled. In some places the fungus had shaded to a dark indigo, and in other patches it was almost blue. There were small fragments of more colorful material in the tank as well, mixed into the moldy stuff.

Alexei pointed into the tank. "What's all that? Did you put something in there?"

"Those are part of the organism. It grows that way," Yuri whispered.

"'Organism'?" Alexei echoed. Odd choice of words. "Isn't it a plant?"

"Oh, I can't be sure just yet...here, watch this..."

Yuri lifted the corner of the lid away. A strangely sweet smell, almost like honey, wafted out from the tank. A shred of white mist slipped out through the opened crack.

Looking closer, nearly touching his nose to the glass, Alexei discovered that the colorful bits were indeed some kind of organic material. What he had taken for tiny pieces of glass were actually minuscule flowers, little half-opened blossoms scattered throughout the black fuzz. They were translucent as cut gemstones, shaded in sapphire and amethyst and ruby and emerald hues. Under the brilliance of the lab lighting the little jeweled flowers seemed almost to sparkle, to gleam with their own internal light, pulsing brighter and dimmer with a regular rhythm that was almost like a heartbeat...

Movement caught Alexei's eye, and he looked up. Yuri had picked up a slice of apple with a pair of long forceps and was lowering it into the tank.

"You're feeding it?"

"Sshh...yes."

The apple brushed against the uppermost tips of the black tendrils, and Yuri held it there. Alexei started to say something -- what, he couldn't recall -- and then the black stuff began to move.

Slowly, with an undersea motion that reminded him of anemones, the tendrils shifted. Reaching, elongating as they stretched upwards, they coiled over and around the slice of fruit, as if feeling their way by touch. Once they had wrapped it completely Yuri released the apple, and the tendrils carried it down into the dense black carpet where it sank out of sight.

"Did you see it?" Yuri whispered reverently.

Alexei could only nod. Every last one of his hairs was standing on end. Yuri withdrew the forceps and closed the lid of the tank.

" -- wh-what *is* it?"

"I haven't the faintest clue," said Yuri. His eyes were glowing, cheeks flushed. "Fascinating stuff though, isn't it?"

Alexei swallowed and nodded again.

"Some kind of unknown organism, obviously. I know it looks plantlike, but that kind of motor capacity isn't found in any but a handful of plants. Besides, when you get its cells under a microscope they're lacking the hard cell walls that plants rely on for their structure -- given the way the thing moves, that makes sense. Some kind of primitive animal from a radically divergent evolutionary strain is my best guess. Do you know the significance of a discovery like this?"

Alexei had some notion, but he didn't care so very much at the moment. "Uh, where did you get this?" he asked, edging away from the table.

Yuri looked back at the tankful of blackness and fog. "It came from Vadim," he said.

Alexei gave him a blank look. "...what?"

"You remember how we took tissue samples when we started studying the blight?" Yuri laid a hand on the side of the tank. "Well, I cultured some of the cells we took from Vadim. It outgrew a petri dish in two days and I transferred it to this tank. This organism grew from those cells."

Alexei didn't understand, didn't want to understand. A cold sweat was breaking out all over his chest and back. "This...this thing...what it is?"

Yuri shrugged. "I think this stuff *is* the blight."

Alexei's stomach lurched. "You're kidding." The thought that *this* -- this black, tentacled mass of horror -- was growing on people, thousands of them, was too much. Worse than a virus or bacteria, those black stains on the skin were actually a complex living organism...parasiting on human flesh, feeding on it, invading it...forcing its inky tendrils into the skin, the muscles, the brain --

"I'm going to be sick," Alexei croaked, stumbling back from the table. Some small part of him was aware how unscientific he was being, but nausea overwhelmed his rational mind.

Yuri caught him with one hand on his arm, steadying him before he fell. "Don't worry," he said brightly. "That's a good thing."

"Wha-?"

"If it's alive, that means you can kill the stuff." Yuri rapped on the tank with his knuckles. "You hear that?" he called out. "We're going to get you!"

"...how are we going to do that?"

"Oh, I've got lots of ideas. We just need to make the human body inhospitable to this thing, and our unwanted tenants will pack up and leave." He waved at the tank. "For starters, I've just given our fuzzy volunteer here a nice dose of pesticide along with that apple. If we come back tomorrow and the blight is dying off in the tank, we'll know it's sensitive to those chemicals. We can develop therapies based on its weaknesses."

In spite of the churning of his stomach even Alexei could see the logic in this approach. He steadied himself, willing his dinner to stay where it belonged. "I really hope it dies."

"Me too." Yuri was leaning on his elbows on the tabletop, peering into the foggy depths of the tank. "Just think about it -- if we do develop a cure, our lab's going to be famous for saving thousands of Khostok citizens." He gave a short laugh. "My father must be spinning in his grave."

Alexei came over to him, eyeing the tank warily. "Why's that?"

"He said I'd never amount to anything, especially not as a scientist. And he never could stand being wrong about anything." Yuri grinned. "What about your dad?"

"What about him?"

"Did he want you to become a scientist?"

"No idea," Alexei admitted. "He disappeared when I was twelve."

"Oh. Run off with a woman?"

"I don't know. I guess so."

"What do you mean, you guess? What else could have happened to him?"

Alexei stuck his hands into his pockets. "My mom always said the DIO took him."

"Oh." Almost automatically Yuri looked away, checking the door, the corners of the room. "For what?" he asked, in a half-whisper.

"She never did say." The memory always made him feel shamefully helpless, petrified with remembered fear. "But she always told me he was getting tortured...like, getting his ears cut off and his tongue torn out and stuff." He dug his fingernails into the palms of his hands. "And that after they'd broken him the DIO was going to come take me away, and do the same to me."

Alexei looked up from the tank to find Yuri boggling at him. "That's awful," he said at last.

"Yeah, I guess so." Now why had he shared all that? He hadn't even been drinking. "Well, obviously the DIO never got me," he said flippantly. "And I got older and realized, how would my mom know what happened to him? It wasn't like the DIO was going to tell anyone. So my dad probably *did* run away with some woman."

Yuri's pitying expression was almost unbearable. Alexei hadn't even told him about the worst of his mother's stories, or about the nightmares that drove him screaming back into consciousness. "You believe all kinds of nonsense when you're little," Alexei said.

"Yeah, we all do," Yuri agreed, too gently. "And it's late at night, after all."

"It is."

"Let's get back to the dorms then, eh?" As if to lighten the mood Yuri clapped Alexei across the back. "Oh!" He drew back suddenly. "I forgot -- how's your shoulder? still healing?"

"It's getting there." Alexei managed a smile.

"Ahh, good, good."

They maintained silence in the elevator, on the way back down to the dormitory. Alexei hoped that Yuri was daydreaming of ways to kill the thing in the tank, and not thinking about his comrade's embarrassing confessions. Yuri was his coworker, after all, not his therapist.

The two of them stepped from the elevator into the hallway. "We're all under a lot of stress," Yuri said, and Alexei cringed. "Yeah."

"Pity we don't have anything to drink down here. With all this talk about 'the importance of our mission', you'd think the CSF could spare a few bottles for us."

A drink sounded wonderful right about now. "Didn't Boris have something stashed away?" Alexei asked. Yuri's face brightened. "I think so! at least, he looked like he was getting into something." He quickened his step, and Alexei hurried to keep up with his long stride.

"He should be back from that meeting with the officer by now," Yuri said, pushing open the door to their four-person dormitory. "Let's ask him. Maybe he can spare -- "

Whatever Yuri had meant to say died out on his lips. He froze in his tracks, blocking the doorway. Alexei halted too. He couldn't see past him into the room, but he heard Yuri make a strangled sort of noise, as if choking.

"What? what is it?" Alexei tried to squeeze past him and a hand came down on his chest, holding him back. A spike of anger went through him -- he wasn't a child, after all -- and he twisted away from the hand, pushing past Yuri and into the room.

Boris was there, lying on his back in the bed, fully dressed. Alexei spent fifteen seconds wondering why Boris' bedsheets were red when everyone else's were white, and then he understood.

Like a man in a dream, Alexei crossed the room. Afterward he would wonder how he could have remained so calm, but the simple truth was that his brain had processed the color of the bedsheets and then seized up completely, sparing his sanity for awhile.

Boris lay on his pillow like a man asleep, his face the grey-white of window putty. In the light of the lone bulb overhead, the shaving razor in Boris' hand winked and glittered up at Alexei. A piece of paper lay on Boris's chest.

"He wrote something," Alexei said. His locked-up brain gave no help in deciphering the writing. From the doorway behind him there came a muffled sob.

It would be several minutes before either of them recovered enough to read the note that had been left behind. There were only four words, but in those four words was all the justification a man might have needed for doing as Boris had done.

WE ARE ALL INFECTED

# CHAPTER SIX

Alexei could see his brother clearly through the chain-link fence that separated them. The man looked lost, stricken, as if a witness to something inexpressible. He opened his mouth to shout.

"Everyone! Listen to me!! Listen! everyone, listen!"

Now Alexei was aware of the crowds around them, CSF soldiers and civilians. His brother's voice carried over the din, silencing it, turning their heads toward the haunted-looking man in the center of the grassy yard.

"You're all going to die," said Alexei's brother. "They're going to kill you all."

There was a hush. The world seemed to hold its collective breath.

"I've seen it," said the man. "They're going to poison-gas the city once they've evacuated everyone who didn't catch the blight. You're all going to be murdered."

And then there was chaos. Gas-masked soldiers were everywhere, falling on the man like wolves on a bear, flailing at him with fists and truncheons. Others began firing into the air, shouting for order as the crowd became a living thing, insane with fear.

Gunfire crackled, and Alexei saw his brother fall. He acted without thinking -- or, rather, his body acted. Alexei struck the chain-link fence and went up, hand over hand, scaling the fence as nimbly as a monkey. He almost thought he would make it, but the barbed wire at the top of the fence seemed to reach out for him, catching itself on his pants, digging its barbs into his skin. He pitched over the fence, onto the other side, and lost his grip. The barbed wire sliced at his legs as the ground came rushing up to meet him.

Alexei awoke with a gasp.

Heart pounding, he pushed himself into a sitting position. His bedsheets were clammy with sweat. "Ugh," he said, still half-asleep, and waited for the adrenaline to wear off.

The dream itself was strange enough -- though if anyone was going to dream about the CSF gunning people down, it would probably be him. But strangest of all had been his complete conviction that the man in the dream was his brother. Alexei had been positive enough to challenge a mess of barbed wire and a six-foot drop in order to save the fellow. Alexei, who was an only child.

He needed a shower, or to wash his face at least. Alexei got halfway to the dormitory sink before he remembered the water was shut off, and cursed under his breath. Squinting around the dorm room in the half-light that slipped under the door, he found that only Anatoly was still in his bed, snoring away.

Boris's bed was empty, stripped of its sheets. Something clenched painfully around Alexei's heart and he looked away. Yuri's bed was empty too. It couldn't be later than two or three a.m., so where was he?

Alexei was starting to shiver. Abandoning the idea of sleep, he pulled on a shirt and a pair of pants and let himself out of the dormitory, into the vacant hallway.

But if he had had a brother, would he have charged straight towards armed soldiers to save him? Alexei knew the answer to that one.

Lubukov Agricultural Labs were as hushed as a tomb at this hour. Only one bulb in every four was still lit, and the hallways were tunnels of darkness broken by puddles of light. Alexei padded down the hall to the elevators.

The ping of the arriving elevator was three times louder than normal. Every noise Alexei made was amplified; he might as well have been the only living thing in the building.

Yuri, surprisingly, was not in his lab. The tanks full of blight fungus sat on one of the lab tables, spotlighted in the gloom.

Was it his imagination, or was the blight moving? Had it seen him open the door, or heard him somehow? Or did it move constantly, feeling around the inside of its prison, looking for a way to escape the tank?

With ice-water trickling through his spine Alexei closed the lab door.

Alexei's second guess was the lunchroom, and it seemed his intuition was correct. As he approached he could hear voices, echoing strangely in the pervasive silence.

"So you see, Vadik, it's not so terrible after all. We're all helping each other out, and nobody has to be alone."

"I think I get it now, sir. But why's it taking so long?"

"Ahh, you know, we've got to get everyone down to the river first..."

Groggy as he was, Alexei didn't place the two voices until he'd stepped into the lunchroom. The two men seated at one of the lunch tables both turned to him, and smiled.

It was Boris and Vadim.

The lunchroom was half-lit like the rest of the facility, but there was no mistaking those faces. Boris was rosy-cheeked as usual, and Vadim's face had gone back to its old self, before the blight had discolored him.

"See, here's Alexei Nikolaevich," Boris said, waving him over. "Soon we're all going to be here."

" -- Lyosha?"

Stunned beyond words, Alexei turned toward the sound of his name. Yuri was sitting at another table, cradling a coffee cup in both hands. "You alright?"

He almost laughed out loud. Couldn't Yuri see them? But when he looked back, Alexei found that Boris and Vadim had vanished.

"Lyosha?"

He felt his sanity beginning to fray and scrambled to get a grip on himself. You were sleepwalking, Alexei shouted mentally. You sleepwalked down to the lunchroom and dreamed you saw them. They disappeared because you woke up.

"Lyosha!" Yuri rose from his chair.

"I'm okay!" Alexei's voice echoed in the empty lunchroom. "I'm okay."

"You sure?" Yuri gave him a searching look as Alexei came up to the table. "Seriously, you've gone white. What's wrong? feeling sick?"

"I'm fine." Seeing ghosts, is all.

"What're you doing up so early?"

"I had a nightmare," Alexei said, and instantly regretted it. Yes, he was about six years old, and went running to his parents' bed whenever the bad dreams scared him.

"Oh...me too." Yuri smiled weakly. "Crazy stuff."

Alexei slid into the chair across from Yuri. "Yeah?"

"Uh-huh." Yuri was looking down at the tabletop. Beside his coffee cup was a small glass jar, its bottom filled with the fuzzy black growth that Alexei was now very familiar with. He picked this up, turning it in his hands. "I dreamed I was stuck in one of the tanks," he said. "I must've been about the size of a lab rat, I guess. I was just trying to get out -- it was really important to get out -- but the walls were all glass, and slippery. I don't think I knew where I was until someone came into the lab -- he was enormous compared to me, and the surprise woke me up." He gave Alexei a sheepish look. "Isn't that weird?"

It was about as weird as hallucinating one's dead comrades. "It's the stress," Alexei offered. "We're all getting a little strange."

Yuri nodded, still considering the jar. "You remember the pesticide experiment we did, right?" he asked suddenly.

"Huh? of course."

"You remember how it turned gray and started to die off? It killed nearly the entire tank."

"That's right."

Yuri was scowling at the jar. "It's immune now," he said.

Alexei remembered how delighted Yuri had been when the poisoned apple had begun to kill the blight, and how crushed he had been when the blight had recovered. He had gone to the point of dumping straight pesticide directly into the tank, all to no avail.

"Plants -- I mean, living things -- they can develop resistances." Alexei said. "Bacteria do it all the time." And Yuri should have known this.

"No, no...I mean the blight itself is immune now." His frown deepened. He held the jar up for Alexei to see it, and Alexei shrank back. "This sample never did get any pesticide in the original tests -- it was one of my controls. Yesterday I gave this thing six ounces of pesticide and look at it -- completely fine."

Now that, Alexei had to admit, made little sense. "Maybe the original tank was a fluke? all of the blight could be immune to pesticides, and the first batch just had an atypical reaction. Or maybe the first round of pesticide was contaminated with something."

"I suppose you're right." Yuri sighed. "So far, the only thing that kills the stuff is burning it and starving it -- it needs food. And when it's growing on a human body, you can't really separate it from its food supply." He set the jar back down.

"I guess not," said Alexei, feeling his stomach clench.

"But the blight doesn't behave like a typical parasite, either. You know that one patient, the one in Storage 8?"

"The young girl? what about her?"

"Well, you remember how she was when she came in, right?"

Alexei knew precisely what Yuri meant. The senior researcher had gotten into it with the CSF when they had brought the girl to the Labs for study -- "I don't care how much equipment you give us, this is not a hospital. You can't be bringing people here when they're half-dead already. I know what you're doing -- you just don't want it on your heads when she dies."

He hadn't said anything at the time, but privately Alexei had agreed with Yuri on all counts. Their newest 'patient' had come with a broken arm, fractured ribs, a concussion, lacerations on both legs and internal bleeding, in addition to one of the most advanced cases of the blight they had seen. In spite of all they had done for her, neither of them expected her to live more than a week.

"Well, her wounds are healing."

Alexei perked up. "They are?"

"Uh-huh." Yuri looked bewildered. "Pretty rapidly too. And they shouldn't be."

"Why not?"

"Well, you know how it goes with parasites...anything hitching a ride on the human body has to share its resources with the host. And parasites are often pretty bad at sharing. They steal too many calories, or destroy healthy organs, or dump their waste products back into the host."

"Right, of course."

"But the blight isn't doing any of those things. In fact, the girl in Storage 8 is healing much faster than she should be." Yuri made a helpless gesture. "Aside from the skin discoloration, psychosis and insomnia, she's the picture of health."

"And you think the blight is responsible for that?"

"I can't explain it any other way."

Alexei couldn't explain it either, but after the ghosts he was about ready to believe anything. "Well, once we figure out a cure for the thing, maybe they can use the blight therapeutically," he said.

That earned a weak smile from Yuri. "Maybe they can," he admitted. "Once we cure it."

It was a lame joke and Alexei knew it. Nobody on earth would willingly subject themselves to infestation with that nightmarish tentacled parasite, no matter what the health benefits. Anyone in their right mind would choose death before submitting to that.

~~~~~

There was something distinctly unethical about keeping human beings in the storage rooms.

It had been the CSF's decision, of course. And they had defended their choice -- the storage rooms were airtight, ventilated, climate-controlled. With their heavy steel doors they were secure against escape from within, once the inner door handle was removed. And since many of the Lab's research compounds had needed different storage environments they had built no fewer than ten storage rooms, each one about ten by ten feet square.

Now that the Labs were dedicated to study of the blight, there was no need to keep those research chemicals in storage anymore. This left plenty of space in the now-empty storage rooms to incarcerate human beings, locking them into the windowless little cells as if they were no more than lab specimens.

But regardless of how well they worked for their new purpose, their architects had clearly not designed the rooms to hold suffering, psychotic blight victims. Soundproofing was a feature the storage rooms prominently lacked, and Alexei was reminded of this whenever they had to venture into the storage area of the Labs. Sometimes the area was quiet, but more often than not it was bedlam, and the halls resounded with laughter, screams, furious arguments, hysterical sobbing. Today all was still, at least at the moment, but this did very little to relax him.

"What are *they* doing here?" Anatoly was asking Yuri. As Boris's replacement it was Anatoly's first time to deal directly with the blight victims, and he was doing a poor job at hiding his nerves. He jerked his head towards the two CSF officers at the door of Storage Room 8. The one codenamed Eagle was kneeling at the door to fiddle with the door lock; Hawk stood behind him with folded arms, supervising.

"They're here for security," Yuri explained. "They always come with us."

"Security? whose security?"

"Ours."

" -- Ahh, there it is." Eagle straightened up. He pressed down on the handle -- the bolts clunked open -- and opened the door a fraction. Hawk slipped inside the storage room at once. "In you go," Eagle prompted the researchers. Yuri was the next one inside, followed by Alexei, and after a bit more prodding Anatoly squeezed into the room as well. Eagle stood guard in the doorway, holding the door open with the toe of his boot, ready to thwart an attempted escape.

Yuri bent down next to the pitiful bundle of rags on the grated metal floor. "How are you feeling, Veronika?"

The bundle stirred. A hand emerged, blotched with patches of ink. With a sideways motion the bundle rolled over, revealing a young woman who might have been attractive if she hadn't been so discolored and so wild-looking. One arm and both legs were so blighted they were entirely black, contrasting against the whiteness of her hospital gown. Her long black hair hung down in tangles, like a feral child. Her pupils were huge.

Yuri straightened up. "She's having an episode," he said quickly. "I wouldn't -- "

Everything happened at once. The woman let loose the shriek of a damned soul, Anatoly yelped in surprise, and Alexei leapt back. Eagle, alarmed, tried to poke his head into the storage room, and all at once the woman coiled up like a spring and leapt for him.

It happened too fast to see. The next thing they knew Eagle was bawling in fear, trying to backpedal out of the room and shut the door. One of the Veronika's hands was clenched on Eagle's chest, holding a fistful of his protective suit in a death grip.

Yuri saw the door closing on the woman and reached out to grab her. "Don't, you'll cut her arm off!"

From where Alexei stood it looked like Yuri had caught hold of the Veronika's wrist -- and then immediately snatched his hand back, as if stung. Almost at the same instant Eagle broke free of her grip and ducked out of the room, shutting the storage door on the five of them. Veronika tumbled to the grated floor.

Hawk had unslung her AKS-47 and was aiming it at point-blank range. "Don't shoot!" Yuri shouted, clutching his hand. Anatoly gave a squeal.

Alexei flattened himself against the metal shelves as Veronika made another leap, aiming herself directly at Hawk. But instead of grabbing her suit the woman dove at Hawk's knees, wrapping both arms around her leg.

"Sister!!" Veronika wailed. "Help me!"

Everyone halted. Still holding her rifle in one hand, Hawk looked down at the woman. Veronika was stretched out on the floor, clutching at Hawk's boot as if to save herself from drowning. "Help me, help me..."

Awkwardly, Hawk reslung her rifle and knelt down. "Calm down now," she said gruffly. As the researchers watched in amazement Hawk loosened the woman's fingers from her boot and held her hands. "Nobody is going to hurt you."

Veronika looked up into Hawk's mask, her face shining with tears. "You've got to help me!" she whispered.

Hawk's uneasiness was evident in her voice, distorted though it was. "...help you? how?"

"Get me out of here." Veronika grasped Hawk's fingers. "Please!"

"You know I can't do that, comrade."

"Oh please..." Fresh tears started in the woman's eyes. "You don't know -- "

"Hawk!!" It was Eagle, recovered from his fright, pounding on the storage room door from the outside. "*Hawk*! Sir, are you okay in there?!"

"I'm fine, you moron!" Hawk shouted back. "I've got it under control!! Stand by! I'll let you know when to open the door."

"Roger that, sir."

"...you don't know, you don't know..." Veronika was whimpering.

"I don't know what?"

The woman checked back over her shoulder. Alexei saw that her pupils were still dilated. "...you don't know what they've been doing to me."

"They're only trying to help," Hawk explained, but Veronika was already shaking her head. "No, not that...they've been coming to me...at night...nobody will listen to me, but it's true..."

Hawk's spine stiffened. And then Anatoly gave a shrill giggle -- more out of nervousness than anything else -- and Hawk was on her feet at once, brandishing her AKS.

"So you think it's funny? It must have been you, then."

Anatoly squealed again and threw his hands in the air, visibly shaking. Yuri stepped up to Hawk, reaching out to push the rifle down. His other hand was stuffed into his pants pocket. "Hold on, comrade, hold on -- let's think this through."

"No-one believes me!" Veronika sobbed. Anatoly was practically sobbing himself. "I'm sorry I laughed! I swear I didn't! I never saw her before today!"

"What makes you think it's one of *us*?" Alexei threw in. Hawk turned in his direction. "We can't even get into the rooms without a soldier -- you guys have all the keys. If anyone's been into storage, it's going to be one of your own men!"

Alexei only had a moment to congratulate himself on his reasoning before Hawk took aim at his chest, and he nearly soiled himself. "Wait, think about it!" Yuri made another swipe for the rifle. "He's right, you know! we can't even get in here without the CSF!"

Unreadable in her gas mask, Hawk stared Alexei down. "All right," she growled at last, putting her rifle away. Alexei's knees buckled and he sank to the floor.

Hawk raked the three of them with her gaze before kneeling down again. "Calm down," she said, pulling Veronika into a sitting position. "I believe you. Tell me who's been bothering you."

Veronika scrubbed at her eyes with the back of an inkstained hand. "I don't know their names...it's the men in the black hats. There's so many of them."

Yuri cocked his head "...hats?"

Alexei was confused...the DIO wore hats, but they were even less likely than the researchers to be sneaking into storage.

"It's true!" Veronika insisted. "They come and ask me to confess, or to do...things, or to burn me with their cigarettes...look, look, they pulled out my fingernails last time!" She thrust her hand in front of Hawk's mask. "Look!"

Hawk took the woman's hand, bringing it right up to the mask's eyepieces. She gave the other hand the same careful scrutiny. Both were perfectly intact, though blighted, and all ten fingernails were still there.

"I see," Hawk said, finally beginning to understand. She released the woman and stood again. "I'll personally see to it that I find the men who've been bothering you."

Veronika's eyes were liquid. "You can't just take me away?"

Hawk shook her head. "We're going to use a different test subject today," she announced to the rest, in a completely different tone of voice. "Let's get going."

"You're leaving me?" Veronika whimpered, and Hawk looked down at her once more. "I have to. But I'll come back to check on you."

"Promise?"

Hawk leaned down and petted the young woman's head. "I promise," she said firmly, then turned to the researchers. "Well, what are you all waiting for? Let's go!" Squaring off her shoulders, Hawk pounded on the storage room door. "Eagle! open up, soldier! we're coming out!"

"Yes sir!" Eagle replied, and the door swung open again. Hawk marched out without looking back, followed by the three men in lab coats. The door clanged shut behind them.

"I've never seen her act that way," Alexei whispered to Yuri.

"I think it's safer not to talk about it," Yuri whispered back. A little half-smile crossed his lips.

"...that big soldier's a *woman*?" Anatoly whispered to no-one in particular. "I can't believe it!"

~~~~~

A warrior trapped in enemy territory should be like a shadow, leaving no trace behind. And when he struck he should be silent as the snake, unseen and just as deadly.

Thinking of himself in terms of snakes and shadows gave Mikhail a private thrill. He grinned to himself as he snuck through the alleyway behind the hotel. He was General Mikhail Ilyich Litvinenko, the decorated stealth warrior, out on a supply run to restock his fortified hideout.

He was every inch a warrior, just like that fellow in the American movie he'd liked so much. Mikhail had even ripped up one of the hotel's red tablecloths and tied the makeshift bandanna around his head, just like the actor. When he shook his head the tails of the bandanna fluttered around his shoulder. It made him more visible, of course, but he felt so manly while wearing it he wouldn't have taken it off. All he needed to complete the look was a bow and arrow.

With the CSF so close at hand stealth was of the essence. Laying to rest the afflicted citizens, poisoned by the DIO's drugs, was a risky undertaking -- twice already the soldiers seemed to have heard his gunfire, and once they had almost come across one of the bodies before he had disposed of it. His mission of mercy had nearly gotten him caught, but he couldn't give it up. He couldn't let his fellow citizens suffer without hope of release.

Stealth, above all. He had to choose his restock points carefully; any obvious signs of looting might bring the CSF to investigate. The convenience store down the street, already half ransacked, seemed a safe enough bet, and Mikhail had taken special care to restrict his shopping to the shelves that faced away from the glass front of the store.

Checking around to make sure the coast was clear, Mikhail let himself into the store, stepping carefully on the broken glass that littered the welcome mat. His list was short, only essential supplies: bandages, canned food, solid fuel, painkillers and antibiotics. Knives and scissors. And clean, pure water, untainted by government chemicals -- that most precious of commodities.

General Mikhail Ilyich Litvinenko, decorated war veteran and indomitable survivalist, skittered around behind the rows of shelving in search of potato chips. Each reclaimed resource was placed carefully into his backpack, heavier items near the bottom. He got down onto his stomach and commando-crawled past a moldering display of once fresh-baked goods.

He reflected that he probably should have commando-crawled in through the front door, to avoid being seen, but there had been glass on the floor. At any rate, the radio receivers implanted in his back molars were broadcasting only static, so it was unlikely that an aerial stealth camera was anywhere nearby.

His eye fell on a bank of glass-fronted refrigerated coolers, filled with row upon colorful row of bottled sodas. They weren't water, but liquid was liquid, and his pack had room for one or two. Hitching up onto his knees, Mikhail opened the door of the cooler.

Cold, humid air gusted into his face. The CSF had shut off the water, but the power was still running, and for that he counted his blessings. The bottles near the front of the row were warmer, and Mikhail reached back into the chilly depths of the cooler, searching for the coldest one.

Something brushed across his knuckles. A piece of string, it felt like, or a scrap of labeling torn from one of the bottles. Still on his knees, Mikhail continued to reach back, feeling his way by touch across the bottle-caps. Then the tickling sensation returned with a vengeance and Mikhail withdrew, empty-handed. He scratched at the back of his knuckles and bent down, peering across the underside of the shelf.

He found the underside coated in something black and fuzzy-looking. Some kind of synthetic insulation, no doubt. The coating wasn't very even, and in some places long strings of the stuff hung down almost to the tops of the bottles beneath them, stirring in a slight breeze that wafted through the cooler.

Except there was no breeze. And the black stuff was definitely moving, the strings coiling and uncoiling slowly, like lazy worms.

And Mikhail had touched it.

General Mikhail Ilyich Litvinenko, decorated war veteran and indomitable survivalist, let out an eardrum-fracturing scream. He scrabbled to his feet, charging back through the store, knocking into the baked-goods display stand and sending muffins and cupcakes bouncing away in all directions. Groaning deep in his throat, he pelted down one of the aisles and snatched up a bottle of rubbing alcohol. When the top refused to unscrew Mikhail simply broke the neck completely away, then dumped the contents over his hand.

The fumes made him cough, but Mikhail persisted until he'd drenched his entire hand in the alcohol. He doused the other hand too, just to be sure, and glanced back at the cooler.

Those rows of colorful bottles gave no clue as to the horror the cooler concealed. Mikhail heard a rising tide of noise as his radio reception began to kick in, and clenched his teeth to dampen the signal.

Sweet merciful savior! This was worse than the CSF, worse than the hideous experiments of the Chorman Defenders Army, worse than callous cruelty of the Veterans' Welfare Board, worse even than the DIO and their poisoned water and aerial stealth drones. Oh, how wrong Mikhail had been.

This was something not of this earth, and the innocent citizenry of Khostok had no clue.

~~~~~

The announcement came around noon, when the researchers at the Lubukov Agricultural Labs were just starting their lunch. Alexei had barely set his tray down when the facility-wide intercom system crackled to life.

"ATTENTION, EMPLOYEES," the amplified voice boomed.

One or two people sighed, and Yuri dropped his fork onto his tray, but for the most part there was little reaction.

"PLEASE STAND BY FOR AN IMPORTANT ANNOUNCEMENT. THIS CONCERNS THE SANITATION PROCEDURES FOR THE BUILDING, SO IT IS IN YOUR BEST INTERESTS TO LISTEN."

He couldn't be sure, but Alexei thought it was Hawk herself making the announcement.

"IT HAS COME TO OUR ATTENTION THAT EMPLOYEES HAVE BEEN DISPOSING OF BIOHAZARDOUS MEDICAL WASTE IN UNAPPROVED TRASH CANS THROUGHOUT THE FACILITY. THIS IS IN CLEAR VIOLATION OF SAFETY PROTOCOL WHICH SPECIFIES THAT MEDICAL WASTE MAY ONLY BE DEPOSITED IN THE BLUE LABELED BINS. IF YOU NEED ASSISTANCE IN LOCATING THE CORRECT BINS, PLEASE ASK ONE OF THE CSF PERSONNEL.

"IMPROPER DISPOSAL OF WASTE PRESENTS A SERIOUS HEALTH RISK TO THE ENTIRE STAFF OF THIS FACILITY. GOING FORWARD, FAILURE TO COMPLY WITH THE GUIDELINES FOR WASTE DISPOSAL WILL RESULT IN PUNITIVE ACTION."

The announcement concluded with a crackle and the click of the intercom being turned off. "That guy's on a power trip," muttered someone who'd yet to receive the memo about Hawk.

Alexei shrugged and occupied himself with his stew. Halfway through the bowl he realized why the far corner of the lunchroom kept on catching his eye.

"Hey, look -- the trashcan's gone."

Only one other person cared enough to look, but the rest were more than eager to grumble about it.

"Ah, they're revoking our trashcan privileges! soon our beds will be revoked too."

"Who bothers to dump their lab trash in the lunchroom? Unless this stew counts as medical waste."

"Sure it does, since they've been tossing cadavers into the stew pot."

"No, they haven't -- the stew would taste better if they had."

"Ssh!" someone hissed, tilting their head in Yuri's direction. Word had gotten around that he had been fairly close to both of the Lab's recent suicide cases, and nobody wanted to remind him.

Yuri dropped his fork again, clattering into the plastic tray. Was he half-asleep or something? Alexei peered at him, and that's when he noticed it: Yuri was eating with his left hand. His right hand was tucked under the table, out of sight.

He would have mentioned it, but at that moment Yuri looked up. Their eyes met and the older man gave his head a barely perceptible shake, as if to say *Don't ask*.

Alexei didn't ask, but it chewed at him afterward. Partly because he was seeing Yuri less and less, and finding him much less talkative when they did meet. And partly because Yuri's right hand was always hidden in his pocket.

Something was bothering Yuri, and it bothered Alexei that he seemed to be trying to hide it. Of course, not everyone liked to blather on about their feelings the way that Alexei habitually did. As unusual as his behavior was, Alexei blamed the deaths of their two comrades and chose not to confront Yuri about it.

As it turned out, Alexei didn't need to ask. His questions were answered three days later, when he awoke in the middle of the night.

~~~~~

An amazing thing, how quickly one's sympathy could be exhausted.

It was nighttime in the repurposed auditorium known as Red Camp Three, but from the sound of things only Nikita was trying to sleep. He lay on his cot with his eyes stubbornly closed and his blanket bunched up around his ears, beset on all sides by the noise of the other inmates.

"The bombs! the bombs are falling! everyone into the shelter!"

"But what about the cake? we can't have a birthday party without cake!"

"So we're all going to be together? everyone?"

"Just let me sleep five more minutes, Mom! I'll get up in a second!"

"Charge! over the top of the hill, men, let's go!"

Nikita's opinion of his fellow camp inmates had undergone a complete transformation since his arrival. He'd begun by seeing the others as honest citizens, suffering unfair circumstances through no fault of their own. Then he'd started to view them as lowlifes, diseased scoundrels who would squabble over a pan of watery soup or steal your shoes while you slept.

At the moment they were little more than bellowing cattle to him, and he earnestly hoped for a CSF soldier to come down the rows of cots and bash each and every one of them in the head if it would shut them up long enough for him to get some goddamn sleep.

The soldiers' enforcement of the camp's "quiet hours" policy was purely dependent on who was on guard, and how drunk they were. For all that they were better armed and armored the CSF were clearly outnumbered by the inmates, and certain individuals assigned to the night watch could not have cared less than the auditorium turned into a zoo at night.

Groaning, Nikita pushed himself up into a sitting position, the blanket still draped over his head. He knew that all the shrieking and gabbling was not a deliberate effort to rob him of his rest; it was psychosis brought on by the blight. He blamed the inmates anyway. The CSF could take the lot of them and line them up against the back wall of the auditorium, and he would only be grateful for the silence. Hell, another night of this and Nikita would be willing to go up against the wall himself if it meant getting some rest. Quite frankly he did not know why the CSF hadn't done so already.

Of course, they claimed there was a cure being developed. They soldiers in charge of their incarceration had made the announcement just the other day, to a chorus of eager shouts and demands. The Lubukov Agricultural Labs was testing a potential cure now, the CSF asserted, and once it was determined to be both safe and effective it would be distributed to the afflicted of Red Camp Three. (Several people had loudly offered themselves as guinea pigs, but they were turned down.) After they were all cured, the evacuation would proceed as scheduled.

Of course Nikita doubted that the cure was real. But then a sinister little voice whispered to him that there was no reason to keep the camp inmates alive if the cure was *not* real, since they were doing nothing but draining the CSF's resources.

Or maybe, the little voice insinuated, the CSF was playing a waiting game instead. In his sleepless nights Nikita had heard people sobbing, had seen the inhuman silhouette of masked soldiers as they carried the bodies out of the auditorium. The empty cots he found in the morning were proof that he had not dreamed these things. Stained skin and madness were not the only effects of the blight -- it was apparently lethal. Nikita did not know *how* deadly it was, but he had yet to see anyone recover from it.

Anxiety lanced through him like razorblades in his stomach. Unable to stop himself, he turned to Elena's cot. She lay there in apparent sleep, her face as smooth as an angel's. A blotch the size of a thumbprint discolored the side of her mouth.

Nikita now knew with complete conviction that he could never be a parent. If being an uncle -- a glorified babysitter, really -- could cause this kind of agony, Hell itself would pale in comparison to actual parenthood. Elena depended on him so completely, and that the world had become so dangerous and so alien in the past few weeks. Children's faith in the competence of adults was entirely undeserved.

Elena whimpered. Nikita bent over her and her eyes flickered open.

"You're awake?" Given the ruckus in the auditorium this wasn't surprising.

Elena nodded and snuffled. "I had a bad dream."

"Aw, that's no good. But it was just a dream, right? dreams aren't real." He stroked her hair, trying to soothe her.

"It just felt really real."

"Well, what did you dream about?"

She looked up at him from her pillow. "I dreamed the soldiers made you stand against the wall and then they shot you."

Nikita's hand stilled.

"They're not going to shoot you, right?"

"No, no, of course not. Nobody's getting shot." Nikita glanced around the room as he spoke, but the distinctive silhouettes of the CSF soldiers were nowhere to be seen. "We're just waiting here for that cure, remember? then we can all go home."

Elena nodded, but her expression said she did not believe it.

"Now, be a good girl and close your eyes. You need more sleep than that."

Obedient to a fault, Elena did so. Nikita continued patting her head, willing her to sleep.

Really, she was such a sweet kid. She acted so trusting when -- suddenly Nikita was positive about it -- she knew her uncle was feeding her nothing but lies.

~~~~~

In contrast to Red Camp Three, the Lubokov Agricultural Labs were peaceful. Still, Alexei couldn't sleep. There was no peace when your nightmares followed you into the waking world.

He opened his eyes for the third time that night. All was quiet in the dormitory; Anatoly must have rolled over on his stomach, for he was no longer sawing logs. Yuri's bed, as he might have expected, was empty. Boris's bed was empty also.

Alexei stared into the darkness at that bare mattress, stripped of bedsheets. He had half-expected the bed to be occupied again, to open his eyes and find the rosy-cheeked old man grinning at him in the dim obscurity of the dorm room.

"None of us have to be alone again..."

Alexei knew he was losing his mind. He could feel himself unraveling, coming to pieces at the seams. 'It's just the stress' was his mantra, his hope that when the quarantine was lifted and they were finally released from the Labs he could recover something of his old self again. Not that his old self had been so terribly well-adjusted either.

God, who wouldn't be going crazy under such conditions? how many weeks had it been since they had seen the sunlight? the researchers were all going to be raving lunatics at this rate, blight or no blight.

Something hissed.

Adrenaline jetted into Alexei's blood, and his heart took off like a rabbit. He was sitting upright in a flash. Boris had not yet materialized in his old bed, but there was definitely something moving on the mattress. An undulating patch of darkness against the grey fabric, like a bloodstain...or the blight.

Or a shadow.

Fully awake now, Alexei realized there was light in the dormitory, more than there should have been. A sort of muted glow was coming from behind him, throwing shadows into the room and onto the bare mattress. Alexei turned around and discovered the source -- the curtain that concealed the sink and toilet. Something (some*one*, of course, it had to be a person) behind the curtain was wielding what seemed to be a flashlight; they were the ones responsible for the shadow puppetry that had startled Alexei so badly.

Alexei slid out of bed and stepped into his pants. If this was a practical joke he was going to let the joker know exactly what he thought of their sense of humor.

When Alexei whipped open the curtain and discovered Yuri there it was hard to say who was more startled. Alexei was surprised, of course, but for an instant Yuri looked petrified enough to faint.

"Lyosha!" he panted, wide-eyed. "Trying to give me a heart attack?"

"Sorry -- what are you doing?"

Instead of answering Yuri looked down. Alexei looked down too, and wished he hadn't.

Yuri was standing over the sink, which was filled with loops of ink-stained white gauze. His flashlight lay in the sink, half-covered by the fabric. The end of the unwound bandage trailed over the cracked edge of the bowl, next to Yuri's hand.

His right hand.

Black and blue smudges had swallowed nearly the entire hand, reaching as far up as the wrist. Only Yuri's fingertips were still pink. The discoloration looked like bruising for the most part, but here and there were half-healed lacerations that had darkened to a shiny jet-black, like polished rubber.

Yuri had caught the blight.

Alexei gasped and took an involuntary step backward. Yuri looked away, ashamed.

"...how?"

"It was when I tried to grab that woman, remember?" He turned his hand over. In the palm of his hand were three dots of a deeper black, all in a row. "Something on her arm stabbed me...it went right through the latex glove." He flexed his fingers. "I have no clue how it happened, but...here I am."

"Oh god." Alexei looked away now, unable to stand it, and Yuri sat down on the lid of the toilet. "What are you going to do?"

"No clue," Yuri said, with a little shrug. "Cut my hand off?"

Alexei gave him a horrified look. "You're kidding."

"Yeah, I am. You know how the blight works -- this stuff's in my bloodstream already. It'd do no good." He was watching his fingers move, studying the hand as if it was an alien lifeform.

"But we have to do something!" Alexei insisted.

"Lyosha, I am fresh out of ideas at this point." Yuri closed his hand into a fist. "And out of clean gauze, too." He glanced at the sink. "It's not like I can cover it up indefinitely anyway; they already found the bandages I threw out. I just hope they don't put me into one of the storage rooms."

"I'll get you more gauze tomorrow," Alexei said. The gears in his mind were engaging again, one by one. "We'll figure something out."

Yuri looked up at Alexei. Behind his oversized glasses his eyes were childishly blue.

"What are you going to do?"

"...something," Alexei said, with a lot more conviction than he felt.

~~~~~

But "something" was still the extent of Alexei's plans when he awoke the next morning.

Yuri was still sleeping, his tainted right hand hidden under the blankets. Fine, he'd let him sleep. Alexei had to get him some more gauze -- and to think. He'd figure something out if only he could think.

Alexei jumped into his cleanest pants and shirt and headed up to the ground floor.

It wasn't really "confidence" that he was feeling -- more like an awareness of how limited his options were. He knew beyond a doubt that there wouldn't be any cure for the blight without Yuri, and without a cure Alexei was never going to see the sunlight again. Understanding this, his next course of action was simple.

And it couldn't do him any harm to ask for more cotton gauze. If the CSF expected them to treat the blight victims then gauze was something they would need. And Alexei himself was clean, after all.

Once he reached the first floor Alexei turned at once toward the back of the building. The CSF had established what they called their "requisitions office" near the loading docks in back. Originally meant for delivery of heavy lab equipment, the docks now received daily shipments of water, medical supplies and tasteless military rations for the imprisoned researchers at the Labs.

Alexei marched right through the door of the requisitions office and up to the desk. The soldier behind the desk looked up. "Name?" he said, reaching automatically for one of the jugs of water on the floor beside his chair.

"Alexei Nikolaevich Raikov," he said. "But I need more cotton gauze, not water."

The soldier set the jug back down. "Cotton gauze?"

"A couple rolls, if you've got it."

That masked head gave a half-turn, as if considering the request. "I think there's some in the back," he said, rising from his chair. "Take a seat. I'll be right back."

Alexei nodded and sat down as the soldier ducked through a door in back of the office.

Left alone, he slouched back in the chair, letting his gaze wander around the room. It looked much the same as before the occupation -- dusty shelves, generic artwork on the wall over the desk, yellowed delivery schedule tacked to the cork bulletin board. The only new details were the boxes of military rations stacked six and seven deep on the floor behind the desk, crates of drugs and medical instruments from the local hospital, and the ever-precious green plastic jugs of water.

When you really considered it, the Chorman Special Forces were being used as glorified relief workers. Setting up camps and handing out water -- this was hardly a military operation.

"Hello, citizen."

He spun around in his chair. Hawk was standing in the doorway of the requisitions office. Flanking her were Kestrel and another subordinate who might have been codenamed Shrike.

Alexei's mouth went dry. "Hello," he said.

"Trying to pick up more bandages?"

He nodded. Hawk took a step back, sweeping her arm toward the door. "This way."

Alexei didn't even remember leaving the office. The next thing he knew he was already in the hallway, following Hawk, with Kestrel and Shrike a half-step behind him. His heart was bashing itself to death against the inside of his ribcage.

*Keep it together,* he warned himself. *You have a reason to ask for the gauze. You haven't done anything wrong. And you don't have the blight.*

*Most especially, don't run. You know what happens when you try to run.*

In silence the four of them packed into an elevator car. Hawk pressed the button for U2 and they began to sink.

Now Alexei was pleading with himself. *Don't say anything, don't say a word. Anything you say will make you sound guiltier. Your conscience is clear. Just keep your mouth shut.*

Hawk ushered them out onto the second underground level and led the way down the hall. For a brief, wild moment Alexei thought they were just going to throw him into a storage room with the rest of the blight victims, but they bypassed Storage and turned into the shower room. Shrike was the last one into the shower room, and he closed the door behind him. Alexei heard the door lock and teetered on the brink of panic, but brought himself back with a violent effort.

"Here we are," Hawk said. She turned to Alexei and the fluorescent lights flashed whitely on her eyepieces, gleamed on the black rubber of her mask and her suit.

"Now...tell me why you need more bandages."

Alexei tested his voice and found it completely broken. "We need them for the blight victims," he managed.

Hawk was already shaking her head. "No, you don't -- their bandages were changed yesterday. I personally saw to that."

"But we'll need some more at some point. In the future."

"But that's not why you're here," Hawk said. "You remember my announcement yesterday?"

"I do," Alexei replied, and followed quickly with " -- sir."

"As I'm sure you know, I made that announcement because we have been finding soiled bandages in all sorts of non-approved trash cans. I'm sure you don't need me to tell you about the health risk that kind of thing presents."

"No, sir."

"The work you people are doing is essential to the future of many thousands of fellow Khostok citizens. If we feel that the blight may break out among the employees at the Labs, we have to deal with such risk factors immediately."

"Yes, sir." The shower room was not well insulated -- in fact it was downright cold -- but

Alexei was starting to sweat all the same.

Hawk clasped her hands behind her back. "So," she said, "this is why I took it upon myself to conduct an experiment of my own. For the past two days, I have personally supervised the treatment of every single test subject. I have personally made sure that all contaminated materials taken from them, including cotton bandages, have been placed into the incinerator immediately. And do you know what results I found from this experiment?"

Oh, Alexei knew already. He had a sudden vision of himself getting sick all over the white-tiled floor, all over Hawk's boots. He certainly felt like doing that right about now.

Hawk raised her hands in mock-surprise. "More bandages appeared in the trash cans!" she said. "It was amazing! And the only conclusion I can draw..." Here she bent down, putting her inhuman masked face at eye-level with Alexei. "...is that someone here, working at the Labs, has caught the blight."

Alexei had had enough. Besides, even an ignorant person could have figured out what Hawk was implying. "I don't have it," he croaked.

"That's good to hear." Hawk straightened up again. "If that's the case, I'm sure you wouldn't mind if we took a moment to examine you?"

"...Go ahead," Alexei said. For a tiny moment he felt proud of himself and his own bravery. Then Shrike stepped forward, grabbed Alexei's arm and handcuffed one of his wrists. Pulling his arm upward, Shrike locked the other cuff around the exposed pipework on the shower room ceiling.

"*Hey*! What -- "

Shrike produced another set of cuffs and chained Alexei's other wrist to the ceiling as well. Caught off guard and off balance, Alexei fought to free himself. He staggered and fell to one side, wrenching both his arms.

He wasn't especially tall, and could only keep both feet on the floor by standing on tiptoe. Once he regained his footing, breathing hard, he gave the soldiers a look of bewildered disbelief. This was his nightmare -- for this to actually happen to him in real life was almost comically surreal.

"Scissors," Hawk said, and Kestrel placed a pair into her hand. They flashed in the shower room lighting. Alexei could feel himself shriveling up, dizzy with mounting terror. The CSF had never looked less like human beings to him; they were living nightmares now, with long animal snouts and soulless eyes.

Hawk opened the scissors with a snicking sound. She inserted one of the blades into the collar of Alexei's shirt -- he gasped at the cold touch of the metal on his bare skin -- and closed them against the fabric. His collar fell open with a rustling sound.

" -- what are you doing?!"

Hawk was already making another cut, slicing downward along the front of his shirt. Alexei sucked his stomach in, away from the scissors. "We can't very well inspect you for blight with your clothes on, now can we?"

She was cutting his clothes off.

"I would have gotten undressed." Alexei was mortified to hear how badly his voice was shaking. The front of his shirt hung completely open now. Hawk put a hand on his bare stomach, to steady him, and he flinched. She reached up and clipped through both of his shirtsleeves, then tugged down on the fabric. What remained of Alexei's shirt slid away to land on the tile floor.

"Looks clean so far," Shrike observed.

Hawk stood back to observe her work, scissors snipping at the air with a metallic sound. Alexei knew he would never hear that noise again without feeling this same gut-wrenching fear. "We're not done yet," she said.

When she reached for him again Alexei danced backwards on his tiptoes. Hawk grabbed his belt and yanked him forward, causing him to fall against his cuffs again. Pain lanced down both arms.

"Hold still," Hawk told him, unbuckling his belt.

Of course he knew what they were doing. Simply asking him to undress would have defeated the purpose. The point here was to scare him, to humiliate him, to make him feel helpless and degraded.

It was working.

With his belt undone, Alexei's pants dropped to his ankles, hobbling him. He felt the icy blade of the scissors slide under the band of his underwear and he clenched his eyes shut, unable to bear it. Unshed tears prickled in his eyes.

As his underwear went the way of his pants Alexei realized how very chilly the shower room was. He squeezed his legs together, his skin puckering up in goosebumps.

"Now, let's have a look at you."

Hawk grabbed Alexei's chin and brought his head up, pried his clenched teeth apart and inserted two fingers into his mouth. "Hmm," she said. "Clean." She released his chin and wiped her fingers off on Alexei's cheek; against his burning skin the spittle was shockingly cold.

What astounded Alexei the most was how impersonal the soldiers were. There was no laughing, no crude comments, no threats. Just this brutal medical exam, in a freezing shower room, in total silence. He would almost have preferred it if they had laughed; they would have seemed more human if they had.

He found it was easier to keep his eyes shut. The examination stretched on for what felt like hours, and at times it seemed like Hawk's rubber-gloved hands were everywhere, poking him, prodding him, groping him, invading him. When those hands finally left him Alexei was at the end of his tether, little sobbing noises escaping through his clenched teeth.

"Clean so far," Hawk observed, and in that moment he hated her in a way he had never hated anything else in his life. "Men?"

Kestrel and Shrike both responded in the affirmative. "Well, Alexei, you've passed the first part of the exam."

Alexei's stomach plummeted.

"Of course, the blight isn't always visible from the outside. Internal infections might not appear on the skin until later. Isn't that right, men?"

Kestrel and Shrike gave another 'Yes, sir' and Alexei had the sudden conviction that they were about to kill him. He couldn't breathe.

A hand seized his hair and Alexei's eyes flew open. "Wait! wait! what are you doing?!"

Hawk looked at him, scissors in hand. "We need a blood sample," she explained. Still holding his hair, she slid the points of the scissors across his cheek. "Now, hold still." She fitted the blades around the tip of Alexei's ear, adjusting her grip. "If we don't get enough blood to test, we're going to have to take another sample."

" -- Yuri," Alexei gasped.

Hawk hesitated, turning to face him. "What?"

"It's Yuri. He's got the blight."

Hawk stepped back, releasing him. Alexei still hung from the ceiling in his cuffs but it felt like he was falling through the floor, dropping away into empty space.

"...Yuri?!" she said, and she almost sounded disappointed. "He's the one?"

"We can go pick him up, sir," Kestrel offered. Hawk was silent for a moment before she replied. "No, I want to do this personally. You two, come with me." She turned back to Alexei. "Wait here a minute," she said, and Alexei almost laughed. "We'll be back shortly."

And they left him there, locking the shower room door behind them.

In truth, Alexei hung there for about twenty minutes before anyone came back to get him. When Shrike returned to release him Alexei's arms had gone completely numb and his legs were headed there. Shrike unlocked his handcuffs and dropped a shirt and pair of pants into Alexei's insensate arms. If he noticed that Alexei had been crying he gave no sign of it; in fact, he didn't say a word. Once he'd handed over the clothes Shrike turned and left the room again, leaving the door unlocked this time.

Slowly, dully, Alexei dressed himself again. His hands were shaking so badly that he took nearly five minutes just buttoning his shirt, but there was no need to hurry. He was trying not to think about it, but the clothes and the unlocked door could only have meant one thing: that the CSF was done with him.

He'd already given them what they wanted.

# CHAPTER SEVEN

"Papa!"

Nikita was instantly awake. For a moment he was lost -- he was facing a high ceiling set with tiny skylights -- and then he got his bearings. The auditorium. Red Camp Three. They were still under quarantine.

"Papa!"

Elena. Pushing his blanket away, Nikita sat up and leaned toward her cot. "Lena, sshh, sshh," he whispered, shaking her shoulder. "You're having a nightmare."

Elena continued to cry out, kicking her legs. Nikita gave her a firmer shake and suddenly Elena's hand shot out, grabbing his wrist. He gasped; her grip was incredibly strong, much more than it should have been. Nikita tried to break free and couldn't.

"Lena, wake up!"

"Is there a problem here?" rasped the voice of a CSF soldier. Nikita looked up directly into the beam of a flashlight, blinding himself for a second.

"No problem," he said. "She's just having a bad dream."

The soldier grunted. "We need to keep the noise level down in here." He kept the flashlight trained on Nikita's face, forcing him to turn away. "Talking during the designated quiet hours is not permitted."

Obviously the night watch was sober tonight. Naturally they turned a deaf ear when all of the other inmates were running amok, but they had to terrorize a little girl for having nightmares. "She's just a child," Nikita muttered, still trying to get his hand free.

All at once Elena released him, jolting upright on her cot. "Get away from my father!" she snarled.

The soldier swung the flashlight over to her face, but Elena didn't flinch. "You are both already in violation of the quiet hours policy; being insubordinate is not a good idea."

Nikita rose from his cot, stepping between the two of them. "She's clearly not feeling well -- I'm not even her father, just her uncle. I'll make sure she stays quiet, I promise."

The soldier looked down at Nikita in silence, but at least he was no longer shining the flashlight into his eyes. "See that she does," he said, and turned away to resume his patrol.

Sighing, Nikita dropped back down onto Elena's cot. She had lain back down again, but her eyes were still open. "Elena? are you awake?"

"Where's papa?" she asked, and something nipped at Nikita's heart. Well, at least she was awake now. "He's not here, Lena. It's just me."

Elena's eyes were black and glittering in the dim light. "He was here! I saw him!"

"No, you were dreaming."

"I wasn't! he was right there!" Her expression was tragic. "The soldiers had gotten him!"

It seemed like humoring her might be the best option. "Well...if the soldiers had him, he must have been getting evacuated too, right?"

"No, he's not."

"He's not what?"

Elena's eyes were closing again. "He's not getting 'vacuated."

"What? why wouldn't they evacuate him?"

But there was no answer -- Elena was asleep again. Nikita watched her steady breathing for a couple minutes more, just to be sure, and then he laid back down as well.

But it was a long time before Nikita got back to sleep.

~~~~~

Five years, all for this. Anatoly had attended the Science and Technology Vocational College for five years, and spent untold amounts of his late grandfather's inheritance, for this. So he could stand at a sink scrubbing out glassware like a lowly dishwasher at an all-night diner.

"Hey, comrade!" someone hailed him. Dripping soapy water from both hands, Anatoly turned and found Leonid, one of the other junior researchers. Judging by the state of his lab coat -- he was not the most careful of eaters -- Leonid was just returning from lunch.

"Hey."

"Need a hand?"

"Of course."

Puzzled, Anatoly watched as Leonid donned his own pair of rubber gloves and stepped up to the sink alongside him. He plunged his hands into the water, drew out a beaker, and began attacking it with one of the sponges.

"You scrub in this sink, rinse in that one. And careful -- this is all the water we're getting."

"Got it, got it." Leonid was already scrubbing away. "How've you been?"

"Fine, just fine."

"Good to hear." Leonid paused. "I hear you've got a dormitory all to yourself now."

Ahh, so that explained this sudden show of camaraderie. Anatoly picked up a beaker of his own, dumping out the collected water. "Not to myself, no."

"But -- " Leonid glanced over his shoulder, lowering his voice. "I heard the soldiers came for Yuri Ivanovich."

Anatoly nodded. "That they did."

"Do you know why?"

"Of course not." Anatoly couldn't resist the urge to check the room over his own shoulder. "Nobody knows. They just know not to ask about it."

"Of course, of course." Leonid placed his beaker on the drying rack and reached for another one. "But who else is there? With him and Boris Grigorievich both gone..."

"Alexei Nikolaevich's still in the dorm with me."

"Who?"

"One of the juniors. About this tall, grey eyes..."

"Oh, the one who doesn't talk?"

"That's the one."

"Ah, I didn't know he was in your room." Leonid scratched his head, leaving soap bubbles clinging to his hair. "But I don't think I've seen *him* around either. You sure he's still there?"

"Of course. I see him every day."

"Doing what?"

"Nothing." Anatoly dunked his beaker into the cleaner pool of water, swirling it around. "He stays in bed all day."

"Sleeping?"

"Probably. Or staring at the wall -- there's nothing else to do in there."

Leonid put another beaker into the drying rack. "Is he sick?"

Anatoly gave a half-shrug. "I can't say. He won't talk to me."

"But he never talks to anyone."

"No, he used to talk to Yuri Ivanovich." Anatoly frowned. "I don't think he's gotten out of bed since Yuri disappeared."

"Oh, I see. You think he knows what happened?"

"I don't know. Why don't *you* go ask him?"

Leonid laughed and splashed some of the foamy water in Anatoly's direction. "That's a good one!"

"Hey! what did I tell you about wasting that water?"

~~~~

There was a grating sound of metal-on-metal as the door bolts slid out of their sockets. Veronika lay in her rags on the floor of her cell, eyes closed, listening as the door was unlocked.

That soldier woman was coming to visit her.

She knew, but didn't know how she knew. It seemed obvious in some intangible way. A lot of things had seemed obvious to her recently, when she was lucid enough to care. She just told herself there had been clues, tiny ones -- she must have known that the soldier was a woman from her voice, her stance, her attitude. She had guessed correctly, that was all.

And now the same woman was coming back to see her. Of course, she had promised to visit, hadn't she? It only made sense to assume that it was her.

The door squeaked on its hinges as it swung inward. Boots rang out on the grated flooring.

"Are you awake, little sister?"

Veronika smiled. She let the soldier come up to her and kneel down to touch her shoulder; then, putting on a surprised face, she rolled over.

"Oh, you came back!" she said.

"Of course."

Veronika sat up, drawing her knees up to her chest. Now she could see that the door had been propped open with of those green jugs, filled with sand instead of water. The gap was about twelve inches wide...she could have gotten out, if she'd been inclined to make a break for it. She knew somehow that she was much faster than this suit-encumbered soldier, much faster than she'd even been before.

But not yet, not yet. She wasn't faster than rifle fire, after all.

"...how are you feeling?" the soldier asked. She seemed about to touch her again, then drew back.

"Better today," said Veronika, and smiled. "Thanks for coming to see me."

"No problem. I had a couple minutes to spare."

Reading the soldier should have been difficult -- the gas mask distorted their voices, and there was no facial expression to interpret -- but Veronika's intuition told her that she was headed in the right direction. "Are the doctors coming today?"

"...no." That masked head dipped downward. "Not today."

"So...you came to see me by yourself?"

The soldier was nodding. Of course, the green jug made it obvious that this was the case: there would be no need for a doorstopper if one of her subordinates had been available to open the door once she was through visiting.

Slowly, her protective suit creaking in protest, the soldier sat down on her heels beside the rag-bundle that served as Veronika's bed. "So, your name is...Veronika Stepanevna, right?"

The name brought back a little tempest of memories, though the weather wasn't as bad today as on other days. "That's right," she said.

"I heard about what happened at the Dragovich Park Provisional Processing Center," the soldier said, and lightning flashed suddenly out of the stormclouds. Veronika looked away. "I'm sorry about what happened to your -- your friend," the soldier went on hastily, seeing her expression.

"My brother."

"...What?"

"Grigori Stepanovich. He was my brother." She hadn't said his name aloud since that day, and it hurt about as much as she had expected. Nonetheless the news provoked some sort of reaction from the soldier, who sat up straighter all at once.

"Your brother!"

"Yeah." Veronika looked back at her. Something tickled at the back of her mind. "You thought he was my husband, didn't you?"

The soldier leaned back. "I -- well, I didn't know," she protested, and even through the gas mask her tone gave her away. "They just said you came in with a man."

"Oh. Well, can I tell you something?"

She nodded, and Veronika leaned forward to whisper it.

" -- I don't care for men."

This had the desired effect. "Well, that's -- I mean -- everyone's different," the soldier stammered, and Veronika knew her aim had been true. "You're entitled to like whoever you wish."

"Thank you," Veronika said. "And now that I've told you my dark secret, you could at least tell me your name."

The soldier at least gave it some thought. "Hawk," she said.

"'Hawk'? What parent names their child that?"

"It's only my codename," Hawk said defensively.

"So it's not your real name then."

Hawk rose to her feet, and for a moment Veronika thought she'd gone too far. "Our real names are classified, sister. We're here on military business."

"Nobody would ever know you told me," Veronika insisted.

"Because you'd keep it a secret?"

Veronika hiked her hospital gown all the way up to her thighs, showing how far the inkstains had spread. "Because I'll be dead before I have a chance to tell anyone. And nobody listens to the crazy girl anyway." She smiled. "Nobody except you."

Hawk had paused when she pulled her gown up, but she was moving toward the door again. "I've got work to do now," she said, "but I'll try to come back and visit sometime."

"I'll try to be here when you get back," Veronika called after her.

Standing half-in and half-out of the doorway, the soldier hesitated. " -- Tatyana Igorevna," she said, and stepped out of the storage room. The door thudded shut again, and the bolts ground along the insides of their sockets as they slid home.

Smiling to herself, Veronika lay back down on her rags. "Hello, Tatyana," she whispered at the ceiling.

~~~~~

"Hey, comrade!"

"Hello again."

"What're you up to?"

Anatoly gave Leonid a pointed look from over his sandwich. "I am eating my lunch."

"That's fine; I'll wait." Leonid dropped into the seat across from him.

"Mmm?" said Anatoly around a mouthful of bread.

"Oh, there was this stuff I found in the upstairs lab -- I wanted to show you. It's pretty bizarre."

"Mmmmff."

"Oh, no hurry; take your time." Leonid eyed the other half of Anatoly's sandwich. "You must be pretty hungry today, eh?"

"Actually, I'm done." Anatoly wrapped a napkin around the other half of his sandwich and dropped it into the pocket of his lab coat. He dusted his hands against his slacks. "Let's go see this thing."

Leonid led the way up to the lab in question, checking to make sure Anatoly was still following him. "I promise, you've never seen anything like this."

"Just show me."

They pushed through the door and into an empty laboratory. A series of glass tanks in assorted sizes stood on the lab tables, everything from a fifty-gallon monster to squat sixteen-ounce glass jars. Most of them were half-filled with what looked like dark plant life, though the fogginess of the glass made it hard to see. One of the blue plastic bins labeled 'BIOHAZARDOUS WASTE ONLY' stood off to one side, its hinged lid thrown open. The air was filled with a mellow, sweetish scent that reminded Anatoly of honey.

"This is where Yuri Ivanovich was working," Leonid explained.

"...Terrariums?" Anatoly stepped into the room, bending down to peer into the closest tank. "You interrupted my lunch for this?"

But when he took a closer look, Anatoly found that these were no terrariums he had ever seen before.

The stuff in the tanks certainly resembled plant life. Through the clouded glass Anatoly could see featherlike growths that reminded him of ferns, long delicate stems bearing many-petaled flowers, tangled vines drooping under the weight of marble-sized berries. But though the shape was correct...the colors were wrong. Most of the plant life was black at its roots, shading to royal blues and ruby reds near the tips of the leaves. The fruits and flowers were stranger still, bright primary hues with a sort of gleaming translucency, like polished glass.

"He hasn't been in here in a week, so I suppose he fed them all before he left." Leonid was hovering nearby, pleased that Anatoly was taking such an interest in his find. "Today I was supposed to be clearing out this lab so someone else could take it over, and...I found all this."

"What was he *working* on?" Anatoly picked up a jar -- it was surprisingly warm -- and peered at its contents. This one resembled mushrooms of deepest violet, with caps so rounded they were almost spherical.

"No idea," Leonid said cheerily. "He didn't start this until after the occupation though; we'd have heard about it long ago."

Anatoly set the jar down. "Do you suppose it's got to do with the blight?"

"I can't see how." Leonid was tapping on the glass of the big tank with his fingernail. "Pity we've got to throw it all away."

"...what?"

Leonid shrugged. "That's what I was told. They need all these tanks, and Yuri Ivanovich...well, he won't be needing them."

Anatoly looked around the room. There must have been at least twenty tanks of the strange-colored plant stuff. "Suppose this research was something big? doesn't anyone have his lab notes?"

"I looked; I didn't find any. Either he didn't keep any notes or he destroyed them all at some point."

Sighing, Anatoly sank into a chair. Leonid came up beside him. "I mean, I suppose we could ask Alexei Nikolaevich what he was working on before we dump everything into the wastebin."

Anatoly laughed. "Have *you* tried talking to him recently?" He paused. "And what do you mean, 'we'?"

"Obviously I can't clean this mess up myself." Leonid made a helpless gesture. "Holding the tank over the bin and scraping it out is at least a two-person job."

"So you just assume...oh, nevermind. Let's get it over with."

With Anatoly grumbling under his breath, the two of them wheeled the biohazard bin over to the lab table and donned their gloves. Grabbing the closest tank, a modest five gallons in size, they carefully removed the lid. White mist floated up out of the tank, dissipating into the room, and the aroma of honey grew thicker. Anatoly and Leonid exchanged a look. The they picked up the tank, upended it over the bin, and waited.

Other than a few dried bits of plant, nothing came out. The growth remained at the bottom of the tank.

"It's stuck," Leonid observed.

"I can see that." Anatoly glanced around the room. "If we just had something...ah, here, hold on." Still holding his side of the inverted tank with one hand, Anatoly reached across the lab table for the pair of long forceps he'd spotted.

"Here, we'll use this." Carefully, Anatoly reached up inside the tank with the forceps. The metal tips dug into the spongy black stuff. "We just need to pry it off the bottom and it'll all come out." He pushed the forceps in deeper. "Just a little -- "

What happened next is a matter of debate. As he later retold the story to his comrades, Leonid would insist that Anatoly shouted when he realized he was losing his grip on the tank. A moment later Anatoly dropped his end, letting the entire tank fall into the wastebin with a resounding crash, taking the forceps with it.

Anatoly would not offer a contradicting story, mainly because he was too shaken by his experience to give a personal account of the events. But privately he was completely convinced that one of the black "vines" in the tank came snaking out, wrapping around the prongs of the forceps like the tail of a snake.

The vine had whipped itself three times around Anatoly's fingers before he found the sense enough to scream, snatching his hands away. Leonid lost his grip at the same time, and the tank plunged into the bin. The vine was yanked away from Anatoly's hand as the tank fell, though its grip was strong enough to pull his latex glove right off his fingers, taking it down the bottom of the biohazard waste disposal bin.

Leonid swore out loud. Clutching his now-naked hand, Anatoly gurgled something incoherent and backed away from the bin.

"You dropped it!"

"It *grabbed* me!" Anatoly stammered. "Something in there grabbed me! I swear!!"

Leonid gave him a look usually reserved for small children and the elderly, then went to peer into the bin. "Gah, what a mess. Guess they won't be using that tank."

Anatoly was sidling toward the lab door. "I'd g-get away from it if I were you."

"But we've still got -- hey! you're not leaving?"

"You can do this yourself." Anatoly slapped at the wall, feeling for the door handle without taking his eyes from the blue bin. "I'm done here."

Leonid looked forlorn. "You're kidding! How am I supposed to empty these all on my own?!"

Anatoly wondered at the logic of whoever had tasked Leonid with cleaning this lab. "Just throw everything into the bin. Tanks and all. Throw it all away," he said. His fingers brushed the handle and Anatoly threw the door open. He spared one last backwards glance at the lab, the tanks, and Leonid standing in the middle of it all.

"And light the bin on fire when you're done," Anatoly suggested, and slammed the door behind him.

~~~~~

"Colonel Akimov here."

"Colonel sir -- this is Heron reporting from Unit Five."

"Go ahead, Heron."

"Sir, I wanted to personally give you some of the details from the reports we received from the first Volgin River Exploratory Squad. There's been some...unexpected information coming back to us from the river."

Akimov had a reputation for being cold, but this was entirely undeserved. He had great affection for all of the soldiers under his command. If Akimov was the processing center in the great machine that was his Special Forces division, then the individual soldiers were not only the gears and levers of that machine -- they were also the sensors. Each little arm of the machine was equipped with a set of precision instruments meant for gathering data. The destruction of any of its sensors spelled a loss of precious data for the processing center. And a processing center which ignored the signals received from any of its sensors was a flawed piece of equipment.

"I'm listening, comrade."

"Yes sir. Initial reports show, as predicted, significant environmental impact from the leaked UEC-571. Plant and animal life in and around the Volgin River exhibit signs of pronounced genetic alteration. Many species could not be classified and are believed to be radical mutations from existing types. Presence of UEC-571 in the water was confirmed, and the analysis reflects that the contamination level is rising, not falling."

"As we expected," Akimov put in. "The ink is a microorganism -- it's reproducing."

"Yes, sir." Heron began to sound uncomfortable. "Also noted by the Volgin River Exploratory Squad was the presence of fog or mist on the water and in the river valley.

Preliminary analysis pointed to weather phenomena as being responsible, but it is the opinion of the Exploratory Squad that the fog is unnatural. Several members of the squad reported psychological symptoms after returning from the expedition, and one had to be sedated."

" -- Have their suits been checked for leaks?"

"Yes sir, Colonel. All protective gear used in the operation was tested and found airtight."

"And what kind of symptoms were exhibited by these soldiers?" Akimov asked. The sensors were the eyes and ears of the processing center; they were one of its most valuable assets.

Heron cleared his throat. "Most reported ringing in the ears, headache, earache, dizziness, nausea and nosebleeds. Several mentioned visual and auditory disturbances as well."

"Hallucinations," Akimov said.

"Yes, sir."

"Of what nature?"

Heron coughed again, and the Colonel waited. "Sir, they claimed to have heard voices."

"Voices."

"Yes, sir." Heron knew how unprofessional this sounded; you could hear it in his tone. "They claim to have heard human voices, and experienced unusual thoughts and impulses -- mainly, intense fear. Several of them reported seeing humanoid figures in the area. These seem to have resolved after leaving the exclusion zone surrounding the Volgin River."

Akimov considered this. "Hearing and seeing people could mean the squads encountered unprocessed Khostok citizens, or escaped quarantines from one of the Red Camps. Why did we conclude that these soldiers were hallucinating?"

The rustling of papers on Heron's end sounded distinctly uneasy. "Sir, my men did not claim they had seen people. The reports describe encounters with unknown humanoid entities."

"'Entities'?" Akimov echoed.

"Yes, sir," Heron said weakly. "The men who saw these apparitions claimed they were all black...and had no faces."

Akimov sat back in his desk chair. "We considered the possibility that these were unevacuated citizens, but the nature of the descriptions suggests otherwise. But we do think it's possible the men became confused, and may have misidentified fellow soldiers due to the foggy conditions and possible toxic effects from an unknown source," Heron offered.

Akimov was silent. The dynamos in his mind began to rotate, sending sparks arcing through the air, setting the gears to turning, the pistons surging up and down. Instrument panels full of gauges came to life, needles dancing back and forth, indicator lights glowing like tiny coals.

"...Sir?"

"I hear you, soldier. Were the soldiers tested for the blight?"

"Yes, sir. They were tested multiple times and all turned up negative."

"Good. But we still want to keep all personnel exhibiting signs of psychological disturbance under observation."

"Copy that, sir."

"I also want another squad sent in to investigate these claims. Have them provided with heavy-duty protective suits. I'll expect a new report in a week's time."

"Copy, sir."

"Oh, and Heron?"

"...yes, sir?"

"Excellent work."

"Thank you sir!" Relief had flooded his voice -- you could just about hear Heron saluting the microphone.

Akimov signed off and disconnected the call. So this was much worse than damaged sensors, after all. The sensors were malfunctioning, throwing back bad data, the way a vehicle's sensors behaved when fouled with carbon. Still, like every problem, this too had a solution. Sensors were costly assets, but they were not irreplaceable.

~~~~~

There was smoke on the horizon, dense and black. From his vantage point on the seventh floor penthouse of the Hotel Litvinenko Mikhail had seen it clearly. When the wind blew the right way he had even smelled it, the aroma of burning with an undertone of sweetness.

Even before the CSF's invasion of Khostok this smoke would have been unusual. The old industrial district that housed his hotel had long been abandoned, the garment factories and warehouses standing empty. Businesses created during a boom of patriotic economic fervor had a way of collapsing when the patriotism, like the government funding, dried up.

But now that the jackboot of the Special Forces was planted firmly in his native city such smoke was very unexpected. Moreover, from his balcony Mikhail had pinpointed its source: the smokestacks of the New Industrial State Bread Company. This factory, like the others around it, had not seen a single employee nor produced a single loaf of bread in over a decade. For its stack to be puffing out clouds of smoke today was very unexpected indeed.

It took Mikhail over an hour to hike from his fortified hideout to the factory. He could have gotten there in half the time but the factory's proximity to Red Camp Three -- known in other times as the Victor Kurylenko Concert Hall -- gave him ample reason to proceed cautiously. He moved along side-streets and alleyways as he approached the factory, detouring to approach it from the east, placing the building itself between him and the camp.

Time and rain had not yet fully erased the white-painted slogans that adorned the red brick facade of the New Industrial State Bread Company.

FINEST PRODUCTS -- MADE USING CHORMAN INGREDIENTS ONLY

WE FEED THE LABORERS WHO BUILD THIS GREAT NATION

STRONG CHILDREN ARE RAISED ON NEW INDUSTRIAL STATE BREAD

SUPERIOR NUTRITION HELPS EACH CITIZEN WORK HARDER

The loading docks lay on the east side of the building. It was a simple matter to wedge his crowbar under one of the unlocked loading bay doors and pry it up far enough for him to wriggle through the gap. Inside the building the smell of smoke was stronger, and Mikhail flicked on his flashlight. Golden dust motes swirled in the beam of light.

He wasn't sure what he expected to find here. Mikhail knew that something was poisoning the inhabitants of Khostok -- the black stains he'd seen on the faces of his fellow citizens confirmed this suspicion. But since the encounter with that unearthly thing in the convenience store he had begun to have second thoughts about the nature of this inky plague. Could any kind of chemical weapon, even one developed by the DIO, result in such a horror? Mikhail was not at all certain of that.

In spite of the belching smokestack, the factory itself still maintained the look of a vacant building. His footsteps muffled by the dust, Mikhail crept along past cobwebbed rolling carts, conveyor belts whose rubber was cracked and splitting with age, mixing vats that held only insects and the desiccated bodies of rats. What little light leaked in through the grimy windows was yellowed and somehow insubstantial.

Ten minutes into his exploration Mikhail came upon a surprise: he was going in circles. His own footprints were there in front of him, standing out clearly in the dust of the floor.

But wait; there were two sets of footprints. Had he doubled around once already without realizing it? or maybe...

Mikhail set his boot down beside one of the prints, then lifted it to inspect his mark. No, the footprints were different -- these weren't his tracks at all. Whoever had lit the factory's furnace had left these marks. And judging by their size, these prints could only have come from the jackboots of the CSF.

With his pulse suddenly thrumming in his ears Mikhail began tracing the path the soldiers had taken. The freshest prints wasted no time in heading straight for the back of the factory. Mikhail was tracking them so closely, and his visibility inside the factory was so poor, that he nearly ran headfirst into a set double doors that seemed to materialize from nowhere.

Taking a step back, Mikhail found the words 'BAKING OVENS' painted above the double doors. And sure enough, the footprints he'd been following disappeared beneath these doors. Mikhail was just reaching for the handle when he spotted the large, shiny new padlock that someone had mounted there, holding the doors shut.

Mikhail fiddled with the lock and found it solid -- he doubted if even a dozen blows with his crowbar would be enough to smash it. Besides, someone would overhear, or find the broken lock afterward -- and did he want to call attention to his investigations? the last thing he needed was the CSF sweeping the city for him.

Frustrated, he turned away. But not all the footprints led to the ovens, he discovered: there were several tracks that branched away from the main trail, heading for a room to the right of the oven doors. Giving the lock a final longing glance, Mikhail headed off after this second trail.

These tracks were not like the first set. At several points Mikhail found evidence that something, apparently a heavy sack, had been dragged along through the dust. And here on the edge of the trail was a print left by someone much smaller, and....barefoot?

Mikhail stopped and squatted down for a better look. He was no expert tracker, but the print left by a naked human foot was easy to identify. And though the bootprints marched on in an even row, these bare footprints seemed to be randomly placed, with wide gaps between each pair. But unless the shoeless person was leaping around the factory like a rabbit this made no sense whatsoever.

There was a scraping sound and Mikhail jerked himself upright, fumbling for his handgun. Holding the flashlight in one hand and the gun in the other, he swept the beam around the factory floor. Dust churned around him, obscuring the walls.

" -- hello?"

No reply. Mikhail turned this way and that, breath wheezing in his throat, straining to hear the noise again. As the dust settled out of the air he finally had to conclude that there was nobody else on the factory floor but him. He reholstered his gun. Perhaps it had only been a rat.

He began to walk again, forcing himself to pay attention to the tracks. Those little bare footprints popped up again here and there, sometimes separated by ten feet or more. Mikhail had a mental image of a shoeless teenage girl bounding around inside the New Industrial State Bread Company factory like a human grasshopper, but even this picture failed to amuse him.

If only that rat had stayed in its nest. There was no sense in a rat scratching around during the day, making noises like that.

The second trail led between another pair of double doors, though these ones were propped open. STORAGE, said the white-painted letters above the doorway. He stepped inside.

Mikhail's flashlight beam landed on a small mountain, composed of something -- or a series of things -- that had been piled onto the floor in the storage room. The pile was darker in some places and lighter in others, and the dust all around it had been disturbed; a clear sign that the departed bread factory workers were not responsible for this.

Puzzled, he aimed his flashlight at the closer edge of the pile. A rectangular object shone red in the light, and silver locks glinted up at him.

It was a suitcase.

In fact, as he looked more closely, most of the pile was suitcases. Scattered among them were backpacks, purses, messenger bags, laundry sacks, even pillowcases tied off with twine. A few of the bags were opened, but most were in their original state, and many had their owners' names still attached. Mikhail had come upon a mountain of luggage, sitting there gathering dust in the storage room of an abandoned bread factory.

Obviously the CSF had placed it here; but he couldn't tell the reason. And though he'd traced the anachronistic smoke to the ovens at the factory, the reason the CSF had for lighting the fires was likewise obscure to him.

Something clanged loudly, the noise echoing through the storage room. Mikhail squeaked in alarm. He snatched his gun out of his holster and dropped it right away, sending him onto his hands and knees on the concrete floor in a frantic attempt to recover it. Choking on dust, he seized the gun and lurched back to his feet again, brandishing it at the corners of the room.

"Come out and face me!"

A scraping noise answered his challenge. Mikhail spun so fast he almost fell down, but other than the dust and the mountain of luggage he was alone. He ran around to the other side of the pile just to be sure, but nothing was lurking back there except more suitcases.

He was not a young man, and Mikhail's heart was racing fit to explode. The beam of the flashlight wobbled back and forth as his hand shook; if he actually had to shoot anything he was almost guaranteed to miss.

" -- come out!"

Something brushed against the back of his neck. This time it was the flashlight he dropped, and unlike the gun it went to pieces the moment it struck the floor. Plastic flew in all directions and semidarkness fell at once, broken only by the amber light that trickled in through the factory windows.

Mikhail slapped at the back of his neck and found that his collar was full of gritty dirt. He turned again, looking behind him. As his eyes adjusted to the weak light he saw bits of dirt and paint raining down on the spot where he had been standing.

He clapped a hand over his heart. What a relief -- so nothing had crept up behind him after all. It was just a little dirt. He had acted like such a baby...

The scraping noise came again, followed by another rain of dirt, and Mikhail's breath stuck in his throat. Now he understood why he'd never been able to spot the thing that had apparently been stalking him the whole time.

It was up above him, in the rafters.

With painful slowness, Mikhail tilted his head back. The sunlight that came in through the windows didn't quite reach the steel rafters that supported the factory roof, and the space beneath the ceiling was almost entirely swallowed up in darkness. Mikhail saw nothing but shadows up above. Besides, the rafters were a good twenty feet off the floor; anything that was able to get up there surely couldn't be --

That was when a shadow detached itself from the other shadows, slipping along the steel beam. It moved with all the grace of a cat, though it was far too big for one. And the round head and broad shoulders were distinctly uncatlike.

The shadow had no facial features, at least none that Mikhail could see. And yet he knew -- would have sworn on his immortal soul -- that the inhuman thing crawling along the rafters twenty feet above was looking straight down at him.

Luckily for Mikhail there were no CSF soldiers in the factory at that time, or they certainly would have heard him making his exit. With a scream that shivered the dust down from every shelf Mikhail stampeded back through the factory in the direction he'd come. Without his flashlight he was practically blind, and every bread cart that blocked his way was a living shadow reaching out to stop him; the cobwebs were their inky fingers on his arms and his face. He struck out at the obstacles in his path like a man possessed, stumbling, falling, staggering back to his feet again.

By some miracle he found his way back to the loading docks. When he tried to worm his way under the loading bay door his pack caught on the bottom edge, and Mikhail squealed in dismay. With a mighty effort that ripped open his pack in the process he squirmed free of the door and took off down the alley, pelting away from the New Industrial State Bread Company factory without daring a single backwards glance.

Anyone who happened to be in the neighborhood around that time would have seen a novel sight: a man in his fifties, absolutely grey with dust and fright, flying along the pavement as if the Devil himself were after him. Tools and maps fell out through the tear in Mikhail's bag, clunking or fluttering to the pavement, but he did not stop to retrieve them.

It had taken him over an hour to get from his hideout to the New Industrial State Bread Company's factory, but Mikhail accomplished the return trip in less than twenty-eight minutes.

~~~~

It was the middle of the night, and the loading docks of the the Lubukov Agricultural Labs were uninhabited, their jointed metal overhead doors lowered to seal off the exits. The CSF's black-painted flatbed trucks sat waiting in the loading area, their beds covered in green tarps or stacked with blue bins that read CAUTION: BIOHAZARDOUS WASTE.

Though most of the soldiers had departed for the night and the captive employees were sleeping, the docks were not quite lifeless. Soft scuffling noises could be heard from time to time, emanating from one of the blue plastic bins. These noises might have been blamed on rats; at least until the hinged lid on one of the bins started to lift upward.

A black tendril snaked its way out of the crack beneath the lid. It went slowly, feeling its way, curling back against itself as if unsure of its progress. Once half a meter of tendril had emerged it rested on the lid of the wastebin, as though the effort had tired it.

Spaced evenly along the length of the vine were a series of dark green nodules. As the vine rested these began to swell, expanding by millimeters as their color grew more vibrant. At last the nodules split along their tops, the sections peeling backward to reveal a center of luminescent emerald, pulsing brighter and dimmer.

Anyone present would have noticed an aroma reminiscent of honey. A spectator at this strange blooming might also have described it as beautiful, if they hadn't known what exactly they were seeing.

But nobody was there. The vine lay contentedly on the plastic lid, glowing greenly in the darkness like a string of tiny stars.

# CHAPTER EIGHT

Alexei was awake when they came for him.

He had anticipated this, of course, but it was insomnia rather than anxiety that had kept him from sleeping. He heard the door of the dorm room bang open -- Anatoly's snoring broke off and then resumed again -- and the thump of boots on the carpeted floor.

Gloved hands seized his shoulder, shook him, and pulled him into a sitting position. Alexei didn't resist. In fact, he was almost relieved.

A flashlight was shining into his face, but he could just make out the silhouettes of two CSF soldiers somewhere beyond the glare.

"Get dressed."

Was it Hawk? it certainly sounded like her. He wondered why they would bother to make him get dressed at all; surely it would have been easier to take care of him right here. If they were worried about having Anatoly as a witness, Alexei was positive that the man would sleep through an earthquake, let alone a gunshot or two.

But no, there would be stains on the bedsheets if they did it here. The DIO didn't do things that way, and the CSF seemed to be following their example. They didn't want it known that Alexei had been dragged out of bed in the middle of the night and shot...they simply wanted him to vanish. Nobody would know where he'd gone, or why, or whether he was still alive or not, and they would be too afraid to ask. The mystery would keep everyone on their toes.

"Come on." The hand on his shoulder jerked him back and forth, trying to wake him. Someone tossed a shirt into his lap. "Put on your clothes. Quickly."

So they were probably going to take him down to the shower room. With its tile walls and floors they could sponge all the evidence away in minutes, wash all traces down the shower drain. Making him get dressed for that could only have been a formality.

Alexei put on his clothes. Once he'd gotten his shirt and shoes on -- he had slept in his pants -- Hawk yanked him up onto his feet, steering him out of the room. Out in the hall Alexei could see that she had brought Kestrel along with her.

The door had barely closed behind them when Hawk shoved Alexei against the wall. "Listen," she said. "We need your help."

Alexei listened; he was too surprised to do anything else.

"The test subject in Storage Room 8 has become violently psychotic. We need you to do something to sedate her, or she may not survive."

"...what?" Alexei said, trying to collect himself. Storage Room 8 sounded familiar. "...you mean Veronika Stepanevna, right?"

"Yes."

And then it clicked. Alexei looked up into the mirrored eyepieces of Hawk's mask. "No," he said.

Hawk hesitated. "What?"

"I'm not helping you. If you're not going to shoot me, then piss off and leave me alone." He moved to push past Hawk.

Grabbing his shoulders, Hawk slammed him back against the wall hard enough to set his ears ringing. "You *are* going to help us," she snarled.

Alexei smirked up at her. It was a tiny vengeance, but it was still more than he'd dreamed of getting. "If you don't want her to suffer anymore, best thing you can do is shoot her." He chuckled. "But that would be too humane for y-- "

Hawk didn't wait for him to finish. Fortunately for his teeth, she openhanded him rather than punching him, but the blow still send him sprawling onto the tile. Before Alexei could pick himself back up Hawk grabbed his shirt, dragging him upright and throwing him back against the wall again.

"Sir..." Kestrel put in, sounding uneasy.

"Shut up."

Alexei tasted copper. He spat. "Does he know why you're doing this?" Alexei pointed his chin at the soldier who stood behind Hawk. "He's very supportive, if he does."

He braced himself for another slap, but this one didn't come. Hawk squeezed Alexei's shoulders, lowering her head until she was eye-level with him. "You're going to help us," she repeated.

"Why me?" In spite of his throbbing lip Alexei was almost enjoying this, but that didn't mean it made sense to him. "Why not -- hell, anyone else?"

It was a moment before Hawk replied. Releasing him, she straightened back up again. "We've already asked all the other researchers," she admitted.

Gingerly, Alexei felt his bleeding lip. "And you think I know something they don't?" He was incredulous; Hawk must have known he wouldn't help her. For her to even be asking him she had to be truly desperate.

"You used to work with Yuri Ivanovich," Hawk said. "I thought he might have figured something out."

Hearing his name brought everything back into focus again. And suddenly Alexei had an idea. "I'll help you," he said, and Hawk turned to him. " -- but only if you let Yura go."

She was already shaking her head. "Absolutely not."

Alexei's heart sank. So Yuri was probably dead -- he'd suspected as much. "Then nevermind."

Hawk put a hand on Alexei's shoulder, though he wasn't trying to leave. "You don't understand -- your friend is highly infectious at this point. He could contaminate the whole building if we released him. His quarantining was only to protect the other employees."

"He...he's still alive?"

"Yes."

Alexei swallowed, not daring to believe it. "Then let me see him."

Hawk and Kestrel exchanged looks. Kestrel shrugged and Hawk sighed through her air filter. "Fine," Hawk said. "If you help the girl, you can see him afterward."

That was far better than Alexei had hoped for. "Then take me to the requisitions office," he ordered. "I'll need some supplies."

They agreed easily. Now all Alexei needed was to come up with something nobody else had yet discovered -- a palliative treatment for the blight. And he had about five minutes to do so.

~~~~

"She just started screaming. That was about an hour ago. Of course, we didn't check on her right away...that kind of thing is pretty normal for blight victims," the soldier explained, turning nervously toward Hawk.

Alexei nodded. The three of them were back from the requisitions office, his pockets full of randomly-selected medical supplies, and the soldier on guard duty at the storage rooms was giving Alexei a summary of Veronika's condition. Behind them Kestrel was busying himself at the lock of Storage Room 8.

"What makes -- " Alexei began, and a hoarse shriek interrupted him. The cry broke up just as suddenly into a series of coughing noises, and Hawk took a step towards the door. "Hurry up!" she shouted.

"Yes sir!" Kestrel replied.

" -- what makes you think she's in serious condition?" Alexei finished.

"She's suffocating," Hawk said over her shoulder.

"On what?"

"No idea. There's nothing in her throat, nothing around her neck. But she acts like she can't breathe."

"Is she asthmatic?"

"Maybe. I don't know." Hawk turned back to the door. "Kestrel!"

"It's open, it's open!" Kestrel grabbed the handle of the door and threw his weight backwards, lugging it open. Hawk pushed him aside and stepped into the storage room first, followed by Alexei. Kestrel followed, and the soldier on guard duty took up a position at the open door.

Veronika lay sprawled on her back on the floor, clutching at her throat. Her breath wheezed in and out of her lungs. Alexei knelt down next to her, painfully aware that he had no clue what he was doing.

"Veronika Stepanevna? can you hear me?"

She looked up at Alexei and right through him. Her pupils were dark and glassy, her lips blue. "Fire," she whispered, and followed this up with a fit of coughing. "Got to get -- get out -- "

Alexei sat back. "She's hallucinating," he said.

"Yeah. I think she thinks the room's on fire," Hawk said. Much to Alexei's surprise, she came to kneel down on the grating beside him. She brushed the hair back from Veronika's face. "But how can a hallucination be choking her?"

"It's psychosomatic."

"...What?"

Alexei sighed. "It's all in her head."

"Oh." Hawk sounded relieved. "So it can't hurt her?"

"Well...actually, it can." Alexei reached into his pants pocket and pulled out a foil-topped glass bottle. Producing a disposable syringe from the other pocket, he unwrapped it and punctured the bottle's foil top with the needle. "Placebo effect can make people sick as well as cure them. If she really believes she's suffocating, she might actually die from it."

Alexei tore open an alcohol swab and passed it across Veronika's bicep. Hawk was watching him closely, and almost moved to stop him as he leaned in with the syringe. "What's that?"

"Sodium thiopental."

"...What?"

"It's a barbiturate," Alexei said. "It'll knock her out."

Veronika twitched when the needle went in, but that was all. The sound of her ragged breathing filled the little storage room. Hawk had pried her inkstained hands away from her throat and was holding them. "I thought they said that medication didn't work on blight victims."

"This is one we hadn't tried yet." Alexei drew out the needle and hunted in his pocket for the bandaids he'd brought. Not that Hawk would have known, but they *had* tried barbiturates before, along with a wealth of other medicines. What hadn't tried was thiopental at a dose massive enough to trigger a coma.

The idea had come to Alexei in those days after Yuri's disappearance. For all the time he had spent in bed, he had done very little sleeping. Lying under his blankets, staring at the wall and listening to Anatoly snoring, he had thought about torture.

Sleep deprivation was one of those interrogation methods considered 'humane' enough that even the Americans would admit to using it. But the sleep studies in his human biology textbook had been unambiguous: other than medical freaks, no human being could go completely without sleep for any length of time without dying. There were even prion diseases that killed through this mechanism alone -- they destroyed the victim's ability to sleep, killing them in the process.

And Alexei knew that the blight victims did not sleep, at least not very much. It was only a theory, but he thought they might have been dying due to insomnia rather than the ravages of the disease itself.

To test his theory, all that remained was to get the blight victims to sleep and see if regular rest prolonged their life. Alexei, like everyone else at the Labs, knew that the victims were strangely immune to painkillers and sedatives. But they were still human -- unless their biochemistry had undergone some radical changes in the course of their infection, they had to respond to these medications at some point. Alexei just hoped he'd landed on a therapeutic dose of thiopental rather than a lethal one.

His knees were aching from sitting on the floor, but Veronika's breathing had already begun to slow. Hawk was down on her hands and knees, peering into the young woman's face. "Veronika?" she said, sounding alarmed.

"She's just falling asleep." Alexei mentally crossed his fingers. If he'd just murdered this woman Hawk might kill him after all, witnesses or no witnesses.

"Is that supposed to happen?"

"Yes, of course." He looked and saw that Veronika's eyes had closed. Her chest rose and fell in deep, even breaths. Alexei swore softly. "It worked."

"When will she wake up?"

"Depends on how exhausted she is." Alexei stood again, wincing as his knees cracked. "Could be six hours, could be twelve. Probably should just let her sleep."

Hawk nodded. "Thank you," she said.

" -- when can I see him?"

"...Tomorrow."

Alexei rubbed a hand over his face -- God, he was tired. He also had no idea what he was going to say to Yuri either, but he'd deal with that when he came to it. He just knew that he had to see him. If the universe denied him even that little bit of atonement he was really going to lose every last one of his marbles.

"Am I done?"

"Yes, you're done." Hawk was rearranging the bundle of rags that Veronika slept in, tucking her into her pathetic bed. "Kestrel, take Alexei Nikolaevich back to his dorm."

Alexei left the storage room ahead of his escort. Kestrel tagged along behind him only as far as the hallway, then turned back, apparently deciding that Alexei could find his own way back to the dormitory. Back to the room with the two empty beds.

She'd thanked him. Why had Hawk bothered to thank him?

The blood on his mouth had dried, but his lip still burned. I didn't do it for her, Alexei reminded himself. I don't care how important that woman is to her. I did it for Yuri -- so I could meet him and tell him...what? that it's not my fault the CSF caught him? that they tortured me into a confession? that I'm sorry he saved my life for no reason?

Alexei pushed through the door and Anatoly's snoring hit him like a pillow. Kicking off his shoes, he fell facefirst into his bed. The bottle of thiopental was still in his pocket, pressing into his hip like a stone. Alexei rolled over, took it out and set the bottle on the floor beside his shoes. He dropped the rest of the bandages, swabs and syringes beside it.

Maybe I'll tell Yuri that high doses of thiopental put the patients to sleep. He might like to hear that.

And with that thought, Alexei passed out.

~~~~~

Mikhail was prepared.

He had been unprepared last time; there was no shame in that. Even the most battle-hardened generals would have called for a strategic withdrawal and regrouping of forces in the face of an overwhelming ambush.

But this time, there would be no retreat, no quarter given.

Mikhail was making his approach on the New Industrial State Bread Company factory, stealthy as a shadow. Or at least as stealthy as he could be, given that he was loaded down with enough military surplus gear to outfit a small platoon. And the machete strapped to his thigh was likewise creeping closer and closer to his knee with every step, forcing him to hold it up with one hand so he could walk normally. But at least the stock of his Mosin-Nagant was no longer clunking against the grenades on his belt.

The tails of his red bandanna fluttered masculinely in the breeze as he crept along. He was downwind from the bread factory and getting closer -- the tang of smoke in the air told him that.

Privately Mikhail was not sure what he had seen that day in the abandoned factory. It had been thoroughly evil; of that much he was certain. The thing in the factory called to mind all the suppressed literature he had read about the Great War, about the blasphemous weaponry their enemy had supposedly been developing. Black magic, the pamphlets had alleged. Perverse rituals. Human sacrifices. Satanic pacts. They would have damned their entire population to Hell if it had meant winning the war.

If the thing had been some sort of remnant of unholy enemy technology Mikhail would not have been one bit surprised. Nor would he have wavered an inch. If anything the possibility only strengthened his resolve. He was not only defending his city against something malevolent -- no, he was safeguarding the very souls of his fellow citizens against the forces of darkness. Mikhail had suspected demonic plagues from the moment he first spotted those black stains on the faces of the afflicted...finding that nightmarish thing in the factory had only served to solidify his unformed fears.

Though he was a warrior for light and justice, the sight of the red brick building with its faded white slogans still filled his stomach with butterflies. Pressing his back to the brick wall, he slid sideways around the building, moving toward the loading docks. Nobody had come along to shut the loading bay door since his last visit, and the gap that yawned beneath the door was impenetrably black. Mikhail was just bending down to crawl beneath it -- careful not to let the grenades around his waist scrape against the pavement -- when he heard voices.

Gasping, he leapt away, flattening himself back against the wall. He stood there holding his breath and listened.

"...more this week than last week. I think there's something..."

"...not actually working on it, of course, but you know we can't..."

"...keeps up for much longer...out of supplies. We'll have to..."

Mikhail breathed out in a silent whoosh. That croaking tone of voice was distinctive: those were CSF soldiers. He knew they were using the baking ovens and storage room in the building, but hadn't expected to run into them today.

Still, his mission wasn't a total loss just yet. Even if entering the factory presented too great a risk, he could still hear pieces of the soldiers' conversations. That gave him an unparalleled chance to conduct some espionage. At any moment the soldiers might disclose some detail of their plans for Khostok, or some vital bit of information about the horrible thing he had seen the other day. And Mikhail would overhear it.

With his back to the wall, Mikhail shimmied away from the loading bay door. There was a window to his right, and he hoped that he might be able to peek through and spot the soldiers inside the building. He could have wished it were nighttime -- that would have given him an excellent chance to use his night-vision goggles under cover of darkness -- but even a hardened warrior would be reluctant to engage with demonic entities after the sun had gone down.

But when he reached the window, Mikhail discovered two things. One, the window was broken, though in such a neighborhood that was not so unusual. And two, there was a dusty footprint on the brick windowsill. It was the print of something humanoid, and barefoot.

His heart leapt. Here it was! and the print faced outward, too, as if the thing had exited the factory through the window. Mikhail looked around. Sure enough, he found a second footprint in a bare patch of dirt not five feet away.

The alleyway the loading docks opened into was relatively narrow. Across the alley from the docks was the backside of another warehouse once used as a furniture factory. The warehouse's fire escape staircase, orange and pitted with rust, lay directly across from the broken window.

Even before he reached the fire escape, Mikhail's instinct told him he was right. And he was -- there on the first step of the staircase was another dusty, bare footprint.

He looked up. The decrepit staircase zigzagged back and forth across the side of the warehouse, leading up to a landing and a door some thirty feet overhead. The door was closed, but the window beside it had been smashed in as well, a starburst of darkness in the middle of the glass.

Mikhail knew where he had to go. He stomped down experimentally on the first step. The staircase vibrated from the impact, raining down orange dust, but all seemed sound enough to bear his weight.

Alert as a wild animal, Mikhail ascended the stairs. They creaked dramatically once or twice, causing him to freeze for a moment, but everything stayed in place. And the alleyway remained deserted during his ascent as well, which was another blessing. By the time he reached the top he was confident that luck was on his side today.

The door at the top was indeed locked, and getting through the broken window proved to be an undertaking. Mikhail was nowhere near as limber as that demonic thing seemed to be. He broke away the largest pieces of glass with his gloved hands, then laboriously removed his pack and dropped it inside the window. Then he shucked off his jacket and laid it on the windowsill. Grunting, he kicked one leg over the sill, straddled it, and dropped down inside the warehouse, stumbling over his pack where it lay on the floor.

Mikhail snatched up his pack at once, retrieving his brand-new flashlight and handgun. When he clicked the light on he found himself on the third floor of the warehouse, in a maze of forgotten office furniture. It looked as if most of the stock had been left behind when the warehouse was vacated; perhaps the factory chiefs, unable to distribute their goods, had locked them away in hopes of some future economic revival.

He doubted the state even remembered the warehouse anymore, but if they did, the condition that it had fallen into would certainly have shocked them. Dust lay like a blanket on the overturned swivel chairs and the orderly rows of office desks, the filing cabinets with their drawers rusted shut, boardroom tables which would never see a single meeting.

The darkness inside the warehouse was thick, almost a tangible thing. It seemed like the only sources of light were the yellow glow of the flashlight and the sickly sunbeams that streamed in through the broken window. Come to think of it, the window Mikhail had entered through seemed to be the only one on the entire third floor -- he could see no others.

Moving cautiously through the jungle of furniture, Mikhail swept the flashlight in a wide arc, trying to get a feel for his surroundings. The ceiling in the warehouse was low and cluttered with narrow pipes, offering no space for demons to hide in, though he kept his eye on it anyway. Here and there were little footprints in the thick dust -- some on the floor, some on the desks and chairs -- reminding him that he was still in the presence of something unholy.

At length Mikhail crossed the third floor and came across the interior staircase that led down to the lower floors of the warehouse. Determined to confront the thing he'd seen, he was just about to start down the steps when something ahead of him glinted in the dark.

He pointed his flashlight at it. The patch of light turned out to be sunlight, leaking in through a window almost completely overgrown with some sort of plant.

As he looked, Mikhail realized that the walls of the staircase were covered in the growth. It was everywhere, long vines overlapping in a tangled mesh, clinging to the bare brick like ivy, growing so thickly near the landing of the staircase that they nearly choked off the stairs themselves.

And it wasn't just in the staircase, either. Turning, Mikhail found the wall on his right-hand side was carpeted in the same growth as well, close enough for him to reach out and touch its leaves.

That explained the obscurity inside the warehouse, at least. The weird ivy must have grown over all of the windows, sealing the building's interior in darkness.

He was no botanist, but Mikhail was curious anyway. The plants looked strangely healthy for something growing in such a lightless environment. He peered at the wall beside him, shining his flashlight on a cluster of pointed, glossy leaves as long as his finger. Small flowerbuds nestled in the junctures of these leaves, and hanging below this cluster was a spray of what seemed to be berries, nearly as large as pigeons' eggs.

The shape of the plants was familiar, but the colors were all wrong. At first he assumed it was a trick of the light, but the more he looked the more Mikhail realized he wasn't mistaken. The leaves and vines were all black, dark as onyx. Fruits and flowers alike were slightly more normal hues of blue and purple, but the light of the flashlight seemed to be refracting through them as if through a stained-glass window. It was certainly his eyes playing tricks on him, but it looked like the little blossoms were almost glowing...

No, it wasn't his eyes. Mikhail switched his flashlight off and stood there staring, awestruck. He must have triggered something when he'd shone the flashlight on them, because the flowers on the wall were ALL beginning to light up, petals opening as their glow intensified. There were yellows and greens, red and blues, purples and pinks, shades of orange and turquoise and magenta and white and every other color conceivable. The wall in the warehouse was a garden of light, a multicolored ocean of stars.

Mikhail was so entranced that he barely noticed that his ears had begun to ring. As a consequence, the rustling in the stairwell went entirely unheard. It was only when a patch of luminous flowers down near the floor began to quiver that he registered the sound. Then a blotch of darkness moved between him and the lights, and fear shot like icicles into Mikhail's brain.

When he finally switched his flashlight back on, the thing was standing right in front of him.

He would realize later, much later, that it must have been lurking in the ivy until he approached. The thing had two legs, two arms and a head, hands and feet, but there the resemblance to a human being ended. For one, its "skin" was a seamless coat of glossy black, as if the thing were carved of polished stone. And second, it had no face.

No eyes, no nose, no mouth. There wasn't so much as the suggestion of a face; the front of the thing's head was as smooth and featureless as a black egg.

But it could see. And it was looking straight at Mikhail.

The memory of that shiny body and faceless face did not come back to him until that night, until Mikhail was safe in his hideout with an empty bottle of vodka tucked into his sleeping bag beside him. At the time, confronting the black thing, Mikhail had a moment of primal terror before his higher brain functions went into standby and something more primitive took the wheel.

Mikhail exited through the broken warehouse window with a headfirst rolling dive that would have impressed even the most jaded of American moviegoers. The rusting fire escape stairs squealed as he took them four at a time, then decided this wasn't fast enough and leapt over the railing to fall the last six feet to reach the ground. With the tails of his red bandanna fluttering behind him Mikhail sprinted the rest of the way back to his hideout, narrowly avoiding a run-in with a CSF patrol.

He surpassed his previous record for the return trip by a factor of three-point-five minutes.

~~~~~

It was late afternoon in the Volgin River valley. The waning sunlight shone through the curtain of fog that lay over the valley, setting it afire with amber and gold.

He was the river.

That wasn't quite accurate, but it was the only way to describe what he was feeling. A billion sensations were all competing for his attention. The water streaming through the riverbed was like blood rushing through his veins; the growing and blossoming of the plant life was the long, slow stretching of cramped muscles. The things that walked along the river were seeing it, hearing it, smelling it, and this was refracted back to him in a hundred different sights and sounds and scents.

One of the living creatures he "inhabited" -- he wasn't certain what they were, but they were definitely sentient -- crept up to the water's edge and lowered their head to drink. This simple movement sent multiplied echoes rippling across his awareness: he was in the water as well as in the creature, he discovered.

For any being limited to a single body, describing the experience would have been impossible. He wasn't sure quite how *he* was registering all this, given that he vaguely remembered having had a single body at some point. He could no longer locate that body, but it hardly seemed to matter, not when his consciousness was stretched across thousands upon thousands of organisms...

( -- *It's all my fault, it's all my fault* -- )

The litany broke into his thoughts, interrupting them. What? his fault? no, not his -- this was someone else's. And what were they blaming themselves for?

( -- *all my fault* -- )

He concentrated on the sound. Once he'd gotten a grip on it he felt himself drawn, like a magnet, slipping away from the river and the plants and creatures and the golden mist. There was something he was forgetting about, something important, and as the voice grew louder the forgotten thing was coming back to him more and more clearly --

( -- *my fault* -- )

He opened his eyes. There was just one pair of eyes now, one field of vision, and he blinked several times in an effort to adjust to it.

"Oh, you're awake?"

He turned and found something dark and blurry beside him. "Are you alright?" the blur was asking. "Here, I've got your glasses..." It reached out toward him. Something settled onto his nose and his vision sharpened all at once, throwing the metal walls and ceiling into focus.

The blur had turned into Alexei, sitting crosslegged on the floor.

"...Lyosha?"

Alexei smiled weakly. "Hello, Yura."

"...how?..." Yuri went to sit up -- he seemed to be lying on his back on the floor -- and his arms refused to hold him. Alexei leaned forward to help him up, pulling him into a sitting position. He felt incredibly weak all of a sudden, like he was ten times heavier than he'd been a minute ago. His head was swimming.

"Easy, take it easy."

"How'd...you get in here?" Yuri asked.

Alexei shrugged. "The soldiers let me in," he said.

Yuri took a good long look at him. Alexei looked exhausted, somehow drained, and several pounds thinner than he remembered. "What happened to your mouth?"

"Huh?" Alexei covered his lower lip for a moment. "Oh -- nothing." He looked away. "Um...how are you feeling?"

"Strange," Yuri admitted. Vague dreamlike traces floated through his memory, just below his consciousness. Something about rivers and honey-colored fog. He pushed it to the back of his mind. "Thanks for coming to see me."

Alexei flinched. "Don't thank me," he said. "It's my fault you're in here."

"What? how?"

"I told them you were infected."

"Oh." Yuri considered this. "So that's what happened to your mouth."

Alexei was silent. "I'm sorry," Yuri said.

"I'm fine, I'm fine," Alexei looked pained. "Don't apologize. Please."

The two of them sat in silence for a moment. "I, uh, have some good news," Alexei said.

"You do?"

"Yeah. You remember how we couldn't sedate any of the patients?" He produced a small bottle and a disposable syringe from his lab coat pocket. "I found out that high doses of sodium thiopental will actually put them to sleep, if you use two or three times the usual dose. It worked on the woman in Storage Room 8 when I tried it."

Yuri smiled. "That's a big discovery," he said.

Alexei seemed encouraged. "Thanks...I thought so. I even think that someone of the fatalities we've had are due to their insomnia, so maybe putting them to sleep might help them live longer." He handed the bottle and the wrapped syringe to Yuri. "Here. Don't let them see it."

"Oh...thanks." Yuri took the gifts and held the little glass bottle up between an inkstained finger and thumb. He was wearing a short-sleeved shirt and Alexei could see that the blight had reached all the way up into his sleeve, and perhaps further up his arm than that.

"We don't have a cure for it though, do we?"

Alexei shook his head. Yuri was still staring at the vial of thiopental, rolling it back and forth between his fingers.

"Lyosha...would you do me a favor?"

"Anything."

Yuri gave him a look. "You haven't heard what it is yet."

"Doesn't matter. I'll do it."

"Alright." Sighing, Yuri stashed the bottle and syringe in the pile of blankets he'd been sleeping in. "I want you to find my daughter and my brother. And if they're still in the city -- I want you to get them out of Khostok."

Alexei's gray eyes widened.

"If you don't think you can --

" -- I said I'll do it," Alexei cut in. "But...what are *you* going to do?"

"I'm not going anywhere." Yuri gestured at the metal walls of Storage Room 7. "I had planned on getting them out myself, but right now I can't even get out of the Labs. Even if I did get out, I can't get very far. Most of the time I'm not..." He groped for the right words. "...I'm not myself."

Alexei looked defeated. Rummaging in the pile of blankets, Yuri came up with a creased photograph which he pressed into Alexei's hands. It was a pink-cheeked young girl in a brand-new schooldress, her blond hair plaited into twin braids. Her eyes were the same color as her father's.

"Remember, her name's Elena. She's ten years old. You should find her together with my older brother, Nikita. He's about my height, but darker hair and no glasses. You can tell him I sent you. If they're still in the city get them as far as Byatin, at least -- Nikita's got an apartment there."

Alexei nodded, staring at the photo.

"Listen -- I'm sorry to ask you to do this." Yuri put his unstained hand on Alexei's shoulder. "But you need to get out of the city too, while you still can. I don't think the CSF is letting any of us out of the Labs. If Elena and Nikita are still here in Khostok, it might be the same for them, too."

"I'll do it," Alexei repeated, and pocketed the photograph. "But after I get them out, I'm going to come back for you."

Yuri blinked at him, then broke into a grin. "Fine, Lyosha, that's fine," he chuckled, easing himself back down onto the blankets. "After they're safe, you do whatever you like."

"...are you okay?"

"Yes, I'm alright. Just going to take a rest for a minute." Yuri waved him away, letting his eyes slip closed. "Thanks again for the visit."

Alexei got back to his feet again. "I promise I'll come back," he insisted.

But Yuri didn't reply. He'd already returned to the river.

~~~~~

"Now see here," Nikita said. "I need to have some aspirin and sedatives for my niece, and I'm not leaving until I get them. I'm a very reasonable man, but she's feverish and hasn't slept in days and I can't stand to see a child suffering like this. Either let me have something right away, or let me speak to your superior."

It all sounded perfect to Nikita -- firm, but rational, and spoken with conviction. Once he'd gotten his chance to talk to the CSF soldier in charge of the infirmary he would say it out loud instead of muttering it under his breath.

Of course, he had to wait in line first. Though it was nothing more than a series of curtained partitions, planted where the auditorium's refreshment stands had once stood, it seemed like there was always a line at the camp clinic. Unsurprising, given that the CSF had culled the sick from among the healthy and boxed them all up in the same giant room.

He'd been in line for better than a half-hour, and being away from Elena for so long was making him nervous. Of course under normal conditions she could take care of herself, but the situation at hand was anything but normal. The CSF couldn't control all of the camp inmates, and it seemed like more and more of them were descending into psychosis as the days wore on.

Not to mention Elena's illness: she'd been unable to sleep for the past three days, and this morning Nikita had woken up to discover that she was running a fever as well. He wasn't even sure that the blight was to blame for it -- the stress and insomnia and nauseating food they'd been eating were certainly enough by themselves to make anyone ill.

And now he had to wait in line to ask for medication. In spite of the CSF's transparent desire to dismiss their "patients" as quickly as possible, the queue was still barely creeping along. Nikita had been staring at the same cocktail advertisement -- a leftover from the vacant refreshment stands -- for the past ten minutes, and the longer he waited the more he daydreamed about pulling the illustration off the cardboard sign and drinking it.

"Next," growled the soldier, and Nikita moved forward another ten inches. At least he was next in line; after the portly fellow ahead of him was through making his demands of the infirmary "receptionist", he would be next.

The fat man stepped up to the soldier. "Now you listen here!" he barked, and Nikita groaned inwardly. Another one of those. "My father's very elderly, he needs his insulin, and you're going to give it to us! And none of this crap about being out of supplies! I've had quite enough of you people, and if you push me any further you're going to regret it!"

Nikita had to give the soldier credit for his patience. He sat behind the card table that served as a reception desk, listening, and at the end of the speech he nodded. "I understand your concern, comrade, but unfortunately we *are* out of insulin at the moment. We expect the next shipment -- "

The man cut him short. "No! I told you, I'm not taking any more of your bullshit excuses! We have a goddamn medical emergency on our hands, and you're just going to sit by -- "

"If there are no other medical requests. please step out of line." The soldier's voice distorted voice carried over the sound of his protests. The little fat man looked fit to explode, his face darkening from red to purple. "I *have* a medical request! I already *told* you what I needed! You're not listening to me! I'll have you know -- "

"Sir, please step out of line now."

The man responded with a string of rage-garbled invective. Nikita took a step back from the escalating confrontation, and the people behind him in line did the same. The man was punctuating each sentence by slamming his fists down onto the card table, and the pens laid out beside the blank admittance forms danced around on the tabletop with each blow.

Nikita saw the soldier pressing the button on the side of his gas mask, switching the radio on. He couldn't hear the soldier's conversation over the noise the fat man was making, but he imagined he knew what was being said.

"I'll wait! I can wait all day!" howled the man, and several people behind him in line began to grumble. "Nobody's getting any medication until I get that insulin! Now, you can get *off* your ass and find some for me, or -- "

"Excuse us, comrade."

The three CSF soldiers seemed to materialize from nowhere, stepping out from a side door somewhere behind the infirmary's curtains. Flushed and sweating, the man looked up at the soldiers in clear surprise.

"Were you asking for insulin?" said one of the three.

"...well, of course." The fat man's expression turned sulky, and he jabbed a finger at the reception desk soldier. "This moron was trying to tell me you're out of it, but I know that can't be true."

A barely perceptible nod passed between the standing soldier and the receptionist. "I do apologize for the inconvenience," said the soldier, placing a hand on the little man's shoulder. "Come right this way and we'll provide you with some."

The man looked somehow less than pleased to have his request granted. As he stepped out of line he glanced back at the rest of the queue, but everyone avoided his gaze. Flanked by the three dark silhouettes, he stepped behind the infirmary curtains and was lost from view.

"Next," the receptionist said pleasantly.

Nikita stepped up, wondering why his knees were shaking. "...just some sedatives and some aspirin please," he asked.

The soldier bent down to a box beneath the card table and came back up with a paper envelope. "Here's the aspirin," he said. "We're out of sedatives at the moment, but we expect the next shipment by Tuesday."

Nikita took the aspirin and pocketed it. "Thank you," he said meekly, and stepped out of line. He'd gotten halfway back to Elena's cot before it occurred to him that he had no idea what day of the week it was.

Elena wasn't really sleeping, but Nikita still had to shake her a little before she came around. She gave him a glazed look as he helped her into a sitting position. "...papa?"

"No, Lena, just your uncle. I've brought you some medicine -- be a good kid and take it, okay?"

Elena took the aspirin and swallowed it with a mouthful of their water ration. When she lay back down again Nikita stayed beside her, feeling her forehead, trying to tell if the fever had gone up or down since he'd last checked. Was it just his imagination, or had the black spot near her mouth gotten bigger?

"Where did he go?"

"Who?"

"Papa."

"...oh, he's not here, Lena. He's not here."

Elena's brow creased up in a frown. "But he was here! I was talking to him!"

Nikita decided not to argue the point. Delirium or not, if it made her feel better he'd let her think that Yuri had been here. Nikita wished he was.

"Is he gonna come back?"

Nikita brushed Elena's bangs from her forehead. "Sure he will."

Two rows away, a bewildered-looking older man with a fuzzy gray beard was wandering from cot to cot, talking to people. He seemed to be searching for something. Nikita watched him approach one young mother and ask her a question; when she shook her head in reply, he moved on to the next person. Whatever he was asking, everyone answered in the negative.

Elena murmured something, and Nikita looked down. "Huh?"

"Are we gonna go too?" Elena asked. Nikita noticed that her eyes were closing, and wasn't sure whether to be relieved or alarmed.

"Go where? to Byatin?"

"No...to the river."

The river? Maybe she was dreaming of a vacation. Hadn't Yuri and Ekaterina taken her down to visit some river when she was little? Nikita could remember that his sister-in-law had loved going on picnics...

"We're all going down to the river," Elena said, her tone full of conviction now.

"Sure, we'll go there." Nikita kept on petting her hair. "Try to get some sleep."

Elena seemed to be asleep already, but he couldn't be sure. The lost little man was asking someone else his question, getting turned away again. Nikita was too far away to hear him, but he could just about read his lips. He wasn't sure why he cared, but something about the man --

"Papa says he'll be waiting for us there," Elena whispered. "At the river."

Goosebumps prickled along Nikita's arms. It was just something about the way she said it. "What, Lena?" he asked, but Elena lay silently on her pillow and did not answer him. He checked her forehead again.

"Have you seen my son?"

The question seemed to float above the rest of the hubbub in the auditorium. Nikita looked up at the old man again, realizing. That's why he looked familiar -- this must have been the diabetic father of the angry little fat man who had held up the line at the infirmary. The one who'd gone off with an escort of three CSF soldiers.

At last the old man gave up, returning to his cot. He was pale and out of breath, and even at this distance Nikita could see that he was shaking. The cot beside him was empty.

Nikita wanted to go talk to him, but there was nothing he could really say. Knowing where his son had gone couldn't have helped the man.

Still, the old man with the fuzzy beard kept on popping back into his thoughts. Nikita checked on him several times, waiting to see if the cot beside him would become reoccupied. He hoped it would. The CSF couldn't very well shoot you for causing a ruckus in line, could they? Maybe the little man would get scolded, maybe thrashed about a bit -- all that was to be expected. But they would have to let him come back sometime.

But when Nikita lay down to sleep that night, the cot beside the old man was still vacant. The next morning, both cots were empty.

In truth, Nikita didn't know how lucky he was. He may have thought the inmates at Red Camp Three to be brutally oppressed, but it paled in comparison to Red Camp One.

~~~~~

" -- your cousin's making boots?" asked one of the CSF soldiers.

The second soldier nodded his head. "It's not as hard as it sounds. He mainly does the quality inspection -- makes sure the boots aren't coming off the assembly line inside-out, things like that."

The first soldier oh'ed thoughtfully. The two of them were walking side-by-side along the second-floor hallway of the Gurlukovich Memorial Hospital, pushing a wheeled cart full of boxes. Or more accurately the first soldier, codenamed Penguin, was the one pushing the cart, while the soldier codenamed Bluejay explained the finer points of his cousin's profession.

"And do they pay him well?"

"Pretty well, pretty well," Bluejay said. "Gets decent hours too."

"Ah, that's good," Penguin observed. He glanced back over his shoulder, but the hallway was empty, the exam room doors all closed. "Are they hiring now?"

"He says they're always hiring." Bluejay checked over his shoulder too. "You thinking about it?"

The cart's wheels squeaked over a scattering of clinic admittance forms, likely dropped there during the hasty evacuation of the building. "I might be," Penguin said.

"Wouldn't blame you."

"Or I could just apply for a transfer."

Bluejay snorted. "You think any of us would be here if they let us transfer out?" He stepped ahead of the cart to hold open the double doors at the end of the hallway. "Keep dreaming."

Sighing, Penguin pushed the cart through the doorway. He tossed a one-handed salute to the CSF soldiers stationed as guards just outside the doors.

The two had reached the physical therapy gymnasium, what had once been the shining jewel of the Gurlukovich Memorial Hospital. Stroke and auto accident victims had come from miles around to participate in the hospital's therapy program, exercising on the padded gym floor as well as in the state-of-the-art swimming pool. With its wide open space and reinforced steel doors this famous gym had been one of the first choices for housing quarantined Khostok citizens.

Looking down onto the gym floor from the second-story walkway, Bluejay and Penguin could see how just a few short weeks as a Red Camp had transformed it from its former glory. The brightly painted murals along the concrete walls had been defaced with a number of slurs, slogans, drawings and demands, mostly for food or medication. The hospital's spacious swimming pool had been drained to provide extra floor space for the sleeping cots, and trash was gathering along the bottom between the beds. The carpeting on the gym floor was ripped and gouged, and the locked steel doors leading out of the gym were scarred and dented from multiple attempts to bash through them.

By Penguin's estimate there must have been close to a thousand souls down there on the gym floor, milling about like animals in a zoo. He knew there had been nine hundred and seventy four inmates at its peak, but obviously the number had declined since then. Even from the second floor walkway, a good fifteen feet above the gym floor, the soldiers could see how severely blighted the inmates were -- there was scarcely one person in twenty whose arms and face were still clear, and several of the inmates were so covered in blight that they looked to have been drenched in ink.

Even through their gas masks the smell was awful. Obviously the overcrowding and difficulty in bathing were partly responsible, but most of the stench emanated from the growing pile of bodies in a far corner of the room. The ones near the bottom had been wrapped in bedsheets, though nobody had bothered to do this with the fresher corpses.

"Poor bastards," Penguin remarked.

Bluejay made a derisive noise. "You want to go down there? you forgot what happened to Sandpiper and Wren?"

Penguin hadn't forgotten. And neither had the camp inmates, it seemed. Someone on spotted the two new arrivals, and a cry went up from the gym floor. Heads turned, people leapt up from their cots, and within minutes a sizable crowd had gathered on the floor below the walkway where Bluejay and Penguin stood, all of them shouting their demands.

"Soap and water! we need soap and water!

"My grandmother needs medical attention! I know you can hear me!"

"You have to let us go! we need to get down to the river!"

"Throw down the boxes already!"

"I demand that you release me! My husband works for the DIO, and he'll hear about this!"

"The shadows are coming! the shadows are coming!"

"My son is dying! what do you people think you're doing?! this is inhumane!"

"Help us! if you have any human hearts at all, help us!"

One of the CSF soldiers guarding the second-floor walkway fired a burst into the air, and the shouting died down. He gestured for Penguin and Bluejay to start unloading the boxes.

Penguin tore open the first box and lifted out a plastic bag of dehydrated soup mix. He looked at it for a moment, then sighed and pitched it over the railing.

The crowd roared as the first bag came sailing down towards them, followed by a second and a third. A small riot erupted on the gym floor below. People were climbing atop each other, wrestling for possession of the rations, screaming and swearing. One of the bags ripped open, flinging a wave of bright yellow soup powder all over the mass of squirming bodies. The crowd shrieked in rage.

"Like rats in a barrel," Bluejay commented to himself, watching the chaos below. At least they didn't have to heft jugs of water over the railing. They had Falcon to thank for that -- Falcon was the officer in charge of Red Camp One, and he had gone to Colonel Akimov and explained the situation personally.

The inmates of Red Camp One had become uncontrollable, Falcon had told the Colonel. They had rioted and nearly killed two of his best men over the lack of medicine in the camp. The blight was at least partly responsible; a good number of the inmates were downright psychotic by this point, so covered in blight they scarcely looked human anymore. Even with their superior firepower it had become dangerous for the CSF to be down among the incarcerated, especially when they were outnumbered almost fifty to one.

Akimov was a rational man, above all, and had understood completely. He had permitted Falcon to seal off the gym, letting the soldiers throw down supplies from the safety of the second-floor walkway. More importantly, he had given the order for the water in Khostok to be partially restored, letting the inmates held at the former Gurlukovich Memorial Hospital use the restroom facilities that adjoined the gym. To be sure, drinking the ink-tainted water out of the sinks had predictably worsened their infections, but there seemed to be few alternatives.

With a grunt, Penguin hurled the last bag of rations over the railing. A minute later the masses seemed to realize that no more food was forthcoming, and a series of angry exclamations went up from the floor.

"That's all today!" The second-floor guard fired off another short burst. "That's all! get back!"

Protesting loudly, the crowd began to dissolve. Several stragglers remained behind, shouting their demands up to Penguin and Bluejay.

"What a madhouse." Bluejay was shaking his head.

Penguin acknowledged this with a solemn nod. "Isn't Falcon going back to talk to the Colonel?"

"Next week."

"Not soon enough." Bluejay's tone was dark. "They'll have torn the place down by then."

"Well, maybe they'll let us transfer out if that happens," Penguin said.

# CHAPTER NINE

Alexei had gone from nightmare to nightmare. He was fairly sure that he had been sleeping up until a minute ago; he'd dreamed about running through a hospital, looking for a doctor. It had been critically important that he find someone, but all of the offices had been closed and locked. He had supposed all the closures were due to the bad weather -- the air had been thick with fog, shrouding the floors, cutting off the ends of the hallways. But just as Alexei was beginning to wonder how it could be foggy *inside* the building, something had grabbed him.

He woke up kicking and fighting. When he opened his eyes and found the soulless masked face of a CSF soldier hovering over him Alexei lashed out instinctively. He got one good punch on the end of their respirator before the soldier grabbed his wrist.

"Wake *up*, you idiot! It's me!"

Alexei stopped thrashing. "...Hawk?" he panted.

"Yes, of course. Awake now?"

"Let go of me."

Satisfied, Hawk released his arm and stepped back. "Get dressed."

Alexei sat up in bed. "What's going on?" he asked, reaching for his shirt. He could see Kestrel standing at the doorway of the dorm, silhouetted in the light from the hallway, and Alexei felt his guts clench up in sudden anxiety. Something had happened to that woman that Hawk was so preoccupied with; they would never have bothered him at this hour for anything else.

"We need you to do an exam on the test subject in Storage Room 8," Hawk explained.

Alexei pulled his shirt down around his ears. "What? an exam? what time is it?" He stood and hunted around on the floor for his shoes. "This couldn't wait until the morning?"

"Just get dressed."

Still blinking the sleep out of his eyes, Alexei laced his shoes up. "If she's having another episode we'll need to make a stop by the requisitions office again," he said. "I'm out of the thiopental."

"She appears to be cured."

Alexei lost his grip on the shoelaces. "...what?" he asked, straightening again. "Who's cured?"

"The girl in Room 8. Veronika Stepanevna."

For an insane moment Alexei almost decided that he was still dreaming. "She's cured? cured of the blight?"

"That's what it looks like," Hawk said. Now that he was more alert Alexei could hear the change in Hawk's tone. She almost sounded excited. "The black stains are all gone. We need an actual exam to confirm it, but -- "

" -- but how? who cured her? what'd they give her?"

Hawk shrugged. "She hasn't been treated since the last time you saw her."

"But I didn't give her anything but thiopental." Alexei looked back and forth between the two soldiers. "That shouldn't have cured anything. It was just to make her sleep. Are you sure she's cured? I mean..."

"See for yourself," Hawk said, and half-dragged him out the door with one shoe still untied.

At the door of Storage Room 8 Hawk waited with barely concealed impatience as Kestrel unlocked the door. Once it was open she darted inside, pulling Alexei along into the room after her.

Veronika sat crosslegged on her pile of blankets, as if awaiting an audience. She still had the long tangled hair and rumpled hospital gown of a mental patient, but when she looked up at Alexei her eyes were clear and alert.

"Good morning," she said, holding up a very pink and very unblighted hand. Alexei stared at it for a long moment before it struck him that she was offering a handshake. Carefully, as if in fear of getting bitten, he reached out and shook hands with the woman.

"Alexei Nikolaevich, right?"

"Um, yeah."

"My name is Veronika Stepanevna." The woman smiled up at him. Her pupils were of normal size. In fact she appeared perfectly healthy -- her face was clear and glowing, her visible skin completely free of stains. Alexei realized that he had never seen her in good health before. It turned out that Veronika was somewhat attractive without the discoloration brought on by the blight, but Alexei found he was more unnerved than charmed. This woman was someone he'd never seen before; a stranger.

Alexei cleared his throat. "Uh, pleased to meet you." He took a step back. "...How are you feeling?"

"Fine," Veronika said. "Thanks to the two of you."

Hawk made a delighted little noise. Still trying to wrap his brain around this miraculously unblighted woman, Alexei knelt down next to her on the floor. "Comrade...do you have any idea why you became cured?"

Something flashed in Veronika's eyes and was gone before he could identify it. "How would I know?" Veronika asked, still smiling. "I assumed you gave me something."

It didn't make sense, but at the moment Alexei couldn't wonder about it. "Well, congratulations -- if you *are* cured, this is wonderful news," Alexei said, trying to return her smile. "If you could please take your clothes off, I'd like to examine the rest of you."

Veronika nodded. She started to hike up her gown, then stopped, casting a glance between Alexei and Hawk.

"...something wrong?"

She looked at him. "Um...well, you're a man, and...I'd rather not take my clothes off while you're here."

Alexei felt himself starting to blush. "But -- this is purely for medical reasons," he insisted.

"You're still a man though. Couldn't you leave?"

" -- but I can't conduct the exam from outside the room." Alexei was getting flustered in spite of himself.

Hawk stepped forward "I'll do it!"

Alexei gave her an astounded look. "Be serious."

"I mean it. There's no need to force this girl to undress in front of a strange man."

"Both of you are crazy," Alexei rose to his feet again. He had an inkling that he was missing something, but he couldn't tell precisely what. "You've hardly got the training to conduct an exam yourself."

"Are *you* a doctor?" Hawk shot back. "Last I checked, you were just a lab assistant."

"I am a junior researcher here, and I have a damn sight more medical knowledge than you do." The conversation was getting ridiculous and Alexei was suddenly tired of it. "Fine, I don't care -- do the exam yourself and I'll go back to bed."

Hawk nodded smugly and gestured to Kestrel, who was still standing in the open door of the storage room. "Let him out. Standby outside until I need you."

"Roger that," Kestrel said. If he found his superior's behavior to be puzzling he gave no sign of it. He obediently stepped aside to let Alexei out of the room and eased the door shut, closing Hawk and Veronika into Storage Room 8 together.

Alexei's frustration only lasted until his next thought struck him. "I need to get into the requisitions office again," he said, turning to Kestrel. "If we did really cure her, I want to test the same treatment on the guy in Storage Room 7."

For a moment it seemed Kestrel hadn't heard him. "...Yuri Ivanovich, right?"

"Yes, that's the one."

Kestrel was examining the tips of his gloves with sudden interest. "I'll take you to requisitions, but you'll have to test it on someone else."

A tiny alarm bell, shrill and insistent, had begun to ring in Alexei's head. "...Why?"

Kestrel sighed. "I thought Hawk was going to tell you," he said irritably. "He's dead."

The news hit Alexei like a sledgehammer. "...what?"

"He died last night."

"...who?"

Kestrel stared at him. "...Yuri Ivanovich," he said softly. "He's dead."

A roaring darkness was filling Alexei's senses, blotting out all sight, all sound. It seemed like Kestrel was growing taller, looming over him, but this was only because Alexei had slumped back against the storage room door and was sliding down to the floor.

"I'm sorry," Kestrel said. "We found a needle and an empty medicine bottle in his cell. Not sure how he got ahold of them but it looked like a deliberate overdose."

But Alexei was not home at the moment, and did not respond. "Sorry," Kestrel repeated, and went back to inspecting his gloves.

There is no telling how long Alexei might have sat there, staring into nothing, if someone in Room 8 hadn't started screaming. Alexei, perhaps understandably, did not react, but Kestrel yelped in surprise and ran to the door. Grabbing Alexei by the collar, he yanked the young man away from the door and flung it open.

"Sir! what -- "

With dreamlike slowness, Alexei picked himself up off the floor and looked into the open storage room.

He spotted Veronika first -- she was cowering in one corner, arms crossed over her bare chest, naked save for a pair of grey underpants. Blood ran from her mouth and trickled down the side of her chin. Her eyes were wild and triumphant.

Hawk was wedged into the opposite corner. She'd unslung her rifle and was trying to hold Veronika at gunpoint, but the way Hawk was shaking made it impossible for her to aim.

" -- Sir?!" Kestrel ventured. Hawk turned to them and it was then that Alexei spotted the tear in her protective suit, right at the juncture of her throat and shoulder. White skin and red blood showed vividly for an instant before Hawk dropped the forward grip of her rifle and reached up to cover the tear.

Kestrel swore and took a step back.

" -- she -- she -- she -- " Hawk said indistinctly. Even her voice was shaking.

Veronika giggled madly. She moved as if to leave and Hawk thrust the firearm in her direction. "You stay right there or I swear I will blow your goddamn head off."

Still grinning, Veronika sagged back into the corner of the room. Hawk released her neck for a moment to stare at her bloodied glove. Two dark crescents stood out clearly on the skin that showed through the ripped suit.

"She *bit* me," Hawk said, and her voice cracked. She clasped her hand back over the wounds. "Right through my suit. She's completely crazy." She glanced at Kestrel, then at Alexei. "Check her back -- she's still infected with something."

Nobody moved. "You didn't tell me Yura had died," Alexei murmured.

Hawk turned toward Alexei and quickly looked away. " -- I wasn't sure how to tell you," she growled.

"Who?" Veronika's smile had faded. "The one with the long hair?"

Alexei nodded, and Veronika shot Hawk a truly venomous look.

"He killed himself," Hawk protested. Blood shone wetly on the black rubber of her suit, trickling between her gloved fingers. "If I'd known he was suicidal I would have set someone to watch him."

"Sir, uh..." That was Kestrel, sounding strained. "Do you need a bandage for that?"

"Don't bother," Veronika said. "The stuff's in your bloodstream already. Soon you'll be showing symptoms."

Hawk stiffened and for a moment Alexei thought Veronika would get shot after all. "Sir!" Kestrel shouted, lunging to grab the gun away from Hawk.

"You deranged bitch." Hawk snarled. Kestrel was fighting to get the AKS away from her. She wasn't giving it up, but the blood on her gloves made it difficult for her to keep her grip.

"You people killed my brother," Veronika said clearly. "You can all go to hell."

"I wasn't there -- I had nothing to do with what happened at the processing center," Hawk insisted, and there was pleading in her voice now. "I was trying to *help* you. Why me?"

Veronika shrugged. "You were convenient."

" -- 'convenient'?!" Hawk echoed. "Someone killed your brother and you're taking it out on the first person you find?"

"No -- this isn't vengeance."

"No? then what is it?"

"I'm getting out of here." Veronika indicated the storage room. "I'm not gonna die here in Khostok. And you're going to help me escape," she smiled sweetly, " -- or everyone's going to know you've got the blight."

Kestrel knocked Hawk's arm out of the way a split-second before the gun went off. The report was deafening, and the bullet pinged off of the wall before ricocheting into the grated floor.

"You're not telling anyone anything," Hawk snarled. Kestrel had both hands on her rifle and was keeping it aimed at the ground. "You're gonna be too dead to talk."

"Are you going to shoot me too?" Alexei asked.

Hawk whirled on him. She made a valiant effort to train the gun sights on his forehead, but with her subordinate fighting her for control of the weapon she wasn't able to do so.

"Don't tempt me." Hawk said through what sounded like clenched teeth, trying to pry Kestrel's fingers from the gun. "I'll kill you both."

"But I'm the only one who could cure you," Alexei said tonelessly. "You can't do it yourself -- you don't know what the dosage should be."

Hawk's gloves were slippery with blood, and in the end Kestrel finally succeeded in wresting the gun from her. Panting through her respirator, she stared Alexei down. "But you're not going to cure me," she said.

"No, I'll do it." Alexei was amazed at how much easier everything became the moment he stopped caring. "If you get us out of the Labs and help me find Yura's family -- and get them out of Khostok -- I'll cure you the same way I cured her."

" -- his family?" Veronika spoke up.

Alexei nodded. "His daughter and his brother were in Khostok when the quarantine came down." That boiling black cloud was gathering in his brain once more, swamping his thoughts, and Alexei forced it back. "He thinks they might still be in the city."

"Oh god," Veronika whispered. "I -- I think I saw them. The girl was named Elena, right?"

Surprised, Alexei turned to her. "A man and his niece were with me at the processing center." Veronika's dark eyes were liquid. "They both got quarantined. I knew your friend had to be related to that man -- they looked so much alike." Her expression turned hard again. "I'll help you find them."

"You will?" Alexei said. "...um, thank you."

Hawk was looking back and forth between the two of them. "Even *if* I help you idiots, you're forgetting there isn't any cure." She pointed an accusing finger. "Look at the girl's back. I don't know what's happened to her, but she's not cured."

Veronika gave Hawk a contemptuous look. Before anyone else could move Veronika spun on her heel, sweeping her hair in front of her shoulders and presenting them with her bare back.

As it turned out, the woman was not completely free of the blight. There was a large, perfectly symmetrical blotch of shiny blackness right in the middle of her upper back, between her shoulder-blades It radiated outward along the length of her spine like a black sunburst, disappearing at the nape of her neck where her hair began.

"I don't care what it looks like," Veronika was saying over her shoulder. She turned to face them again, hair falling over her bare chest. "I've stopped hallucinating, and now I can sleep again. Maybe I'm not totally cured, but I'm not losing my mind anymore either."

Hawk was silent. "...That might be your best chance, sir," Kestrel suggested.

"What?" Hawk turned to her subordinate. "You *want* me to help these two break through the quarantine?"

"Well...we went through training together, didn't we?" Kestrel handed her rifle back. "I don't want to see anything happen to you. And you know what'll happen if the Forces find out you've got the blight."

Hawk looked down at the rifle, its wooden grip already stained with blood, and touched the ripped fabric at her throat. Sighing, she made a sign to Kestrel and he nodded, ducking out of the room. Hawk followed him out, and Alexei narrowly avoided losing a foot when Hawk slammed the door shut in his face, locking him in the storage room.

"...I'm sure they'll be back," Veronika said, bending to retrieve her discarded hospital gown.

Alexei looked at the angular hole in the door where the inner handle had once been. He poked at it, then turned listlessly away and sank down to sit on the floor.

There was a rustling of papery fabric as Veronika slipped back into her gown. She took the water jug down from one of the shelves and splashed a little into her hand, washing Hawk's blood from her face.

"That was a good idea you had, offering to cure her. I really think she might've killed me otherwise."

Alexei was staring at his shoes. The laces on the left one were still untied, but he made no move to tie it. Veronika padded across the room and crouched down beside him.

"Listen," Veronika said. "Really, I'm sorry about -- "

" -- please leave me alone," Alexei whispered. The thunderheads were rolling in again, rumbling in his ears. He drew his legs up to his chest, wrapping his arms around them, and put his head down on his knees.

Veronika seemed to understand, and retreated to take a seat in her own corner of the storage room. They were still sitting in their corners fifteen minutes later when someone unlocked the door.

~~~~~

Mikhail saw it all vividly, as real as if it had actually happened.

The setting was a Khostok city street, empty of cars and pedestrians. The buildings were all still standing, though with shattered windows and concrete scarred by shrapnel from the bombs lately fallen in the air raids. From far away came the sound of a barking dog, and from further still there was the rattling of machinegun fire and the distant whoomph of an occasional mortar.

In the middle of the street, a manhole cover inched upward from its socket. The cover slid to the right, revealing a well of darkness leading down into the sewers. Footsteps rang out on the ladder as a black peaked visor cap emerged from the depths. Decorating the cap was a silver death's-head pin, the skull grinning vacantly down at the uninhabited street.

The owner of the cap stepped up from the ladder and onto the asphalt. With the toe of one leather boot he nudged the manhole cover back into place, then readjusted his leather trenchcoat with a couple of brisk tugs, brushing the dirt and cobwebs from his shoulders.

"Is everything ready, Herr Obersturmbannführer?"

The officer in the visor cap jumped a little, then snapped into a smart salute. "Heil, o powerful one! Ja, all is in place."

To describe the person who'd greeted the officer would have been difficult. They wore a broad-brimmed hat, and a long coat with the collar turned up, but other than that their features were indistinct, as if seen underwater. An observant bystander might have commented on the smell of sulfur in the air, but Obersturmbannführer Klein would hardly have dared to be so tactless.

"All two hundred packages have been placed, in the locations indicated by your maps." Klein thought it safe to drop his salute now, and produced said map from the pocket of his trenchcoat. "Your employer's generosity is most gracious."

The thing in the trenchcoat smiled, or gave the impression that it was smiling. "This was not charity," it said.

"Nein, of course not!" Klein stammered. "Your payment is ready and waiting for you; you have the Führer's word."

Satisfied with that, the thing waved a vaguely-defined hand at the manhole cover. "These presents you have concealed will unwrap themselves once the time is right. The delay will be enough to allow your men a safe retreat."

Klein nodded and snuck a glance at the manhole. "...and then?"

" -- 'and then'?" The thing's face split horizontally as it gave a gurgling laugh. "You will count yourselves fortunate that you were not the ones to incur the wrath of my employer."

A breeze wafted down the street, and Klein drew his leather trenchcoat closer around him. "...Mein Gott..."

The thing snorted. "...not quite."

"But what if someone were to find these...presents?" Klein looked worried. "Some handsome, misunderstood Chorman soldier may uncover them, and make it his mission to cleanse his city of the dark plague unleashed by your packages."

"Mmm." The broad-brimmed hat was nodding. "Truly, Herr Obersturmbannführer, we must hope this does not happen."

Mikhail savored the daydream for a final moment before letting it go. This, he was sure, was more or less precisely how their current situation had come to pass. His dear departed comrades, fellow soldiers as wronged by the Veterans' Welfare Board as he had been, had told him everything.

Old Tomasz in particular had been a fount of information when it came to the unspeakable dealings of Chorma's mortal enemy. Of course Old Tomasz had also attributed his knowledge to direct communications from the Archangel Michael and the benevolent intervention of sentient telepathic whales, but that didn't mean his information was unsound.

But now was not the time for daydreaming. His newest weapon in the battle against the unholy legions had just been completed, and Mikhail was itching with eagerness. In truth there might have been a little anxiety in the itch as well, but not very much. There were very solid and very elementary engineering principles behind the little toy he'd built. And besides, the forces of Light were on his side.

There was the compressed-air tank, easily rechargeable with a hand pump borrowed from an abandoned auto repair shop. From the same shop he had also taken several rubber tires and a trifling amount of gasoline to dissolve the tires in. A metal canister attached to the air tank held the jellied cocktail of gas and rubber, and a sturdy hose snaked away from the fuel canister to terminate in a nozzle garnished by Mikhail's most prized find: a butane welding torch he had found on a bench at a machine shop, obviously unwanted by its former owner.

With the air tank and fuel canister strapped into a military pack on his back, Mikhail tightened his red bandanna around his forehead, grasped the handle of the butane torch, and strode proudly out the door of his seventh-floor penthouse apartment. His head held high, humming snatches of something patriotic, he made a beeline for the spiraling staircase of his hotel.

The stairs groaned beneath him as Mikhail descended from the seventh floor of the Hotel Litvinenko. Floors seven through five passed uneventfully, but on the landing of the fourth floor Mikhail began picking up that faint aroma of overripe fruit, mingling with the less-pleasant fragrance of gasoline and melted rubber. He crept the last ten steps down to reach the landing of the third floor.

Ahead of him on the stairs, the blockade that barred the way down was a jagged mass of deeper blackness in the dim stairwell. He trained his flashlight on the pile of broken furniture, searching for what he already knew was there. And though he expected it, was prepared for it, even welcomed it at this point, the sudden snakelike movement from within the tangle of wood and fabric still made his heart skip a beat.

It knew that he was here. Was it the vibration of his footsteps that gave him away, or the light from the flashlight? could it hear him, or smell him somehow? Of course the infernal growth couldn't *see* him, could it? Plants couldn't see...and this thing was a plant, wasn't it? how could it have been anything else?

Mikhail steeled himself as the slithering thing worked its way through the blockade towards him. The handle of his homemade weapon felt slippery against his palm. I'll teach you to invade my home, he said to himself. Teach you to come into my native country, my hometown, poisoning the very souls of my countrymen.

The thing reached the edge of the blockade and emerged into the open air, extending itself upward like a cobra charmed by a flute-player. In its movements it was indeed snakelike, long and slender like the arm of a black octopus. Reaching a height of better than six feet, the tentacle swayed closer to him, and Mikhail gave his bladder strictest orders not to betray him.

Time stood still. The black ropy thing seemed to hesitate, swelled up in a dozen places, and all at once burst into bloom. Gleaming yellow flowers the size of baseballs suddenly unfurled themselves along the length of the tentacle, their petals translucent as amber. Compared to the flashlight, the glow from the flowers was bright enough to dazzle him. That honeyed scent washed over Mikhail's senses, strong enough to taste it on his tongue.

Ignoring the ringing in his ears, he leveled the nozzle of his new weapon at the bizarre flora growing out of his barricade. Though he had learnt the design of his new toy from his study of enemy weaponry, Mikhail would never have referred to it by anything so un-Chorman as a 'flammenwerfer'.

"Return to the Pit from whence ye came!" Mikhail shouted, and pressed the trigger on his weapon.

A stream of liquid fire blossomed from the end of Mikhail's flamethrower, and rushed out to embrace the unearthly flower.

~~~~~

Metal ground against metal as the bolts slid out of their sockets, unlocking the door. The sound reverberated along the metal walls inside Storage Room 8. Veronika leapt to her feet; Alexei remained sitting.

The door cracked open and Hawk poked the muzzle of her gas mask into the storage room. "Here," she said, and threw a khaki-colored something directly at Veronika's head. The young woman caught the bundle in midair and unrolled it -- it was a mechanic's zip-up coveralls, stained with oil on both knees.

"Get dressed." Hawk flung a pair of well-worn boots onto the floor and stood with folded arms in the doorway, Kestrel peering over her shoulder. Her protective suit was no longer ripped at the throat -- clearly she'd changed into a fresh one while absent -- and there was the slightest of bulges on her shoulder that spoke of a bandage underneath the rubberized fabric.

Smirking, Veronika hopped into the overalls, zipping them up over her hospital gown. The boots were clearly too large and she tugged on the laces, trying to tighten them.

"I've got the sodium-whatever stuff that you were using," Hawk told Alexei. He nodded without looking at her and rose to his feet.

"Ready," Veronika said brightly. Hawk half-turned to her, and though Alexei couldn't see her face her voice gave away her expression.

"You two are going to follow me and do *exactly* as I say," Hawk growled. "I am helping you because it is easier for me to do things this way. If you give me the slightest difficulty you are going to become liabilities very very quickly, and I will take the first available opportunity to shoot you both in the head and do things my own way. Do we understand each other?"

Alexei and Veronika both nodded. Unslinging her AKS-47, Hawk stepped back from the doorway. "Then let's go."

Veronika was first out of the room, clomping along in her oversized boots, and Alexei followed close behind. The muzzle of Hawk's rifle dug in between his shoulder-blades "March. To the loading docks -- quickly now."

In a way it made sense. Anyone who happened to be in the halls of the Lubukov Agricultural Labs would not have realized they were witnessing the escape of a patient, a researcher and a renegade soldier. To all outward appearances Hawk and Kestrel were carrying out CSF business, leading two Lab employees along at gunpoint, perhaps for a round of questioning in the shower rooms.

Alexei was more familiar with the Labs and wound up leading the way to the docking area, just behind the requisitions office. The indoor garage at the docks had been seldom used before the CSF's arrival and was cluttered with both lab trucks and the assorted black vehicles CSF had brought. The air was dim and somehow foggy, bitter with diesel fumes. Rows of blue biohazardous-waste bins stood along one wall.

Veronika stopped short, and Hawk turned her rifle sideways to give her a shove. "Keep moving."

" -- what's *that*?" Veronika asked, pointing.

"Nothing. Let's go."

"No, seriously! look above the bins! right there!"

"She's right, sir -- look up there." Kestrel stepped down into the garage with the rest of them, indicating the wall above the wastebins. Hawk looked where he was pointing.

A dark mesh, like a giant irregular fishing net, was clinging to the brick wall above the bins. Though the docks were only half-lit the growth on the wall escaped notice at first glance due to its sheer size: it could have been a pattern on the brick, maybe discoloration caused by water or mold. Only a more careful inspection revealed the leaves growing on the net, the grapelike clusters of berries, flowers of improbable colors. The growth seemed to extend all the way up to the ceiling, where the unusual fogginess of the air made it difficult to make out.

"...some kind of weed," Hawk pronounced at last.

Veronika was unconvinced. "Why's it all black?"

"Because that's the blight," Alexei said, and everyone turned to him. He was staring up at the wall, hands hanging at his sides.

"...but the blight only grows on people." Hawk sounded uneasy.

"Hey, -- d'you think it might be that 'inkweed' stuff they were talking about on the radio?" Kestrel touched the side of his mask. "Remember? the squads who were doing the neighborhood sweeps kept finding mold growing in the houses. Maybe that's the stuff they were seeing."

"Probably." Keys jingling in her hand, Hawk unlocked the door of one flatbed CSF trucks. She gestured impatiently at the green tarp lying in the truckbed. "You two! In the back, under the tarp!"

Veronika clambered over the truck's tailgate, followed by Alexei. When she peeled up the tarp a sour odor wafted out from underneath it, and Veronika wrinkled up her nose. "This thing is hardly going to hide us." She looked to Alexei for support, but he was already lying down on the truckbed, one arm tucked under his head. "Any idiot can just look in the back and see there's two people back here under the tarp. If you think -- "

Hawk pointed her AKS in Veronika's direction and flicked off the safety. Veronika ducked down into the truckbed, pulling the tarp over her body with a rustle of plastic sheeting.

"Ugh," Veronika muttered, holding her breath. The sour smell was much stronger now, and sickly-sweet in a way that made her stomach churn. Beneath her cheek the metal floor of the truckbed was sticky. She felt it when the engine turned over, the vibrations traveling up through the metal into her bones.

In the stinking green darkness under the tarp Veronika listened to Hawk and Kestrel saying their goodbyes. She missed most of the conversation due to the engine noise, but she thought Kestrel might have been wishing his superior good luck, and promising to find her after the quarantine was over.

Hawk threw the truck into gear and it lurched backwards, and Veronika splayed out her arms and legs to stop from rolling into Alexei. She heard the whine of electric motors and the rattling of metal slats as the overhead door slid open, letting the three refugees out of the loading docks.

There was an indefinite length of time where the truck stopped and started, turned corner after corner, and more than once Hawk slowed down to speak to someone who replied in the croaking tones of a gas-masked CSF soldier. Just as Veronika was starting to suspect Hawk had gotten lost in the complex the truck made another sharp turn and suddenly began to pick up speed. A whiff of fresh air snuck under the tarp.

They were out of the Labs!

After weeks in the storage room Veronika was desperate to see the outdoors -- to catch a glimpse of the sky at least, if not the houses and trees -- but common sense held her head down. She lifted the edge of the tarp with one finger, inhaling the early-morning scent of dew-soaked grass.

Veronika had only the vaguest idea where the Lubukov Agricultural Labs were in relation to her house, though she had never visited them before. Nonetheless she remembered that the Labs were a bit north of downtown Khostok. There were big office buildings all around the Labs, she recalled, and some industrial factories, an elementary school not too far away.

And yet there was silence.

Veronika realized she had no clue what time it was. Early morning, judging by the sunlight that seeped under the tarp, but how early? Early enough to account for this complete stillness, this vacuum of sound? Aside from the dull roaring of the engine and the humming of their tires against the asphalt there were no noises -- no honking horns, no pedestrian chatter, no other vehicles. They were traveling along in a dead city, a world without life.

In this stillness Veronika could clearly hear it when the radio in the truck's cab began to hiss and crackle. "Albatross, come in Albatross," Hawk was calling.

"Albatross here," the radio replied.

"Albatross, this is Hawk." She paused. "I've picked up two civilians -- they say they were with an evac group but I think they're from a Red camp."

Veronika's mouth went dry. She glanced over at Alexei but he was lying with his back to her, curled up in the truckbed.

"Copy that, Hawk. Are they clean?"

"Can't tell. Gonna bring them in anyway. They've got no papers though -- can you ID them for me?"

She could leap out of the truck, right now. Veronika couldn't tell how fast they were going, but the adrenaline told her she would make it out alright if she just vaulted over the tailgate and took off down the street. Were they still downtown, or had Hawk diverted off into the suburbs at some point? in what direction were they traveling? how far had they gone?

"Go ahead with the names," Albatross was saying.

"Names are Elena Yuryevna and Nikita Ivanovich," Hawk said. "Last names Sokolov. At least that's what they're telling me -- I've got nothing to confirm that."

"Let me check." The radio buzzed with static for a long minute. When Albatross came back on he was chuckling. "That's a negative, Hawk. Elena and Nikita Sokolov were already admitted to Red Camp Three. I checked with the officer on duty at the Camp and he says the Sokolovs are present and accounted for. You picked up a couple of liars."

Hawk grunted. "I thought so. Thanks for checking."

"No problem. Albatross out."

"Over and out." The radio clicked and went dead. Veronika felt the truck slowing, tilting to one side as Hawk pulled a U-turn and drove off in the opposite direction.

Veronika let out the breath she'd been holding in a long sigh. Then she coughed. "Ugh...why does it smell so bad in here?" she muttered, half to herself.

Beside her under the tarp, Alexei stirred. "They use these trucks to transport the bodies."

So he hadn't been sleeping after all. " -- 'bodies'?" Veronika whispered. The little hairs rose up on the back of her neck. "What bodies?"

"When people die at the Labs, they have to move the corpses someplace." Alexei's voice was hollow. "They use these trucks to take them away."

That was the smell she had noticed: the scent of decay, of death. That's why Hawk hadn't bothered to conceal them any better than this -- they weren't supposed to be invisible. The two of them were disguised as corpses.

In the darkness under the tarp Veronika could just make out the silhouette of Alexei's back. She inched closer to him, grimacing at the stickiness of the metal floor.

"Alexei," she whispered. "What happened to your friend -- "

" -- I don't want to talk about it," he hissed back. "Just leave me alone."

Veronika fell silent. They were picking up speed now, flying along the road toward Red Camp Three.

Alexei did not know or care where Red Camp Three was located. In fact he was trying his hardest not to think. About the camps, about the Sokolovs, about anything. He knew he could hold everything together if he didn't think about any of it.

He had almost succeeded when he felt Veronika's arm slipping over his waist.

Alexei fought back, trying to push her away, but Veronika noticed that he didn't fight very hard. She dragged him backwards into the hug, wrapping both arms around him. Alexei doubled over. "Let go," he said weakly, his voice breaking.

Veronika didn't let go. A moment later Alexei began to shudder, and put both hands over his face.

"It wasn't your fault," Veronika said.

Alexei said nothing. The truck sped onward through an unseen and noiseless Khostok.

~~~~~

"Pelican, this is Osprey. Do you read me?"

"Loud and clear, sir."

"Good. Seagull, do you copy?"

"Yeah -- I'm half suffocated but I copy."

"Say again?"

"I said, I'm half dead from suffocation but I do copy you, sir."

"That breathing equipment may save your life, comrade." Osprey's tone was icy. "You'll be grateful for it soon enough."

"Sorry, sir. I'm ready when you are."

Osprey, commander of the second Volgin River Exploratory Squad, nodded his head. Though he'd never have admitted it, the advanced-protection suits they currently wore made their normal suits seem as comfortable as pajamas in comparison.

Per Akimov's explicit orders the three of them were decked out in heavy-duty metallic protective suits meant to resist high heat and radiation as well as biological and chemical hazards. And as if the suits weren't cumbersome enough there was also the body armor and the wide array of weapons each soldier had been equipped with. A long air hose ran down from the muzzle of their gas masks and into a portable oxygen tank in each soldier's pack, adding to the weight.

It was a bit like wearing a heavy quilt, and not a particularly flexible quilt either. But orders were orders, even if those orders specified dressing up like an astronaut for a simple exploratory mission into a perfectly normal river valley.

Or at least that was how Osprey had felt after receiving his mission guidelines. Now, standing on the bank of the Volgin River, he experienced a new and unexpected thankfulness for their stupid NBC suits. Because somehow, in the interval between the CSF's arrival and this moment, the Volgin River valley had become something other than perfectly normal.

Osprey had been told to expect "poor visibility", but the truth of the matter was that the valley was filled with a fog so opaque it was almost liquid, like a river of milk. From where they stood on the high point of the hill that sloped down into the valley, the trio could see that the fog had risen some twenty feet above where the river had once been. Supposedly the water was still down there, somewhere, though you couldn't see it anymore.

Ten feet below where they stood, the fog began. It was thinner at this height, transparent enough for them to see the weedy tangle of plant life that sprawled over the ground, reaching up toward the top of the hill. The shapes were organic and familiar though the colors were not: the plants in the mist were all black, shading to dark reds and blues at the tips of their leaves.

Inkweed, the men had begun calling the stuff. Suddenly all the reports were full of it -- the black plants seemed to be turning up everywhere in the city, indoors and out.

In spite of its color and sudden appearance nobody had *officially* stated that the inkweed was connected to the ink. In fact that was half the reason that Osprey was here today, preparing to lead his men down into god-knew-what: Akimov wanted some confirmation that the crashed car, the site of the UEC-571 leak, was the origin point for this strange infestation.

Looking down into the mist and the half-seen black foliage it concealed, Osprey realized how appropriate their suits were. If they were geared up like astronauts it was only because they were venturing into what might as well have been alien territory.

Osprey looked to his right and found Pelican standing there, head held high, awaiting orders. Seagull was to Osprey's left -- he was fidgeting with his air hose, tugging on his mask.

Osprey's voice crackled out of the speaker inside Seagull's helmet. "If you break that seal you'll be sorry, I promise you."

Seagull dropped his hands. "Understood, sir!"

"Nevermind." Osprey waved a hand in the air. "Let's move out!"

The three of them began to make their way down the hill, Osprey in the lead. Through the suit everything sounded muffled, faraway; the loudest thing Osprey heard was his own breathing, hissing through the air hose.

He almost expected to feel the temperature drop when they waded into the fog, but from inside his suit he felt nothing. If he'd stepped into water there might have been a change in pressure, squeezing his suit around his legs, but there was none of that here. The mist rolled around his legs, creeping up over his knees, eddying around his hips. Still Osprey pushed forward, in silence.

Halfway submerged in the mist, Osprey lost sight of his feet. The inkweed grew nearly to his waist in some places, thick stalks bearing glossy black leaves with ruby tips. Some trick of the sunlight refracting through the mist made the flowerbuds on the inkweed seem to shimmer as the soldiers passed them by. The ground underfoot was choked with other sorts of inkweed, crisscrossing the ground like creeper vines, and Osprey felt it tugging at his boots as he shuffled downhill.

"Pelican?"

"Here, sir."

"Seagull?"

"I'm here too." Their voices on the radio were tinny, indistinct, but at least he could hear them. Osprey turned and saw that Pelican was chest-deep in the milky fog, his metallic suit gleaming in the weakening sunlight.

"Let's stay together men," Osprey said gruffly. "We don't want to lose sight of each other in this stuff."

Both soldiers answered in the affirmative. Now the mist was lapping at the eyepieces of Osprey's gas mask, rolling over his head like waves breaking at the shore. There must have been a breeze blowing. He found himself tilting his chin up, as if trying to keep his face above water. Feeling ashamed, Osprey pulled his head down and let the mist swallow him up.

'Low Visibility.' What a joke. Osprey couldn't see five feet in front of him. He put both hands out, feeling his way, pushing past the taller and sturdier inkweed plants. The leaves brushed over his eyepieces, scraping softly along his arms. Some of the plants were ridiculously large, and as they progressed toward the river they seemed to be getting bigger. A few were even taller than he was. It had been just over a month since the CSF had been called into Khostok; could this jungle really have grown in just a few weeks?

The sunlight dimmed the further down the riverbank they went. Though it was growing darker, the strange refraction on the inkweed flowers seemed to be intensifying, the glow piercing through the blanketing fog around them. Pinpricks of light gleamed and vanished in the mist, winking on and off like Christmas lights. Watching them was beginning to make Osprey dizzy, and he forced himself to look straight ahead.

At least they were walking on a slope, he told himself. At least there was no possible way to get lost down here in the valley. If you were walking downhill, you were moving toward the river, and if you walked uphill, you were moving away from it. How he wished he were walking uphill right about now.

"Pelican?"

"Here, sir."

"Seagull?"

"Right next to you, sir."

Osprey stopped, looking left and right. Whiteness surrounded him, impaled through and through by the spiny black shapes of the inkweed. Multicolored fireflies danced in the billowing whiteness around him. "Eh? You're where?"

"I'm right next to you," Seagull replied.

"Negative -- you must be next to Pelican." Osprey checked over his shoulder and found nothing but fog. "I can't see anyone."

"...neither can I, sir." Even over the radio he could hear the uneasiness in Pelican's voice.

"Seagull," Osprey called out. "Are you sure it's one of us? could be one of these goddamn weeds. There's a lot of -- "

"-- no, it's definitely a person." Seagull hesitated. "...uh, Osprey sir, would you wave your arms, please?"

" -- Say again?"

"Just wave your arms in the air for a second. Please."

Osprey waved a hand overhead. "I'm waving. Do you see it?"

"...no." Now Seagull was the one to sound nervous. "Pelican, you wave your arms now."

"Okay, I'm waving."

Osprey was still looking around, trying to place his men. Seagull and Pelican were nowhere to be seen -- the two of them might as well have been on the moon. "Seagull? was it Pelican you saw?"

"...no," Seagull replied. "It's gotta be someone else."

"Who? a soldier? civilian?"

"Can't tell." His tone grew bolder. "Shit, I'm gonna go see who this is. Could be someone got lost down here -- can't see your hand in front of your face, it'd be easy to lose your way. Gimme a second..."

Osprey strained himself trying to hear. Seagull's raspy breathing came to him over the radio link, mingling with the sound of his own ragged breaths, but other than that the stillness was absolute. Colored sparks swirled around him in a ceaseless ballet.

"Hey there," Seagull called softly. "Hey, you! can you hear me? are you lost?" He paused. "We're with the CSF -- don't worry, we're not going to hurt you. If you just -- ah!"

Osprey jumped. "What? what?!"

"I-it moved!" Seagull stammered. "It's coming towards me."

"Dammit, Seagull!" Osprey felt like he was wound tight enough to snap. "Who *is* this person?"

"I can't tell, sir!"

"What do you mean, you can't tell? what are they wearing?"

"I-I can't really see them..." Seagull's voice was shaking. "Looks like they've got some sort of helmet on...like a motorcycle helmet...it's tinted, you can't see the face..."

"...motorcycle helmet?" Pelican echoed.

"That's what it looks like...they're still coming towards me, they're...they're...oh..."

"Seagull?!" Osprey shouted. "...Seagull!"

Over the radio link Osprey heard Pelican calling out to his comrade as well, his voice taut with fear. Suddenly it felt like the fog was pressing in on him, the inkweed crowding closer. The sound of his own breathing thundered in his ears.

"*Seagull*!!"

When he finally answered, Seagull's voice was barely above a whisper. "...it's not a helmet."

"What? say again! repeat that!"

"The thing is right here in front of me," Seagull sounded dazed. "It's not wearing a helmet. That's its face." He groaned. "It has no face."

Osprey couldn't breathe. Static crackled over their radio link, loud in the stillness.

"S-sir," Pelican broke in, and he sounded about as terrified as Osprey felt. "Some of the re-reports we've gotten...it's possible that the..." he swallowed audibly. "...the...the atmosphere down here could be toxic...it-it could be causing visual disturbances, hallucinations, delusions...it's possible that's what's happening..."

"I hear you," Osprey replied, and felt the tiniest bit braver. He hadn't even considered that. And hadn't Seagull been fiddling with his oxygen hose before they went down? If his apparatus had sprung a leak he could have been breathing in toxic fumes from the beginning. Plenty of chemicals could cause a soldier to hallucinate. And a faceless stranger could only have been a hallucination.

Come to think of it, Osprey himself was beginning to feel dizzy, even lightheaded. His ears were ringing too. He'd been too frightened to notice it beforehand, but maybe the swirling lights and the oppressive silence weren't entirely to blame for it. And here they were, three grown men who'd gotten drunk on poisonous gases and were jumping at their own shadows.

"Seagull, Pelican!" Osprey said. "I'm ordering a retreat! One or more of us may have been compromised by hazardous fumes in the air. Let's regroup on the riverbank above the fog line! Do you copy?"

"Copy, sir," Pelican replied, his voice tremulous with relief.

"Seagull?"

There was no answer. The mist flowed around him like a noiseless river.

"*Seagull*!!"

"He may have fainted, sir..." Pelican sounded desperate to believe this was true. "The fumes in the air...he may have passed out. Uh, h-how should we proceed?"

What he meant was, do we have to go find Seagull and carry him out? A cold hand reached into Osprey's abdomen, squeezing around his intestines. He knew the protocol for this kind of thing, of course. And yet --

In the end, the commander of the second Volgin River Exploratory Squad did not have to make that call. All of a sudden Seagull gave out the loudest and most terrified scream he had ever heard, and before he knew it Osprey was sprinting up the hill, back the way he'd come, slapping inkweed out of his way as he ran.

Nothing, not even the bulkiness of his protective suit, could have slowed him down. He tripped on a tangle of weeds, fell, and scrambled on his hands and knees for several yards before regaining his feet and continuing his mad uphill dash.

Seagull screamed again, and the sound inside Osprey's helmet was earsplitting. Osprey screamed back, clawing at his mask as he ran, trying to tear it off.

He felt like he'd been running for hours when his head finally broke through above the mist. Osprey looked around wildly, realized he'd been running almost parallel to the river, and bolted off to the right, towards the top of the hill. Wheezing, gasping for air, he stumbled up out of the inkweed and collapsed onto the green grass.

"Sir! Osprey! Sir! Can you hear me?"

Osprey rolled over onto his back, chest heaving. Little puffs of white cloud drifted past in the blueness overhead. Pelican was still calling him, but at the moment all Osprey could do to was lie there panting.

"Sir! sir!" The ground shook as Pelican came pelting up to him -- it seemed that they'd emerged from the mist several yards apart from each other, and a good quarter-mile downriver from their original entry point. Slope or no slope, they were lucky to have found their way out of the river valley at all.

"Sir!" Pelican's masked and helmeted face loomed over him, blotting out the sunlight. "Sir! are you hurt?!"

" -- fine -- " Osprey managed. He took Pelican's offered hand and let himself be pulled into a sitting position. His head was still spinning, but the dizziness and the ringing in his ears had subsided.

"Sir, I, uh...I didn't see..." Pelican didn't finish the thought. Both men turned together toward the river, toward the line where the grass stopped and the mist and inkweed began. Neither of them spoke for a long, long time. Somewhere faraway a bird started to sing.

"We'll have to report this," Osprey said, once he'd caught his breath. Pelican nodded.

"We'll report that...the three of us went down to the Volgin River, as ordered." Osprey grunted as he heaved himself back onto his feet. "Shortly after entering the area, all parties involved became intoxicated by what we suspected to be hazardous gases. The decision was made to withdraw, but the soldier codenamed Seagull succumbed to the effects and was unable to retreat."

"Understood, sir." Pelican offered Osprey his shoulder, and the commander tossed an arm over Pelican's back for support. Together they started to trudge away from the river, back to their waiting vehicle. Osprey kept his eyes on the ground as he walked -- he was so grateful to see plants of a normal, healthy shade of green that he could almost have wept.

"And what about...that thing?" Pelican asked.

"What thing?"

"You know...the thing that Seagull found."

Osprey closed his eyes briefly. "That was a hallucination," he said, and prayed that this was true.

~~~~~

Veronika must have dozed off in the back of the truck while riding to Red Camp Three, though she didn't recall falling asleep. It seemed that she was awake one moment, holding Alexei, and the next thing she knew the truck had stopped, the tarp was gone and Hawk was kneeling over her, twisting her arms up behind her back.

"*Hey*! What -- "

Cold steel slid around her wrists, and Veronika heard the click as the handcuffs were locked. When she started to thrash Hawk struck her over the ear, and her head rebounded off the truckbed with a metalling *pang*. A knee came down in the middle of her back, pinning her as her other wrist was cuffed.

"There," said Hawk, and stopped kneeling on her. Her head throbbing, seething with outrage, Veronika flopped over onto her side and found Alexei lying there beside her, already handcuffed like she was. He looked exhausted, red-eyed.

Hawk bent down next to them. "Don't say a word," she whispered, then grabbed both of them by one arm. Alexei and Veronika were dragged out of the truckbed, over the lowered tailgate and plopped down on their feet on the asphalt.

She was still half-awake, and Veronika's surroundings came to her in a blur of impressions. They were in a parking lot, surrounded by black CSF vehicles like the truck that had brought them here. The lot was ringed by a tall chain-link fence that was clearly a recent addition. Beside the lot was a vast domed building gaily painted in red and decorated with golden stars. The building was set about with double doors, most of which were sealed over with nailed wooden planks and coils of barbed wire.

"...the concert hall?" she murmured under her breath. Hawk jabbed her in the back with the muzzle of her rifle and Veronika stumbled forward. Prodding them along, Hawk herded her two captives toward the building entrance, up a flight of steps to the largest pair of double doors.

Two guards were stationed at the entrance, leaning back against the wall as they chatted with each other. Above the double doors, covering the metal letters that spelled out VICTOR KURYLENKO CONCERT HALL, someone had hung a hand-painted cloth banner that proclaimed the building's new name to be RED CAMP THREE.

One of the slouching guards tilted his head in Hawk's direction. "Good morning, comrade. What's this here?"

Hawk gave Veronika a shove that almost sent her sprawling facefirst onto the marble floor. "Found these two trying to sneak into one of the Blue camps. Pretty sure they're not clean. We've got extra beds here?"

The guards looked at each other. "Sure, we've got beds to spare," said the second one, a hint of laughter in his voice. "There's more and more vacancies everyday."

"Go on in," said the first soldier, and held open one of the doors. Hawk saluted them and Veronika hurried forward lest Hawk decide to push her again. Alexei came after her, dragging his feet, and as Hawk stepped inside the door boomed shut behind them.

~~~~~

Nikita was not a religious man, but he'd quietly given thanks to whatever gods were listening when Elena's fever had broken. The stains on her chin had not gone away, of course -- it couldn't be said that the heavens were excessively merciful -- but at least she had slept a little, and Nikita was not ungrateful for that small blessing.

Still, she had been very weak afterward, and that had alarmed him. He had supplemented the increasingly watery stews the soldiers provided with the few bags of nuts and dried fruit that he had found in the camp. Of course he had not told Elena that the treats had been "found" in the suitcases left beside one of the recently-emptied cots; that might have upset her, and in her condition he didn't want her to overtax herself.

She didn't need to know that her uncle had been sitting up at night, watching the other inmates sleeping, waiting for the CSF soldiers to stop at someone's bed and check their vital signs before quietly bearing the body away. There was no need to bother her with such morbid stuff.

But when Elena woke him that morning, Nikita's first impression was surprise. "You're out of bed!" he said sleepily, rolling over. Automatically he felt her forehead. "How are you doing? did you sleep?"

Elena looked brighter and more awake than she had in days. "Veronika's here!" she declared, tugging on his shirt.

"...who?"

"Veronika -- you know, the lady we met at the park!"

"Oh, her..." Nikita remembered now; the woman at the processing center with the inkstained arm. The one who'd been buried alive under a pile of CSF soldiers. He wouldn't have imagined Veronika had lived through that, let alone that she would somehow turn up at Red Camp Three.

He would have explained this to Elena, but by the time he was fully awake she was halfway across the auditorium already, weaving through the rows of beds. Nikita pushed himself up on his elbows, alarmed, and then he saw where Elena was heading.

On the far side of the room were two people, hands behind their backs, waiting while a CSF soldier unlocked their handcuffs. One of the people was a skinny young man with dark hair, unknown to Nikita, but beside him was a woman in mechanic's coveralls who looked startlingly familiar. Of course the resemblance might have been coincidental -- Veronika couldn't have been the only person in Khostok with hair that long -- but then the woman in coveralls caught sight of Nikita's niece.

"Elena!"

The woman knelt down and Elena ran right into her open arms. Nikita heaved himself out of the cot, took a second to straighten his rumpled clothing, and jogged across the auditorium to meet her.

Veronika -- and it was indeed her -- looked up as Nikita arrived. "Hey there!" she said, beaming at him. "Good to see you both!" Elena was clinging to Veronika's waist, and the young woman gave her an affectionate little squeeze. "How've you been?"

"Um, we're fine." Nikita didn't want to be rude, but he was more than a little bewildered. Not only was she still alive, but Veronika looked entirely too healthy for someone who'd tangled with a barbed-wire fence and six CSF soldiers not so very long ago. Of course the coveralls concealed most of her skin, but there were no scars on her face or her arms or --

-- her arms!

Nikita did a quick double-take. Her arms! both of them were clear, a normal healthy shade of tan. It was as if she'd never had the blight at all.

"You -- " Nikita caught himself an instant before he blurted out something stupid. The soldier who'd uncuffed Veronika was still standing behind her, as if waiting for something, and the young man who'd come with her was staring at Nikita with an unreadable expression in his gray eyes.

"Don't worry -- they're OK." Veronika tilted her head towards the auditorium doors. "Why don't we talk out there?"

Nikita followed as Veronika led them all out into the hallway, several yards down from where the portable chemical toilets had been planted. The doors at the end of the hall had been locked and barricaded, and as a result the far end of the hallway didn't see much traffic. If you didn't mind the proximity to the toilets it was a good place to get some privacy.

Nikita glanced back and forth between Veronika, the soldier, and the young man. Elena was still clutching Veronika's hand. "...what's going on?" Nikita asked at last.

Veronika smiled. "Sorry, I should have introduced you. This is Alexei Nikolaevich -- " she tapped the young man on the shoulder. " -- and this is Tatyana Igorevna."

The soldier gave a warning growl, and Nikita took a step back. Veronika didn't seem to notice. "Alexei, Tatyana, meet Nikita Ivanovich and Elena Yuryevna."

"Hullo," said the strange young man, looking away.

"Um, hello," Nikita replied.

"You're a girl?" Elena was wide-eyed in astonishment. The soldier -- Tatyana -- looked down at her and nodded, once.

Nikita scratched the back of his head. "Nice to meet you both, but..." he looked helplessly at Veronika. "...how did you get here? the last time we saw you..." He didn't want to say more. Veronika had claimed the two strangers were okay, but talking about a cure for the blight seemed especially dangerous.

"I got some help from these two," Veronika gestured at her strange companions. Nikita thought he heard Tatyana give a snort of disgust but he might have been mistaken. Veronika's voice dropped to a conspiratorial whisper. "The three of us are here to get you and Elena out of Khostok."

"We get to leave?!" Elena squeaked, and Veronika shushed her gently. "Yes, we're going to leave!" she said. "We're going to Byatin -- how does that sound?"

"Great!" Elena was bouncing on her toes. "When are we going?"

"Soon, very soon."

"You're not serious!" This was a bit too much for Nikita to take in all at once, and not all of it was making sense to him."...why would these people want to help us?"

Alexei coughed. "Um...the truth is, I used to work at the Labs."

"Eh? You did? at the Lubukov Agricultural Labs?" Nikita leaned forward. "You worked with my brother then! Yuri Ivanovich -- you must have met him there, he's one of the senior researchers..."

Alexei nodded. He was looking down at his shoes, hands in his pockets.

"Well -- where is he?" Nikita checked over his shoulder, as if his brother might be lurking somewhere nearby. "Did he come with you?"

Alexei said nothing. Veronika had suddenly become absorbed in a loose thread on the cuff of her coveralls and even Tatyana was looking off toward the chemical toilets, as if lost in thought.

Elena tugged on the hem of Alexei's shirt, and he looked at her. "Do you know where my papa is?" she asked.

A kind of spasm passed through the young man's face. "He....he's...he's still at the Labs," Alexei said. He shot a glance in Nikita's direction. "He asked me to help get you two out of the city."

"He did?" Nikita frowned. "Why wouldn't he come himself?"

"Uh, they were watching him too closely for him to get away." Alexei scuffed the toe of his shoe along the tiled floor. "He was working on the blight, you know...important stuff. He said he'd catch up with us later."

Elena's face fell. Nikita reached out and pulled her closer to him, patting her head. "And what about you?" he said, looking up at the silent soldier.

Tatyana shrugged. "I'm being blackmailed," she said sullenly.

"She's still helping us though," Veronika added. "So don't worry."

Oh, Nikita was still plenty worried. Not worried enough to pass up the offer of escaping the camp, but still... "Well, thank you both," he said. "For being willing to help us."

Tatyana grunted something in reply, then leaned over and tapped Alexei on the shoulder. "Can I speak to you for a minute?"

Nikita stepped back as the soldier excused herself and went off with Alexei, disappearing around a bend in the hallway. Once they were out of earshot he sighed. "They're...a little odd, aren't they?"

Veronika nodded sympathetically. "I know this is all kind of sudden...sorry about that."

"No, no, it's fine -- better than fine, really." He took another look at her arms, marveling "Really, how'd you get rid of the blight? You *are* cured, aren't you? at the processing center your whole arm was..."

Veronika rolled her sleeves back to show him. "Ask Alexei -- he gave me something that did this. Once we're in a safe place we can do the same for your niece." She winked at Elena. "Just don't tell anyone I was cured, eh? People here would kill to know how it's done, and there's not a lot of medicine to go around."

Before the evacuation Nikita might have objected. *Let's cure everyone*, he might have said. *There's no reason to keep the cure to ourselves. Other people deserve it just as much as we do.*

But that was the old Nikita, the one who didn't know what it was like to eat watery cabbage stew for weeks on end, or to see men vanish for trying to save their fathers, or to watch his niece getting sicker without being able to help her. Now he knew better -- nobody deserved the cure more than his brother's daughter.

Meanwhile, thirty paces away, Tatyana ducked into a doorway and pulled Alexei in after her. " -- do you hear anything?" she asked urgently.

"Huh?"

"Do. You. Hear. Anything." Tatyana shook him a little for emphasis. "Like music, orchestra music."

Alexei shook his head. Tatyana swore colorfully and clutched at her mask with one hand.

"What's wrong?"

"*I* am hearing music," she said. "I thought they might have been playing it over the loudspeakers in here." She chuckled. "I think it's Tchaikovsky, but it's hard to tell."

Alexei just stared at her. "I didn't know you liked classical music."

"There's a lot you don't know."

Alexei ignored the remark. "Is your shoulder itching?"

Tatyana nodded. "Like the devil. That's bad, isn't it?" She searched Alexei's face, then swore again when she saw his expression. "I need you to have a look at my shoulder." She turned both directions, scanning the hallway. "You can't do it while I'm in uniform -- I'll have to dress like a civilian. I've got to get out of my suit."

Before Alexei could object Tatyana was already moving off down the hallway. "But you don't have any other clothes..." he muttered, watching her retreating back.

~~~~~

"We'll have to go soon," Veronika was saying.

"Of course."

Nikita had located three empty cots in the auditorium, all standing side by side, for the three newcomers to use until they were rested enough to make their escape together. Nikita had reasons to anticipate that the cots' former occupants, a married couple and their teenage son, would not be returning to reclaim them.

Veronika was sitting on one of the cots, Elena at her side, leaning forward to whisper with Nikita. Alexei was sitting crosslegged on another cot, shoes off, looking blankly into the distance.

"Now, the Volgin River Bridge is probably going to be guarded," Veronika murmured. "They'll be expecting people to try and escape the city that way. That leaves two options: going north up into the mountains, or trying to cross the river to the south."

Nikita frowned thoughtfully. "We could spend days trying to get over the mountains, and we're hardly equipped to be camping out in the woods."

"I like camping," Elena put in, and Veronika petted her head. "Camping with no tents isn't a lot of fun, sweetheart."

"So how about the river, then? If we find someplace shallow enough..."

" -- then you can expect to be picked off by the Special Forces as soon as you're across," someone interjected.

Everyone jumped. A tall and powerfully built woman was standing beside their cots, looking down at them in disdain. Her blonde hair was tied back in a loose ponytail and the flush on her cheeks contrasted with the brilliant blue of her eyes. She carried a bulging khaki backpack slung over one shoulder. In spite of her clothes -- she wore a rumpled men's tee shirt, jeans and heavy boots -- and her sour expression, the woman was uncommonly attractive.

"They'll be patrolling the riverbanks too, not just the bridge," the Valkyrie sneered. "You won't last ten minutes."

"Uh..." Nikita had gone pale. "...excuse me, comrade...we were just..."

"It's me, it's me." The woman dropped her backpack on the floor and sat down on Alexei's cot.

Nikita coughed. "Wait -- Tatyana?"

Tatyana nodded. Elena's eyes were huge. "You're that soldier!"

"Sshh -- it's a secret!" Veronika said quickly. Elena clapped both hands over her mouth. Nikita was still boggling at Tatyana, blushing as he did so.

Ignoring them all, Tatyana poked Alexei in the arm, snapping him out of his trance. "Would you take a look at me now?"

"Oh...okay." Alexei turned to her. If he was at all startled by her unmasked appearance there was no sign of it in his grey eyes. Tatyana pulled open the collar of her tee-shirt, exposing her shoulder, and Nikita gave a little hiss.

"She's...how did she get infected?" he whispered to Veronika. "I mean, she was wearing a protection suit..."

Tatyana gave the two of them a look of purest venom. "Why don't we give them some privacy," Veronika suggested, standing up. "We can go over to your cots to talk, how about that?"

Tatyana continued to glare as Nikita, Veronika and Elena moved away to a different part of the room.

"Where'd you get the clothes from?" Alexei asked.

"Oh, that," Tatyana grunted. "There's a bunch of spare luggage in the CSF offices here at the camp. They don't throw any of it away."

"You mean, it belonged to one of the people being held here."

"He won't be needing it anymore."

Alexei gave up. "Lie down," he said, and with a sigh Tatyana did so. Bending over her, he tugged down the collar of her shirt to get a better look at the bite wound. The two dark semicircles left by Veronika's teeth were barely even visible now; they had melted into the shiny black patch of ink that covered Tatyana's shoulder, almost as large as the palm of Alexei's hand. He shook his head. "That's...not good."

"What? what?"

"I don't know how she did that." Alexei bit his lower lip. "You've definitely caught the blight, but...it's progressing way faster than normal."

Tatyana glowered up at the ceiling. "I'll kill her."

"That wouldn't do anything to cure you."

"No, but it'd make me feel a whole lot better." She reached into the pocket of her jeans for something which she pressed into Alexei's hand. "Here. Use this."

Alexei looked at what she'd handed him: a small bottle and a disposable syringe. Sodium thiopental. A cold shudder passed through him and was gone.

"I said I'd use this on you when we got out of the city," Alexei reminded her. "Besides, you saw the girl...if anyone needs this, it's her."

Tatyana's eyes flashed. "You're not *getting* out of the city unless you use this on me right now," she said. "I'm not going anywhere like this. And you heard those two talking -- they couldn't escape from an unlocked car. You're all as good as dead without my help, *including* that girl."

Alexei went to stand up and Tatyana seized his wrist, dragging him down until they were face-to-face.

"You give that to me," she snarled, "or I'm going march right over there and tell that kid that she's an orphan now."

Halfway across the auditorium, on his own cot. Nikita was out of ideas. "That soldier woman was probably right about the river," he admitted. "They'll be patrolling."

Veronika glanced over at Elena, who was napping peacefully on her cot. "But we can't take the mountains," she protested. "Even if we knew the route -- which we don't -- we'll come out to the north of Khostok. Byatin's to the south of us."

"We could try for Kurgitzky?"

"We'll be on foot," Veronika reminded him. "Kurgitzky's sixty miles away."

Nikita groaned. "But if we take the -- hey, what's going on?" He lifted his head. There was a minor commotion in the auditorium, six rows away from where they sat. People were standing up, laughing and hooting, some of them shouting encouragement.

"Sounds like a fight."

"Yeah, that happens a lot here. I think people are...wait a second." Nikita rose to his feet. "Shit, it's your friends! they're the ones fighting!"

Veronika leapt up from the cot.

Perhaps nobody was more surprised than Alexei when he realized he'd actually punched Tatyana in the face. But he only had a moment to reflect on his newfound impulsiveness before two hands seized his shirt and Tatyana tackled him to the floor of the auditorium. The little bottle of thiopental rolled away under the cot as Tatyana shook him by the collar, banging his head against the floor.

"You want to fight with me?!" she spat, red-faced. Alexei thrashed and kicked but with Tatyana straddling his waist there wasn't much else he could do. He swiped at her face and she released his shirt to grab his hands, pinning them over his head. Someone nearby was cheering them on.

"You're insane." Tatyana held him down, watching Alexei struggle. There was little doubt who was stronger. "I could kill you."

Alexei surged upwards, arching his back, then collapsed again. He was panting. Tatyana studied him carefully. "That's what you want, huh?"

Their eyes met for a second. Alexei turned his head away.

"I thought so." Tatyana's flush was fading, her breathing returning to normal. One corner of her mouth was reddening where Alexei had hit her. "You *are* crazy."

Alexei stubbornly refused to look at her.

"Listen...what happened to your friend was not my fault. It wasn't your fault either."

Alexei still wouldn't meet her gaze, but Tatyana could see him clenching his teeth. She released him and stood again, dusting off her jeans. One of the auditorium hecklers gave a shout of disappointment that the fight had ended so quickly. Alexei lay where he'd fallen.

Tatyana checked her lip, found that she wasn't bleeding, and lay back down on the cot once more. "Guys!" Veronika exclaimed, hurrying up to them. "What's going on?!"

Tatyana waved her away. "Nothing."

"'Nothing'?!" Veronika looked down as Alexei pushed himself back upright again, rubbing the back of his skull. "What happened?"

"Nothing," Tatyana repeated. "Just leave us alone."

Veronika looked to Alexei, but he wouldn't face her either. After a minute's hesitation Veronika huffed and stalked away, glancing back over her shoulder in case they two started up again.

Tatyana waited until they were alone. "I'm sorry," she mumbled.

Alexei reached under the cot to retrieve the thiopental and the syringe from where they had fallen. His hands were shaking.

"I really will get you all out of the city...I promise," Tatyana went on. "I just can't think straight with symphony going on in my head." She closed her eyes for a moment, wincing. "There's cannons going off now -- you have no idea what it's like."

Alexei rose and seated himself on the edge of the cot. "Cannons?"

"Sounds like it."

Unwrapping the syringe, Alexei fitted the needle in place and carefully pierced the top of the bottle. Clear liquid flowed into the syringe chamber. "If it's Tchaikovsky, then that must be the 1812 Overture."

Tatyana's eyes opened. "...I think you're right," she said.

Alexei pulled the syringe out of the bottle and jabbed it into Tatyana's arm. She flinched as it went in, but didn't complain. The moment he withdrew the needle Tatyana's hand shot out and seized his wrist.

"How much did you give me?" she demanded.

"Enough."

"The same dose you gave that woman?"

"Of course."

Tatyana searched his face and, just for an instant, Alexei could see how frightened she was. Not that he'd given her too little, but that he'd given her too much.

Alexei pulled out of her grasp. He resealed the bottle of thiopental and disassembled the needle, putting it back into its envelope for safekeeping. He rose to leave and Tatyana grabbed the hem of his shirt.

"Stay here," she mumbled.

Alexei sat back down. He watched as her eyelids flickered shut -- she was trying to fight it, he could tell -- and her breathing grew deep and even. It took less than five minutes before Tatyana was out cold, snoring quietly on the pillow. At least she wasn't as loud as Anatoly had been.

"Don't worry," Alexei told her, tugging his shirt free of her hand. "I need to save the rest for Elena."

## CHAPTER TEN

Nikita almost thought the CSF were joking amongst themselves when they referred to the camp rations as "stew". The slop they served the inmates had gone past "stew" and past "soup" and was hovering somewhere around "salty water with shreds of cabbage in it." At least it warmed you to drink it, he supposed.

It had been twenty-four hours since Veronika and her strange acquaintances had arrived. They were no closer to agreeing on an escape route, and now that the soldier woman had slipped into a medical coma Nikita had resigned himself to waiting just a little longer. Elena seemed to have perked up considerably with Veronika here to tell her stories and jokes, and this cheered Nikita more than anything. He was almost feeling optimistic this morning, the "stew" notwithstanding

Elena had gobbled down her breakfast and gone off with Veronika immediately afterward, leaving Nikita to have his hot cabbage water by himself. Bowl in hand, he searched the auditorium and found Alexei on his own cot, having his breakfast alone. Nikita threaded his way through the rows of cots and came up beside the young man.

"Need any company?"

Alexei glanced up and then looked away. He nodded. Balancing his bowl carefully, Nikita took a seat beside him. "How's the food?"

"Awful," Alexei said. Nikita laughed out loud. "Yeah, I know. You've been staying at the Labs since the quarantine came down, right? I'll bet they were feeding you better than this."

Alexei gazed into his bowl. "A little better maybe," he admitted. "Not by a lot."

"Too bad." The two of them ate in silence for a moment. "The soldiers were keeping you all there, huh? the same way we're locked up in here?" Nikita kept his voice down, in case anyone happened to be listening.

"Pretty much. They wanted us to find a cure for them."

"And you did, right?"

Both of them looked over at the cot beside them, where Tatyana's unconscious silhouette was visible under the blankets. Alexei didn't know the odds of one of the CSF soldiers recognizing her, but he had laid a sheet over her head anyway. "I hope so."

"You don't know?"

Alexei shook his head. "Veronika Stepanevna's the only one who's been cured so far," he confessed. "She could have just been a fluke -- a stroke of luck. But if the soldier woman gets better, we'll know it works...and it's safe to use on Elena."

Nikita could appreciate the wisdom in that approach. "Was Yura the one who discovered this?"

Alexei dropped his spoon into his bowl, where it sank of out of sight beneath the cabbage bits. He didn't seem to care. "No, someone else did."

"But you worked with him, right?"

"Yeah."

"Tell me...how's Yura doing?" Nikita prodded. "It's been awhile since I've seen him -- I live in Byatin, you know. I'd just come up to Khostok for a visit when the quarantine hit."

"Um." Alexei was looking into his bowl again. "He's...he's a great guy. Very smart."

"Yeah, that sounds like my brother. You know him pretty well?"

"I guess so."

Nikita couldn't tell if Alexei was standoffish or just very shy. "Well, I know he'll be glad to see his kid again," he said. "And once he gets here we can make some serious plans to get out of this dump and down to Byatin."

Alexei's gray eyes fixed on Nikita. "Uh...well...I don't think he wants us to wait up for him."

"Huh?" Nikita was puzzled. "He's not going to get out of the city by himself, is he?"

"That's what he said," Alexei murmured. "He's not meeting us here -- he said he wanted us to leave Khostok without him."

"Then he's nuts."

Alexei shrugged. His stew had gone cold already, and he bent forward to set the bowl on the ground. "I think...he wants to make sure Elena gets out of here as soon as possible," he said slowly.

Nikita was unconvinced. "You're sure about that?"

Alexei's reached into his pocket and brought out a crumpled color photograph, which he passed over to Nikita. It was of a pink-cheeked young girl in a brand new schooldress, her blond hair plaited into twin braids.

"...this came out of Yura's wallet," Nikita said after a pause. "He always keeps her photo with him -- how'd you get this?"

"He gave it to me."

"Huh." Nikita tucked the photo into his own pocket. "And he asked you to get his daughter out of Khostok without his help?"

Alexei nodded.

Nikita gave the young man a good long look. "He must really trust you."

Alexei shrugged and turned away.

"...something wrong?"

Muttering an apology, Alexei stood up and bolted from the room, capsizing his stew bowl in his hurry. It clattered across the floor as Alexei pushed past two people, leapt over a cot and dashed out of the auditorium without looking back.

"...well, you're a strange one," Nikita muttered, looking down at the spreading puddle of cabbage water.

~~~~~

When you got right down to it, the human body was mechanical in nature. There were rotating joints and hinges, a pressurized circulatory network, complex sensory equipment, a data processing center, even a primitive system for converting organic matter to energy. The body was a badly designed machine, it was true, inefficient and prone to breakage, but it was a machine all the same. All of the uncomfortably unpredictable realities of the human body could be sanitized by thinking of them in these terms.

And machines consumed resources; that was an inescapable fact. Something as straightforward as an automobile needed a wide range of oils and fluids for its proper function, to say nothing of its fuel requirements.

But it wasn't entirely accurate to think of tea in terms of a fuel source, since it had no calories. Rather, Colonel Akimov preferred to think of it as something like a fuel additive. It improved the efficiency of his digestive system and enhanced cardiovascular performance, so the metaphor seemed to fit.

With peerless mechanical precision, Akimov measured out the water from the green ration jug and poured it into the tea kettle that Police Chief Petrenko had provided him with. The chief had been more than helpful when it came to such requests: all Akimov had to do was call down to his office and ask for it. Petrenko had provided the hotplate, the kettle, and a box of Motherland's Finest Black Tea, all of them personally delivered to the door of Akimov's command post by Chief Petrenko himself. Anything that can speed along the evacuation process, Petrenko had said with a smile.

The tea kettle was bubbling away on the hotplate when the call came in through the radio in his gas mask.

"Akimov here."

"Sir, this is Heron again, with Unit Five."

"Ah, yes."

"If you have the time, I wanted to make my report on the second Volgin River Exploratory Squad."

Akimov consulted the clock -- Falcon would not be due into his office for another few minutes. "Go ahead, comrade."

Heron cleared his throat. "As per your orders, the second squad received heavy-duty protection suits with portable oxygen supply." The sound of shuffling documents came through the connection. "Unfortunately, sir, the second squad did about as well as the first. Of the three soldiers sent into the Volgin River area, only two came out."

"We lost one?" This was unexpected. "What was the cause?"

"The survivors weren't very clear on that, sir. The missing soldier supposedly began to hallucinate shortly before his disappearance -- his comrades heard him over the radio -- so it's not unlikely he succumbed to some sort of toxic effects from the fog."

The tea kettle had begun to whistle, and Akimov moved it from the hotplate, folding a dishcloth to set underneath it. "Did he report the same hallucinations as the others?"

Heron hesitated.

"I'm asking if he talked about seeing those 'entities', comrade. The ones with no faces."

"...as a matter of fact, sir, he did."

"I see." Akimov set out a teacup and dropped a tea bag into it. Clouds of steam rose from the cup as he poured in the hot water.

"Sir, I still think there must be a rational explanation for these reports," Heron insisted. "There's been all kinds of rumors going around; the soldiers say the bodybags are going missing from the transport trucks, the inkweed's taking over the city, all sorts of things. I'm sure the men are telling each other about these faceless humanoids they think they're seeing -- the soldiers must be hearing this, and then hallucinating whatever they've heard."

Akimov regarded his teatime layout. As an afterthought, he set out a second teacup beside the first. "And when was I going to be informed about the missing bodybags?"

It sounded like Heron had choked on his own tongue. "Sir, I -- that was just a rumor! I didn't want -- I mean, I didn't think you'd want -- since you'd given orders to burn them, I didn't think you needed us to keep track of every dead body we -- "

"Enough, enough." Heron wasn't a bad soldier, just imprecise. Like a firearm made without quality control: a little too much space in the mechanism here, a component of the wrong shape there. Small errors stacked together could impact the function of the entire device. But Akimov understood that not everyone had been manufactured to the same strict standards.

Heron was still apologizing when someone knocked on the door of Akimov's command post. Falcon was here. " -- is that your entire report, soldier?"

Heron's tone was miserable. "...yes, sir."

"Get me more details on those missing bodies," the Colonel said sternly.

"Roger that, sir."

"And the Volgin River is to be off-limits until further notice. No more exploratory squads."

"Copy, sir."

"Akimov out." He cut the connection before Heron could apologize again. "Enter."

The door of the former Emergency Public Broadcast System office squeaked open, and Falcon poked the muzzle of his gas mask into the room. "Falcon, sir." He saluted.

"At ease, at ease." Akimov beckoned Falcon into the office. "Come have a seat."

Falcon shut the office door behind him, then drew up a chair in front of Akimov's desk and seated himself. "Thank you for seeing me on such short notice," he said.

"Don't mention it. How have you been?"

"Ah...it's been difficult, sir," Falcon admitted.

"So I hear." Akimov's tea had taken on a lovely golden color, and he lifted the teabag out of the cup and tossed it into the trashcan. "Tea?" he offered, indicating the kettle.

"Uh?" Falcon seemed puzzled. "Um...no, thank you, sir."

"Suit yourself." Reaching into his desk, Akimov brought out a length of flexible tubing. He screwed one end into the special gasket on the left side of his mask, then poked the other end of the hose into his teacup. He took a sip, found it to his liking, and smiled inside his mask. "You're sure? It's very good."

"Ah...yes, sir. Quite sure. Thank you anyway."

"Don't mention it. Now...you wanted to see me."

"Yes, of course." Falcon sat up straighter. "It's about Red Camp One."

Akimov tented his fingers together.

"Sir, the situation is out of control. There's not enough food or medicine for all of the incarcerated and they're getting more and more belligerent by the day. We had to shoot several of them last week when they tried to use the cots as a battering ram to break down the doors of their confinement area. The inmates are so heavily blighted some of them aren't even afraid of gunfire anymore."

Akimov nodded to show he was listening. The fluid level in his teacup dropped as he took another sip.

"They can't get to my men anymore, but the inmates are tearing each other to pieces fighting over the rations. The bodies keep piling up and we can't retrieve them. And besides, the hospital atrium's completely overgrown with inkweed -- my men refuse to go in there, even under direct orders."

"Why is that?"

Falcon threw up his hands. "They say there's something living in there, sir. They won't go near that atrium. Short of holding them at gunpoint, I've tried everything I can think of, but they're scared witless. These things they think they're seeing -- "

" -- black things with no faces?"

Falcon sat back in his chair. "...how did you know?" he asked at last, in a tiny voice.

Akimov waved the question away. "In your opinion, comrade, what would have to be done to salvage the camp?"

"...you want my honest opinion, sir?"

"Always."

Falcon took a deep breath. "We'd have to cure them all immediately, then evacuate them to Byatin. That's the only way. "

"You know there's no cure for the blight yet."

Falcon nodded. "I know, sir. But they're going to start eating each other in a few days." He paused. "Actually, they might be doing that already. We can't get close enough to tell."

"I know our budget is inadequate for an undertaking of this magnitude," Akimov said.

"I've made sure the Regional Secretary is aware of it."

"Of course, sir." Falcon said quickly.

Akimov nodded to himself and fell silent. Minutes passed without another word from either party; Falcon could almost have thought that his commander was sleeping. He craned his neck and saw that the fluid level in the teacup continued to decrease, millimeter by millimeter. Not asleep.

In truth Colonel Akimov was chewing over the available data with all the singlemindedness of a high-speed computer. He'd known this was coming, had had the data on Red Camp One well in advance of Falcon's visit, but as yet had produced no satisfactory solution.

Regional Secretary Glukhovsky had been explicit about his orders: first and foremost, the contamination was to be contained in Khostok. The secondary objective was the complete sanitizing of the city -- an order which Akimov interpreted to mean the eventual cure and evacuation of those infected. But Akimov couldn't take forever in accomplishing this second goal; even if he had been allowed an indefinite amount of time, their supplies were not unlimited.

"...comrade Colonel?"

Akimov held up a hand for silence. All in a flash it had come to him: he was laboring under a commitment bias, a sunken-cost fallacy. How embarrassingly organic of him. Akimov knew that human beings were prejudiced in favor of absolute solutions -- no loss of life, no wasted expenses, everything accounted for and neatly tied up -- even when such things were impossible under the present circumstances.

But wasting time and resources while holding out for a mythically ideal resolution was not what a machine would do. Not even when that machine was being graded on its performance, and might run into severe penalties for failing to fill all of its mission parameters. No, a true machine would not hesitate to divert its course in favor of the best possible option.

"...I've also made provisions for this situation," Akimov pronounced at last, and Falcon thought he might have detected a bit of weariness in his commander's tone. "There's no sense in exhausting our meager resources trying to prolong the existence of these few, clearly terminal cases. Our duty is not to these few...it is to the city of Khostok, and to the country of Chorma itself."

"Of course, sir."

"The needs of the many, Falcon." Air bubbles gurgled through his drinking hose as Akimov reached the bottom of his teacup. "You're familiar with the phrase?"

"...of course, sir."

"Good man." Akimov unscrewed the hose and replaced it in his desk drawer. Suddenly he was brisk. "Tomorrow, you will be available at 0800 hours to accept delivery of a package -- I'll arrange to have it brought to Red Camp One."

"Yes, sir."

"There will be directions in the box. This device will not be complicated to use. You will have your most trusted associates unpack it, program it as directed, and place it above the confinement area where the inmates are kept, so that they cannot reach it to damage or disable the device."

Falcon was silent.

"There will be little risk to your men so long as they wear their masks, but I would have them withdraw to other areas anyway. After an interval of forty-eight hours you may reenter the area, though masks should be worn at all times. I would appreciate a personal report on the device's effectiveness."

Still no response.

"Do you understand your orders, comrade?"

Falcon jumped. "Y-yes, sir," he stammered.

"Also, if you hear anything else about these faceless things your men claim to be seeing, you will report that to me directly."

"Yes, sir."

Akimov smiled again, though Falcon couldn't see it. He knew that Falcon was built to more stringent quality control standards than Heron was. He was the ideal man to carry out the initial -- and hopefully final -- implementation of the Stardust device.

"Excellent. You are dismissed."

Falcon rose from his desk chair and saluted with a trembling arm. Akimov saluted in return, and the soldier turned toward the door.

"Oh, and Falcon?"

Falcon looked back.

"Do take some of these with you." Akimov reached over the desk to hand him three bags of Motherland's Finest black tea. "You really should try them; you don't know what you're missing."

~~~~~

At this late hour the soldier codenamed Crane was the only one working at the New Industrial State Bread Company factory. But Crane didn't mind working alone; in fact, he preferred it that way. He wasn't a very social person, and things went so much more smoothly when there was just Crane, the ovens, and the pile of cloth sacks waiting to be loaded into the flames.

He wasn't *embarrassed* about his line of work, oh no. That wasn't the reason he preferred to be alone. But to have other soldiers hanging around trying to make conversation would only have made the job that much more awkward. Working the overnight shift meant he could take as long as he liked, treading and retreading the same path between the pile of bags and the open door of the blazing bread ovens.

Crane's protective suit was both a blessing and a curse under these circumstances. The respirator on his gas mask shielded him from the worst of the stench wafting up out of the sacks, along with whatever contagions might have been present. On the other hand he was confronting an open fire while dressed head-to-toe in rubber and non-breathable fabrics. By the end of his shift he was always just about swimming inside his protective suit. And no matter what he did to them the eyepieces of his mask always fogged up. Yet the peace and quiet he enjoyed made it all worthwhile.

Crane picked up the next cloth sack and frowned to himself. It was a small one, perhaps fifty pounds at the most, with sharp angles jutting out against the cloth. He hated the small ones. Crane chucked the bag into the fiery maw of the oven and paused to take a breather, hands on his knees.

He would tell Mum that he was training for rescue work, Crane decided. Military exercises preparing them for snatching orphans out of burning buildings, things like that. Mum was always complaining that his letters were too short, after all. She didn't seem to grasp that he was not "too busy" to write more; he was making sure that he didn't wake up one day in a roomful of DIO agents. Mum didn't understand that most of the Special Forces missions were too highly classified to write home about.

Like the one he was engaged in right now. Mum wanted to hear all about it, and all he could tell her to do was read the newspapers. Then again, Crane doubted that the situation in Khostok would even make the front page -- the government would likely slip it into a second-page article spinning it as a false alarm, portraying the quarantine and evacuation as simple precautionary measures and depicting those recovered from the blight as victims of mass hysteria and dissident fearmongering.

Of course, all that depended on the blight being cured. If the quarantined citizens couldn't be disinfected then there was a good chance that Operation Starlight would be enacted. And if the Politburo did authorize Starlight, well, the government would have to come up with a better cover story than that.

The flickering glow from the ovens threw dancing shadows on the walls around him. The rest of the NISBC factory was unlit, disconnected from the power grid, forcing him to use his flashlight to get around inside the building. In here in the baking room the open ovens provided light enough, and usually Crane was grateful for that.

Tonight, for some reason, he was not. Tonight something was bothering him. It was probably that small bundle, he decided. Crane didn't know why they couldn't just pack each bag to capacity. He recalled with a shudder the almost-empty sack he'd come across the night before. He had thought that someone had neglected to fill it until he realized there was a tiny fifteen-pound weight sagging at the bottom of the bag. Just a dog, Crane had said to himself. It was only the corpse of someone's pet dog.

The eyepieces of his gas mask were starting to cloud up and Crane moved away from the oven's mouth, toward the orderly row of wheeled bread racks that stood along the left-hand wall. On second thought he would rather have used his flashlight in here. The beam from a flashlight was steady and unwavering, and didn't make it look like the shadows were leaping about on the walls, or that the cloth sacks were squirming around like giant maggots in the orange half-light...

Sudden fright seized him, and Crane kicked the oven door shut. It clanged like a a death knell in the relative stillness of the empty factory, throwing the room into near-absolute darkness. Groping in his utility belt, Crane found his flashlight and switched it on, training the beam on the pile of white cloth sacks. A millisecond after the light struck them everything was still, but in that millisecond he thought he saw something there.

Movement. Something in the sacks had been moving.

His breath snagged in his throat. He swept the light back and forth over the sacks, trying to catch another glimpse, but all was motionless. There was a sidearm holstered on his hip, and Crane's hand unconsciously came to rest on the butt of the gun.

"Hello?"

Even through the mask his voice sounded thin and reedy, full of fear. The sound of it annoyed him. (*You big baby*,) Crane scolded himself. He was probably seeing things.

Still, there was no reason not to check. As a diligent soldier it was his duty to check, maybe even stab a couple of the sacks with the bayonet of his rifle. They were all going to go up in flames in a moment anyway, but it wouldn't hurt to make double-sure that nothing in the pile was still kicking.

Crane slid his firearm out of his holster and flicked the safety off. Feeling slightly foolish, he crept up on the pile and gave the nearest sack a thump with the toe of his boot. Nothing.

"Huh," said Crane. He hesitated, then kicked another bag. Still nothing; no movement, no response. Almost satisfied, he walked around to the other side of the pile and gave the lowest sack a good solid boot.

And something slid off the top of the pile. As it plopped onto the floor in front of him Crane yelped into his mask and leapt backwards, brandishing his gun, preparing to blow the thing away. Then he took a better look at the slithering thing and the full force of his stupidity hit him.

It was only a loose sack. His kicking had dislodged it, no doubt, There was no reason to be so twitchy. Grumbling at himself, Crane bent over to retrieve it.

For a horrid moment the sack felt so light that he was certain he'd come across another one of those fifteen-pound bundles, but closer inspection proved this wasn't the case -- this one was genuinely empty. There was nothing in the bag at all.

One of the truck loaders must have slipped up and tossed an empty bag in with the filled ones. But if that were the case, why was the top of the empty bag still tied off with string? Puzzled, Crane turned the fabric over in his hands and discovered that the sack was damaged: it had split open all along one side.

So perhaps the sack hadn't always been empty -- perhaps it had ripped open and its contents fallen out. Crane dropped the sack and looked around, as if expecting to see those contents lying around somewhere nearby. Maybe it had fallen out on the truck during the trip here, but wouldn't someone have noticed that? or maybe --

Something halfway across the room bumped into one of the abandoned bread racks. The cart struck its neighbor and capsized with heart-stopping crash. This time Crane didn't yelp; he screamed.

When he pinned it with the flashlight beam he found the cart lying on its side on the dusty floor, one wheel squeaking back and forth. Crane gulped and thrust his gun in the general direction of the noise.

"Freeze!"

Of course, since he couldn't see who had toppled the rack, he couldn't tell if they'd frozen or not. Nonetheless he was starting to grasp what was going on. The ripped sack must have been occupied until just very recently, and its contents were now up and stumbling around the baking room, knocking into things. That was probably the movement he'd seen earlier.

All at once Crane regretted his decision to join the Chorman Special Forces. He had objected to working the ovens initially, but that he had gotten used to. The sacks were all tightly closed, after all, and if you didn't think about the shape or the weight it was an easy job to do. He was just the guy who tossed the bags into the oven; nothing to be ashamed about.

But now that something -- some*one* -- had apparently been lively enough to fight their way out of their bag, his job description had changed. Because Crane knew the higher-ups wouldn't allow a non-soldier to leave the New Industrial State Bread Company factory after they'd seen the baking room. The scandal would be immense.

Crane groaned inwardly. He started to advance on the row of bread carts, sweeping the dusty metal racks with his flashlight. He prayed that it was an adult who'd escaped, hopefully a man -- an old man -- but not too old, not a kindly old grandpa or anything -- someone out of shape and preferably ugly. Yes, that would make it easiest.

"Hello?" Crane called out. He stepped behind the bread carts and shone his flashlight into the darkness there. Nothing.

"Is anyone here?"

Silence answered him. Suddenly Crane was aware of how clammy he felt inside his suit, notwithstanding the heat from the nearby ovens. The eyepieces of his mask were still partly clouded. The sound of his own breath, whistling in and out of the respirator, was thunderously loud in his ears.

Crane sidled along the wall behind the bread carts, shining his flashlight on the mildewed boxes and behind the dusty countertops. It would be an ugly old man, he decided. Someone rude and aggressive enough to rush out and fight him, forcing him to shoot the man in self-defense. Not the sort of person who would cry or beg to be spared.

"Come out -- I won't hurt you," Crane said, and cringed inwardly.

Or better yet, the old man would be deranged by the blight, like so many late-stage victims were. Yes, he would stagger towards Crane like the monsters in those splendid American movies his uncle had smuggled from overseas. That would be the best of all -- rather than shooting an innocent and frightened civilian in cold blood, Crane would be a hero, blasting away at something that was practically already a mindless corpse.

There was a clang, a squeak of hinges, and suddenly the room was full of bloody light. Crane's own shadow leapt up on the wall beside him, sending his heart up into his throat.

Someone had opened the oven doors again.

Crane nearly knocked over the entire row of bread carts in his rush to confront the escapee. But there was no need to hurry -- as he popped out from behind the carts he spotted their silhouette at once, standing directly in front of the oven.

Switching the flashlight off, Crane jammed it back into his belt. He gripped his sidearm with both hands. "Freeze," he said, advancing towards the ovens.

The person obligingly held still. Backlit by the wavering orange glow from the fire, Crane could only see their outline: they were thin and young and not especially tall. Female, perhaps, though it was hard to tell. And they seemed to be facing him.

Naturally logic dictated that he shoot first and make observations later, but Crane did not do this. In his defense he was initially curious -- he wanted to see the person's face before he shot them down like a dog -- and then he was too confused to remember to shoot.

Because the person appeared to be naked. The silhouette showed no telltale outline of clothes, no wrinkles that would indicate pants or shirt. Matter of fact, they didn't even seem to have any hair. Just skin, smooth skin...and even that was wrong. For as Crane drew closer, like a moth to a candle, he could see in the flickering light that the person's skin was black all over, black as ink, and shiny as the toe of a polished rubber boot.

Crane struggled to understand what he was seeing, but it was as if his brain had frozen over. Between the ringing in his ears -- when had that started? -- and the fogging of his eyepieces the room seemed suddenly faraway, indistinct.

"You...are you alright?" Crane asked, and his own voice echoed back to him from miles away. The person was coming closer to him, though Crane couldn't tell which of them was moving anymore. He was searching their face, trying to make out their features, not comprehending why he couldn't find any.

Maybe the heat was getting to him. It was so terribly hot in the baking room, after all, and he was so incredibly tired all of a sudden. He was sweating inside his gas mask; he could feel liquid trickling down over his face, running over his upper lip.

But when the sweat ran into the corner of his mouth, the taste was wrong. Metallic, coppery. Not sweat...blood. His nose was bleeding. Crane reached up to touch his face and his fingers bumped into the rubber of his gas mask instead. He'd quite forgotten about the gun in his other hand.

That person was still standing there, waiting for Crane, watching him. He knew they were watching him even though he couldn't see their face, couldn't see their eyes. Why couldn't he see their face? He could see the rest of their body, even if what he saw was incomprehensible: they were black and shiny all over, sexless as a doll.

"...what are you?" Crane whispered.

The thing -- he was no longer sure it was a person at all -- looked at him. And its shoulders began to move. No, not its shoulders...something behind them. Something long and ropy was emerging from the thing's back, rising into the air overhead, curling and uncurling against the backdrop of the oven's glow.

Like the arms of an octopus, Crane thought vaguely. That's what they look like.

One of the tentacles came snaking through the shimmering air towards him. It nosed up against his shoulder like a curious puppy, and at that touch the spell was broken. His brain thawed in an instant. Crane looked at the thing and his mind fractured in a half-dozen places.

"Oh god -- "

A tentacle zipped backward and struck the oven door, closing it. The clang echoed from the rafters as darkness fell like the blade of a guillotine.

There was no time to scream.

~~~~

"It looks like a trashcan," Penguin commented.

Bluejay snorted into his mask. "Maybe."

"I think that's intentional," Falcon said slowly.

The three of them regarded the device in silence. They were in Falcon's office at Red Camp One, formerly the Gurlukovich Memorial Hospital, with the door securely closed. The floor was littered with packing peanuts and instruction sheets were spread across Falcon's desk. An opened box stood off to one side.

To say the device looked like a trashcan was somewhat accurate; it was about the correct size and shape. It was a straight-sided cylinder of metal painted a matte black, and a seam around the top resembled a closed lid. A hinged panel had been opened on one side, and Bluejay was poking around inside while the other two watched.

"A half-hour, right?"

Falcon nodded. Bluejay double-checked the instruction sheet and pressed a sequence of buttons. The LCD display changed from 00:00 to 00:30. A tiny red light began to flash.

Penguin and Falcon both took a step back. "That looks like it's done it," Bluejay observed, shutting the panel.

Working together, the three of them lifted the black canister onto the wheeled cart they used for transporting rations. It was surprisingly heavy. Penguin pushed the cart toward the door as Falcon stepped forward to open it; it was just barely the right size to fit through the door, and the cart bumped against the doorframe as it slid out of the room.

Falcon jumped. " -- careful!!" he hissed.

"...sorry!"

They moved in silence down the hall toward the physical therapy gym. Falcon was fidgeting with his gas mask, feeling the straps to make sure they were in place, screwing his respirator filter down more tightly, checking the seal around the hood of his protective suit.

"...is everyone else out of the building, sir?" Bluejay asked.

"Just about everyone." Falcon was holding the sleeve of his suit up against his eyepiece, inspecting what looked like a tiny rip. "Except the guards in the containment area. We're going to clear them out right now."

"Plenty of time," Penguin said.

Falcon and Bluejay rushed forward to open the double doors that led out into the second-floor walkway above the gym floor. With infinite care Penguin navigated the cart through the doorway.

There were three guards standing on the walkway, and all three of them turned as the cart wheeled into view. They had all heard the announcements over their mask radios and from their postures they were clearly anxious to be dismissed.

"That's the device?" one of the guards asked, drifting over to the cart. "Looks kinda like a trashcan."

Penguin, Bluejay and Falcon lifted the device and gingerly set it down in the middle of the walkway, some distance back from the railing. "We can't put it too close," Falcon said in a low voice. "We don't want someone to throw something up here and knock it over."

As if on command, a shout went up from the gym floor -- one of the inmates had spotted the additional soldiers up on the walkway. If the inmates realized it was too early for the CSF to be throwing rations down they did not seem to care.

Penguin peered over the railing at the swiftly-growing crowd under the walkway. People pointed and shouted; some were raising their fists at him, others were holding up small children. They were so dirty and ragged they could have been war refugees, fleeing their homeland ahead of the waves of enemy soldiers.

No, not refugees -- prisoners. Suddenly they reminded Penguin of all those photos he'd seen in the history textbooks, of prisoners incarcerated in enemy internment camps during the Great Patriotic War. The hollow eyes and hopeless expressions were the almost same.

He backed away from the railing, stomach tumbling. But they're diseased, he reminded himself. We didn't lock them up for their ideology or nationality. They're infected with something bad, something deadly and contagious that we can't cure.

It didn't make him feel much better.

"Penguin!" Falcon called out, and Penguin turned to his superior. Everyone had gathered at the door already, watching the black device as if expecting it to attack. "Come on, comrade! let's move!"

Penguin didn't dare a backwards glance. He hurried to rejoin the others and the knot of soldiers moved out through the doors, guards and all, deserting the walkway above the gym. A half-dozen cries of protest followed them as they left.

Falcon led the group down the hall, toward the elevators at the front of the building. His march turned into a brisk walk and then into a jog, and the rest of his men sprinted to keep up. Nobody spoke, and so when Falcon began to mutter under his breath the lot of them overheard him clearly, even through his mask.

"God forgive me...God forgive me...God forgive me..."

~~~~~

Natasha was asleep when the commotion started. She had been napping a lot recently; there wasn't much else to do in Red Camp One except sleep. She supposed that the lack of food that was making her so tired. Either that, or the steadily-growing dark stains on her stomach and chest. She supposed she should have been worried about the latter, even alarmed, but most of the time she was too groggy to care very much. And she had been having such lovely dreams lately.

The young girl had gotten quite adept at sleeping through the perpetual ruckus in the repurposed gymnasium. As long as she had her head buried under her pillow she could have slept through just about anything. So when her mother awakened her that day it was by snatching the pillow from Natasha's head and whacking her in the face with it.

"Muh!" Natasha threw out both hands, blinking and squinting. "Uhh?"

"Wake up, wake up, wake up," her mother hissed. Natasha kicked her legs out of the cot and her mother grabbed her shoulders, dragging her upright. "Mom, what's -- ow!"

"Hush!" the older woman put a finger to her lips. "Something's wrong."

"Wha?"

"Look over there. Just look."

Bewildered and still half-asleep, Natasha looked where her mother was pointing. "The walkway?" Natasha asked. "They throwing the rations down already?"

"No. Look harder."

Something in her mother's tone had a sobering effect on her. The teenage girl rubbed her eyes and looked again, and at last she saw it.

A thin yellow mist, almost too transparent to see, was pouring in a slow-motion waterfall over the railing of the second-floor walkway. It reminded Natasha of the fog machines at the magic show she'd once seen, the time they had vacationed in Byatin. They made it using dry ice, her mother had explained. But there was no reason for anyone to keep dry ice on the walkway above.

"What is it?"

Her mother had started dragging Natasha away from the cot, away from the misty waterfall. "I don't know," she whispered. Her mouth had tightened into a thin line. "I don't know."

Natasha and her mother weren't the only ones to notice the mist. Though many of the inmates were too sickened by that strange black growth to care very much, a growing number of people were getting up from their cots, pointing and muttering to their neighbors, backing away from the slow downpour. As they retreated they tapped their comrades on the shoulders, shaking them awake, explaining with gestures and whispers. They reminded Natasha of herd animals edging away from a predator, afraid to take their eyes off it.

Several people must have known the mist for what it was, but nobody dared speak it aloud. Moon-eyed, edging towards the further wall of the gymnasium, the inmates watched as the yellow clouds rolled across the carpeted floor toward the drained swimming pool. The mist seemed to be heavier than air, and when it reached the pool it cascaded down into the empty basin, towards the cots assembled along the bottom.

"There's still people in their beds," Natasha commented. Her mother seized her arm, as if to stop her from going to them, but Natasha had no intention of that.

Someone in the pool began coughing.

The effect on the crowd was instantaneous. "It's gas!" someone shrieked, "Gas! they're trying to kill us!"

Three more people took up the cry before the rest of the crowd started trying to hush them.

"Now let's stay calm! we don't know -- "

"Gas! gas!"

"Just like in the war!"

"Now, people, we can't panic!"

"Where's my son?! have you seen my son? he was right here!!"

A wave of people came hurrying up out of the pool. They bottlenecked at the concrete steps leading up to the gym floor, jostling and pushing each other out of the way. As they clambered up they joined the ranks of other inmates already moving towards the furthest wall.

The mist continued flowing down into the pool -- the waterfall had widened now, turning into a cloudy torrent. Several more people had begun coughing, and many of those who weren't coughing were shouting in alarm.

"I can't breathe! I can't breathe!"

A man broke away from Natasha's group and ran straight for the pool, leaping down into the basin. Natasha heard him shouting a woman's name. The crowd was pressing closer around her, tense and whimpering. Someone in the group had started to sob.

"Help! help! help!"

"For God's sake!"

"I can't breathe!!"

"Gas! gas!"

The bottleneck at the pool stairs had become a crush, packed with frantic people. The volume of noise was steadily rising -- people were shouting, swearing, calling out names, frantically begging for help.

An elderly man heaved himself up from the edge of the pool, bypassing the crowd at the steps to clamber out onto the gym floor. He got to his feet, took three steps and fell flat on his face, convulsing violently.

The crowd went insane.

Natasha was shoved aside by a sudden surge of bodies, stampeding like cattle away from from the danger. It sounded like everyone was screaming at once. A cohort broke away from the larger mass of people, charging toward the door of the restrooms. Several of them reached the doorway at the same time and all tried to cram themselves into the restrooms at once, and the crowd behind them hit them like a tidal wave.

More stragglers came stumbling up out of the pool, retching and coughing, collapsing atop one-another to the sound of onlookers' horrified cries. Though she couldn't hear herself over the din Natasha knew that she was shrieking too. Someone lifted her bodily and slammed her up against the nearest wall, and she fought back for a moment before she realized it was her own mother, trying to keep her from getting trampled. She was shouting something to Natasha, face contorted, but the roar of the crowd drowned out the words.

The chaos subsided as the greater mass of people ran out of places to retreat to, but the panic remained. The people at the wall were huddling together like frightened sheep, trying to get as far away from the mist as possible. Those who'd come out of the pool too late remained where they'd fallen, twitching reflexively. Nobody went to help them.

A scuffle broke out over the door to the restrooms -- those packed inside were trying to shut the door, as if that would save them from suffocation, while those outside were still fighting to get in. From all sides came the sound of crying, shouted names, loud wailing, hysterical prayers.

"Comrades! comrades, listen to me! Listen!!"

A man's voice carried over the din. Her mother was half-smothering her in an effort to shield her, and Natasha pushed her back, trying to see where the voice was coming from.

"Comrades! if you listen to me, we can escape! we can still escape!!"

Natasha found the speaker standing in a clear spot on the gym floor, waving his hands over his head. Her blood chilled a few degrees when she spotted him -- the man was one of those late-stage blight cases, so discolored he scarcely looked human anymore. The blotches on his skin had darkened past the bruise-like stains and into a shiny uniform blackness that covered three-fourths of his body. His face was half-stained, as if wearing a mask, and one eyeball had darkened into a black glassy orb like the eye of a rat.

"Listen to me, everyone!" the man bellowed, hands cupped around his mouth. "There's windows on the doors! We can break through the windows and unlock the doors!" He gestured wildly. "We can get out! we can get to the river!!"

Down to the river! that's where they had to go! Natasha took a step towards the man and her mother tugged sharply on her arm, holding her back.

"Come on! someone help me!"

The chorus of panicked voices had died down, though there was still wailing and sobbing. People were listening to the man, at least, even if nobody was moving to assist him. Natasha had seen the doors he was referring to -- they were made of heavy steel, with tiny glass windows set above the doorknobs. And they were on the on the opposite side of the gym, under the walkway that was silently pouring down that lethal yellow torrent into the room.

"Come on!" said the man, beckoning. "The gas is gonna fill the pool first -- we've still got time! if we get the doors open, we can all get to the river!"

A man and a woman broke away from the crowd, charging towards the speaker. Natasha made up her mind and sidestepped her mother, wrenching her arm free. She couldn't close her ears to her mother's frantic shouts but she knew she wouldn't be followed. Not in the direction she was heading.

The moment he saw people hurrying towards him the man turned and ran, heading for the cots. "Grab one of the beds!" he shouted, bending down to seize the metal frame of an upturned cot. The other man caught up to him and snatched up the opposite end of the bed and both of them sprinted off toward the doors.

Natasha followed on their heels as the group swung wide to avoid the downpour of the mist, sliding along the wall to get under the walkway and up to the doors of the gym. Her eyes and lungs began to burn once she was within fifteen steps of that yellow fog, but if she was going to get to the river it hardly mattered.

The steel doors in question were battered and dented from numerous attempts to do precisely what this man was suggesting. Nonetheless Natasha held out a small hope -- the last time someone had tried to use a cot as a battering ram on these doors, a bullet from a CSF soldier had ended the attempt. Now that there were no soldiers anymore they might actually have a chance. Besides, they weren't targeting the doors themselves: they were trying to break the windows.

"On three!" called the blighted man, clutching the cot's frame in both hands. The other man and woman took up their positions behind him, alongside the cot.

"...one! Two! *Three*!!"

They charged, driving the cot forward and into the window. There was a jarring impact. When they drew back the reinforced glass was shot through with cracks, but still holding. "Again!" the ringleader shouted, and the group danced backwards to get a running start. This time the cot missed the window entirely, putting a vertical dent in the window's metal molding.

"Again! We can do it comrades! Lift it high on three! ...ready, one! Two! *Three*!!"

The sound of splintering glass was almost musical. People cheered, and Natasha turned to see a small cluster of people gathered some yards behind them, watching their efforts. The improvised battering ram dropped to the floor as the laborers shouted in joy.

"Good work, comrades! Now let's unlock the doors!" Stepping forward, the blighted man thrust his arm through the narrow opening of the broken window, fumbling around on the outside of the door. More and more people were arriving behind them, holding shirts and handkerchiefs over their mouths, watching in hopeful silence. "You can do it!" someone exclaimed.

The man found the door handle and began yanking on it, wincing as the broken glass stabbed into his shoulder. He fought with the handle for several minutes before withdrawing his arm with a grimace.

"No good," he said, clutching at his arm. Blood was streaming down over his hand. "It's locked from the outside too."

His audience groaned. Natasha could almost hear the rushing of the river; that's how close it was. She felt it in her veins. "I can get through!" she burst out, startling herself. "Put me through the window -- I can go get help!"

Faces turned to her. "Yes, the girl can fit through!" the crowd agreed. The blighted man sized Natasha up, comparing her size to the narrow gap offered by the window. "There's a lot of broken glass," he said. "Are you sure?"

Natasha couldn't have explained how, but she was. "If it means we can all get to the river, then I am."

"Ahh," The man broke into a grin, his black eye glittering. "Come on then, comrade! Let's get you through!"

Natasha stepped forward and was lifted into the air by a half-dozen hands. She reached out herself as they guided her into the window, trying to steer herself through the opening. Other hands gripped the windowframe, closing over the jagged edges, helping her along. Little glass teeth scraped along her shoulder, slicing through her shirt, and Natasha bit down on her lip.

Once her head and shoulders had passed through the window Natasha's weight shifted forward. The people on other side of the door held her legs as she bent at the waist, hands flat against the door, working her way down to touch the floor. "I've got it!" she called back, balancing in a handstand on the tiles. "Let go!"

The helpers released her legs and Natasha tumbled to the ground in an ungainly somersault. Her hands and shoulder were gouged and bleeding and her throat still burned, but she was out of the gym.

Natasha stood. The window behind her was full of faces, peering through at her. "I'm through!" she called out, and a chorus of cheers answered her from the other side of the door.

"Go then, comrade!" The blighted man waved her away. "Go and get help!"

Natasha nodded and, with scarcely any idea where she was headed, turned and ran.

Gurlukovich Memorial Hospital was entirely vacant, and echoes pursued Natasha as she pelted down the hallway. Most of the lights had been shut off and this left her running in darkness or under the crimson glow of emergency lighting. She had the vague notion that the physical therapy gymnasium where she had spent so many weeks was toward the back of the building, which meant she was running toward the entrance.

Red 'EXIT' signs shone at the ends of hallways, tempting her. Natasha tried several of these and found them locked, and she was forced to keep going. The entrance wouldn't be locked, she reasoned. The CSF had to have ways of getting in and out of the building. Of course

Natasha couldn't have known that the CSF had forsaken the ground floor of the hospital some weeks ago, in favor of occupying the second floor exclusively. And she couldn't have known their reasons for doing so, either.

An overhead sign pointing her towards the atrium filled Natasha with sudden hope. Yes, she remembered now -- in addition to the gymnasium the hospital also boasted a giant atrium housing an indoor garden, two-story trees and exotic plants stretching up skyward under a glass ceiling. Natasha remembered that the soldiers had led her through that famous atrium on the way to the gym, and if her blurred memory still served her it was nearly at the entrance to the building.

The pulse pounding in her ears was a drumbeat urging her forward. Natasha dashed around a bend in the hallway and saw a tangle of plant life through a darkened doorway at the end of the hall. She was almost there. Another fifteen seconds --

Natasha flew through the doorway and tripped immediately, sprawling onto her stomach. With a grunt she heaved herself back onto her hands and knees. She was kneeling under a canopy of branches, the leaves tickling her arms and face, rustling as they stirred against each other.

Well, no wonder she'd tripped: it seemed that she had bypassed the stone walkway bordering the atrium garden and gone hurtling directly into the garden itself. She was just lucky she'd landed on the grass and not in a rosebush or something. Holding the leafy branches away from her face, Natasha rose to her feet again, looking around.

There seemed to be no end to the garden -- it stretched on above her and around her as far as she could see. The glass roof of the atrium was lost overhead in what looked like a silvery fog. How big was this garden? and how deep had she gotten? It seemed impossible that she'd gone more than three steps before stumbling and falling. And besides, the last time she'd seen the atrium garden it hadn't looked anywhere near this big.

The growth was thick enough to blot out all but a trickle of the sunlight that streamed in through the glass ceiling above. In the misty gloom Natasha could just make out the silhouettes of the leaves, looking dark and strange in the dim light...

Or was that a trick of the light? Squinting, Natasha leaned towards a nearby branch, trying to make out the color of its soft oval leaves. They almost looked...black. Not a healthy green like plants should be, but a glossy black like the wings of crows.

As she stared, the cluster of berries hanging above the leaves took on a different color. It was a gradual change, unnoticeable at first, but the more Natasha stared the more she was certain that the berries were changing color before her very eyes. They began as nearly the same color of the leaves, shifting slowly to a bloodred and then to a cherry-red hue, and then by slow degrees taking on a brightening gleam until the berries were glowing like red-hot coals.

And then, as if all that were not improbable enough, the "berries" split open, unfurling flame-colored petals that shone with an unearthly brilliance.

The scent of honey struck her nose, and Natasha blinked. What was she doing? There were hundreds of people suffocating in the gymnasium, and here she was mooning over a flower. Giving herself a shake, she pushed the branch aside and struck off in what she assumed was the right direction. Even if she was headed the wrong way, she reasoned, she would eventually reach the stone walkway that bordered the atrium garden, and from there she could get to the lobby.

Guilt had started nibbling at her. It was unforgivable to zone out like that, especially when so many lives depended on her. It didn't matter that she had started to feel weak and dizzy -- inhaling that gas had probably done that to her. And after all that ruckus in the gym it was no wonder her ears were ringing. Regardless, she had to push forward.

The black foliage that grew thickly on all sides slowed Natasha's progress a great deal, forcing her to push past or duck under their branches as she waded through the garden. But the overgrowth wasn't without its merits: when she stumbled the branches were there at hand, letting her catch herself before she fell. And as she moved towards the walkway Natasha seemed to be doing an awful lot of stumbling.

She just had to reach someone, that was all. As long as it wasn't a soldier it didn't matter who she found. A policeman -- they hadn't evacuated the police yet, had they? -- or even a civilian. Someone who could raise an alarm, who could bring tools that would release those trapped and awaiting a slow choking death in the gymnasium. Someone, anyone...

When she pushed aside the next branch and caught a glimpse of that pale oval, hovering some six feet off the ground and looking so like a human face, her first thought was that she'd found someone. Natasha went staggering forward into what she assumed were a person's arms. Her consciousness was slipping already when struck her that the touch of these "arms" was wrong -- warm enough, but too smooth, almost slick.

Natasha tugged herself back from the edge, pulling away from that embrace. She looked up and froze: she had been hugging the stem and leaves of a gargantuan flower. The white oval had been its flowerbud, not a human face.

And as she stepped backward, the flower *moved*. No amount of dizziness and confusion could convince her otherwise...the flower's stem was bending, the bud leaning towards her like the head of a snake. With her heartbeat crashing in her ears Natasha watched it blossom, petals spreading to reveal a center of such pearlescent brilliance it dazzled her almost into blindness. A honeyed breeze gusted against her face, carrying notes of sweet fruit and clover.

Natasha fell.

Someone caught her. This time she could feel hands and arms -- certainly this was a human, not a plant. Natasha's mind sank into the void, then bobbed back up into consciousness for the final time. "...in the gym!" she croaked. The person holding her did not reply, and Natasha opened her eyes to see their face.

But there was no face. Where the person's face should have been was only a smooth black blankness, gleaming under the light that shone out of the bizarre flower.

Natasha went under again, and was lost to the world.

~~~~~

"I can't breathe! I can't breathe!"

"Lena, wake up!"

"Help me!"

"Wake up!" Nikita whispered, shaking his niece.

Veronika stirred in her cot. "Something wrong?" she asked sleepily, lifting her head.

"She's having another nightmare." Nikita's brow furrowed up.

And Elena had been doing so well since Veronika's arrival. For the past forty-eight hours she had seemed almost like her old self again. Encouraged by this, Nikita had moved Elena and himself into the two newly-vacant cots beside the ones occupied by Veronika, Alexei and Tatyana.

Elena wore a bandaid on her chin now, covering the stain, and at times Nikita could just about imagine that she didn't have the blight at all, that the whole ordeal of the camp was simply a prolonged misunderstanding. And then things like this would happen and the daydream would come down around his ears.

"Help...help..." Elena was coughing, tugging at the neck of her tee-shirt. Veronika leaned over her. "Is she asthmatic?"

"No, no...it's just the nightmare." Nikita grimaced in sympathy. "Wake up, Lena, wake up..."

Veronika looked thoughtful. She reached out to Elena's cot and slid one hand under the girl's head, cradling the back of her neck.

Nikita didn't understand. "What are you -- "

"Sshh," Veronika hushed him. She was concentrating intensely now, peering into Elena's troubled face. Nikita saw her tighten her grip on the nape of Elena's neck and the girl flinched as if stung.

"Hey!"

Veronika waved him off with her free hand. "Look at her now," she whispered, letting go.

And surely enough, Elena was relaxing. As the tension drained out of her body she stopped clutching at her throat, letting her hands fall by her sides. Her expression became peaceful.

"...what did you do?" Nikita breathed.

Veronika just shrugged, glancing up at him. As their eyes met a shock ran through Nikita -- Veronika's eyes were all black, her brown irises swallowed up by the pupils. With a shout of surprise he jerked away from her, and a startled Veronika did the same.

"What? what?!"

"You -- " he began, then took a second look. No, Veronika's eyes were perfectly normal now. The pupils were of regular size and the irises were still visible. He'd been mistaken...he was still only half-awake. Or he had been until a moment ago. "Nevermind...sorry."

"YOUR ATTENTION PLEASE," boomed a voice, and they both jumped again. The CSF soldiers had used the auditorium's announcement system only a handful of times since they'd arrived at the camp; it always caught Nikita off-guard.

"YOUR ATTENTION PLEASE," the voice over the announcement system repeated. People were sitting up in their cots, rubbing their eyes, complaining in cracked voices. His watch had been stolen some days ago while he slept but by Nikita's estimate it was no later than 8am.

"IT HAS COME TO OUR ATTENTION THAT THERE HAVE BEEN COMPLAINTS MADE REGARDING THE FOOD AND WATER QUALITY AT THIS EVACUATION CAMP."

Loud cursing, laughter, jeers. Awakened by the noise, Elena's eyes flickered open. She sat up and blinked vaguely at the howling adults around her. "We getting 'vacuated now?"

"No, Lena -- they're making an announcement," Nikita explained. "Ssshhh."

"THE CHORMAN SPECIAL FORCES DO ACKNOWLEDGE THESE COMPLAINTS. WE WISH TO INFORM YOU THAT WE ARE PRESENTLY RUNNING LOW ON ALL SUPPLIES, AND YOUR PATIENCE IS APPRECIATED."

More hooting and cursing. Nikita thought he detected a note of sarcasm in the announcer's tone, but the audio was too distorted to tell. Yawning, Elena moved over to Veronika's cot and sat down beside her, setting her head on the woman's shoulder. Veronika petted her absently.

"HOWEVER, WE DO HAVE GOOD NEWS."

A hush settled over the inmates.

"WE HAVE JUST BEEN INFORMED THAT THE VOLUNTEER RESEARCHERS AT THE LUBUKOV AGRICULTURAL LABORATORIES HAVE DEVELOPED A CURE FOR THE BLIGHT SYNDROME. WE CAN EXPECT THIS TO BE DISTRIBUTED -- "

The rest of the announcement was lost under a torrent of cheering and applause. People were leaping up from their cots, clapping wildly, embracing each other, dancing. Only a scattered few seemed to be concerned about hearing the rest of the message.

As the listeners hushed the celebrants and the hubbub gradually died down, the loudspeaker became audible once more. " -- YOUR PATIENCE IN WAITING UNTIL THEN," it said. "MESSAGE REPEATS. WE HAVE JUST BEEN INFORMED THAT THE VOLUNTEER RESEARCHERS AT THE LUBUKOV AGRICULTURAL LABORATORIES HAVE DEVELOPED A CURE FOR THE BLIGHT SYNDROME." A smaller burst of enthusiasm, quickly stifled. "WE CAN EXPECT THIS TO BE DISTRIBUTED IN SEVEN DAYS' TIME. WE UNDERSTAND THE NEED FOR URGENCY, AND WE ARE WORKING AS FAST AS WE CAN. WE APPRECIATE YOUR PATIENCE IN WAITING UNTIL THEN."

The loudspeakers clicked off and the celebration resumed, building louder and louder until  auditorium echoed with the sound of people rejoicing. A bit overwhelmed, Nikita ducked his head and exchanged a puzzled look with Veronika. "Do you think..."

" -- They're lying," Alexei murmured.

So the young man was awake after all. Nikita looked over to where Alexei lay on his back in his cot, staring up at the ceiling. "There's no cure," he said.

"...well, you cured *her*, didn't you?" Nikita tilted his head in Veronika's direction. "Maybe your comrades found the same solution."

"She's not cured."

Veronika's expression darkened.

"...what?" Nikita said. "She's not? but -- "

"She's not cured." Alexei sighed. "She's...in remission or something. We really don't understand anything about it. But she's still got the blight. There's no cure for it."

Nikita looked at her, but Veronika wouldn't meet his gaze. Elena looked confused.

"I...then what are you doing for that woman soldier, if you're not trying to cure her?" Nikita scratched his head.

"Trying to put her in remission," Alexei explained. "That seems to stop the hallucinations, and might let the victims live longer."

Nikita's already slim hopes were growing thinner by the moment. "Then why would the CSF lie about having a cure?"

Alexei shrugged his shoulders. "Buying time, I imagine."

"A week?"

"That's probably all they need."

"But that doesn't make sense," Nikita protested. "There's still going to be riots a week from now when they don't have anything to give the inmates."

"Oh...I'm sure they'll have something to give them."

"Well, what?"

Alexei blinked, then turned to look at Nikita. "I don't know... but we need to be out of here before then," he said in a hushed tone. "In fact, we need to leave right away." He lurched into a sitting position, rubbing his face with both hands. "Is Tatyana awake?"

When Nikita reached her cot and lifted the blanket that concealed Tatyana's face, he found the soldier fidgeting and muttering in her sleep. "Looks like she's waking up," he called over to Alexei. It would have surprised him if *any*one could have slept through the commotion those announcements had caused. Bending over, he shook Tatyana's shoulder. "Uh, comrade? are you awake?"

Tatyana's blue eyes slitted open. Nikita didn't notice the size of her pupils until a moment too late. "Oh, good, you are," he said. "We need to -- "

Her hand closed on his shirt collar and yanked downward, and Nikita found himself face-to-face with the soldier. "I could break you in half, old man," she snarled.

Nikita opened his mouth, but no words came out. He heard Elena squealing in alarm, and similar exclamations of dismay from Veronika and Alexei.

"You think you can stop me?" Tatyana seemed to be having trouble focusing on his face. Nikita pushed against her shoulders, straining upward, but her grip held. A couple stitches popped in his shirt collar. "Go ahead. I don't give a rat's ass about the inheritance."

Alexei leapt over the cot, dropped down beside Nikita and grabbed Tatyana's hands, trying to pry them loose from his collar. "Shit shit shit," he muttered. "She's having an episode. It didn't work...I don't know why, but it didn't work...shit..."

"You're pathetic," Tatyana went on. "But I'm *going* to join your precious Special Forces, old man, and there's not a goddamn thing you can do about it. I just hope you live to see me outrank you."

Veronika seemed to drop out of nowhere, landing on Tatyana's cot. In a flash she'd reached up and clapped a hand on either side of the soldier's neck. Nikita both felt and saw the jolt that shook Tatyana's body -- like she'd been shocked with electricity, he reflected afterward. Her eyes rolled back in their sockets. Moment later she'd gone limp, and Alexei was able to wrest Nikita's shirt collar out of her hands.

"Sheesh." Nikita backed away from the cot.

Alexei was leaning over Tatyana's unconscious form, frowning. "It didn't work," he repeated. He looked back over his shoulder. "Are you okay?"

"Fine, fine, just fine." Nikita busied himself straightening out his rumpled collar, wondering why his hands were shaking so badly. He glanced at Veronika, who was just climbing down from the cot -- he wanted to see her eyes again, just to be sure, but she wouldn't look at him. "What did you *do*?" he repeated.

"Nothing," Veronika said evasively. She sat down next to Elena, pulling the distressed girl into her arms. Elena hugged her back at once. "Your uncle's okay, Lena, don't worry."

Nikita turned to Alexei. "What *was* that?!" he demanded.

"She had a hallucinatory episode." Alexei was tugging the blanket back over Tatyana's face. "It doesn't make sense -- I gave her the exact same -- "

"No, not that -- what Veronika did to her."

"Huh? What do you mean?"

"Didn't you see her?" Nikita was swiftly becoming exasperated. "She -- she just touched her, and Tatyana passed out!"

Alexei looked to Veronika for an explanation, but none was offered. "Maybe she choked her or something."

"No, she -- ah, forget it." Nikita sat down heavily on his own cot. "So she's not cured -- or in remission, or however you called it. What now?"

Alexei came to sit down beside him. He propped his elbows on his knees and buried his face in his hands. "I don't have enough thiopental to dose her again," he admitted at last. "And we can't move her out of the camp like this. We'll need to find more medication, and soon."

"Where are we going to get more?"

"...I imagine the camp infirmary has some," Alexei said. "It's a pretty common drug."

"What, are we going to go ask them for it?" Nikita looked over his shoulder at the guards beside the auditorium doors -- they were watching the celebrating inmates with cool detachment. He hadn't forgotten what happened to the little fat man and his diabetic father. "You heard the announcement -- they're out of everything."

"Oh, I'm sure they're holding out on us."

"Of course. But we'd have to break into their supply storage to get to it."

Alexei just nodded. Nikita gave the young man a look. "We'll get shot."

"Probably," Alexei sighed. "That's why I'm going to do it by myself."

"You're crazy."

"No doubt."

Nikita saw there was no point in arguing. "Don't we have any other options?" He glanced over at the blanket-covered silhouette that was Tatyana.

"No, we can't."

"Can't what?"

Alexei picked his head up out of his hands. "We can't leave her," he said. "I promised."

Nikita reddened. "I didn't -- I wasn't going to suggest that."

"Oh. Sorry."

"It's okay." Nikita considered him. "You must feel pretty bad about blackmailing her, huh?"

"Actually, it was my idea." Veronika plopped herself down on the cot on Nikita's other side. The woman's eyes were a perfectly normal shade of brown, but Nikita still couldn't suppress the shudder that passed through him. "I was the one who thought of blackmailing her. Alexei just helped."

"Oh...I see."

Veronika leaned over him to talk to Alexei. "I think we should try for it tonight."

"Try what?"

"Breaking into the infirmary," Veronika whispered. "I'll bet there's not many guards scheduled for the graveyard shift, I bet -- that's our best chance."

Alexei blinked at her. "You're coming with me?"

"Of course." She grinned. "It doesn't help anything if you get shot."

Alexei almost smiled. "No," he said, "I suppose it doesn't."

## CHAPTER ELEVEN

The city of Khostok had been cursed. Yes, that was an accurate way of putting it. The fascist armies had laid a curse upon the fair city prior to their withdrawal, a curse authorized by their amphetamine-crazed Führer and paid for with the souls of millions of the fascists' own countrymen. They had followed their leader down into the pits of Hell itself, seduced by promises of glory and luxury.

But General Mikhail Ilyich Litvinenko would not stand idly by while honest God-fearing Chormans suffered the same fate. The DIO and the CSF might have been powerless to stop the plagues they had so ignorantly unleashed, but Mikhail was not. He had his tools, his brilliant intellect, and the forces of righteousness on his side. There was no way he could fail in lifting the curse.

As he crept along the alleyways of the empty city, following the route highlighted by his map, Mikhail savored the freshness of the early morning air. It was doing him no small benefit to be out in such weather: Mikhail had not slept much on the night before. Several hours had been spent locked in glorious battle against the infernal weeds that encroached upon his hideout.

In the end, of course, Mikhail had emerged victorious, but it had cost him a good night's sleep. Another consequence of the battle was the stench of gasoline and carbonized wood that hung in an almost-visible cloud around him, alerting everything downwind to his presence, but this Mikhail failed to notice.

The tattered map that guided him was one of his most precious documents. It had been bequeathed to Mikhail by his dear departed comrade and fellow war veteran, Old Tomasz. The original map had been stolen at great risk from the vaults of the DIO, Tomasz had explained, during a harrowing escape from their underground torture chambers. Only by the blessing of the Archangel Gabriel, who had transformed Old Tomasz into a frog, had he been able to evade his captors and escape with the map.

Of course the original map had had to be destroyed, naturally, to prevent its falling into the wrong hands. But Old Tomasz had cleverly copied the details onto a piece of cardboard torn from a Crunchy Stars cereal box, reproducing every street and landmark in blue and green crayon. Some of his notes were illegible, and it seemed that Tomasz had been using the box as a combination diary and grocery list before deciding to make it into a map, but in general his information had been sound.

The map was a tourist's-guide to Khostok's hidden landmarks, unlabeled monuments to government corruption and wickedness. Here was the Air-Polluter, cleverly disguised as a patriotic statue, which exhaled noxious gases from concealed ports in its base and thus disbanded groups of protesters. There was the Supersonic Ear-Splitter, hidden within a lamppost, which emitted blasts of sound undetectable by average citizens but crippling to those installed with the DIO's mind-controlling hardware. Mikhail himself had wandered by this lamppost and experienced firsthand the deafening roar of static from the radio equipment in his head, forcing him to clench his teeth and hurry away.

And there was Mikhail's target -- the entrance to B-20, otherwise known as The Warrens. Here Old Tomasz had been vague, circling an entire block with red crayon as the probable vicinity of an entry point to this vast and mysterious underground complex. He had only been there once, Tomasz had explained to Mikhail, and he had been a frog at the time, so of course he wasn't entirely clear on which building housed that entrance. But it was somewhere around here; he had been sure of that.

It had all come to Mikhail last night, fatigued as he was from fighting those black weeds. His inspiration had had all the qualities of a vision -- he had seen the black-uniformed Obersturmbannführer emerging once again from underground, had seen those unholy plants pushing their way up from beneath the asphalt, had seen those demons crawling up out of the sewers and drains and wells all over the city. As creatures of Hell, naturally they must have come straight up from their native realm -- up out of the pit itself.

And then the lightbulb had flared in his brain. What better way to unleash demons into Khostok than to open a portal to Hades directly below the city itself? And what better place for such a portal than those subterranean bomb shelters known collectively as B-20, built during wartime at a depth of several hundred feet? Why, the warrens were halfway to Hell already -- all the fascists had had to do was blast the rest of the way down to create a convenient highway straight from Hell to Khostok.

Realizing this, it was easy to see what the DIO had done. The demon-infested warrens must have been sealed off after the Great War ended, locking the plague into the shelters. And then a few weeks ago the DIO had come along and blithely opened Pandora's Box.

No wonder they were engaging in this coverup! he could imagine the gossip if word ever got out that the government had unleashed Hell on Earth in an effort to weaponize it.

Mikhail had had enough of trying to combat the demons individually: he was going to go to the source. Cut them off at the root. If he could find the entrance to the warrens he could seal it off again, trapping the demons inside and singlehandedly rescuing every man, woman and child in Khostok.

*If* he could find the entrance. The red crayon scribble on Tomasz's map was less than specific, and Mikhail was reduced to wandering the streets, checking each and every building on the block. Fortunately most of the buildings here in the medical district were abandoned like those in the old industrial neighborhood, victims of the bursting postwar economic bubble some years prior. From the boarded-up windows and chained-up doors Mikhail could tell that no DIO agent had come along to disturb these places in some time.

Of course several buildings on this street had been in use right up until the quarantine, and these were more likely places to hide the entrance to an underground shelter system. The doors had all been locked as their workers evacuated, but that did not stop Mikhail. He entered and exited these shops as stealthily as a ghost, leaving only smashed windows, sooty footprints and the stench of gasoline to mark his presence. Not even the most highly trained professional could have detected his intrusion, Mikhail felt.

In this manner he worked his way down the street highlighted on Tomasz's map, searching for anything that resembled an entrance to the shelter network. As he approached the traffic light on the streetcorner Mikhail drew closer to the blue-and-white painted concrete of the Gurlukovich Memorial Hospital, easily the largest building on the block. When he reached the optometry clinic beside the hospital and found it had not seen any customers in some seven or eight years, he knew where he would explore next. Hitching his backpack into a more comfortable position Mikhail struck out toward the hospital.

As soon as he caught sight of the parking lot a terrible fear seized him, and he ducked back around the corner of the building. The CSF were there! they had taken the hospital! In that glimpse Mikhail had seen all the signs he needed: the barbed-wire fencing around the parking lot, the black armored vehicles within the lot itself, the padlocks on the main entrance doors.

Once the surge of adrenaline had faded and Mikhail realized what the CSF's presence here meant, he was elated. So Old Tomasz had been right all along -- there *was* an entrance to the warrens here on this block. And the CSF were here to guard it. Perhaps they still held futile hopes of weaponizing the demons, or perhaps they simply didn't want anyone stumbling across the truth behind the evacuation. Regardless, all the barbed wire in the world would not stop Mikhail.

Drawing upon his warrior's courage, Mikhail peeked back around the corner of the building again. The parking lot was empty of soldiers and civilians, thankfully, and there were fewer CSF vehicles parked there than he'd first thought -- he only saw two of them at the moment. A banner above the main doors to the hospital flapped in the morning breeze, making the words RED CAMP ONE ripple as if underwater.

They had disguised the entrance to Hell as an evacuee camp. Mikhail almost caught himself marveling at their deception: it was a perfect justification for taking over the building. He only hoped that they had not gone to the lengths of housing actual evacuees, or victims of that inky brain-devouring plague, in the hospital. Or perhaps they were -- perhaps the demons needed regular sacrifices of children or maidens to keep them placated. Old Tomasz had hinted as much in some of his stories.

Scarcely daring to breathe, Mikhail slipped through a gap in the temporary fencing and tiptoed toward the front door of the building, pausing every ten steps to sweep the sights of his

Mosin-Nagant across his surroundings. For an occupied building, the hospital seemed strangely quiet: Mikhail heard no voices, no engines, no movement at all. The few vehicles left in the parking lot were empty. The ground-floor windows had all been boarded up, and no shadows stirred in the upper-floor windows that overlooked the lot. All the signs of occupation remained except the people...it was as if they'd vanished into the earth.

*Had* they?

A bit bolder now, Mikhail ventured up the steps and right up to the padlocked doors of the main entrance. He could almost have laughed -- the doors were so heavily secured they might as well have hung a sign reading "DANGER - ENTRANCE TO THE FIERY ABYSS."

Upon closer inspection Mikhail realized they *had* hung a sign beside the door, though it didn't read as he anticipated. "Attention soldiers," the notice said. "This building off limits until further notice by order of Colonel Akimov of the Chorman Special Forces. Entry strictly prohibited." Below the warning was the note's author, someone named Falcon, and a date.

Now Mikhail doubted that the CSF were even inside anymore. True, the posted warning could have been a ruse, but then there would have been some signs of life. There should have been guards outside, at least. And the parking lot looked awfully empty too.

But why abandon the location? If the soldiers had become overwhelmed by waves of demons or infernal brain-rotting plagues that forced them to flee for their lives, would they have taken the time to bar the door and post warnings outside? Mikhail doubted they had cleared the area for anything so altruistic as blasting the entrance closed, but it still paid to be cautious. One never knew --

The morning breeze had stilled, but it wasn't until Mikhail's throat and eyes began to burn that he noticed it. A certain smell had been bothering him for the past few minutes, and now that the wind had died down it was growing more and more overpowering. It was the smell of something bitter and acrid; a sharp chemical smell. Within seconds the stench had driven him from the steps of the Gurlukovich Memorial Hospital, choking and coughing.

Back in the alleyway he retched a couple of times, then felt better. Blotting his eyes on his sleeve, Mikhail looked up at the blue-and-white wall of the hospital's eastern side. The painted facade gave no clue as to the horrors within, but now Mikhail knew with certainty: the entrance to the warrens -- and the adjoining tunnel to Hell -- was here, somewhere in the building. After nearly being suffocated by the sulfurous fumes belching up out of the Pit he would not doubt any longer.

With a shudder Mikhail turned back homeward again, vowing to return. If his crusade took him into the bowels of the earth he would not waver. He just had to hurry home and pick up a few things. A crucifix, for example. And decent gas mask.

And dynamite. Lots and lots of dynamite.

~~~~~

"How may I help you?"

Alexei took a deep breath. "I think I've recovered," he said, "I don't have the blight anymore."

Behind the card table which served as the camp infirmary's reception desk was a single CSF soldier. After considering Alexei for a moment this soldier shrugged, picked up his pen and went back to filling out his paperwork.

"I'm serious!"

"I'm sure you are." The soldier didn't look up.

Alexei could hardly blame him for his attitude. It was the middle of the night, after all, and the soldier had probably chosen the graveyard shift so he could avoid having to deal with the inmates. Alexei couldn't see beyond the temporary curtained partitions that separated the "clinic" from the rest of the former refreshment stands, but it looked like the receptionist was the only one in the infirmary right now. At least he hoped this was the case.

"I had the blight, of course, but it went away," Alexei explained. He was starting to realize that the camp clinic had no doubt heard similar stories hundreds of times before, and this one was lame at best. Not that it mattered -- he didn't have to convince this surly desk clerk that he had truly recovered. He only had to distract him long enough for Veronika to slip past.

"Mmm-hmm," said the soldier, still looking down at his paperwork. He tapped the pen against the side of his respirator filter.

Alexei was sharply aware of Veronika's presence nearby, hiding behind one of the refreshment stand signs that advertised popcorn and drinks. "I'm not asking you to release me," Alexei argued, "but don't you think the Labs should know about it? If someone gets over the blight all on their own, they should be studied."

The soldier glanced up at him. " -- this could be the key to developing a cure," Alexei hurried on. "If I've recovered because I'm producing antibodies to combat the disease, or because my immune system -- "

" -- but they've already found a cure," the soldier interrupted. "Didn't you hear the announcement? It's going to be distributed in just a few days -- you'll have to sit tight until then, comrade."

Alexei remembered the announcement, and a trickle of ice water ran down his spine. Maybe he was being paranoid -- it wouldn't have been the first time -- but he didn't want to stick around and find out what exactly the CSF meant by a 'cure'.

"Can you at least test me for the blight?" Alexei leaned forward, hands on the desk. "I know the Labs developed a blood test for it. Come on, you've got to have some testing kits lying around back there."

The soldier looked up at him again. " -- and if you test me, I'll leave you alone," Alexei promised.

Sighing through his respirator, the soldier dropped his pen and rose to his feet. "Wait here," he growled, and turned to duck behind the curtained partition.

Alexei's heart leapt. He looked back over his shoulder and found Veronika already in motion, sneaking along in a catlike crouch. She skirted the reception desk and noiselessly slipped in behind the partition, and Alexei finally let himself exhale. It was halfway over -- now she just had to find the thiopental and get out with it.

The receptionist reappeared a minute later, holding a vial and a syringe and looking none the wiser. "Thanks," Alexei said. "I just want to be sure, you know?"

"Just roll up your sleeve."

"Actually, I can do it myself," Alexei held out a hand for the equipment. The soldier hesitated. "I'm a doctor, you know."

"Yeah?" The soldier dropped the vial and syringe into Alexei's hand and reseated himself behind the desk. "Where do you work?"

Alexei caught himself before he gave an honest answer. "Oh...at the Gurlukovich Memorial Hospital. I'm a psychiatrist."

"Yeah? that's the hospital with the big gymnasium, right?"

"That's the one." Alexei was feeling more and more optimistic. If he could keep the soldier talking until Veronika had gotten back out again they might actually both survive this. "Ever been there?"

"No, but my aunt has. Did you know they converted it into an evacuation camp?"

"Huh? the hospital?"

"Yup. It was the first place they picked." The soldier's head quirked to one side. "Say...how'd you wind up in this camp, if you were working at the hospital?"

Alexei swallowed. "I, uh...well, I wasn't at work when they announced the quarantine."

"Mm, I see. You must live near here, then, if they had you shipped to Camp Three after processing."

"Exactly -- exactly." Alexei could see the soldier's attention waning, and scrambled to think of something. "Frankly, I'm glad I'm not at Camp One."

"Why's that?"

"Well, most of my patients probably wound up there. I probably wouldn't get any peace at all...everyone would be wanting me to look at them, asking me to write prescriptions, all sorts of nonsense...and me without any of my equipment."

That earned a chuckle out of the soldier. "I'll bet you're right."

Alexei was encouraged. "People think it's so prestigious to have a medical degree, but there's a lot of stress that comes with the job, you know. Having to listen to other people's problems all day is pretty draining." He leaned over the desk. "But you already know that, don't you? you're here all day taking complaints, having to tell people you're out of supplies..."

"Absolutely!" The soldier nodded with conviction. "And they don't pay you hardly enough to eat, either. I tell you, the other day I said to -- "

From somewhere back behind the curtained partitions there came a crash. Alexei's heart skipped a beat. The soldier's head snapped up into the air, alert as a hunting dog.

" -- what were you saying?" Alexei asked weakly, but the soldier was already getting to his feet, looking back toward the curtains. A gloved hand rested on the sidearm holstered at his belt. "One moment," he said, and ducked behind the curtains again.

Quiet panic seized Alexei. Damn it! so they were all going to wind up shot in the head after all. Or at least Veronika was going to wind up that way. Matter of fact, the soldier might not have any clue that Alexei had been working with her, distracting him so the theft could take place. If Alexei walked away now --

His brain rambled on in this manner even as Alexei slid around the edge of the reception desk and behind the curtains, following the soldier. Behind the partitions he found a small makeshift clinic rather like a field hospital, with wheeled folding beds and rolling carts holding instrument trays. Aside from a half-empty bottle on one of the rolling carts there were no medicines in sight. All of the beds were empty, and the clinic area itself was vacant. At the far end of the room was a half-open door.

He looked around in search of a weapon. (*You're going to get yourself killed,*) scolded an internal voice that sounded curiously like his mother's. (*You won't even get a decent death -- you're going to get shot down in the hall like a petty criminal. And this time there's nobody to come and save you.*)

A glint of silver on a nearby tray caught Alexei's eye. The scissors and tweezers would be useless to him, but beside these was a scalpel that looked like it could be dangerous. When he picked it up the metal was so cold it burned.

(*Just pray they've got good aim*,) the voice sneered. (*If they hit you in the stomach it's going to take ages for you to* die.)

Clutching the scalpel in his fist, Alexei snuck over to the door and eased it open, wincing as the hinges squeaked. Once the gap was wide enough he poked his head through and found himself staring down a long hallway lined with doors. Employee offices, from the looks of them. One of the office doors stood ajar, opened toward Alexei so it blocked his view of the office's interior. There were no soldiers in sight.

Alexei stepped out into the hallway. He hadn't gone ten paces when he heard a shout, immediately followed by a shriek of mortal terror. Before he could decide whether to pursue or flee from the noises something huge and black came hurtling out of the open office door. With an impact more felt than heard the thing struck the opposite wall and slithered to the ground.

It was the soldier from the reception desk. Wide-eyed, Alexei crept over to him, but the man lay where he'd fallen: he was either unconscious or quite dead.

Veronika stood in the open doorway of the office, chest heaving, looking pale and shaken. The zip-pockets of her coveralls were stuffed with bottles, and over her shoulder one could see that the office behind her was crammed full of drugs and other medical supplies. The contents of several torn-open boxes littered the desk.

Alexei's scalpel slipped out of his fingers and clattered across the tile floor. He looked between the skinny young woman and the muscular armed soldier who had just been inexplicably catapulted across the hallway. There was nobody else around.

"...what happened?" Alexei asked. Veronika looked straight through him, then focused on his face.

"...I think he saw me," she panted. Alexei glanced back at the motionless soldier. "He's not dead," Veronika added. "If he saw me, we'll have to get out of the camp."

As if on cue, there was a faraway shout from back in the direction of the infirmary. "Puffin? Puffin, where'd you go?"

Veronika snarled like a cat, and her brown eyes appeared to darken suddenly. Alexei shrank away from her. "Get back to the clinic -- quickly -- hide under one of the beds!" she hissed at him, retreating back into the office. "We'll have to leave tonight -- try to get the others awake. I'll get your drugs and meet up with you in the auditorium."

" -- but -- "

"Go! I'll meet you there!" Veronika ducked back into the office and swung the door shut after her. Alexei took a last look at the closed door and the heap of unconscious soldier on the ground before it, then turned and pelted back toward the clinic.

From the sound of their voices the soldiers were right beside him, but when Alexei peeked back into the infirmary he found it still empty. Then someone's shadow slid across the front of the partitioning curtains and he threw himself on the floor, ducking behind one of the rolling beds as the CSF soldiers appeared from behind the curtains.

"Puffin?" called the first soldier. The second one was chuckling to himself. "Probably gone off to sample some of the medical alcohol -- testing it for purity, you know."

The two of them strode towards the door in back of the infirmary. Fortunately for Alexei those imposing masks somewhat limited the soldiers' peripheral vision and they completely overlooked the young man crouching behind one of the beds. The first soldier was still muttering and grumbling as they passed through the doorway. "He's gonna need it when he gets demoted to janitorial duty, I tell you..."

Holding his breath, Alexei waited until the two soldiers came across Puffin's unconscious body. As their shouts echoed down the hallway Alexei scrambled back onto his feet and sprinted out of the clinic, through the concessions area and back into the auditorium. As late as it was, scarcely anyone was awake to see him take a running dive and slide into the relative safety beneath Nikita's cot.

Alexei curled up beside someone's backpack and lay there catching his breath. Nikita's upside-down head appeared over the edge of the cot, blinking at him. "You okay?" he whispered.

"Yeah...but Veronika's still back there."

Nikita frowned. "Had trouble?"

"Uh-huh. Soldiers."

"Do we need to go help her?"

Alexei shook his head. "She told me to run...she was gonna meet us here." He swallowed against the dryness in his throat, collecting himself. "Listen...Veronika thinks the soldiers are gonna be looking for her. She's getting the drugs, but she says we need to leave."

"Oh hell." Nikita's head disappeared.

"I'm sorry."

Nikita said nothing for a long moment. "I'll wake Elena and get her shoes on," he said. "But what about -- shit!"

"Huh? what?!"

"...I don't believe it."

"What?" Alexei wormed his way out of his hiding place. Nikita was sitting on his own cot, gaping at the auditorium wall. He pointed and Alexei looked.

The auditorium's ventilation ducts were mounted on the wall some ten feet above the floor. As Alexei squinted in the low light he saw what Nikita had seen -- one of the metal grills that shielded the ducts was moving. The grill rocked back and forth by a centimeter in each direction, then suddenly pivoted on its lower left-hand corner, swinging down and away. A head materialized from out of the darkness of the ventilation shaft.

"God in heaven," Nikita said.

Veronika worked her way carefully out of the ventilation system, grabbing the lip of the shaft so she could pull her legs out. She seemed to take the ten-foot drop to the floor in slow-motion, her shadow stretching out like black taffy behind her, shrinking back to normal size again when she touched down on the floor.

Nikita was speechless. Alexei was too, but after seeing a two-hundred-pound soldier hurled across a hallway nothing much surprised him anymore. Keeping her head low, Veronika scurried up to them and promptly ducked out of sight between the cots. "Did he tell you?" she asked.

"Yeah," Nikita found his voice at last. "...This time I'm gonna let *you* two wake up that woman. I'll get Elena ready."

Veronika nodded, checking in all directions for the masked silhouette of a soldier. Finding none, she lifted the blanket from Tatyana's face and slipped up onto the cot alongside her.

"Wake up, Tanya," she murmured, patting Tatyana's cheek. "Wake up, wake up."

Tatyana groaned, shaking her head. Veronika gave her another half-dozen light slaps. Finally Tatyana's eyes slitted open, revealing black pupils surrounded by a thin ring of blue.

Instinctively Veronika clapped a hand over Tatyana's mouth. Moments later the female soldier came to life, shrieking a series of oddly-accented curses that came out muffled by Veronika's hand. Alexei couldn't tell for sure, but the expletives sounded more German than Chorman.

"Oh no," Nikita murmured. Elena was sitting up in her cot, face puffy with sleep, brushing her tangled hair out of her eyes.

Veronika held on as Tatyana bucked and kicked, trying to throw her off. She pressed the palm of her hand against Tatyana's forehead and shut her eyes.

This time both Alexei and Nikita saw it. Tatyana kicked a final time and went rigid, muscles clenching, back arching. Then the spasm passed as quickly as it had come and Tatyana went limp as an old rag. Veronika cautiously lifted her hand.

"Is the soldier lady okay?" Elena asked. Nobody answered her.

Tatyana gasped, coughed and opened her eyes again, looking around the room. Her skin shone with sweat but her pupils had shrunk to normal size again.

"You awake now?" Veronika asked.

Tatyana glared up at the woman astride her. "Get 'way from me." She swung an arm and knocked Veronika onto the floor. Unruffled, Veronika rolled back under the cot again. Alexei breathed a silent sigh and scooted over to speak to Tatyana.

"Listen...we need to get out now. The soldiers are going to be looking for us."

Tatyana turned and fixed Alexei with a frosty look. "What did you clowns do this time?"

"They caught us breaking into the medical supplies," Alexei said simply. "We were looking for more thiopental."

Tatyana had been asleep or incoherent for better than two days and Alexei could almost see her sifting through her memories, trying to remember what she was doing here. Her glare lost a little of its iciness. "...I thought you already gave me the thiotempal."

"I did. It didn't work."

Tatyana shut her eyes. "I'm going to try it again," Alexei offered, "but we need to get out before -- "

"Here they come," Nikita whispered, low and urgent. He dropped down flat on his cot and tugged Elena down beside him. "Lie down, Lena, lie down and be quiet."

"But I've got my shoes on!"

"Sshh, I know. We've got to pretend we're sleeping now...just be still for a moment."

Alexei ducked instinctively. Over the rows of cots he saw the white beam of a flashlight roving back and forth across the sleepers, and behind the beam was the distinctive silhouette of a masked CSF soldier. If they were lucky Puffin wouldn't have recovered enough to be searching on his own, and whoever was out hunting for the thieves might not identify them. And yet...

"This is insane," Tatyana growled. All in one motion she sat up, swung her legs over the edge of the cot, seized her backpack and lurched onto her feet. Before Alexei could call her back she was marching off into the darkened auditorium, heading for the doors.

Alexei slid himself back under Nikita's cot. Veronika was curled up beneath Elena's cot, her head pillowed on one arm, waiting.

The four of them lay without speaking for several long minutes. Near as they could tell from listening, the soldier with the flashlight was going down the rows of cots, shining the light into people's faces. They could hear him asking questions but the distance was too great to hear what was being said.

"Do you think she's turning us in?" Nikita whispered from above.

Alexei bit his lip. "...I don't know."

"No, she isn't," Veronika whispered back. Alexei could barely see her in the obscurity under the cot, but he could see that she was smiling. "She wants us to cure her; she won't take any chances with that."

"If you say so." Nikita sounded less than convinced. "Does anyone have *any* idea where we're going once we're out of here?"

"To Byatin," Veronika suggested.

"I know, but how? The river's too heavily guarded, and we don't have the right supplies to be hiking in the mountains."

Alexei cleared his throat. "...I have an idea," he said softly. "Why don't we hide out in the city for a few days? we might be able to scavenge the equipment we need for getting across the mountains."

Nikita grunted. "That won't be scavenging...to get what we need we'd have to do actual looting."

"Yeah. Are we okay with that?"

Nikita and Veronika both confirmed that they were. "We might get lucky," Alexei went on. "I don't know how long the quarantine's going to last, but we might be able to get by in Khostok long enough to wait it out. Then the river won't be guarded anymore."

"If we do wait it out, we could even 'scavenge' a car and drive it south," Nikita sounded like he was warming to the idea. "Hell -- if we wait until they lift the quarantine, then we can join up with Yura before we leave. Let's do that."

Alexei said nothing.

"...I don't think the city is safe, either," Veronika murmured.

"Why not?" Nikita asked. "It's a big enough place to hide in. You think they're going to be combing the city for us?"

"No, that's not it." Veronika sounded troubled. "We need to get completely out of Khostok. We won't be safe until we get to the river."

"...the river?" Nikita echoed. "What difference would -- oh crap. Sssh, everyone, they're coming this way."

Alexei stiffened. From his hiding place beneath the cot he couldn't see anything, but the floor beneath his head had begun to quiver with the distinctive tread of an approaching soldier's boots. He spotted the white circle of a flashlight beam sailing along the floor towards them, a pair of rubber-coated boots following close behind.

The boots slowed as they came closer. (*Keep going, keep going,*) Alexei begged. He suddenly regretted hiding under the cot -- if Puffin hadn't identified him as an accomplice to Veronika's thievery, trying to hide from the CSF made him look very guilty indeed. And he was completely unarmed now that he'd dropped that scalpel; he hadn't so much as a nail file to defend himself with.

The boots stopped directly in front of Nikita's cot. "Get up," the soldier rasped. They tapped the toe of their boot against the leg of the cot, some six inches away from Alexei's face. "Come on, on your feet."

"...uh...sorry, is something wrong?" That was Nikita, doing his best impersonation of a man awakened from sleep.

"Just get up."

Alexei heard Nikita whispering to Elena, trying to reassure her. Both of them rolled out of the cot. Then the soldier unslung their rifle and rapped its muzzle against the metal of the cot frame.

"Get out from under there, both of you."

Alexei and Veronika exchanged identical looks of alarm. A hundred mad ideas went through his brain, but before Alexei could settle on any of them the soldier bent down and whispered "It's *me*, you idiots. Get out here before I drag you out."

Alexei crawled out from under the cot and stood upright, his knees wobbling under him. Veronika appeared at his side. In the darkened room Tatyana's black CSF protective suit turned her into a shadow, a moving blotch of darkness. The only details were the fragments of light that glinted from her gas mask's eyepieces and the metal on her rifle. That was why she'd taken her backpack when she stormed off -- she'd kept her suit with her.

"You could have told us you were getting into your uniform," Veronika muttered.

Tatyana pointed the rifle at Veronika's face and Elena gave a mouselike squeak. Nikita held her close. "No talking," Tatyana said. "We're going to go out those doors there -- see them?

-- and I'll direct you from there. Let's go."

The five of them fell into line and began their march out of the auditorium. Alexei caught sight of the other soldier with the flashlight, still scanning the faces of the sleepy inmates in search of the thief. He waved casually to Tatyana and she waved back. It seemed that inmates being led away at gunpoint was a common enough practice here at the camp.

And from the looks the other inmates were giving them, this must have been a frequent sight indeed. Those inmates who weren't sleeping lifted their heads as the five passed their cots, watching the procession with guarded faces. Alexei made eye contact with a few of them, and every single person dropped their gaze when he did.

They didn't want to see it, he realized. The other inmates knew what was happening -- or thought they knew -- and didn't want to get involved. If they pretended not to see the doomed ones they could keep their consciences clear.

Alexei wanted to hate them, but on a personal level he knew exactly how they were feeling. And, really, what could they do?

Tatyana exchanged polite greetings with the door guard as she directed her captives through the auditorium exit, motioning with her rifle to keep them marching along. As they passed through the doors she whispered for them to take a right turn into the adjoining hallway. At the end of the hall lay a glowing red EXIT sign, and below it a pair of double doors guarded by a matching pair of CSF soldiers. The captives hesitated, but Tatyana marched right up to the guards with a salute.

"Morning, comrades."

"Good morning," one of the guards replied. "What's this?"

"I'm taking these four out back," Tatyana said gruffly. "Colonel Akimov's orders."

"Seriously?" The other guard peered at the four civilians standing a cautious distance away. "How old is that girl?"

Tatyana turned on him. "Authorization code nine-zero-five dash four-seven-two-two. Go ahead and call the Colonel himself to confirm that -- I'm sure he'd love to wake up in the middle of the night to answer your questions."

"Alright, alright, at ease there." The first guard drew a key from his pocket and started unlocking the doors. "Just bag them up when you're done, okay?"

"I've got orders to take them to the factory right away."

"Fine, you follow your orders then." The guards stepped back, holding the doors open so Tatyana could escort her captives through. The first one gave her a slightly sarcastic salute as she passed; the second was shaking his head. They could hear him muttering as the doors swung shut again. "That kid had to be about eight years old..."

It was near-dawn and the night sky overhead was paling already, stars fading against the lightening backdrop. A chill breeze whipped around the brightly painted exterior of the Viktor Kurylenko Concert Hall. They'd exited to the rear of the building, looking down into a secondary parking lot filled with CSF vehicles of various sizes and purposes.

"They'll be listening." Tatyana looked around. "Over here -- everyone get over here, up against the wall."

Alexei, Veronika, Nikita and Elena shuffled over to the left of the exit doors, huddling against the red concrete. From their stunned expressions Alexei could tell that Veronika and Nikita had grasped the meaning behind Tatyana's conversation with the door guards. Elena had not understood, of course, but her uncle was holding her so tightly that she must have guessed something wasn't right.

"Cover your ears," Tatyana said. She clicked off the safety on her AKS-47, swung the rifle skyward and fired four short bursts into the air. Everyone cringed away from the noise. Elena shrieked, clapping her hands over her ears, and Nikita grabbed her up to shield her with his body.

Tatyana lowered the rifle. "Sorry," she grunted. She glanced back toward the exit doors, but nobody appeared to confirm the execution. "C'mon this way -- we're taking one of the trucks."

The four of them hurried after her in shaken silence as Tatyana led the way into the parking lot. She reached one of the flatbed CSF trucks and whipped the green tarp out of the truckbed, sending out a gust of sour air. The smell was revoltingly familiar to Alexei.

"Get in there and lie down -- I'm going to cover you with the tarp. No moving, no talking."

Nikita lifted Elena up into the truck and climbed in after her, followed by Veronika and then by Alexei. Elena protested that her clothes would get dirty and Nikita reassured her that it would be alright. There were gummy brownish-red patches here and there on the bottom of the truckbed and Alexei tried not to think too hard about them.

Once they were all lying down Tatyana threw the tarp over them, shutting them into the green darkness together. The truck rocked slightly as she climbed into the driver's seat and slammed the door shut.

Elena coughed. "Smells funny," she said in a small voice.

"Sshh, we have to be quiet now," Nikita hushed her. "Let's pretend we're sleeping again;

can you do that for me?"

"Okay."

The engine sputtered and roared, surging forward with a grinding of gears. Alexei wondered how long they would have to lie there breathing in the smell of death, then realized they hadn't told Tatyana where to go. He assumed she would take them out of Red Camp Three and then consult with the rest of the group once they were a safe distance away.

Of course it did occur to Alexei that Tatyana might have been taking them away someplace to dispose of them, but he was starting to doubt that this was her intention. After all, she'd had a much better opportunity to kill them back there at the wall.

"This truck..." Nikita's voice rose up in the darkness. "Is it used for...what I think it is?"

"Yeah," said Alexei.

"God in Heaven," Nikita whispered.

~~~~~

With a squeal of brakes the black CSF truck pulled to a stop in front of Red Camp Three's exit gate. Beside the exit was a tiny wooden booth inset with glass windows, scarcely big enough for a single chair. The cash register inside the booth showed that it had once been used for collecting parking fees, though its location had made it the logical choice for a makeshift guard post.

Tatyana rolled down the window of her truck. The soldier inside the booth hefted himself to his feet and stepped outside, straightening his protective suit as he ambled over to greet her.

"Hail, comrade!"

"Hello there."

The guard leaned one elbow on the hood of Tatyana's vehicle. "On the way to the factory?" he asked, pointing the muzzle of his gas mask at the tarp-covered truckbed.

"Yeah," Tatyana said. "Got four bags to deliver."

"I see. What's your codename, comrade?"

"Plover. What's this about?"

The gate guard lifted both hands. "Ah, you know, I've got orders to keep a closer eye on the traffic that comes through here."

Tatyana nodded. "Good idea. We've got to stay on our toes -- can't have the inmates slipping out on our watch."

"It's not the inmates we need to worry about." The guard lowered his voice. "It's our own men."

"No kidding?"

He shook his head. "We've had desertions," the guard explained gravely. "Soldiers are just up and vanishing."

"No kidding!"

The guard nodded. "That's why I'm gonna ask you to pop that mask off for a second." He sounded almost apologetic. "We're on the lookout for a couple deserters right now -- anyone coming or going has got to show their face. Colonel's orders, you know."

Tatyana scoffed. "Seriously now, comrade."

"No joke."

"The Colonel's got to know how dangerous it is to have your mask off in an unsecured area," Tatyana protested. "We're not wearing these respirators for peace of mind, are we?"

"I know, I know, but it's only for a second."

Grumbling, Tatyana reached up to undo the drawstring on her hood. Then she paused. "You first."

" -- eh?" The guard took a step back.

Tatyana lowered her hand. "I'm only taking mine off if you take yours off first."

"I -- there's no reason for me to take my mask off!" the guard stammered. He clapped both hands onto his respirator, as if Tatyana might try to pull it off anyway.

"Oh sure there is." Tatyana leaned out of the truck's cabin. "If it's so safe to take it off out here, you might as well join me, eh? Get some fresh air." She chuckled.

" -- nevermind," the guard said thickly. "Just let me take a look under your tarp and you can pass through."

"Oh, sure, you go ahead and have a look." Tatyana sounded amused. "But I'd hold your breath if I were you."

"Eh?" The guard halted in midstep. "...why?"

Tatyana was adjusting her rearview mirror with an air of nonchalance. "I heard about those deserters, but I heard something else, too."

"Yeah?"

"Uh-huh. Someone told me why they deserted."

The guard was drifting away from the truckbed, back Tatyana's window. "And why was that?"

"The way I was told, those soldiers caught the blight." She leaned out and tapped on the guard's gas mask. "And they were wearing their gear, too. If there's enough bugs in the air, the mask's not gonna save you. It's gonna come straight through -- "

The guard jerked away from her. "You're lying." He cupped both hands over the air filter on his gas mask.

"You think so?" Tatyana chuckled. "Go hop in the back with the corpses if you're so sure. You'll know in a few hours if I was telling the truth."

But the guard wasn't interested in verifying her claims, it seemed. He retreated all the way to the little booth and stepped inside, shutting the door securely after him. Tatyana saw him hitting switches and a moment later the chain-link gate began to slide sideways.

Tatyana took her foot off the brake and stepped on the clutch. As the truck rolled through the opened gate she waved goodbye to the guard. He waved back, but the gesture was less "farewell" and more "get away from me." The last she saw of him, the gate guard still had one hand over his air filter.

"Much obliged, comrade," Tatyana whispered to herself.

~~~~~

By the time the black truck came squeaking to a halt again Alexei had lost track of the time. It seemed this trip had taken much longer than their journey from the Labs to Red Camp Three, but since he had certainly napped along the way he couldn't be positive about that. They had been in the truckbed under the tarp for an hour at least, by his reckoning, for when Tatyana whipped the tarp away Alexei was temporarily blinded by the sunlight.

"C'mon, everyone up," Tatyana was saying. She sounded as if she were still wearing her mask, and as his blurred vision sharpened Alexei could see this was true. Sitting up, he looked around and discovered that Nikita, Elena and Veronika were in similar states of disorientation.

"Where are we?"

"Industrial district, according to the map." Tatyana was leaning on the tailgate, surveying their surroundings. "Supposed to be a mostly abandoned area. Shouldn't run into many patrols out here. We all awake now?"

"We're awake, we're awake," Nikita said. Elena yawned and nodded.

relax and move slowly and I won't have to shoot you in the face, okay?"

Mikhail nodded. The person released his arm, scooting back a pace or two, and Mikhail spun around to see them.

Holding him at gunpoint -- with his own damn firearm -- was a slight young woman with masses of long dark hair. She was dressed in a mechanic's zip-up coveralls and oversized boots, and half-smiled when he laid eyes on her. "What's your name?"

Mikhail straightened up to his full height. "General Mikhail Ilyich Litvinenko -- war hero and survivalist."

"Ooh," said the woman. "What are you doing out here, General?"

"Keeping our fair city free of the plagues of Hell, you young ruffian."

"I see." The young woman was certainly smiling now, though Mikhail couldn't see why. "Well, my name is Veronika, and my friends and I were wondering why you didn't come out to introduce yourself."

"Your friends?" Mikhail glanced back at the truck out on the street and found that the other passengers were watching them over the edge of the truckbed. "...don't trust anyone who's 'friends' with the Special Forces," he said suspiciously. "You wouldn't know it, but those soldiers have just about gone and doomed our precious hometown to burn in the fiery pit."

She hesitated for a second, and then the young woman let out a laugh. "I knew it!" she chuckled. "Wait 'till I tell Tatyana that you thought she was a soldier. She won't believe it."

It dawned on Mikhail rather slowly. "...that one's *not* with the CSF?"

"No, of course she isn't," Veronika said merrily. "She stole that uniform off the guard when we broke out of the camp."

"So you *did* escape!" Mikhail exclaimed, and Veronika nodded. "We're just trying to get some supplies before we get out of the city."

"Ahh, now I see." Mikhail broke into a grin. "Well, let me come out and make the proper introductions then! always glad to see more honest citizens getting themselves out of the clutches of those government hounds."

Veronika turned his gun around and handed it back to Mikhail butt-first. "I'm sure they'll be pleased to meet you as well, General."

~~~~~

"I'll bet she's gotten herself killed," Tatyana mused aloud.

"We haven't heard any gunfire though," Nikita whispered.

"There's no gunshot when someone stabs you."

Nikita, Elena and Alexei lay in the bed of the truck, peeking over the edge, and Tatyana was sheltering on the far side of the vehicle. In the five minutes since Veronika had snuck into the TV repair shop the silhouette of their watcher had vanished from the window, but there had been no other signs of confrontation. Tatyana had unslung her AKS-47 and was holding it at the ready.

When the first person emerged from around the side of the building Tatyana popped up and took aim with her rifle. Alexei ducked. Then Veronika appeared, waving her arms in the air. "It's okay!" she shouted across the street. "Don't shoot!"

Tatyana cautiously lowered her rifle, and three heads bobbed up over the edge of the truckbed once again. Elena gave a small giggle and Nikita hushed her.

Their unknown watcher turned out to be a scruffy-looking old man loaded down with a motley array of equipment, weapons and military gear. His belt was sagging under the weight of several homemade grenades and multiple ammo belts were crisscrossed over his chest. A gas mask was pushed up on his forehead like a ridiculous rubber hat. Around his neck were three crucifixes, a rosary, a portrait of the Blessed Virgin strung on a length of parachute cord, and a string of desiccated garlic cloves.

"It's alright, comrades!" the man barked as he drew near to the truck. "Fellow Chormans have nothing to fear from me!"

Veronika was smiling as she came up. "Tatyana -- you'll never believe this," she said loudly. "The General here thought you were an actual soldier! It's just like I told you -- in that uniform you really look the part. You should've enlisted back at home."

Tatyana gave the newcomer a careful once-over, and then her gaze flicked over to Veronika. "...nah, I'm not interested in joining the Special Forces," she said. "Don't pay nearly well enough for what they want from you."

Mikhail reached the truck and snapped into a crisp salute. He gave his audience a moment to return the gesture, but when they didn't he eventually let his arm drop. "General Mikhail Ilyich Litvinenko -- war hero and survivalist, at your service."

The tall individual in the CSF uniform snorted and coughed inside her mask. The three in the truckbed all looked delighted to see him, almost as if they were on the verge of laughter. Relief at finding someone to help them, Mikhail surmised.

"Uh, pleased to meet you...General. My name is Nikita Ivanovich, and this is my niece Elena Yuryevna." The taller of the two civilian men nodded in Mikhail's direction.

"Alexei Nikolaevich. Pleased to meet you," said the second one.

"Tatyana Igorevna," said the uniformed individual.

"Bah!" said Mikhail. "What kind of a man's name is that?"

"It's not a man's name."

"I know! what on earth was wrong with your parents, naming you that?"

Veronika gave a loud chortle and Tatyana glanced sharply in her direction. All in one movement she unbuckled her gas mask and swept it off her head. Under the mask Tatyana's face was flushed, blond hair sticking to her forehead in dark streaks.

"Huh!" Mikhail came closer, squinting up at her. "So they named you Tatyana 'cos you kind of looked like a woman, I suppose?"

Tatyana threw her hands in the air. "I'm going to wait in the truck," she announced. "Once you clowns have decided where we're going, let me know." She marched back around to the cabin, climbed into the driver's seat and slammed the door shut after her.

Mikhail was scratching his stubbly chin. "If he doesn't want people taking him for a woman the boy had better stop shaving," he commented.

"I...uh..." That was Nikita, doing his level best not to laugh out loud. "So, General...Litvinenko...what are you doing out here?"

Mikhail beamed at him. "Safeguarding our fair city, that's what! These are dark times, you know, and impure forces roam the streets."

"You mean the soldiers?" Veronika asked.

"Worse! far worse!" Mikhail stabbed a finger at the sky. "The very spawn of Satan is abroad in these days. I've seen them -- confronted the demons face to face." He wagged his finger at the listeners. "This evil takes many forms. 'Times it looks like flowers, innocent flowers -- except they're black as pitch, and glowing like foxfire..."

" -- inkweed," said the grey-eyed young man. "You've found inkweed growing? where?"

"All over the place." Mikhail spread his arms, demonstrating. "Grows in dark corners, away from the light. Only way to get rid of it is to burn it."

His audience was listening intently. "And then there's the demons themselves," Mikhail intoned, lowering his bushy eyebrows. "Looks like a man, but black, black all over...and they've got no faces." He swept a hand over his features. "None at all. As if God himself had erased 'em from their heads."

Elena's eyes were enormous. Nikita and Veronika exchanged looks. "If you ask me, that's what becomes of those who catch the demon plague," Mikhail declared. "They start with the black spots on their bodies, then the spots spread...the stuff grows into your brain, your heart...into your very *soul*." Mikhail slapped the flat of his hand on the tailgate for emphasis, and Elena jumped. "And then...you become *one of them*."

Nikita held Elena close to his chest. "So you're out here looking for these...devils, am I right?" Veronika asked.

"Yep!" said Mikhail. "Demons, and any that's infested with the Devil's touch. For them, God's mercy is their only hope." He cast a searching look across the truck's passengers. "None of you have got the black spots...do you?"

All four of them emphatically reassured Mikhail that they did not have it. He pointed up toward the truck's cabin. "What about him?"

"Uh, Tatyana is actually a woman," Nikita muttered. "And yes, she's clean too."

"Ahh, good, good," Mikhail's relief was visible. "They must've thrown you in the camps for some other reason, then -- if you don't show up for 'processing' it's into the camps you go, healthy or sick."

" -- that's exactly it," Veronika interjected. "None of us wanted to evacuate, so when they rounded us up they threw us in the camps." She gave Mikhail a winning smile. "Didn't even bother testing us to see that we were clean."

Mikhail nodded sagely...of course he'd been right. "Lucky you didn't catch the plague while you were in there -- those who're blighted can't be helped, you know. Sending 'em to God as quick as possible's the only way to save their souls."

In spite of her uncle's best attempts to comfort her the little girl was looking more and more horrified. Must have been through a lot, Mikhail imagined. "Listen," Nikita began. "We're just trying to get some traveling supplies and get out of Khostok before they catch us again. You wouldn't know of anyplace we could get some food or some camping gear, would you?"

Mikhail's expression turned crafty. "...I might," he said.

"You might?"

Mikhail nodded. "I've got to -- keeping the demons at bay is tiring work, I need all the equipment I can lay hands on."

"...we might be able to work something out," Veronika suggested.

Mikhail turned to her. The young woman unzipped one of the pockets on her coveralls, reached in, and brought out a handful of medicine bottles. "I imagine a demon hunter might be in need of painkillers, antibiotics...all sorts of drugs, I bet. But these are gonna be harder to scavenge than canned food or water, right?"

Mikhail's eyes gleamed.

"So how about it? Interested in trading?"

"I'm sure we can work out some sort of arrangement." Mikhail watched as the bottles disappeared into Veronika's pockets again. "Hell -- I'll even put you up in my secret hideout for the night, until you're kitted out to travel. You're not safe out here on the streets -- not with the kind of things that's roaming the city."

"That's -- very generous of you," Veronika said haltingly. "But I'm not sure we need -- "

" -- got a map you might be interested in," Mikhail went on. "If you're looking to get out of the city, that is. The river and the mountains aren't the only ways out of Khostok."

Mikhail let this sink in. The three adults looked at each other in silence, and then Veronika turned back to him. "We'll at least come have a look," she promised. "We can work out a trade when we get to your place, anyway."

"Alright then!" Mikhail thumped his fist on the tailgate. "I'll lead the way! Tonight, you're all going to be guests of the Hotel Litvinenko!"

He left the three of them to converse amongst themselves and marched around to the passenger side of the truck, knocking on the window. Their driver leaned over and opened the passenger door.

"What?"

"I'll be directing you to my secret hideout," Mikhail announced as he climbed up into the passenger seat. "We're going to see about trading off some of your surplus medicine for some needful supplies I have on hand."

The blonde woman -- if she was indeed a woman -- gave him a glacial look. Without another word she buckled up. Glancing in the rearview to make sure the rest of the passengers were still in the truckbed, she turned the key in the ignition and stepped on the clutch. The vehicle began to roll forward.

Mikhail instructed her where to turn, and Tatyana followed his directions with ease. After several minutes' they were rolling along at a good speed and Mikhail had to admit that she was not unskilled. "Hey, you're not a bad driver," he pointed out. "You sure you're not a man?"

Tatyana slammed on the brakes hard enough to send Mikhail rocketing forward into the footwell. His head rebounded off the dashboard with a thunking sound, and if he hadn't been wearing the gas mask up on his forehead he might have been left with a concussion.

"Sorry about that," Tatyana said, and for the first time since Mikhail had met her she was smiling. "You might want to buckle up."

~~~~~

"Hotel...Komarov," Elena said aloud, reading the tarnished metal letters mounted on the faded wallpaper in the lobby.

"Nah, this is the Hotel Litvinenko!" Mikhail declared. "Last bastion of freedom and security in this whole city."

Their journey had taken the five Camp escapees deep into the heart of the abandoned areas of Khostok. In spite of his manner and appearance Mikhail's sense of direction was seemingly intact, and he had brought them safely to his hideout without so much as a wrong turn. After stashing the truck in an alleyway behind a dumpster he had escorted his five new guests in through the hotel's employee entrance, leading them through the kitchen and laundry rooms to reach the expansive lobby of the vacant hotel.

Mikhail allowed his guests to pause by the reception desk, taking in their surroundings. He knew they would be impressed. If they had the good taste enough to overlook the cobwebs, the dust, the ratholes, the dry rot, the mildew and all the other signs of nature's efforts to reclaim the hotel, its opulence was in clear evidence. He doubted any of the five had ever seen such luxury.

Finally Alexei sneezed, shattering the silence. Tatyana mumbled something about putting her gas mask back on.

"You...live here alone?" Nikita asked. Elena was reaching out to touch the ancient phone on the reception desk and her uncle pulled her hand away.

"Yep," Mikhail said proudly. "Sole owner and proprietor too! C'mon -- I'll show you upstairs."

In awed silence Mikhail's guests followed him upstairs to the second floor. They were obviously not as hardened to the ways of survivalism as he, and little things like the shrieking and splintering sounds that came from the stairs, or the sleek gray rat that skittered across Veronika's foot, seemed to distress them for some reason.

When they reached the tangle of rope and broken furniture that barricaded the staircase the group hesitated. "What happened here?" Veronika asked, eyeing the scorch-marks that blackened the rose-printed wallpaper.

"Here is the site of one of my many battles against the forces of darkness," Mikhail replied. "That black weed's been growing in my hotel down on the lower levels. Only thing it respects is fire."

They seemed suitably impressed by his tale, if Mikhail read their expressions correctly. Ushering them off the stairs and onto the second floor, Mikhail guided the five of them toward the darkness visible behind the half-open doors of the elevator. Here his guests hung back again, somehow reluctant to follow him into the black void of the open elevator shaft.

"Don't worry!" Mikhail called out to them. "It's safe!" By way of illustration he stomped a couple times on the roof of the elevator car beneath his feet, setting the cables to shivering. "Come on in -- you've got to go up the ladder to get upstairs!"

One by one the five of them trickled into the elevator shaft, stepping onto the roof of the car as if it were thin ice. They seemed just as suspicious of Mikhail's makeshift chair-leg-and-drapery-cord ladder as they had been of the creaking staircase, but all five of them made the ascent to the third floor, even the little girl.

From there it was a simple matter of climbing the stairs from the third to the seventh floor, up to the penthouse. Alexei's foot went through a rotted step between the fifth and sixth floors and everyone made a big deal over it, but they nonetheless reached the penthouse all in one piece, as Mikhail knew they would.

"Make yerselves at home!" he cried magnanimously, sweeping an arm at the penthouse suite. He shucked his backpack off and tossed it onto the king-size bed, sending a mushroom cloud of milky dust billowing up from the quilt. Elena pulled her shirt up over her nose and mouth.

"Nice jacket," Tatyana said.

"You like this?" Mikhail spun around, showing off the enormous portrait of the Virgin Mary he had sewn onto the back of his military surplus coat. "Made it myself! One can't be too careful, you know."

Alexei was sitting on a chair picking splinters out of his ankle, and he muttered something that Mikhail didn't catch. Elena peered out through the grimy glass of the patio door at the Khostok cityscape below them. Nikita hovered nearby, enjoying the same view.

"You said you had a map?" Veronika prompted.

"Ahhh..." Mikhail rubbed his hands together. "That I do, yes, that I do."

Heads turned.

"But I say we talk business after we've had lunch -- how does that sound to everyone?"

Elena's response was immediate and enthusiastic, and it seemed that nobody had the heart to disagree with her. Mikhail went into his stores of "reclaimed" goods and brought out an industrial-size can of stewed beef and another of new potatoes. His guests watched with undisguised interest as he assembled the tin pots over a series of tiny camping stoves in the center of the room.

Presently the aroma of hot food began to fill the penthouse. Mikhail even found a package of dried-out bread rolls in his stash and skewered several of these on one of his cleaner bayonets, toasting them over the small open flame.

"Those are gonna taste like canned fuel," Tatyana pointed out. She had stripped out of the soldier's protective suit and was standing around in a tee-shirt and jeans, watching Mikhail's progress.

Veronika had taken a tube of something from her zippered pocket and was applying it to Alexei's ankle. "I'll eat yours if you don't want it," she offered.

Nikita squeezed himself back in through the penthouse door with his arms full of blankets and quilts sourced from the other rooms. "Blankets?" Veronika said, looking up. "What do we need those for?"

"Well, if we're spending the night we'll need someplace to lie down."

Veronika wound a strip of gauze around Alexei's ankle. "I thought we were going to pick up our supplies and go tonight." She tucked the end of the gauze into the bandage. "It's not safe in the city."

"Y' won't be able to go tonight anyway, comrades," Mikhail said.

Tatyana's expression turned wary. "...and why's that?" asked Veronika.

Mikhail glanced up from the simmering pot of stewed beef. "Oh, you'll see when you get a look at the map." So saying, he fetched a bottle of his second-best vodka and laid out some relatively clean glasses beside it. "Gather 'round, everyone, food's just about ready."

All five of them had taken up seats on the floor by the time he'd finished speaking. Elena was bouncing up and down with impatience as Mikhail began ladling the stew into the tin camping plates.

"I, uh..." Nikita tore his eyes away from the meal. "We really appreciate this, but...I don't think there's any way we can repay you."

Mikhail chuckled as he passed Elena the first dish of stew. "Ah, but you're wrong about that too." He lifted the bottle of vodka. "Have a drink?"

They all ate their dinner in voracious silence, gulping down seconds and thirds as soon as they were offered. The toasted bread rolls did indeed taste faintly of camping stove fuel but nobody complained, not even Tatyana.

The only person who turned down the vodka was Veronika. Elena wanted to try it along with the adults, though after Nikita permitted her a sip she immediately began coughing and pronounced it horrible. Her uncle laughed a little. "Serves you right. Next time, don't ask."

Once the plates were empty and the camping stoves had burned themselves out Elena announced that she was sleepy. Nikita rose to assemble a bed out of the blankets he'd brought. Folded into a down comforter that cost more than Nikita's car, Elena slipped easily into sleep. Nikita patted her head and came back to rejoin the circle around the camping stoves.

Veronika cleared her throat. "Now...why can't we leave tonight?"

Mikhail gave her a slightly boozy smile. "Well, now..." He looked around at the expectant faces. "Has anyone here heard of the warrens?"

"...you mean the B-20 system," Tatyana said at last. Judging by the flush on her cheeks she'd had almost as much vodka as Mikhail.

"Right!"

"It's a series of linked bomb shelters. The military built a bunch of underground complexes like that during the war," Tatyana explained, seeing the puzzled looks her companions were giving her. "B-20 was the one under Khostok."

"What does that have to do with us?" Nikita asked. "I thought you knew of a way out of the city."

"I do, indeed I do." Mikhail seemed to relish the attention he was getting. "Y'see, the warrens go aaalllll under our city, and there's multiple ways to get in and out of it. One of the tunnels goes right under the Volgin River and comes out on the other side."

"Oh," Nikita said, realizing. "You think we can bypass the river patrols if we get into this shelter network, is that it?"

"Yup, yup."

" -- the entrances to B-20 are all hidden, though," Tatyana objected. "Even though nobody's using them, the locations are still classified."

"...is that the map you were talking about?" Alexei asked. He hadn't spoken much since he'd begun drinking, and was sitting with his chin resting on his knees. "You have a map showing the entrances -- is that it?"

Mikhail cackled. "Clever boy, you are!"

"But that still doesn't explain why we can't go tonight," Veronika put in.

"I don't see why there's such a hurry." Nikita was looking back over his shoulder at Elena, bundled up in her quilt. "We could probably use the rest."

"Well, let me put it to you like this." With a flourish Mikhail drew Old Tomasz's map from his jacket pocket. He laid it on the floor beside the near-empty bottle of vodka, smoothing out the creases, and motioned for the others to gather around.

"Here," said Mikhail, stabbing the map with his finger, "is one of the entrances to the warrens."

There was a bewildered silence.

"Oh...that's your map, huh?" Veronika sounded disappointed.

"It looks like...is the entrance indoors?" Nikita asked.

"Some of the entrances were in government buildings," Tatyana said. "Made it easier to do the excavating in secret."

Veronika scratched her head. "Which building is that?"

So they couldn't read the map -- as much as Mikhail might have expected from a group of civilians. "That building is a Khostok hospital," he explained. "The entrance is somewhere inside."

"Where?"

"Ahh..." Mikhail was grinning. "That's what I don't know." He sat back on his heels. "I'm not as young as I used to be," he admitted, "and these war wounds of mine like to give me trouble now and then. I'm not fit for poking around in search of the entrance -- that's a big building, and it could be anywhere inside. But that's where you young ones come in."

"You want us to find the entrance for you," Nikita finished for him. He looked around the room. "Well, I don't know about everyone else, but I'm okay with that. Besides, we'd need to find the entrance ourselves if we're getting out of the city."

Tatyana lifted her empty glass in agreement. Veronika was chewing her lower lip, but she nodded too. "Taking the shelter route might be our best way out."

"Now y'see why you need to head out in the morning." Mikhail began refolding his precious map, careful not to smudge the crayon. "You could be explorin' for hours before you find the entrance. Then once you get down in the warrens you're still looking at a good long hike to get out of Khostok. You'll need to be rested up and geared up before you even think about heading down there."

"We can start searching for the entrance tomorrow," Nikita said. "Once we get to the hospital -- "

" -- which hospital is it?"

Everyone turned to Alexei.

"It's the Gurlukovich Memorial Hospital," Mikhail said. "Been there before?"

Alexei's eyes widened. "But -- they're using the Memorial Hospital as a refugee camp."

"How would you know?" Nikita asked.

"No, wait -- he's right." Tatyana was frowning. "Gurlukovich Memorial Hospital was designated Red Camp One. You're sure that's the right building?"

"Positive!"

"Then we can't do it. There's no way to look for trapdoors into hidden shelters when there's soldiers everywhere." Nikita ran a hand through his dark hair. "Escaping from *one* camp was enough for me."

Mikhail gave a mocking laugh. "Comrades, comrades, don't worry. It's not a camp. Sure, there's signs out front that say that, but it's only a ruse -- a way of keepin' noses out of the hospital, keepin' their secrets safe. If you go down there -- "

"Of course it's a real camp." Tatyana gave the old man an incredulous look. "It was the first camp that we -- that the CSF set up in the city."

"But there's nobody there," Mikhail said, thumping his empty glass on the carpet. "I was down there myself just the other day. The building's empty. Everyone's gone."

Tatyana stared at him. "...they're gone?"

"On my honor as a soldier!"

"Um..." Nikita looked uncertain. "You're sure it was *this* hospital they used for Red Camp One?"

Tatyana turned on him. "My memory's fine," she said icily. "Gurlukovich Memorial Hospital is Red Camp One. Or it was, at least." She turned away from everyone, looking out through the sliding glass door of the patio at the rooftops of the city.

"...maybe they were evacuated?" Veronika mused out loud.

Tatyana was shaking her head. Nikita made a helpless gesture. "Well...we'll find out tomorrow, won't we?"

"Sure you will," Mikhail soothed them. "We can make some trades in the morning -- I'll see to it that you're geared up with everything you need to do your exploring."

Nikita thanked him and, in the uneasy silence that followed, rose to his feet to clear away the empty dishes. Tatyana, Veronika and Alexei soon followed suit, picking up plates and cups, throwing out the spent canisters of fuel, scrubbing out the pots with a rag and a little water. It had taken a decent meal and a round of drinks to help them realize it, but they were all indeed exhausted by all they had been through.

But as far as Mikhail was concerned, he had never felt more full of energy. It was better than he'd dared hope for -- these five travelers were a godsend. It was a sign, yes, a sign from above that he'd run into them while on the way down to the hospital himself, in search of the very same entrance they were going to be finding for him.

It was as if God had spoken directly into Mikhail's ear. "My son," He might as well have said, "I have seen thy power and thy virtue, and have reserved for thee a holy mission. Take thee in hand these tools which I have given ye, and use them to light the way to the warrens. Let them brave the dangers of the hospital, my son, to uncover this entrance in thy stead.

"And once they have uncovered thy way, bring to the mouth of that Pit thy homemade grenades, pipe bombs, and other such weapons of righteousness. Cast these into that black chasm, from whence issueth all manner of sin and corruption, and seal the entrance thereof for ever more."

"...thy will be done," Mikhail breathed, transported. "Amen!"

## CHAPTER TWELVE

"Morning, Chief."

"Good morning, Ivana."

"Having some tea?"

"Mm? oh, this isn't for me." Police Chief Petrenko indicated the box of Motherland's Finest Black Tea tucked under his arm. "It's for the Colonel."

"Ah," said Petrenko's secretary. She shot him a sympathetic look before turning back to her typing.

As he rode the elevator up to the fourth floor the Police Chief considered the box of tea. The advertisers had opted for a traditional style of artwork, and the box depicted a painted landscape with blue mountain peaks rising in the background and a vast tea plantation in the foreground. Ruddy-faced, cheerfully nationalistic workers marched along the rows of tea plants with wicker baskets, gathering the leaves.

He couldn't imagine what Akimov saw in this stuff, let alone that he would like it enough to drink cups and cups of it. Petrenko had always thought that tea tasted like water out of a raingutter -- he'd have taken coffee over tea anyday.

When he reached the door of the former Emergency Public Broadcast System office Petrenko knocked politely. "Enter," croaked the Colonel, and the Chief let himself in.

"Ahh, Chief Petrenko." Akimov rose from behind his desk to greet him. "Good to see you."

"Good morning, sir." Now why did he always start to sweat whenever he talked to this man? It was the mask, Petrenko decided. The protective suit was nothing more than a fancy rain slicker, nothing to have nightmares over, but their gas masks were something else. With their faces hidden by those weird contours of black rubber and eyes concealed by mirrored lenses the CSF no longer looked quite human. You couldn't look them in the eyes, couldn't read their expressions. And it certainly didn't help that they all sounded like robots through the mask.

"I've brought you more tea." Petrenko held out the box like an offering.

"Ahh -- thank you, thank you." Akimov took the box and set it aside on the shelf with the hotplate, kettle and teacups. "Have some tea with me?"

Petrenko could feel the sweat welling up in his pores. "Oh, no, thank you sir. I've got to be -- got some work to attend to."

"Of course." Akimov reseated himself. "You must be very busy."

"Yes, sir." Actually Petrenko had been less busy than usual -- crime had markedly reduced as Khostok's population had dwindled away to less than a tenth of its former size. He eyed the scattering of maps and printed reports that covered Akimov's desk. "I'm sure you're pretty swamped yourself."

"Oh, it is what it is." Akimov gestured at the kettle. "That's why I like having something to drink -- helps keep me sane, you know."

Petrenko couldn't imagine handling Akimov's duties, but he pictured himself drinking something a bit stronger than tea under such circumstances. "I'm just glad we're no longer under rationing," Akimov was saying, almost to himself. "You know, during the Great Patriotic War they reserved the real tea leaves for our troops, and let the civilian market have all sorts of different leaves and twigs in their tea bags. Most of them didn't taste a thing like tea."

"I can imagine," Petrenko said.

"You remember the rationing, no doubt?"

"Oh, I do, I do." Petrenko rubbed at the back of his neck and found it clammy. "I was only a boy at the time, but I remember the coupon books. Waiting in lines at the stores, that kind of thing."

"Ahh," said Akimov. "How was the tea back then?"

Petrenko hesitated. "Uh, I don't know -- never drank tea."

"I see."

The chief swallowed hard. "I'll bet you were grateful to have real tea again once the war was over, right sir?"

"Oh -- " Akimov chuckled. "I don't remember. The war ended shortly after I was born."

Petrenko blinked. " -- How old *are* you?" he blurted out.

"Thirty-five."

It was almost impossible. Colonel Akimov was younger than the chief himself! It exploded Petrenko's former mental image of the man as a soft-spoken white-haired old soldier, distinguished by his service in the Great Patriotic War. How on earth had this man gotten to his position by the age of thirty-five?

"Quality," Akimov pronounced slowly, "is the most essential factor in any soldier.

Quality can not be assumed to be present or absent on the basis of race, gender, class, or age." He twined his gloved fingers together, nodding. "Quality is what matters."

A salty trickle ran down Petrenko's spine. "Of course! I didn't mean -- "

" -- take these teabags as an example." Akimov pointed at the box on the shelf. "Before they are packaged and sent to the consumers, they must be inspected by trained professionals to ensure they meet certain quality control standards. Selecting the most advanced processing machinery, the finest grade of leaves, the best-trained workers...none of these things can guarantee that one hundred percent of the finished products will pass quality control."

"Of course not, sir."

"The quality control inspectors have a thankless job," Akimov continued. "Their work is invisible to most people. Very few consumers know how many defective, sub-par or dangerous items have been stopped from reaching their hands. They only see the end result."

Petrenko had no idea where this lecture on quality control had come from, but he suspected he had offended the Colonel in some way. He held his breath as Akimov paused for a moment, lost in thought. "And yet it's strange," the Colonel mused. "The most dangerous weapon of all is rarely if ever quality controlled."

Petrenko was nodding automatically when he caught himself. "...the most dangerous weapon?"

"Yes indeed." Akimov pointed his mask directly at the Chief. "What do you suppose that most dangerous weapon is?"

Surely he must have insulted Akimov by asking about his age -- that was it. He was probably the youngest Colonel with the CSF, if not the youngest in all of Chorma, and it would make sense that he was sensitive about his age. That was why he was putting Petrenko on the spot like this. "Uh...the atomic bomb, sir?"

The mask swung from side to side as Akimov shook his head. "Tell me, Chief Petrenko -- who made that bomb?"

"Th-the Americans, sir."

"...and what are the Americans?"

Petrenko's mouth was growing drier by the moment. He swallowed again. "Uh, capitalists?!"

"You're missing the point."

Petrenko willed the floorboards beneath him to split open, dropping him down through the floor of the former Emergency Public Broadcast System office, all the way down to the ground floor of the station. "S-sir, I -- "

Akimov sighed. "Humans."

"...eh?"

"Humans built that bomb." Akimov leaned over the desk toward the Chief, lowering his voice. "Since the dawn of time, humans have built all the bombs -- all the guns -- all the knives and swords that have ever existed. Even chemical weapons, like the kind currently plaguing your city, would never have endangered mankind to this degree if they had not first been discovered, synthesized, refined and weaponized by human hands."

Petrenko was speechless. "Humans are the most dangerous weapon," Akimov said, sitting back in his chair. "They are directly or indirectly responsible for billions of untimely deaths. And humans are almost never controlled for quality. Doesn't that strike you as strange?"

Several things were striking Petrenko as very strange right now, but humanity's lack of quality inspection was not one of them. "Practically anything you manufacture -- even something so simple as a tea bag -- must meet quality standards. But humans don't have to." Akimov spread his hands in an expansive gesture. "Practically any two individuals who meet certain biological minimums can manufacture a human being. They need no license, no permits. They can, and often do, create both unneeded and unwanted human beings quite by accident.

"And the product they create will not be inspected in any manner before it is installed into human society." The Colonel tilted his head in Petrenko's direction. "You, being the Chief of Police in Khostok, have doubtlessly run across thousands of human products that would have failed inspection if anyone had been tasked with inspecting them. Humans that utterly fail at being productive, functional members of a healthy society. Instead of inspecting them early on -- when their flaws could be easily remedied -- it falls to your department to clean up the aftermath of their failure to integrate."

Petrenko thought that he might have been able to make sense of what Akimov was saying, but the way his mind was reeling he could barely remember his own name. "But I see that I'm boring you," Akimov said, reaching for a stack of papers on his desk. "My apologies."

Petrenko snapped back to himself. "No, I -- I'm sorry, I wasn't -- "

"I'd almost forgotten -- I do have some good news for you." Akimov flipped through the papers, scanning their contents. "The evacuation of the uninfected citizenry is at ninety percent completion. We expect the last few buses to be leaving later on today."

Slowly the fog was clearing from his mind, and when the words finally sank in Petrenko's heart leapt. "You're almost done?" He scarcely dared believe it.

Akimov nodded. "We encourage you and your men to get ready -- you'll be evacuating along with the CSF when we withdraw from Khostok," he said. "Of course we can't withdraw until the city has been sanitized to the satisfaction of the Regional Secretary, but we anticipate that to happen in short order."

"Of course." Petrenko was elated -- he could almost feel himself floating. It was nearly over! "Thank you for letting me know...I'll let you get back to work," he stammered, reaching for the doorknob.

"Good day, Chief Petrenko." Akimov waved to dismiss him.

Petrenko was halfway out the door when a thought struck him. "What about the people who were infected?"

"Oh yes -- they will be dealt with," Akimov said absently.

"...how?"

The Colonel lifted his head. "I'm afraid that's classified," he said. "But per Secretary Glukhovsky's orders, the blight will be cleared from Khostok." Akimov's smile was evident in his tone. "That was the mission I was given, and it will be carried out."

Petrenko nodded slowly. He wasn't sure he understood, not fully, but he was beginning to see that he wasn't meant to.

"Good day, Colonel," said Petrenko, and eased the door shut after himself.

~~~~~

It was happening again. Alexei was twelve years old, and his mother was crying in the kitchen. And he knew  -- as he always knew -- that she was crying over his father.

The skinny young boy whom Alexei had once been hesitated on the threshold of the kitchen, scuffing the toe of his sneaker against the fraying carpet. He didn't want to go into the kitchen, but he knew he would. He knew by heart what his mother would tell him; her own personal account of what had happened to his father, what the DIO had done and were doing and would do to the man. And then, when he was sick and near-fainting with horror, Alexei knew what his mother would tell him next. That his father's fate was his own, as soon as the DIO caught him.

Alexei watched his sneakers move, carrying him into the kitchen, across the yellowed and cracking linoleum with its faded pattern of intertwined violets. His heart drummed in his ears, nearly loud enough to drown out the sound of his mother's sobs.

And then the crying stopped.

That wasn't supposed to happen. Confused, Alexei looked up. The kitchen's threadbare curtains and water-stained wallpaper were the same, but his mother had vanished -- wasn't even in the kitchen at all. In her place was a terrifying apparition: a creature in a hooded coat and pants, all black as ink and shiny as oil. They wore black gloves and black boots, and their face was not a human face at all, but something with hollowly gleaming eyes and a long snout ending in a flattened cylinder.

It took him a moment to recognize the monster for what it was -- a CSF soldier in their suit and gas mask, standing in his mother's kitchen. As soon as Alexei identified it the soldier looked up and caught sight of him.

"I'm sorry," said the soldier. "Yuri's dead."

Alexei jerked back into consciousness.

Darkness surrounded him. Alexei lay there in bed for a long time, catching his breath and trying to stop the runaway jackhammering of his heart. He could see nothing of the room, but the sound of Anatoly's droning snore was somehow comforting to him. It was familiar, at least...it told him that he was still at the Lubukov Agricultural Labs, and they were still under the quarantine.

And small wonder the CSF were invading his nightmares -- they were everywhere in the Labs these days, barking orders, brandishing their rifles, threatening them over the announcement system. How long had they been there at the Labs? weeks? months?

Alexei groaned, rubbing his eyes. He was cracking up and he knew it.

In the darkness of the dorm room someone stirred. "Lyosha?" whispered a voice.

"...Yura?"

"Yeah, it's me," Yuri replied. "You okay?"

"...had another nightmare," Alexei said.

"Ugh. Too bad."

"Yeah."

"What was it this time?"

Alexei thought carefully before answering. "...I dreamed that you were dead," he whispered back.

Yuri hesitated. "...I'm sorry,"

"Nah," Alexei half-smiled, "don't be sorry. Not like it's your fault I get nightmares."

Yuri said nothing.

" -- Yura?"

No reply. The only sound was Anatoly's snoring, a constant low rumble in the darkness.

Alexei turned his head. The room wasn't completely without light, but it still took awhile for his eyes to adjust to the dimness. There were low dark silhouettes scattered here and there: the outlines of sleepers. But that couldn't be right -- for one, there were too many of them. And it looked like they were lying on the floor.

Alexei turned the other way and froze. A spectacular nighttime view of the Khostok skyline lay behind him, visible through the glass of a sliding patio door. Most of the buildings were unlit, but the stars and the moon gave off enough light for him to see.

Goosebumps prickled along his arms. Alexei turned back to the sleepers, more awake and starting to remember now. The snoring wasn't Anatoly -- it must have been the crazy old man, the one who claimed to be fighting demons. That was the potbellied silhouette over to Alexei's right, where the snoring was coming from. They were in his "hotel", up on the seventh floor.

Everything had begun flooding back to him, the weight of grey reality pressing down on his chest, suffocating him. Now he remembered Tatyana and Veronika and the escape they had made from the Labs; meeting Nikita and Elena, and their second escape from Red Camp Three. He was getting Yuri's family out of the city because -- he recalled it clearly now -- that had been Yuri's final wish.

Alexei could see them all in the ghost-light that came from the cityscape behind him: the tall silhouette was Nikita, with Elena's small shape beside him. Veronika was nearby -- Alexei recognized her by the dark spill of her hair. Tatyana lay in her blankets a distance away from the rest of them, her rifle by her side. And the person across the room, the one sitting up and watching him --

A jolt of alarm went through him. Alexei recounted just to be sure, but there was still one extra body. There shouldn't have been a seventh person in the room.

Alexei lunged upright. The watcher jerked in surprise and ducked down. There wasn't enough light to make them out...Alexei couldn't tell if the stranger was young or old, male or female. In fact they didn't seem to have any distinguishing features at all -- it was as if they were nothing but a shadow, an outline of a human being.

"...hello?"

Slowly, moving with a fluid grace that was rather catlike, the stranger crept toward the open doorway of the penthouse. They stopped at the door and looked straight at Alexei, then slipped noiselessly out of the room.

Alexei realized some moments later that his hair was all standing on end. He rubbed at his arms, trying to drive away that skin-crawling feeling. Already he wasn't completely sure what it was he'd seen; the darkness and the silvery light gave everything a sheen of the surreal.

He had been dreaming, he decided. Or hallucinating. If his conversation with Yuri just now hadn't been a dream then he had certainly hallucinated the whole thing. It wouldn't be the first time he'd spoken to his dead coworkers. Alexei had not been right in the head for some time, and he knew he was getting less and less stable as time went by.

But that didn't matter, really. As long as he got Yuri's family to safety before he lost the rest of his marbles, everything would be alright.

Alexei lay back down again to wait for the sunrise. Dream or no dream, he knew he wouldn't be sleeping again tonight.

~~~~~

"Get his mask off," Shrike said.

Eagle looked at Shrike, then glanced down at Kestrel where he knelt on the floor of the shower room. "...you want *me* to do it?" he asked.

Shrike made an impatient noise and motioned with the muzzle of his rifle. "Yes, *you*, you idiot. Take off his mask."

"Okay, okay." Eagle bent down next to Kestrel. "I'm sorry," he whispered.

"No talking!" Shrike barked.

Kestrel held still as Eagle unclasped the buckles on his gas mask and lifted the mask up over his head. The cold air of the shower room rushed across his face, bringing the faint smell of mildew and disinfectant with it, and he gasped at the chill.

Under the mask Kestrel's face was gleaming with sweat, freckles standing out against his flushed cheeks, strands of brown hair sticking to his forehead and temples. He glared up at Shrike. "I told you -- I don't know anything."

Shrike didn't seem to hear him. "Now the suit."

"I can take my own suit off," Kestrel growled. He reached for the zipper of his protective suit and the muzzle of Shrike's rifle swung up, zeroing in on a spot between his eyes. "Don't move."

Kestrel froze.

"Eagle -- take his suit off."

Eagle reached over and tugged down the zipper of Kestrel's protective suit. Fingers of cold air slid over Kestrel's skin, chilling him through his undershirt. Once the zipper was halfway down Eagle started to unbuckle the belt that held the suit around Kestrel's waist. "Just do what he says, okay?" Eagle whispered.

"I said, no talking!"

Eagle helped Kestrel out of the black chemical protection suit, shucking it off over his shoulders and dropping it onto the tile floor behind him. "Gloves, boots, pants -- let's get it all off," Shrike said.

Kestrel stared Shrike down as Eagle undressed him. Once the gloves and boots were off Eagle knelt to undo Kestrel's pants, unzipping them and letting them fall to the floor. Kestrel could feel his skin shrinking away from the chill of the room. Eagle straightened up again, turning away so he wouldn't have to look at Kestrel.

Shrike produced a pair of handcuffs from his suit pocket, their chains jingling musically in the awkward silence. He jerked his chin up. "Hands in the air," he said, tossing the cuffs to Eagle.

A length of exposed piping curved downward from the ceiling of the shower room. Kestrel reached up and grabbed hold of it, the iciness of the bare metal numbing his skin. As Eagle handcuffed him to the pipe overhead Kestrel wondered for an instant if this was how Alexei had felt during his interrogation.

At least they hadn't used scissors to strip him. Kestrel knew that Shrike would have loved to do so -- he seemed to take a special interest in these "interview" sessions -- but the CSF's protective suits were too expensive to mutilate for the sake of a simple interrogation.

Once Kestrel was cuffed Shrike took a step back. "Now we can talk."

Kestrel rolled his eyes. "Seriously, Fedya, I've already told you everything." He jerked on his cuffs a few times, testing the links. "I can't tell you what I don't know."

"You always were a bad liar, Vasya." Shrike walked in a circle around his prisoner, nodding appraisingly. "Where's Hawk?"

"Don't know."

"Forgotten?"

"She didn't *tell* me where she was headed." Kestrel jerked again on his handcuffs. They were solidly made, and the pipe wasn't going anywhere either.

"What a shame." Shrike completed his circuit and came around to stand in front of Kestrel again. He took Kestrel's chin in a finger and thumb, forcing the young man to face him.

"But really -- you were her best friend. Why wouldn't she tell you?"

"Oh, I don't know." Kestrel glowered at his captor. "Maybe she knew they'd give her position to some sick bastard like you, eh?"

Shrike squeezed a little harder on Kestrel's chin. "Some friend she was, then." He chuckled into his mask. "She sabotages the Labs by planting inkweed everywhere, infects all the civilian staff, and then skips out of town...leaving little Vasya to pay her bill."

Kestrel blinked. "...sabotage?"

"Oh, she didn't mention that to you? I'm not surprised." Shrike sounded triumphant.

"You -- she didn't sabotage anything and you know it."

"Colonel Akimov thinks she did." Shrike released Kestrel's face with a little shove. "He's the one who ordered this interrogation."

Kestrel shifted left and right, trying to stop the cuffs from cutting off his circulation. "What's the point? The Labs are going to hell and he wants to pin the blame on someone? How could finding Hawk solve anything right now?"

"...I'm not here to answer your questions," Shrike said, and now he sounded irritated. "I'm giving you a chance to come clean with us before the actual interrogation starts."

"Oh...oh, now I see." In spite of himself Kestrel had begun to smile. He turned to Eagle, who stepped back as if he didn't want to get involved. "Akimov didn't order this," Kestrel explained. "First of all, I know Hawk, and she'd never betray the CSF like this. She had no reason to. Second of all, I know the Colonel, and he trusted Hawk with his life. He'd never have suspected her without evidence. And third, even *if* Hawk had sabotaged the Labs -- which she didn't -- I know Akimov wouldn't waste time and manpower trying to catch her right now. He's too rational for that."

Eagle had shied away from Kestrel, anticipating what was coming. Kestrel turned back to Shrike. "And fourth, I know *you*, and you were just itching for a chance to chain me -- "

Kestrel didn't even see Shrike lashing out. He only saw the dark blur of a gloved hand for an instant before the impact hammered into his face. Something snapped, and Kestrel rocked back in his handcuffs, insensate for a moment. When Shrike seized his hair and dragged him back to his feet the pain helped to clear Kestrel's mind, and by the time he was standing upright again he'd started laughing.

"I knew it!" Kestrel said, somewhat indistinctly. The taste of copper was flooding his mouth and he leaned forward to spit pink-tinged saliva onto the white tiles of the shower room floor. He wouldn't have shared this with anyone, but he hadn't been completely positive about this interrogation being Shrike's own idea. In a way he was almost relieved -- that fist had confirmed his suspicions.

"You hit too early, Fedya," Kestrel scolded. "That should come later, after they're good and scared. You have to work up to it." He smirked at Shrike. "And never let the prisoner see you losing your temper."

Kestrel expected to be punched again, but instead Shrike stepped forward and seized Kestrel's throat, lifting him nearly off his feet. Judging by the tightness of his grip Kestrel had made the man very, very angry indeed.

"You haven't *seen* me lose my temper," Shrike snarled. The masked face was looming closer, close enough for Kestrel to see his own reflection in the mirrored eyepieces. It looked like blood was pouring from his nose, and the way it felt Kestrel would have been surprised if it didn't turn out to be broken. He still managed a smile anyway.

"I know what you're up to," Kestrel whispered. "Everything's gone to pieces since Hawk disappeared. The researchers have all got the blight, there's inkweed everywhere, and suddenly you're the one in charge of this trainwreck." He chuckled. "You know we're pulling out of Khostok any day now. You're thinking that you can blame Hawk for everything that's gone wrong at the Labs and win some points with the Colonel before we all go home."

Shrike had said nothing, but the gloved hand on Kestrel's throat was slowly tightening, making it harder to talk. "But it's not going to work, Fedya," Kestrel managed to say. Grey spots shimmered before his eyes. "...because I know why Hawk ran off."

Kestrel swam in darkness for an instant before the world came rushing back to him. Shrike had released his throat. Kestrel gasped and coughed, gulping in the air.

"I'll give you once chance," Shrike muttered. "Tell me why she left."

"You sure?" Kestrel couldn't resist. "Think about it -- you might not want to know."

Shrike reached out to grab his throat again and Kestrel leaned back. "Alright, I'll tell you!" He coughed again, then fixed Shrike with his broadest grin. "She caught the blight."

"Huh?" Shrike jerked upright. "She -- how?"

"The same way all the researchers caught it, you drooling idiot. It wasn't sabotage."

Shrike was intrigued enough by this new bit of information to overlook the insult. "Tell me how," he demanded.

"It's in the air." Kestrel lifted his chin. Shrike and Eagle both looked up as if expecting to see a black cloud of ink hovering above them. "You remember reading the reports about the air filtration system, right? Or did you sleep through the briefing?"

"The -- the explosion in Storage Room 5!" Eagle interjected. "It ruptured some of the ductwork, right?"

"Right," said Kestrel. "The vaporized ink in Room 5 got vented into the central air system, and from there it got into every single room in the Labs." He gave Shrike a pointed look. "*That's* how the researchers got infected, and how the inkweed started popping up all over the goddamn place. The Labs were full of ink vapor way before the CSF got here. It took weeks for the symptoms to show, but it was the explosion that did it, not Hawk. Unless you think she drove down to Khostok a week before the quarantine -- "

Shrike brushed him off with a gesture. "So the air's contaminated," he grunted. "But Hawk would have known that. You're saying she was stupid enough to take off her mask in a contaminated area?"

"Of course she wasn't."

"Then how..." Shrike broke off in midsentence, realizing. " -- you're not serious."

Kestrel let out a giggle. "Think about it, Fedya. You know Hawk wouldn't abandon her post for no reason. And she would never have taken her mask off in here."

Eagle let out a squeal of dismay. "You mean -- you mean the masks aren't filtering out the ink?" He was clutching his air filter in both hands. Kestrel felt almost sorry for him.

"You think I'd let you two take off my mask if it was doing me any good?" Kestrel shook his head, sending bright drops spattering onto the tile. "We're all doomed. You, me, the researchers, the CSF, and everyone else who's set foot inside the Agricultural Labs."

"You're lying," Shrike said, and Kestrel knew he had won. "You're lying."

"Why don't you go ask the Colonel?" Kestrel suggested. Much to his surprise Shrike backed away a couple paces, moving towards the shower room door. "Better yet, ask him if you should be wasting your time interrogating me. I'm sure he'll tell you -- "

But Shrike had bolted already. Kestrel blinked at the door as it swished back and forth. "It worked," he muttered, surprised.

"Is -- was that true?" Eagle asked in a quavering voice. He still hand both hands on his filter. Kestrel tried to shrug, but with his arms over his head it wasn't possible. "I don't know," he said honestly. "But I'd still get the hell out of the Labs if I were you."

Eagle made a whining noise and began to sidle toward the door.

"Hey -- " Kestrel called out to him. "I don't suppose you can uncuff me, can you?"

"Umm...no, sorry...not without authorization," he said sadly.

"Ahh. Well, doesn't hurt to ask."

Eagle was still retreating. "I'll see if I can get someone to approve it," he said. "You shouldn't be in here too long."

"I'd appreciate that."

"No problem." Eagle hesitated with his hand on the doorknob. "Uh, Kestrel?"

"Mm?"

"You know, I..." He dithered for a moment. "I never did think Hawk sabotaged the Labs," Eagle said finally. "She always seemed really...loyal, I guess. Better soldier than I am."

Kestrel chuckled low in his throat. "Well, now. If I see her again I'll tell her you think so."

"Okay, yeah -- and tell her I said hi, too." With that parting thought, Eagle slipped out of the room.

Kestrel breathed a silent sigh of relief. They were gone, at least for the moment, and he was still conscious. Better than that, he still had all five senses and all four limbs intact -- not everyone who'd been through a CSF interrogation could boast the same advantages.

Hanging there in his chains, Kestrel weighed his odds. If he saw Hawk again he'd have liked to tell her a good many things. But how probable was that?

"Not very likely," he muttered at the empty room.

The only sound was the muted plit, plit, plit of blood dripping onto the tiles. Even still, the scraping sound barely registered in Kestrel's mind. It was only when it stopped that he noticed it, lifting his head.

At first he thought he was hearing things -- he *had* been punched in the face, after all, and might have a concussion on top of all the other aches and pains -- but then the noise came again. Kestrel caught his breath and held it. It was a low grating sound, like something being slowly dragged across a cement floor. And it came from behind him.

Kestrel twisted around, swinging back and forth in his cuffs like a fish on a line. It was no good; he could barely turn more than a few degrees, and with his arms over his head like that he couldn't look back over his shoulder to see what it was. Panting from the exertion, he hung there and tried to think -- was there another door in back of the shower room, one they hadn't noticed? but that was unlikely; the CSF wouldn't have chosen such a room for their interrogations if there was more than one entrance.

Or perhaps someone had been hiding out in the shower room? Kestrel had to admit that this seemed a bit more realistic. Someone had been crouching out of sight in a shower stall during his questioning, and now that the interrogators were gone the eavesdropper was emerging to...to rescue him, maybe?

It was a silly thing to hope for, but one couldn't blame Kestrel for hoping. He cleared his throat. "...hello?" he said, feeling foolish.

The scraping halted again. Kestrel was just about to call out a second time when a loud metallic *clang* nearly made him jump out of his skin. Heart pounding, he squirmed around in his handcuffs, trying to turn around and only succeeding in wrenching his shoulder. Growling in frustration Kestrel let himself go limp again.

The noise kept echoing in his mind, replaying itself. It had sounded like metal -- like metal hitting the tile, in fact. Kestrel glanced eagerly up at the pipes overhead, but they were all still there, and solid as ever. So something else had fallen, then. What else in the room was made of metal? The showerheads, the doorknobs, the faucets, the knobs in the showers...

...and the metal covers on the floor drains.

That was what Kestrel had heard; he recognized it now. The scraping had been someone unscrewing the metal drain cover from its socket, and the clang had been the drain cover hitting the floor. But why would the yet-unseen stranger in the shower room bother taking the cover off the drain? Unless --

Kestrel's hair all stood on end. Unless the person was coming up *out* of the drain, into the shower room.

Kestrel thrashed and fought until a lancing pain in his right shoulder made him stop, his breath hissing through clenched teeth. " -- who's there?" he panted.

No reply. Who in their right mind would be crawling around in the drain system anyway? Were the pipes even wide enough to fit a human being? but if not, then what on earth was coming up out of the drain behind him?

When the hand touched the small of his back Kestrel screamed aloud. Or he tried to, at any rate. Something caught the shriek in his throat and choked it off, and a soundless rush of air escaped in his place.

Dizziness swamped him all at once, muddying his thoughts. His surroundings faded into greyness. That punch must have given him a concussion after all, Kestrel noted with vague surprise. The little hand on his back slipped away. Footsteps echoed in the shower room, coming to his senses over a great distance, the noise nearly drowned out by the buzzing in his ears.

Kestrel hadn't been aware of closing his eyes, but when the hand touched his face he found himself opening them again. He was looking down at a blood-splashed tile floor. Very gently the hand on his chin lifted his head up, until Kestrel was looking at the stranger face-to-face.

Only there was no face there. Where the face should have been was only a smooth and glossy blankness, flawless as a black mirror, reflecting Kestrel's own horrified expression back at him.

This time, he did scream.

~~~~~

"Attention soldiers. This building off limits until further notice by order of Colonel Akimov of the Chorman Special Forces. Entry strictly prohibited." Tatyana paused, squinting at the signature on the posted notice. "Falcon put this up just a few days ago," she said. "He was the officer in charge of Red Camp One."

"So the old man wasn't crazy," Veronika put in.

Tatyana snorted. "I wouldn't say that."

"But he was right about the hospital -- it looks like it really was abandoned." Veronika moved a few paces away from the securely padlocked door of the Gurlukovich Memorial Hospital, scanning the upper-floor windows that overlooked the parking lot. Black and depthless, the windows stared back at her.

Alexei was peeking in through the boards that had been hammered over the hospital's ground-floor windows. He shook his head. "Nobody in there," he said. "The lights are all out, too."

"It doesn't make *sense* though." Tatyana was fingering the safety on her AKS, glaring at the notice. "Where'd they take the inmates?"

Veronika came back to the main entrance doors and bent down to inspect the padlock that held them shut. "Weren't they all supposed to be evacuated?"

"No -- red camps were for the blight victims. Blue camps were evacuees," Tatyana said impatiently, pointing at the banner above the door that declared the building RED CAMP ONE. "They wouldn't have evacuated any of the blight victims without a cure."

"They *did* announce a cure while we were at that camp," Veronika said. "You weren't awake then. They said it was going to be distributed to the victims within a week."

"But that was a lie," Alexei murmured. "There's no cure."

Nikita said nothing. He had barely spoken a word during the drive to the hospital, sitting in silence as they rolled through the empty streets in the CSF truck Tatyana had stolen. Now that they'd arrived Nikita stood guard on the steps of the hospital, gazing off in the direction of Mikhail's hotel.

The streets around the hospital were echoingly vacant. A gust of wind surged down the avenue, blowing a drift of torn paper ahead of it. It had been only a matter of weeks since the quarantine but there were tufts of green grass struggling up through the cracked asphalt already. Without passing traffic to crush them back down the plant life was eager to reclaim the city.

Alexei went over to Nikita. "Um..." He cleared his throat, "I'm sure she'll be alright," he said.

"Uh?" Nikita seemed to come awake. "Yeah...probably." He shrugged.

"The old man probably wants to get out of Khostok as badly as we do," Alexei pointed out. "He wouldn't do anything to risk that."

Nikita did not seem convinced. "Besides," Alexei went on, "Elena's much safer at the hotel than down here with us."

Sighing, Nikita looked back at the hospital's boarded-up windows and padlocked doors. "I guess so," he said.

"Guys!" Veronika was waving to them from the front door. "Get over here!"

Once they'd all gathered at the main hospital entrance Tatyana thumped on the door with her knuckles. "We're not getting in this way," she said. "We don't have the equipment to take this stuff off. Besides, just because they've left the building doesn't mean the patrols aren't keeping an eye on it."

"Let's go around back," Nikita suggested. "They might've left an entrance open back there."

The rest agreed. "So long as we get off the street," Tatyana said, hitching her backpack further up onto her shoulder. "Let's go."

The alleyway that ran alongside the building was grassy and narrow, barely large enough for a single emergency vehicle to pass through. All the ground-floor windows that looked into the alley were boarded up as well, fresh lumber and silver nails showing how recently the work had been done.

"Why would they lock things up after they left?" Veronika asked.

Nikita looked back over his shoulder. "Maybe they left something here."

"Like what?"

Nobody knew. "Or they could be hiding something," Nikita said. He glanced over at Tatyana, who was trudging along with a resigned air. "Could be they don't want anyone getting into the B-20 system."

Tatyana looked sideways at him. "IF the entrance is even *in* there. You saw the 'map' that guy was using."

"He was right about the camp being abandoned," Veronika reminded her.

When Tatyana said nothing Alexei spoke up. "Doesn't the CSF know where the entrances are?"

"Colonel Akimov probably does," Tatyana admitted. "It's need-to-know for the rest of the soldiers, though."

"Who's Colonel Akimov?" Nikita asked.

Alexei thought he recognized the name. Back when she had gone by the codename "Hawk", Tatyana had reported directly to someone named Colonel Akimov. Alexei remembered the time that Yuri had asked for permission to see Elena again, and Tatyana had agreed to bring the request up to the Colonel for approval. Maybe she'd actually done so. Not that it mattered anymore -- Yuri had died without seeing his daughter's face again.

"Akimov's the one in charge of the evacuation," Tatyana was saying. "He's one of the higher-ranking officers in the CSF. In fact -- "

Alexei suddenly broke into a jog. " -- Hey!" Nikita called out, startled, but Alexei stumbled ahead without looking back. "What's gotten into him?"

Tatyana just shrugged. Nikita turned to Veronika. "Is he always like that?"

Veronika seemed to be just about as puzzled as Nikita. "I guess," she said. "I don't know him all that well."

Nikita looked after Alexei's retreating back until he disappeared around the corner of the building. "Why did he come with you, then?"

Veronika marched in silence for a few moments. "Honestly, we're the ones who came with him," she said. "Getting you and Elena out of the city was Alexei's idea."

In back of the building the three of them came across the hospital's emergency entrance, identified by glaringly red letters on a white-painted background. A forgotten ambulance was parked half-under the covered walkway. Alexei sat on the hood of the vehicle, and lifted his head when the others came into view.

"Found something," he called out hoarsely, hopping off the hood of the ambulance.

Tatyana slipped around behind the ambulance to inspect the building's emergency entrance doors. "No good," she shouted back to the group. "These are boarded up too."

"I meant the ambulance," Alexei said.

"Eh?" Tatyana came back, dusting her hands off on her jeans. "We can't use that -- we stick out enough already."

"No, he's right -- look." Nikita pointed. The hood of the ambulance was dented all over, streaked with black from innumerable boot-prints. The roof of the driver's cab was in a similar state.

"They've been walking all over this thing," Veronika observed. The four of them all seemed to make the connection at the same time, tracing the path from the ambulance's hood, to the roof of the driver's cabin, to the top of the vehicle, to the corrugated aluminum awning that covered the emergency entrance, to the second-floor window that stood directly above the awning.

"Aha!" Veronika was the first one onto the ambulance, scrambling up the glass windshield onto the cabin of the vehicle. They watched her crawl from the roof of the ambulance onto the awning, making her way carefully to the second-floor window. She had to stretch to reach it, but the window slid upward with a touch. "It's unlocked," she called back to the rest. "C'mon!"

One by one they all made the climb up onto the awning. Tatyana in particular seemed worried that the roof wouldn't bear their combined weight, but it didn't so much as creak underfoot. "Someone gimme a boost," Veronika prompted them, one hand hooked over the windowsill.

Nikita bent down under the window and laced his fingers together, letting Veronika step into his hand so he could heft her up. Tatyana was next, and though she was considerably heavier than Veronika Nikita boosted her up without trouble. Alexei went up after Tatyana, and the two of them leaned out to grab Nikita's arms and hoist him up.

"Hoo!" Nikita exclaimed once they were all inside. "That's enough exercise for today."

Veronika eased the window closed behind them, shutting out the outside world. Now that they were indoors, away from the birdsong and the fitful breezes, the stillness of the hospital settled onto them like a wool blanket. It was deathly quiet.

A long hallway lay before them. Closed doors lined the walls on either side, most bearing brass nameplates. A scattering of dropped admittance forms littered the floor like bleached autumn leaves. Beside the window there was sunlight enough to see, but the end of the hall terminated in dark obscurity: all the lights in the building were out.

"If the warrens are underground, we'll need to get down to the ground floor to look for that entrance," Nikita whispered. It seemed sacrilegious to speak too loudly inside the building, as if it had been a church rather than a hospital.

The group was in agreement. "Let's be careful," Tatyana whispered back. "They might have posted guards when they left."

Alexei brought his flashlight out of the backpack he wore, flicking it on. The other three followed suit, aiming their lights at the well of blackness at the end of the hallway.

"Come on," Nikita urged, and they all set out together.

Around the first bend in the hall they lost sight of the sunlit window. The group followed the hallway as it snaked back and forth, walking around the piles of spilled paper, moving deeper into the heart of the lifeless building. The bobbing beams of the flashlights were the only illumination here. In places they found the detritus of the CSF's recent occupation: a scattering of empty boxes, those green plastic jugs that held water rations, the discarded filter from someone's gas mask. Nobody spoke.

At last they came to a juncture in the hallway. Various signs overhead pointed them in different directions for the Atrium, the Gymnasium, the Pediatric Ward, the Maternity Ward.

"The atrium should be on the ground floor," Nikita murmured. The flashlight-litten faces around him nodded solemnly.

At first glance the stairwell looked like a dead-end, a gulf of nothingness at the end of the hall. It was only when they pointed their flashlights at the ground that the steps appeared. In single-file the procession descended toward the atrium, footsteps ringing out on the steel staircase.

Nikita had taken the lead. Alexei was right behind him, flashlight trained on Nikita's backpack. They had descended no more than thirty steps when Nikita seemed to evaporate into thin air.

It happened too quickly to see. One moment Alexei was following him, trying to keep quiet, and the next thing Alexei knew he was in the lead. Nikita was gone.

Automatically Alexei threw himself backwards, colliding with Tatyana and nearly knocking her off her feet. She caught him with a hiss of surprise. "What -- "

"Nikita!" Alexei replied in an urgent whisper. "Nikita's gone! look!"

"Huh?" Veronika and Tatyana crowded onto the step with him, shining their lights ahead. There was something dark and massive blocking the stairwell a few steps down, and as the gleam of their flashlights swept over it the thing absorbed and reflected the light in uneven patches.

They heard a muffled curse, and the dark blur seemed to quiver. "Guys?" Nikita called out.

"We're here!" Tatyana said, edging down another step. "Where'd you go?"

"I tripped," Nikita grunted. "There's all these...weeds and things, I guess...it's growing in the stairwell." There came rustling and shuffling noises, like an animal moving about in the undergrowth, and the uneven darkness trembled.

Now that it was moving it became clear that the dark blur was a mass of plant life -- they could make out the shapes of the leaves now, the individual stems and vines. The foliage grew so densely it was almost impossible to see at first glance. There was just a wall of darkness ahead of them, cutting off their descent.

"Inkweed!" Alexei forgot to whisper. He tried to scramble backwards up the steps and tripped, landing on his rear. "Shit -- where'd it *come* from?"

They could hear Nikita fighting his way through the tangle, swearing and cursing. "It's everywhere...uh, I think I'm stuck." More thrashing sounds. "I landed on it when I fell -- it broke my fall, but..." He swore again, more loudly this time. "I think...yeah, I'm stuck. Can you guys help me out?"

A hand burst out of the dark mess, startlingly pale against the inky foliage. Tatyana surged forward and grabbed it. "I got you!"

Another hand emerged beside the first, and Veronika grabbed this one. Alexei just stared. There was just so *much* inkweed, more than Yuri had cultured, far more than he'd seen in the garage at the Labs. He had a sudden vision of the hospital as a human brain with the inkweed growing inside it, hollowing it out, devouring the healthy tissue and replacing it with this dark corruption, until the building was only a shell concealing the diseased madness within.

Veronika and Tatyana leaned backwards, pulling, and Nikita's head broke free of the inkweed, leaves scraping across his face. "Thanks," Nikita managed, red-faced with effort. "I'm just...I got myself tangled up in it somehow. Little further and I think..."

Tatyana was just reaching down to get a better grip when Nikita was suddenly jerked backwards, sinking halfway back into the inkweed again. He let a startled shriek, eyes widening.

"It's got me!" Nikita grabbed at Tatyana's sleeve. The expression on his upturned face was that of a trapped animal. "Something's got me! Help!"

The panic spread to Veronika and Tatyana, overpowering their disbelief. The two of them seized Nikita and began a tug-of-war against the inkweed.

"What? what is it?!" Veronika shouted. "What's got you?!"

But Nikita was in no condition to answer her. Something unseen gave a terrific yank on Nikita's legs and he slipped backward another six inches, up to his neck in the black leaves. His scream echoed in the stairwell. Tatyana had Nikita below both arms and Veronika was pulling on his hand, trying to drag him up the steps, but the unseen thing was clearly much stronger.

Alexei snapped out of his stupor and dropped his backpack onto the steps, unzipping it. He pawed frantically through the supplies Mikhail had equipped them with. "It's the inkweed!" he called out to them. "The inkweed's got him!"

"How can a plant be grabbing him?!" Veronika shouted. Tatyana was straining backward with all of her might, veins standing out at her temples. Nikita was clutching desperately at her shoulders, like a man drowning -- if the thing yanked him under, Tatyana would almost certainly go with him.

Alexei's hand closed on something small and hard. "It's not a plant!" he shouted back, scrambling down the steps toward the black tangle. When he reached the mass of inkweed Alexei flicked the butane lighter on and thrust the small flame directly into the foliage.

Alexei wasn't holding the lighter anywhere near where Nikita was trapped, but the effect was the same. All in one simultaneous movement the inkweed shrank away, the vines rearing back like a nest of snakes. Nikita broke free with such force that he tackled Tatyana onto the steps, knocking Veronika down in the process.

"Got him -- get back, everyone, get away from it!" Tatyana barked, dragging Nikita up onto his feet. The lot of them clawed their way back up the stairs, not stopping until they'd reached the hallway again. When Tatyana released him Nikita collapsed on the floor, chest heaving, his face ashen. Alexei's knees gave out and he sank down to the floor as well, quaking all over. It would be several minutes before he realized he'd left his backpack in the stairwell.

"What was that? what was it? what was it?" Veronika demanded, her voice high and shrill.

"Calm down," said Tatyana, who was clearly at the end of her own tether. She wiped her mouth with the back of one trembling hand. "Just...calm down."

Alexei thought he might be sick. Waves of nausea rolled through his stomach and he curled himself into a ball, head against his knees.

The four of them sat there panting for several minutes. "You okay?" Tatyana asked at last.

"Fine," Nikita replied, though he was obviously anything but. He rolled over onto his back on the floor. Nikita's pants were rumpled and one pant leg was torn below the knee, but he wasn't bleeding anywhere. "Oh Christ," he breathed at the ceiling. "What *was* that?"

"The Special Forces call it 'inkweed'," Tatyana said. Her ponytail had come undone and she was trying to retie it, but her hands were shaking too hard to do so. "It's been growing all over the city since the quarantine."

"But what was grabbing him?" Veronika asked, more quietly now.

"That was the inkweed," Alexei croaked. He was still curled up, but the nausea had receded enough for him to talk.

"But...how can a plant grab someone?" They had had the same conversation in the stairwell, but Veronika couldn't be blamed for not remembering.

Alexei looked up. "Inkweed's not a plant," he said again.

" -- then what *is* it?" Nikita asked.

"I don't know." Alexei forced himself to breathe deeply, shutting his eyes for a moment. "I think it's the same thing as the blight, though."

The group was speechless. "But...the blight only grows on people," Nikita protested weakly.

Alexei was shaking his head. "When it grows on people, it looks like those stains. When it grows somewhere else, you get inkweed."

"Bullshit," said Tatyana. She was clutching her neck with one hand, covering the place where Veronika had bitten her. "How do you know it's the same thing?"

"...Yuri took some samples from the blight victims and cultured them," Alexei murmured, avoiding her gaze. "Those samples grew into inkweed. He was studying it...he was the one who told me it wasn't a plant."

Now Tatyana looked like she might be ill. She turned on Veronika. "You -- " she snarled, lurching to her feet, and Veronika darted away from her.

"Guys, guys -- " Nikita rolled over, standing up again. He stumbled sideways into the wall, righted himself and reached out to Tatyana. "Come on -- we're here to find the entrance to the shelters, remember?"

There was a long tense moment before Tatyana sighed, turning away from Veronika. Alexei let himself exhale. "Alright," Tatyana said. "Let's keep moving."

Working his way up against the wall, Alexei got back onto his feet. His knees were still wobbling but they held him up.

"I dropped my flashlight back there," Nikita said. They all cast nervous glances back toward the stairwell.

"I'll take point," Tatyana said, moving to the head of the group. "Do we wanna try for the gym next? there's gotta be more than one set of stairs."

Nobody objected. Tatyana checked the signs overhead and set out toward the gymnasium, followed by Nikita. Alexei came after him and Veronika was last in line, keeping the two men between Tatyana and herself.

If the exploring party had been cautious before, now they were on edge. Every shadow was full of inkweed, black tendrils reaching out to grab them and drag them down into an unseen maw. Alexei couldn't help but think back to the samples of inkweed Yuri had grown in those glass tanks. He remembered Yuri feeding the stuff, the little tentacles wrapping around the apple slice and pulling it down until it was buried in the black growth. If the inkweed had been a plant it would have been horrific enough, but if it wasn't --

Tatyana coughed. "Ugh," she mumbled. "Wish I had my mask."

"Yeah, I noticed it too," Nikita said. "They were definitely using this place as a camp."

Alexei was about to ask when the scent hit him all at once. It was sickly-sweetish and rank, an organic smell, strong enough to make him gag. Behind him he heard Veronika coughing and choking as well.

"We'll get used to it," Tatyana said over her shoulder, still marching forward. "Let's keep going."

By the unsteady beam of their flashlights the group spotted the double doors at the end of the hall. The sign above the doors read PHYSICAL THERAPY GYMNASIUM. Alexei scanned every last inch of the doors with his flashlight, but there wasn't so much as a leaf of inkweed in sight.

Tatyana pushed the double doors open and immediately reeled backward. Moments later the rest of them were falling back as well. Alexei clapped a hand over his mouth, bile burning at the back of his throat.

"What *is* that?" Nikita gasped.

"Don't know," Tatyana said grimly. Like a person moving against an invisible tide, she pushed through the doors and into the gym. Nikita clenched his teeth and forged ahead after her. Veronika was leaning against the wall, gagging, and Alexei hung back with her until she'd composed herself.

"I'm okay, I'm okay." Veronika gave herself a brisk shake and pushed away from the wall. "Let's go in."

As they passed through the double doors and into the gym the smell hit them like a wave of putrid water. Their flashlights illuminated a narrow strip of tile flooring ahead of them -- they were on a raised second-floor walkway overlooking the gym floor, a railing on their right and office doors on their left.

"The gym must be down there," Tatyana said thickly, leaning over the railing and pointing her flashlight downward. Alexei leaned over as well, but the beams from their flashlights were too weak to light the floor below them. It was like looking down into a well -- the first floor could have been miles below them, for all they could see. Alexei felt a sudden wave of vertigo and backed away from the railing.

"They were probably keeping the inmates down in the gym," Tatyana observed. "With so many of 'em all in one place and no running water, it's bound to smell like this."

Nikita gulped. "Let's have a look around -- there should be stairs leading down somewhere," he said. "Once we get out of here the air should be fresher."

That was incentive enough for them to all begin filing around the walkway, looking for a way down. They reached the end of the walkway without finding a staircase, though Veronika did locate the elevator, useless now that the building was without power. On Nikita's suggestion they retraced their steps again, heading back the way they'd come.

Then Alexei's foot struck something that clanged in the darkness. Everyone froze.

"What was that?" Tatyana asked.

"Kicked something," Alexei said, rubbing the toe of his shoe. "Looks like someone left a trashcan in the middle of the hall here."

The others crowded around, pinning the object with their flashlights. It was a squat metal cylinder, smooth and black. "Kind of a strange trashcan," Veronika remarked. Tatyana crouched down next to the can, studying it with sudden interest.

Nikita was peering over the railing again. "Didn't the old man give us some rope ladders?" he asked, slipping his backpack off his shoulders. "We might have to slide down to the ground floor. The railing seems pretty solid."

"So long as we don't have to take those stairs." Veronika shivered. She held up a flashlight for Nikita as he hunted through his supplies. Presently he uncovered a coil of rope which had been thoughtfully knotted at regular intervals. One end was tied to a stout iron hook, and this Nikita hung over the railing along the edge of the walkway. He gave the ladder a few experimental yanks; the rope was thick and obviously quite sturdy. "Who wants to go down first?"

There were no volunteers. "Tatyana?"

"No," Tatyana said, in a tone of voice Alexei had never heard before. "I'm not going down there."

"Fine," said Nikita. "If nobody else wants to -- "

"Oh, I'll go," Veronika offered. She tucked the end of her flashlight into her pocket and rubbed her hands together. "We used to do rope climbing in gym class. I'll hold the rope while you guys come down."

"Fair enough." Nikita stepped aside and offered a hand, helping Veronika over the railing. She began to climb down, her head bobbing lower and lower until it disappeared below the edge of the walkway.

Tatyana was still kneeling beside the trashcan. Alexei bent down next to her. "Uh, are you -- "

" -- I know what happened here," Tatyana whispered.

"What?"

But Tatyana said nothing. She looked up at Alexei and suddenly he realized why she sounded so different. Her expression said it clearly: Tatyana was horrified.

Alexei couldn't imagine what could have frightened the soldier so badly, but he only had about thirty seconds to ponder it before Veronika started screaming.

Everyone rushed to the edge of the railing. "Veronika!" Nikita called down. "Veronika! What's wrong?!"

The screams went on for a long minute before stopping abruptly, as if clipped off. "Nika!" Tatyana shouted, and there was real panic in her voice. "Talk to us!!"

When Veronika finally answered them her reply was so broken and distorted that it was more of a wail. The listeners on the walkway had to strain to understand what she was saying, and even when they caught the words they still couldn't comprehend what she meant.

"They're dead! they're dead! they're all dead!"

~~~~~

Sliding down that rope ladder was like a descent into Hell. Fortunately the human brain can only handle so much, and most of what Alexei, Nikita, Tatyana and Veronika found there in the Gurlukovich Memorial Hospital Gymnasium did not remain with them. Their sanity would not allow for it.

The horror was slow to dawn on them. When Alexei reached the bottom of the ladder and his shoes touched the gymnasium floor, the first thing his flashlight found was Veronika. She was huddled in a ball on the floor, hands over her face, shaking. Her own flashlight lay beside her on the floor.

Tatyana was next down the ladder. When she called out Veronika's name the young woman came to life again, practically flinging herself into Tatyana's arms. Tatyana caught and held her without seeming to realize what she was doing. With her free hand Tatyana swept the flashlight beam across the darkened gymnasium, illuminating the room. Alexei looked, and wished to God that he hadn't.

The gym was full of corpses. At first glance there seemed to be hundreds, thousands of them, piled atop one another like the unburied victims of some medieval plague. Most were clumped up in the corners of the room, but many were scattered at random across the floor, limbs jutting out in all directions, eyes and mouths wide open. The droning of flies was everywhere.

Nikita reached the gym floor, saw what Tatyana's flashlight had found, and turned away. Seconds later Alexei could hear him noisily losing his breakfast a couple paces off, but as Alexei seemed to have turned to stone there was very little he could do for Nikita. He stood there staring until Tatyana's voice broke in on his thoughts.

"That was a Stardust device," Tatyana said hollowly. Veronika was sobbing against her chest. "The thing on the walkway. It wasn't a trash can."

Alexei said nothing. The world was rocketing away from him, leaving him drifting in empty space, a void without light or heat. Somewhere in the darkness of the gym Nikita was still coughing and retching.

"It releases quick-acting nerve gas. They're used in biological warfare. The camp must have been rioting, staging an uprising, something...they must have gotten out of control, that's the only...but to use Stardust against other Chormans..." Tatyana broke off.

"...who did this?" someone whispered, and Alexei was startled to realize it was his own voice. The room was slipping away from him and he made a belated effort to grab onto something, anything, before his tether broke completely and he lost himself in the abyss.

"The Special Forces did this." Nikita's voice seemed to come swimming out of nowhere. All at once Alexei caught sight of him, red-eyed and face contorted in fury, striding purposefully across the gym floor. Time was crawling by so slowly that he scarcely seemed to move at all, and it seemed to take Alexei forever to realize that Nikita was going to lash out at Tatyana, had his fist in the air already.

His trajectory reversed itself, and Alexei came plummeting back to earth.

Tatyana gave Nikita a blank look as he came marching up. She either didn't realize or didn't care that she was about to get punched, and she barely blinked when Alexei suddenly leapt on Nikita's back, grabbing his wrist.

"Get off me!" Nikita shouted.

"It's not her fault!"

"Get off, dammit, get off!"

"It's not her fault!"

Nikita went down on his knees, still fighting to throw Alexei from his shoulders. If the encounter with the inkweed had strained something in the man then the roomful of cadavers might have broken it entirely. "These were women and children!" Nikita bawled, his voice cracking. "How could you people do this?"

"It's not her fault," Alexei kept repeating. Nikita was shaking all over. "All these people...how many were here? how many?!"

"Around seven hundred. Maybe more."

Nikita made a noise like he was about to be sick again. He seemed to have forgotten about Alexei, or no longer cared about getting away from him. Alexei had Nikita in a one-armed headlock, clutching his wrist in the other hand, and he could feel it as the fight started to go out him. Shaking even harder now, Nikita curled forward, head touching the floor. Alexei released him and slid off his back.

"Where's the rest of them?" asked Veronika in a quavering voice.

Alexei looked up. Veronika had taken the flashlight away from the near-paralyzed Tatyana and was passing it across the room in slow sweeps. "There's..." She gulped and tried again. "There's not even a hundred people in here. Count them."

Alexei got to about ten bodies before he gave up, his stomach tying itself in knots. Nonetheless he saw Veronika's point -- on second glance there weren't thousands or even hundreds of cadavers in the room. There was no way the dead there in the gymnasium accounted for all of the several hundred inmates of Red Camp One.

"Then they took them somewhere," Nikita said brokenly. He had begun picking himself up off the floor, but from the slump of his shoulders Alexei could see that the blind rage was gone. "They have those...those trucks they take the bodies away in." He wiped his eyes off on his sleeve. "Like the one we've been riding around in. That's what it's used for, right?"

"Nikita, there could be survivors," Alexei murmured. "We could go look for them."

In the unsteady glow of the flashlight Alexei could see the sanity filtering back into Nikita's eyes. He snuffled, wiped his face again, and seemed to compose himself. "Alright," he said huskily. "Alright."

Alexei got back to his feet. Veronika nodded at him, her cheeks shining with tearstains, and tugged on Tatyana's sleeve. "Let's see if anyone survived," she said.

Tatyana did not respond. Veronika tugged again, calling her name, but there was still no reply. Tatyana had checked out for the moment, leaving her body to stare out across the gymnasium floor like a statue.

When Veronika slapped her the report was like a gunshot. Spell broken, Tatyana staggered sideways and shook her head. "Akimov did this," she said. She wouldn't look any of them in the eyes.

"Who?" Veronika asked. "The Colonel?"

"He would have had to authorize this." Tatyana lifted a hand toward the piles of bodies. "The inmates must have gotten way out of control. Stardust would only be a last resort, but Akimov might -- if he allowed the use of the device in one camp, he might authorize it in the others."

Nikita spat out a curse too obscene to print. "Then we need to find the entrance to the warrens," Alexei said. "But let's see if there's any survivors first."

Nikita and Veronika were in agreement with that. At the moment Tatyana was little better than a walking corpse herself, and in the end Veronika had to lead her by the hand as they explored the miniature Hell that the gymnasium had become.

Their progress was painfully slow. The floor was sticky, flies swarmed about them in buzzing clouds, and the overpowering stench made each breath a torment. Every low silhouette their flashlights found was another tragedy, another human being converted into rotting meat. From their tortured postures it became clear that most of the victims had died in convulsions, and the twisted bodies cast eldritch shadows when the lights hit them.

But far worse than the bodies were the faces. It was clear that the gas killed very rapidly, and the expressions of panic remained behind after the souls had fled, fear and terror stamped on the lifeless features.

Though they could close their eyes, the smell of the place persisted. It was strong enough to taste it on your tongue, and it was inescapable. Now Alexei knew why it had seemed so familiar -- it was the same one he had encountered under that green tarp, in the back of the CSF's transport truck. It was the scent of decay, the nearest thing to Death made tangible.

The gymnasium was in a total shambles. Being used as a camp was partly to blame, no doubt, but most of the damage had come in the chaos wrought by the state-sanctioned genocide that had taken place there. The rubber floor mats were ripped, trash littered everywhere; it seemed that everything within arm's reach of the inmates had been destroyed or defaced. Those folding cots were scattered around the room, bent and overturned, and even though he hadn't the stomach to count them Alexei could see that there were many more cots than bodies.

The walls of the gymnasium were especially arresting. At one time they had been painted with bright murals, patients in white uniforms stretching and exercising under the watchful eye of white-coated doctors. Over this colorful artwork the camp inmates had scrawled a wide variety of graffiti. Some was simply obscene, but much of it was painful to read: demands for food and water, complaints about the abysmal living conditions.

A few poor souls had apparently scribbled out their last thoughts onto the wall as the deadly fog was rolling into the gym -- in jagged letters half a meter tall these messages read:

POISON GAS

THE CSF HAS KILLED US

HELP HELP HELP

GOD SAVE US

Other messages had been left as final words to their loved ones. Alexei hadn't the heart to read any of these.

Nikita was near his limit already, and when he stumbled over a body much smaller than the rest it pushed him over the edge. "I can't do this," he choked. "There's nobody alive in here."

"It doesn't make sense," Veronika murmured. "They must have been keeping the inmates here...where did they all go?"

"They got out." Tatyana pointed across the room. Everyone turned, and the flashlight beams swept across the gym towards where she was pointing.

The doors of the gymnasium were open, the doorway gaping blackly in the painted wall.

Instantly the group made a beeline for the doors. The desire to find survivors and the lure of fresh air spurred them onward, and Alexei was at the head of the pack, stumbling across the uneven floor in his haste to get out of the gym. He was no more than three yards away from the exit when Nikita seized his shirt collar, yanking him backwards.

Alexei yelped in surprise. "Get back, everyone, get back!" Nikita shouted, dragging Alexei bodily away from the door. "Get away from it!"

Someone shone their flashlight into the doorway, lighting it up. And then Alexei saw what he had almost run headlong into.

Inkweed. The doorway of the gymnasium was clogged with a black jungle of the stuff, growing in riotous profusion, entirely blocking the exit. The room adjoining the gym was packed so full of the growth that it was was spilling into the gymnasium through the open doors, spreading in a black carpet across the floor.

It looked as if some immense force had hit those heavy steel doors, smashing them inward. The impact had crumpled and distorted them to the degree that one door was nearly off its hinges. Inky tendrils of the weed were creeping across the metal, nearly obscuring the large black letters painted onto both doors:

THIS WAY

TO THE RIVER

~~~~~

In the end they found no survivors in the gym, nor any trace of the hundreds of vanished inmates. There was no getting through the gym's proper exit and they resorted to climbing back up the rope ladder to return to the second floor. The exploration in the gym had left them all soiled and exhausted in every sense of the word.

The emptiness of the second-floor hallways were a blessing after the horror of the stairwell and the reeking gymnasium. By common consent the group retraced their steps, heading back to the window they'd used to enter the hospital. It was only by coincidence that Alexei happened to glance down that adjoining hall during their journey, and an even greater coincidence that he caught sight of the thing in the hallway.

"Wait!" Alexei hissed, and everyone came to a halt. He motioned with his flashlight. "Look -- down there!"

"What? what is it?" Nikita and Veronika shone their flashlights into the gloom, lighting up the empty hallway.

"I saw something!" Alexei said. "Someone's down there!"

"I don't see anyone." Nikita sounded dubious. "Are you sure?"

"Wouldn't hurt to check," said Veronika, but Alexei was already creeping forward into the hall. "...hello?" he called out, swinging his light back and forth. "Hello?"

Two more flashlight beams joined Alexei's own as Nikita and Veronika followed him in. "Could be a soldier," Nikita muttered.

"Why would a soldier be hiding from us?" Veronika asked.

"...is anyone there?" Alexei whispered, inching forward. Something under his shoe creaked in protest and Alexei looked down to see what it was.

He'd stepped on the corner of a square metal grill, like the kind used to cover ventilation ducts. Alexei shone his flashlight onto the duct cover, then moved the beam to the right. There at the bottom of the wall was a large square hole of the right size and shape to fit the discarded cover -- and just big enough to admit a human being.

Alexei dropped onto his knees and pointed the flashlight into the duct. "...Aha," he remarked. "There you are."

"You found someone?" Nikita and Veronika crowded in close behind Alexei. "Who is it?"

"Can't see..." Alexei squinted into the duct, trying to make out the silhouette "I think -- let's back up, I think they're coming out."

The three of them scooted backwards, keeping their flashlights trained on the duct as the stranger made their exit. And though they had all been through Hell that day, had been knee-deep in corpses and nearly devoured by the inkweed, none of them were prepared for what came crawling out of that hole.

It resembled a human being, but the resemblance only made the thing that much more horrid. The thing that emerged from the ventilation duct was black and glossy all over, faceless and sexless as a department store mannequin. As it straightened up to its full height the flashlight beams reflected off of the thing's blank face in three spots of brightness. It had no eyes, no nose, no mouth -- not even contours suggesting a face -- but from the angle of its gleaming head the stunned onlookers could tell that it was looking directly at them.

Nikita made a sort of squeaking noise. The rest had forgotten how to breathe, let alone to scream.

The thing turned right and left, examining each of them in turn. Slowly, almost thoughtfully, it canted its head to one side. For an instant the gesture seemed familiar to Alexei, but the thought slipped away before he could place it.

They were all so mesmerized by the apparition that they neglected to notice what was rising into the air behind it. Out of the thing's back there emerged long inky ropes of the same texture and color as its skin, coiling and uncoiling like restless snakes as they rose over its head. One of these ropes slid over the thing's shoulder and reached out towards Alexei.

Alexei had had nightmares like this. The paralysis, the sense of frozen time, the buzzing static that now filled his skull, the sheer alien incomprehensibility of the thing in the hallway. He watched helplessly as the blunt end of the tentacle -- for that's what those ropes were, tentacles -- came towards him, stretching out to touch his cheek --

-- the loud *chok-chok* of a bolt being drawn back and slammed home shattered the stillness. Tatyana stood at the end of the hallway, teeth bared, her AKS-47 leveled at the black thing's face. "Everyone get down!" she commanded.

Alexei and Nikita dropped to the floor. Veronika spun around, arms out. "Don't shoot!" she cried.

Tatyana's expression would have been funnier under different circumstances. " -- what?!" She lowered the rifle a few inches. "Why the hell not?!"

" -- just don't!" Veronika said.

Nikita sat up, grabbed the leg of Veronika's coveralls and yanked, tumbling her onto the ground. Tatyana raised her weapon, sighted along the barrel...and lowered it again, looking dumbfounded.

The black thing's tentacles had disappeared, withdrawn into its back. It raised both hands, palms out, in a gesture of supplication so universal there could be no mistake about it. With its face still pointed towards Tatyana, never lowering its hands, it crept sideways toward the ventilation duct.

No-one moved to stop it. The thing crouched down beside the wall, glanced into the duct, took one final look at the four speechless humans in the hallway -- then darted into the ventilation shaft. Tatyana charged toward the duct to intercept it but the thing was gone already. For a minute they heard it scrabbling and bumping about deep inside the shaft, rather like a very large rat, and then there was nothing but silence.

Alexei's vision greyed out, and he brought himself back just before he fainted. Nikita was mumbling a prayer under his breath.

Tatyana was the first one to speak. " -- what *was* that thing?!" she quavered, flicking the safety toggle on her weapon.

"How should we know?" Alexei said. He went to get up and his legs promptly folded underneath him. On his third try Nikita helped him to stand upright, propping him against the wall.

When Veronika got back to her feet Tatyana turned on her. "Why'd you stop me from shooting it?!"

Veronika was just as pale as the others, but somehow she was calmer. "We don't even know what it was," she said. "Why kill it if you don't know?"

" -- you -- " For a moment Tatyana was too astounded for words. "Why *kill* it?! You saw the thing!! What, did it look like a puppy to you?!"

"It was one of those creatures," Alexei said, realizing. "Remember? the old man told us about them -- all black, with no faces. He thought they were demons."

"A demon -- fine, okay," Nikita echoed with a hysterical little laugh. "I don't know what else it could have been."

Tatyana finally swung her rifle back onto her back. "And you didn't want me to kill it," she said to Veronika.

" -- you're assuming you *could* kill it," Veronika snapped. "What if the old man's right? what if that thing *was* a demon, and you shooting it just makes it angry? what then?"

Everyone turned toward the ventilation shaft. They waited, but there were no sounds to be heard -- whatever they had seen was truly gone now.

"Let's get back to the hotel," Alexei said faintly. "We've done enough for today."

The idea met with unanimous approval.

~~~~~

"Ah, good," Mikhail grunted. "Yer back!"

Alexei, Nikita, Tatyana and Veronika merely looked at him. They had departed the Hotel Litvinenko just six hours earlier, but in that interval the small group had changed completely. Their skin and clothes were streaked with dirt, Nikita's pants were torn at one ankle, and Alexei's backpack was missing. They all stank of death. But the greatest change was in their faces, in the burnt-out, shell-shocked expression each one had brought back.

Certainly, Mikhail said to himself, these youngsters weren't as hardened to the ways of survivalism as he.

"Come in, come in already." Mikhail held open the door of the seventh-floor penthouse. The four came shuffling into the room and dropped their backpacks onto the carpet. "Looks like you had a rough time! Did you -- "

" -- where's Elena?" Nikita cut him off. Mikhail frowned. "Eh, not sure."

Nikita stiffened. "What do you mean, you're not sure?"

"I mean I'm not sure." Mikhail scratched at his stubbly chin. "She got into a tantrum and ran off into the hotel. Haven't seen her since lunchtime. Ya know, I'm no babysitter, and if you -- "

What Mikhail had meant to say was, "if you think a military man like me is fit for playing nursemaid, you'd better think again." However, what actually came out of his throat sounded more like " -- erk!", as Nikita had seized him by the collar yanked him forward until their noses made contact.

"Where. Is. My. Niece?" Nikita growled.

Veronika laid a hand on Nikita's arm. "I know where she is," she said quickly. "Come on -- we'll go get her."

Nikita looked at the woman. "...how would *you* know?"

"I just know. Come on, she's close by."

With a final glare in Mikhail's direction Nikita released him and turned to the woman. Veronika headed right back out the door of the penthouse with the other three youngsters close on her heels. In moments Mikhail's hotel room was empty again.

"Huh!" Mikhail sniffed, adjusting his collar. Fortunately for them, Mikhail had always had excellent restraint -- if his warrior instincts had kicked in, the lot of them would have been lying on the floor with broken bones in a matter of seconds.

"Might not be so lucky next time," Mikhail said darkly, giving the penthouse door a significant look. Then, his ego satisfied, he straightened out his red bandanna and set about preparing for dinner.

Veronika jogged down the seventh-floor hall of the renamed Hotel Komarov, her comrades following close behind. She ran down the stairs to the sixth floor, bypassing the doors of fifteen hotel rooms before stopping suddenly at the door of Room 616. "In here," she said over her shoulder, turning the knob and pushing her way into the room.

They found Elena sitting crosslegged on the floor of Room 616, stacks of moldering books around her. She looked up as the adults came flooding into the room.

"Library's closed," Elena said crossly. Her pupils were the size of dimes. She went back to her books again, opening one large volume and sifting through the mildewed pages. "Clear on out before I get the security man on you."

Nikita let out a trembling sigh. Veronika ran right up to the girl, grabbing her in a tight embrace. Elena's squawk of protest was clipped off in the middle as something intangible shot through her body -- she went rigid and then limp again, head falling back. Veronika passed the girl over to her uncle, who scooped her up into his arms.

"...what did you do to her?" Tatyana asked, confused.

"She's not gonna tell you," Alexei said.

Veronika flashed them both a guilty look. "I can't explain it," she said shortly. "I'm sorry."

"'s alright." Nikita was looking down into Elena's face, biting his lower lip. "Do you think the old guy knows about her?"

"Who, Mikhail?" Veronika asked.

Nikita nodded. "You heard what he said about people who'd caught the blight."

"He's not bright enough to figure it out," Tatyana opined.

"And if he did suspect her, it'd show," Alexei added. "I don't think he'd keep something like that to himself."

Grudgingly, Nikita agreed. "I still don't trust him."

The others felt the same way. "You all saw what we got into at the hospital," Tatyana said. "How do we know he didn't send us out there to get caught by -- by that thing?"

"But why would he do that?" Alexei protested, looking around at the others. "He picked us up off the street -- why bother if he's just going to get rid of us right away? It's not like we left behind anything valuable when we went out."

Nikita's expression turned dark all of a sudden, and he pressed Elena a little more closely against his chest.

" -- that's not what I meant," Alexei hurried to say. "I don't really think -- "

" -- owww," Elena said sleepily, opening her eyes. "You're squishing me."

"Ah, you're awake!" Nikita said. "Are you alright, Lena?"

The little girl nodded, blinking up at the circle of adult faces around her. "You're back already?"

"Yes, we're back."

Elena yawned expansively. "Is it dinnertime yet?"

~~~~~

After dinner, with the smell of cooked sardines and camping stove fuel still lingering in the air, Mikhail passed out the vodka again. Alexei, Nikita and Tatyana all drank twice as much as the night before, and even Veronika participated this time. The four of them sat in a circle around the flickering glow of the oil lantern Mikhail had lit, retelling the tale of what they had found in the hospital. Nikita in particular kept glancing over his shoulder at where Elena lay buried in her blankets, worried that she would wake up and overhear them.

Mikhail listened attentively. "The spawn of Satan," he declared once they were through. "It's as I feared."

"You could have warned us," Tatyana said.

Mikhail clapped a hand to his heart. "On my honor, comrades, I've never been inside that building once in my life. If I'd known you were walkin' into such a nest of snakes I'd never have let you young ones go alone." He thumped his empty glass against the singed carpet. "Next time we go, I'll lead the way! It's the only thing to do."

"With all due respect, General...I'm not sure having an extra person will help," Veronika said.

"Bah!" Mikhail roared. "That's where you're wrong -- you'll see when we get there." He wagged a finger at his audience. "I've been training for years for such a mission...a holy crusade against the armies of darkness. I've got all kinds of weapons here, enough for a whole platoon. Once yer all rested we'll get everyone geared up and we'll all head down there and drive the demons back into the pit of fire!"

For some reason Mikhail's enthusiasm did not seem to be catching. "I'll go back," Nikita said, "but not to the gym." His eyes were liquid. "I just can't believe the Special Forces could do such a thing, even under orders. All those people..."

Mikhail snorted like a horse. "*I* can believe it. They're coverin' up their dirty dealings, that's what's happening."

"What 'dealings' are you talking about?" Tatyana asked icily.

"Well, ones like you and me weren't meant to know, but it was the CSF and the DIO who unleashed the demon plagues," Mikhail explained. "This is black magic we're talkin' about, infernal technology, somethin' the fascists left in the city durin' the Great War -- not that any of you youngsters would remember the war. The CSF and the DIO were tryin' to weaponize this old fascist tech they found, and it got away from 'em. That's the truth, and they're tryin' to bury it deep."

Tatyana's expression was positively wintry, but Alexei spoke up first. "That's all wrong," he protested. "The blight was caused by a chemical leak at the Agricultural Labs. An accident."

Mikhail cocked an eyebrow. "An' how would you know?"

"Because I used to work at the Labs."

For a minute Mikhail considered this. "So the stuff that's causin' the plagues came out of the Labs?"

"Yes."

"An' where did the Labs get it from?"

Alexei opened his mouth and shut it again. "...that I don't know," he said finally.

Mikhail chortled. "Well, now you know." His flushed face glowed with smug conviction. "And now you know what yer Labs have been dealin' with, too. It's the mark of Satan, that's what those black spots are. The stain gets into your soul, eats it away, turns you into one o' them no-face demons." He shook his head. "God have mercy on you if you catch it, cos nothing else is savin' you but Him. Best to put a bullet in yer head while yer still human."

Under the flush of alcohol Tatyana's face had turned chalky-white. "Matter of fact, the CSF mighta saved a bunch of souls that day, gassin' the camp like that," Mikhail mused aloud. "If you kill 'em early enough, before the soul rots away to nothin', you might -- "

Nikita started to lurch to his feet and Alexei grabbed his shirt, holding him back.

"Now, General," Veronika said loudly, in a tone of voice typically used for the senile elderly, "I've heard of a few people who got over the blight on their own."

"Uh? You have?"

"Yes!" Veronika was casually rubbing the back of her neck, smiling at the old man. Nikita saw the gesture and started to relax, sitting back down. Tatyana had noticed as well, Alexei saw, and a little of the color came back to her face. Of course there was no need for the two to get upset over Mikhail's claims -- someone who'd "gotten over" the blight, after a fashion, was right there in their midst.

"Didn't think that was possible," Mikhail said.

"What -- you think God couldn't cure someone if He wanted to?" Veronika pressed him.

"Guess yer right," the old man said grudgingly. "I suppose if He wanted to, it'd be possible."

# CHAPTER THIRTEEN

There seemed to be no end to the nightmares.

For what must have been the hundredth time Alexei jolted up out of sleep with a gasp, his body covered in sweat, his bedsheets sticking to his clammy skin. This last one had been especially bad -- he had dreamt of a roomful of cadavers, mouths gaping wide in silent screams, black clouds of flies filling the air. It had been so real Alexei could have sworn he had smelled the rotting flesh.

With a shudder he rolled out of bed. He found his pants and shirt and pulled them on, still half-awake, and stepped into his shoes. Quietly Alexei let himself out of the dormitory -- he could hear Anatoly snoring away in his bed, and didn't want to awaken him.

It must have been nearly three a.m., and the semi-lit halls of the Lubukov Agricultural Labs were silent as the grave. Alexei reached the lunchroom without encountering another living soul.

His premonition had been correct, and he found Yuri sitting by himself in the otherwise empty cafeteria, warming his hands around a cup of coffee. He perked up as soon as he caught sight of Alexei. "Good morning, Lyosha!" Yuri called out softly. "You up early or up late?"

"Hey, Yura. Up early." Alexei slid into the chair across from Yuri.

"More bad dreams?"

"Of course," Alexei gave him a rueful smile. "How about you? Up early or up late?"

Yuri canted his head to one side. "Oh...I don't sleep much anymore," he admitted.

"Well, that'd be one way to avoid my bad dreams, I guess," Alexei chuckled.

"Oh I still have dreams," Yuri said. "All the time. At least, I used to think they were dreams."

"Huh?" Alexei didn't understand. "What do you mean?"

"Mmm...how to put it?" Yuri pushed his glasses back up into place, and they promptly slid back down his nose again. "I'm awake all the time, but I'm still hearing and seeing things."

"What kind of things?"

Yuri spread his hands. "Everything!" he said. "Everything under the sun. I can't describe it to you, but you wouldn't believe everything I've seen in the last few weeks." His blue eyes were fairly glowing.

Alexei wasn't sure what Yuri was driving at, but it was starting to make him uneasy. "Can you give me an example?"

"Sure." Yuri tapped on the tabletop. "This conversation we're having right now is a good example."

Alexei gave his friend a blank look. "What about it?"

Yuri smiled broadly. "This isn't a dream, Lyosha. Or a hallucination."

"But -- of course this isn't a dream," Alexei said. He glanced nervously around the lunchroom. "Uh, how long have you been...seeing things?"

"Since I caught the blight."

Alexei blinked, looking down at Yuri's hands. There wasn't so much as a smudge anywhere on his skin; Yuri was obviously clean. But then Alexei saw that it wasn't a coffee cup Yuri was holding. He had a small glass jar in his hands, filled with a tangle of black organic matter and small, twinkling lights.

"I think you need more sleep, Yura." Alexei laughed a little. "You don't have the blight."

Yuri just smiled at him. "It's so hard to explain," he said, unscrewing the lid from the glass jar. "And there's only one way to show you..."

Alexei sat back from the table, now genuinely uneasy. "Show me what?"

Yuri glanced up at him. "Just trust me -- okay, Lyosha?"

Before Alexei could answer him Yuri leaned forward, thrusting the jar at his chest.

Alexei jerked back into consciousness again. Panting, heart racing, he lay there in the darkened room, trying to collect his scattered thoughts.

This time, he felt certain, he was actually awake. He could feel the hardness of the carpeted penthouse floor beneath the tangled quilt he was sleeping in, could hear the ebbing murmur of the crazy old man's snoring. It was the snoring that was triggering these nightmares, Alexei decided. He'd been dreaming he was back at the Labs ever since they'd arrived at the dilapidated hotel. And after all they'd been through two days ago, exploring that hospital, anyone in their right mind would be having nightmares.

But it was all okay now, Alexei told himself. Now that he was awake the nightmares were over.

He opened his eyes. There was a black shadow looming over him, blotting out his view of the ceiling, and Alexei's blood froze in his veins.

It took seconds for his eyes to adjust to the dimness of the penthouse, but Alexei didn't need a clear look to know what was crouching over him, straddling his chest, its face inches from his own. He could see the thing's waving tentacles silhouetted against the ceiling tiles above, could see the faraway lights of Khostok reflected in the glossy, featureless surface of its face.

It was the thing from the hospital. It had found him.

Alexei felt his heart stop.

The eyeless thing looked down at him in perfect silence. How long had it been sitting there, watching him sleep, waiting for him to wake up? And what was it waiting for now? It had no reason to hesitate -- doubtlessly the thing could tell that Alexei was helpless. His comrades were sleeping a few feet away, guns and weapons within arm's reach, but they might as well have been on the moon. There was no way to save him now.

As Alexei stared up at it the thing canted its head to one side, like a curious dog. The gesture stirred something in his memory, and for that instant Alexei was more amazed than afraid.

Then its tentacle flashed down like a scorpion's tail, plunging a needle-sharp stinger in between Alexei's ribs.

He had never screamed so loud in his entire life. Adrenaline surged through his body and Alexei lashed out at the thing, kicking and flailing, but it had already bounded out of reach. Alexei gasped and screamed again, doubling over, clutching at the knot of pain on his left side.

"What? who is that?"

"The fascists are comin'! arm yourselves, men!"

"What's wrong?"

"Alexei! it's Alexei!"

Hands came out of the dark to seize him and Alexei fought back, panicking. The room was full of confused voices, people shouting back and forth, calling his name, shaking him. Someone lit the oil lamp and the room flared with yellow light, shadows leaping on the walls.

Alexei was still screaming when Veronika grabbed his shoulder and slapped him twice, quite hard. He let out a squeal and fell back against his blankets, panting for air. He was shaking all over.

"Good God! what on earth -- "

"Everyone hush, hush. Just be quiet."

"What's happening? is he hurt?"

"Alexei!" Veronika was shaking him. "Alexei, what's wrong?"

He'd just about caught his breath, but with his brain still reeling like an unbalanced carousel Alexei was in no way capable of answering. His left side pulsed with a burning heat, spreading slowly across his ribs, over his stomach. The realization was like a high-dive into a bath of ice water -- the thing had *stung* him.

Everything sane that was left in him shrank away from the thought. The faceless thing was like some kind of monstrous wasp. It had followed him all the way here to the hotel to -- to -- to inject him with something, something that was even now under his skin, spreading through his veins. And God alone knew what, or why it had done so.

"...Alexei?"

When he eventually came back to his senses Alexei realized that he'd awakened the entire room. Still clutching his side, he looked up at the circle of anxious faces hovering above him. "Is it..." His throat was raw, though with the way he'd been screaming it was a wonder he could still talk. "Is it...still here?"

Veronika was peering closely at him. "Is what still here?"

Well, that answered his question. Nikita and Tatyana checked over their shoulders anyway, but the thing had clearly vacated the room. Nobody else had seen it.

"What was it, Alexei?"

What, indeed? He had no way of knowing *what* the thing had injected him with, but Alexei could imagine. And if God were merciful Alexei's guess would be wrong, but if he was right --

"...nothing," Alexei croaked. Why couldn't he stop shaking?

"What d'you mean, 'nothing'?" Mikhail's hair was sticking up in every direction, his red bandanna skewed to one side. "Why the hell were you screamin' then?"

"Had a nightmare?" Veronika asked gently. She was petting his face -- probably feeling sorry for having slapped him -- and Alexei drew away from her.

"Must have been some nightmare," Nikita remarked. He was holding his niece in his lap. All the commotion had spooked Elena, no doubt, and she was watching Alexei with wide blue eyes.

"Yeah," Alexei said, curling tighter. The sting had become a steady burning throb in his side, growing larger with every pulse. He could picture his heart pounding away, forcing the blood through his veins, spreading the thing's venom through his limbs. "Sorry to wake you all up."

"'S fine," Tatyana said. "You sure you're okay?"

Alexei nodded and tried to breathe deeply, willing himself to stop trembling. He was miles from 'okay' and getting further by the minute, but he couldn't let them see that. "I'm alright now. Sorry."

They were all plenty suspicious, and had every right to be, but when they got nothing else out of Alexei they eventually gave up. One by one the others returned to their beds. Mikhail gave Alexei a calculating look before leaning over to snuff out the oil lamp, plunging the room into darkness again. Not that it mattered anymore -- the thing had already accomplished what it came to do.

Groaning quietly, Alexei felt his ribs. The wound was neither large nor very deep, but that wasn't what he was afraid of. It never even occurred to him to worry if he'd been poisoned. If it had meant to kill him, he knew, the thing could have easily snapped his neck before he'd even had a chance to scream. It might have been better if it had done so. But killing him had never been the thing's intention anyway.

Clearly it had had other plans for him.

~~~~~

Alexei lay awake until morning. As the eastern sky grew brighter he extricated himself from his tangled blankets and let himself out of the penthouse, tiptoeing down the hall to another hotel room. With the curtains drawn back there was light enough to see himself now, and Alexei pulled up his shirt to inspect his wounds.

The tiny puncture left by the sting had vanished already. In its place was a dark stain about as big as the palm of Alexei's hand, streaks radiating outward from the center like a black sun.

The thing had infected him with the blight.

Alexei felt numb. It wasn't really a surprise to him -- he had been fairly certain that this was the faceless thing's intention -- but the sight still chilled him to the bone. Reluctant to touch it, he prodded around the stain, examining the skin. There was no pain or soreness anymore, though it did tingle a bit.

He drew in a deep breath, held it, and let it out slowly. It was strange, but in a certain way he was almost relieved. The stain meant an end to wondering what to do with himself after Elena and Nikita were out of Khostok.

Alexei would take the Sokolovs to Byatin and dose Elena with sodium thiopental until she went into remission, like Veronika had. He'd treat Tatyana too, if he could. Or maybe he'd just leave Veronika to take care of them both -- it seemed that Veronika could terminate someone's blight hallucinations by touching them. At one time Alexei would have liked to study that phenomenon, but that time had been ages ago.

Now he just wanted to get them all out of Khostok, see that they were safe, and go off someplace to die. If he didn't aggravate his condition by trying to cure it he probably had a good few weeks of sanity left. That would be plenty of time to fulfill his promise to Yuri.

The others were just waking when Alexei came back into the room. Mikhail was up already and there was a pot of coffee simmering away on one of the camping stoves. "Today's the day, comrades," he announced to the room, bayoneting several bread rolls to toast them for their breakfast. "I've got our arsenal ready to go -- once we've eaten up we can head out to find that entrance."

Nikita sat up and yawned. Elena was already out of bed, a gas mask pouch slung over one shoulder, busily hunting around the room for something. Veronika was up as well, her hair disordered from sleeping. "How're you feeling, Alexei?"

Alexei turned away from them. "I'm fine," he said. "Sorry about last night."

"Don't worry about it," Nikita said.

Tatyana rolled over in her sheets. "Get out of the house with those muddy boots!" she exclaimed, the words muffled against her pillow.

"Eh?" Mikhail turned around, a bayonet full of bread rolls in hand. Nikita lifted his head.

"Just wait until your mother sees what you've done to the sofa..." Tatyana mumbled. Mikhail started towards her but Veronika beat him to it, practically leaping onto the woman. She pressed her hand to Tatyana's forehead and the soldier spasmed once, twice, shivered and lay still again.

"...what's goin' on?" Mikhail asked.

Veronika ignored him. "Wake up, Tanya!" Veronika called out, patting the woman's face. "You're talking in your sleep again!"

" -- guh?" said Tatyana. Her eyes slitted open and focused on the woman lying on top of her. Veronika took a close look at Tatyana's pupils and, satisfied, gave her a grin. "Awake now?"

Tatyana nodded slowly. "'m wake. Gettoff."

Veronika stood and pushed her hands through her wild hair. "Don't any of you sleep like normal people?" Mikhail muttered, turning back to his camp stove.

Alexei winced a little. "We've been through a lot," Nikita said defensively. "Lena, come here -- what are you doing?"

Elena came running back to her uncle with the gas mask pouch swinging around her knees. "I'm packing," she said importantly.

"Packing what?"

Elena dropped the pouch on their bedding and opened it, fishing out a water bottle, a knife, a coil of twine, a roll of bandages, a can of salmon, three bags of chips and a chocolate bar. She laid these onto the blanket in even rows, taking stock of her supplies. "We're going today, right?"

Nikita watched as Elena took inventory and carefully repacked the bag. "*We* are going, for a little while, yes," he said. "But you're going to stay here."

"Can't stay here," Mikhail said. He turned the bayonet back and forth, letting the small flame of the camping stove toast the spitted rolls on both sides. "Nobody's gonna be here to watch her."

"We're not bringing her along."

"I'll stay and watch her," Tatyana offered. She was sitting up, rubbing at the spot on her shoulder where Veronika had bitten her. It was probably tingling -- Alexei's own patch of blight certainly was. It was like champagne fizzing away under his skin. He could see the tiniest sliver of an inky stain above the edge of Tatyana's shirt collar and he prayed that Mikhail's vision was bad.

"Wha?" Mikhail frowned. "No reason for you to stay behind!"

"I'm not feeling so well," Tatyana said. Her shirt collar had shifted to one side, uncovering the stain a little more. Tatyana didn't seem to realize it, and none of the others were sitting in a position to see it either. But if Tatyana turned around...

"You sick?" Mikhail was eyeing her warily. Alexei glanced across the room at the guns and ammunition piled underneath the fancy gilt-edged oaken desk. He wasn't sure how Mikhail would react if he realized there was a blight victim in their midst, but he knew he couldn't rely on the old man's understanding. Alexei could probably get across the room to grab a weapon in a few seconds, but Mikhail was already armed -- he slept with that sidearm on, Alexei was pretty sure. Would he kill Tatyana right away? how much time would they have after he noticed?

"No, not sick," Tatyana said irritably.

Nikita squared his shoulders. "I am not bringing my niece into that building."

Mikhail turned to Nikita. "Now just think about it -- your girl is gonna have to go down there sometime, or else how's she getting into the warrens? and you remember, I'm comin' with you -- we're likely gonna find that entrance today, you mark my words. D'you really wanna hike all the way *back* here to get her?"

"He's got a point," Veronika said.

Nikita's jaw was set, but he wasn't arguing anymore. "I *want* to go!" Elena protested.

Her uncle gave her a pained look. "You don't even know where we're going, Lena."

"Yes I do!" Elena slung the gas mask pouch onto her back. "We're going to the river!"

Veronika blinked at her. "...the river?"

Nikita gave her a quizzical look. "Which river is that?"

"*The* river," Elena said, as if that explained everything. "Didn't papa tell you?"

"Tell me what? when?"

"Last night." Elena had adopted the pedantic, scholarly manner of a child explaining something to a typical adult. "Papa came by and told me he was gonna meet us all at the river, and we had to hurry up. He said I should tell everyone to *hurry*," she repeated.

"Ahh, now I see." Nikita reached out and mussed Elena's hair. "You talked to him in your dream, eh?"

Elena pouted. "Wasn't a dream."

"Of course not." Nikita rose to get himself a cup of coffee. Sulking, Elena wandered over to where Alexei was leaning against the glass patio door. "Papa said he talked to *you* last night, too," she told Alexei. "You remember, right?"

Alexei looked up at the little girl in mute amazement. Then he nodded. "Yeah, I remember."

Nikita glanced up as he poured the coffee, winking at Alexei. Of course he'd assume the young man was humoring Elena.

"Did your papa say anything else to you?" Alexei asked her.

Elena nodded. "He said to tell Lyosha that he's very sorry for everything."

"Breakfast's ready!" Mikhail called. Tatyana and Veronika got up from their beds to join the circle around the camping stoves, and Nikita took a seat beside them, careful not to spill his coffee. Elena padded over to sit with the adults, dropping her bag beside her.

"Alexei?" Veronika looked over her shoulder. "You coming?"

Alexei was sitting with his back to them, looking out through the glass of the patio door. Outside the sun was just cresting over the tops of Khostok's tallest buildings, turning the empty windows into squares of molten gold, brightening the green tufts of grass that sprouted in the cracked asphalt of the streets below.

"'m not hungry," he said quietly.

Veronika and Nikita exchanged looks. Mikhail twirled a finger near his temple. "Ah, well, more for us then!" the old man declared, and began passing out the toasted bread.

~~~~~

Little Fedya was only eight years old, and as a natural consequence his perspective was different from an adult's. He was not enjoying his stay in Red Camp Two -- in that regard he and his mother were of the same mind -- but he had his own reasons for that.

There was no TV in camp, for one. Most of his toys had also been left behind at the house during the evacuation, including the ones he had specifically told his mother to pack, like the train set and the army men and the model of the red American sports car with the flashing headlights on it. There were also no gumballs at Red Camp Two, which aside from cars with flashing lights were Fedya's *other* favorite thing.

Of course the camp was not without its merits. There were no baths, for one, and he could appreciate the wisdom of abandoning such a useless practice. And then there were the little beetles that scurried about underneath their folding cots, which were not as exciting as model cars with flashing lights but were better than nothing. He had ceased trying to make pets of the beetles when his mother found one crawling on the cot and screamed loudly enough to bring the soldiers running, but at least Fedya could still watch them skittering around on the floor and pretend they were race cars.

Fedya failed to understand why they couldn't simply drive back home to get his proper race cars; they had gotten to the camp by driving, he reasoned, and should be able to leave the same way. His mother had tearfully confessed that he was "a little sick," pointing to the inky black spot on the back of his left hand.

Fedya was not impressed by the stain and scarcely remembered it except when it itched. He certainly didn't connect it to the increasingly frequent and strange dreams he had been having lately. But when his mother explained that the soldiers wouldn't let them leave, Fedya finally understood -- it was the duty of soldiers to prevent people from doing things, just like policemen.

The soldiers themselves were interesting too. Fedya could understand a little of his mother's fear -- they did look awfully tough in their black uniforms and black gas masks, and they did sound a little bit like robots when they talked. Besides, they had those giant guns. But after Fedya had studied them for a while his fear went away. He'd realized that some of his army men were replicas of Chorman Special Forces soldiers, and afterward they fascinated more than frightened him.

So when the tall CSF soldier came marching in through the doors of Red Camp Two that morning, Fedya did not make much of him. He probably wouldn't have noticed the soldier at all except for the hat: this new soldier wore a peaked visor cap atop the hood of his protective suit, wrapped in clear plastic.

Fedya was too young to decipher the badges of rank on this new soldier's uniform, so he supposed that the hat was responsible for all of the deference the other soldiers showed the newcomer -- they saluted sharply whenever he came nearby and offered him a chair if he so much as paused for a moment. Fedya wondered if they'd have done the same for him if he'd worn the same hat.

But the visor-capped soldier did not sit down. He marched up and down the rows of cots, hands behind his back, looking at the dirt-streaked faces of the inmates. One or two people tried to approach the man and the other CSF soldiers pushed them back with the butts of their rifles.

Fedya remembered something similar from one of his history classes: in the bad old times, before the current era of peace and brotherhood, there had been Noblemen who did not permit themselves to be touched by Peasants. Fedya's history teacher had told them that the nation had entered into an Era of Equality now, and such feudal practices were abolished, so it struck him as strange to see such things.

By the time the visor-capped soldier had reached Fedya there were no fewer than six CSF following him as self-appointed bodyguards. The soldier paused in front of Fedya's cot, looking down at him through the mirrored eyepieces of his gas mask. "Good morning, young comrade," the soldier rasped.

"Good morning," Fedya replied.  He'd always been told to be polite to strangers, especially influential-looking ones.

"And what's your name?"

"Fyodor Grigorievich," Fedya said. "But my mum calls me Fedya."

"Mmm." The soldier nodded. "And where is your mummy now?"

"Getting soup." Fedya pointed to the long queue that snaked back and forth along the far wall of the camp.

"Ahh," said the soldier. "Well, Fedya, would you like a toy car?"

The soldier's bodyguards looked at each-other in clear bewilderment. "Sure!" Fedya replied, perking up at once.

With a flourish the visor-capped soldier drew a small toy car out of the pocket of his protective suit. It was made of real metal with shiny blue and silver details, and though its headlights were painted on it was still a pretty adequate toy car. Fedya took it eagerly and an instant he was kneeling on the cement floor of the camp, making the revving noises, all prepared to embark on his first test drive.

"Hey -- it won't go."

"Hmm?" The soldier braced his hands on his knees and bent down. "What's wrong?"

"It won't go!" Fedya pushed the car forward to illustrate. Its wheels seemed to be locked, and it skidded sideways no matter what he did. "It's broken."

"Let me see."

Fedya placed the car into the soldier's gloved hand. The man straightened up, bringing the car up to eye-level for a closer inspection. His bodyguards watched in puzzled but respectful silence as he tinkered with the little vehicle and finally unscrewed one of its wheels.

"Ahh -- here's the problem." The soldier leaned over to show the wheel to Fedya. "See -- this one's not perfectly round. That's why it won't roll."

"Oh," Fedya said, deflated.

"It's a very tiny component," said the soldier. "Hardly more than eight percent of the toy's entire mass. Its function is exceedingly simple. And yet a slight variation in shape is enough to render the wheel unable to fulfill its intended function."

"Oh."

The soldier nodded his authoritatively decorated head. "Furthermore, the other three wheels -- which appear to be within acceptable tolerance ranges with regard to size and shape -- are rendered useless by this defective fourth. The fourth wheel may only be a few degrees outside of the acceptable range, but those few degrees spell the difference between a functional toy and a nonfunctional one."

"Yeah, it's broken," Fedya agreed.

"Well, if the defective component can be replaced..." Rummaging in the pocket of his protective suit, the soldier brought out another minuscule wheel. With a surprising deftness for someone wearing gloves he screwed the new wheel onto the car's axle, rotated it back and forth, and handed the finished product back to Fedya. "Try it now," he suggested.

Fedya obediently made another test and this time the little car zipped across the cement floor. "Hey, you fixed it!"

"As I thought." Nodding, the soldier held up the wheel he'd removed. "What shall we do with the flawed one, then?"

"Huh?" Fedya shrugged. "It's trash, I guess."

"Indeed, said the soldier. He regarded the bent wheel with a contemplative air, rolling it between his finger and thumb. "As part of a mechanical system, its role was to fulfill a certain function. Failure to do so has rendered its continued existence pointless."

Fedya bobbed his head up and down to show that he was listening. "Vroooooom vr-vroom," he said quietly, nudging the toy car around the leg of the cot.

"Everything in existence fulfills some sort of function. Nothing is exempt, not even humans." He canted his head at Fedya. "You, for example, young comrade -- you function as a child to your mother and a good student to your teachers, am I right?"

"Mum says I'm a good boy," Fedya said absently. In his road trip across the cement floor his vehicle had encountered two beetles fighting over half a dropped cracker, and he was trying to make them scatter so his car could pursue them.

"I'm sure you are." The soldier bent down again, with an air of someone confiding a secret. "Would you care to guess what *my* function is?"

"What?" Fedya looked up. He'd been too busy grinding the cracker to dust beneath the car's wheels to listen to what the visor-capped soldier was saying. His teachers liked to do the same thing -- to look for the one kid who was daydreaming and ask them to parrot back the last five minutes of the lecture -- and now he had no idea what was being asked. "Um..."

"*Fedyenka*!" cried his mother's voice. From halfway across the room she'd spotted him beside the soldier, and that was incentive enough for her to leave the queue without her soup ration and come running to save him. Once he was within reach she swept the boy up into her arms, nearly making him drop his car. She clutched him to her chest as she turned to the soldier.

"Comrade officer, forgive me -- is there some problem? has my Fedya done something wrong? he's just a child, he doesn't know -- "

" -- we're just having a chat," said the soldier, touching the brim of his cap. "At ease."

Fedya's mother had taken in the visor cap and the badges of rank with one look, and they did anything but put her at ease. "Is everything alright?" she repeated, still gripping her child near tight enough to crush him.

"Of course, of course." The soldier inclined his head politely. "Didn't mean to alarm you. I'll be on my way now." The soldier turned to leave.

" -- comrade officer?"

He turned back. "...yes?"

Fedya had finally wriggled free of his maternal restraints to resume test driving his new toy. His mother clasped her hands together. "Forgive me for asking -- it's only for my Fedya's sake, you understand, but -- the cure? when is it being delivered?"

A perceptible hush fell over the nearby cots. Few people were staring, but everyone within a twenty-foot radius was listening as hard as they could.

"Soon," the soldier promised. "Very soon. You have my word that you won't endure these conditions much longer. I have been tasked with eradicating the blight from your city, and I will accomplish this mission."

"Oh thank you, thank you." Fedya's mother looked as if she would have kissed the hem of his protective suit, but thought better of it.

The soldier bowed modestly. "This is merely my function," he said.

Fedya's mother nodded and retreated to her cot, still murmuring thank-yous. The soldier waved to little Fedya -- who was wholly absorbed in running down beetles with his new toy car -- and turned away again. At his gesture the six bodyguards followed after him. All eyes were upon the little entourage as they moved towards the exit doors of Red Camp Two.

At the exit the visor-capped soldier turned to one of the bodyguards. "Is the car ready?"

The bodyguard saluted. "Ready and waiting, Colonel."

"Then bring it around -- I need to get back to the command post right away," Colonel Akimov said softly. "I have an important phone call to make."

~~~~~

"Push, comrades, push!" Mikhail cried. "Put your backs into it!"

"Shut up and climb!" Tatyana shouted back, red-faced.

The six of them -- Alexei, Nikita, Veronika, Tatyana, Elena and Mikhail -- had gotten back to the Gurlukovich Memorial Hospital without incident, but reentering through the window above the emergency entrance proved unexpectedly complicated. Mikhail's not-inconsiderable bulk was nearly impossible to boost up through the second-floor window. After several failed attempts and some heated discussion about leaving him there on the roof of the awning they were finally making some progress, but tempers were growing shorter by the moment.

Elena, Tatyana, Alexei and Veronika had already gotten into the hospital. Tatyana and Alexei were both leaning back of the window, each grabbing one of Mikhail's arms, while Nikita stood on the awning below and attempted to push the old man up through the window. Mikhail's rifle, sidearm, belt full of homemade grenades and rucksack full of additional weapons had all been handed up through the window already, lightening the load as much as possible, but even these measures seemed to be inadequate.

"C'mon, you weaklings!" Mikhail bawled. Lacking any other way to assist in the efforts he had begun shouting his own brand of 'encouragement' to the team.. "Up and over! up and over! c'mon, pull!"

"...I'm just gonna drop him," Tatyana growled through clenched teeth.

"He's gonna yank me right out the window if you do," Alexei replied.

With a shout Nikita shoved the old man upward. Mikhail rose another six inches and Tatyana reached out to seize the back of his collar, bracing both feet against the wall as she leaned backward. "Use your legs!" she barked,

Mikhail's feet pedaled in the air like a swimming dog, nearly booting Nikita square in the face. He was up to his chest on the windowsill now, both Tatyana and Alexei attempting to drag him in by the collar of his jacket, but the greater part of Mikhail's mass was still outside the building.

Panting for air, Nikita stepped back from the window, leaving Mikhail's rear dangling out in space. The old man's eyes bulged. "I'm slipping!" he wailed, clawing at the wall below the window. One of his flailing hands caught Alexei's arm and pulled, yanking the young man after him. Veronika grabbed onto the back of Alexei's shirt and tugged him in the opposite direction.

Nikita had already unslung his rifle and was holding it by the barrel, taking aim. He stepped forward and put all his strength into one final upward thrust, using the rifle butt as a plunger to force the old man up and through. Squalling, Mikhail popped in through the window like a cork from a bottle, half-flattening Alexei beneath him as he landed.

As the dust settled Tatyana picked the old man up off of Alexei. "Hah, finally!" Mikhail said, straightening his bandanna and retrieving his weapons from the floor. He rubbed at the seat of his pants where the rifle butt had connected with his backside. "I knew you could do it!"

Tatyana ignored him. After helping Alexei back onto his feet the two of them leaned back out the window to grab Nikita's hands, pulling him up into the hospital. He was flushed from the exertion and there was a bootprint on the shoulder of his jacket where Mikhail had stepped on him. Once he was inside Elena grabbed her uncle's hand, and Veronika went to close the window.

"This is nothing -- just a little exercise," Mikhail opined. " You kids wouldn't last ten minutes in the military. Wouldn't even make it through basic training."

Nikita rolled his eyes. Tatyana sneered at Mikhail when his back was turned.

"Well!" Mikhail said, clapping his hands together. They all turned at the same time, looking down the dusty hallway that extended toward the heart of the building. Everyone reached for their flashlights and clicked them on. Nothing had changed since their last visit some days ago -- or at least nothing that they could see. The halls were vacant, the office doors all closed, the papers littering the floor still undisturbed.

But Alexei could *hear* that something was different. This time the hospital was not silent. This time Alexei could just make out a low constant humming, just above the threshold of his hearing -- a sound that seemed to be traveling through the walls of the building and up into his bones. He supposed that perhaps a generator had started running somewhere.

Mikhail unslung his rifle and racked the bolt back. The noise echoed up and down the hallway. "Let's split up into three groups," he suggested. "That entrance could be anywhere on the ground floor."

"Okay," said Nikita. "I'll go with Alexei."

Alexei blinked at him, but Nikita was looking at Veronika. "Would you please watch Elena for a bit?" he asked. "I think she'll be safer with you."

Veronika looked surprised too, but she accepted. "Come on Lena," she said, taking the girl's hand from her uncle. Elena nuzzled up against the young woman's side, sheltering under her arm. "You stay with me and Tanya; we'll be alright."

"I never said I'd go with you," Tatyana muttered. "And don't call me that."

"You'd rather go with General Litvinenko?"

Tatyana said nothing. "I don't need anyone's help," Mikhail declared. "More than capable of defendin' myself." He patted his grenade belt significantly. "We'll meet back up here in two hours to share what we've found. Everyone's got their watches, right? and the guns I packed for ya?"

They all did. "Then let's go!" Mikhail said, and immediately marched off down the hall.

"Remember -- steer clear of the atrium!" Veronika called after him. "And the gym too..."

The old man didn't look back. Tatyana muttered something about him getting himself killed and started off down the hall that branched off to their right. Veronika went after her, still holding Elena by the hand. "We'll be alright!" she called back over her shoulder. "You two be careful!"

Nikita nodded, waving. As the three disappeared around a bend in the hallway he turned back to Alexei. "Let's go," he said, hefting his backpack onto his back.

The left-hand hallway led to a series of exam rooms. These halls had not been heavily used by the CSF during the building's stint as a quarantine camp, and not enough time had elapsed for the hospital to begin showing the signs of neglect. One who didn't know any better might have guessed that the doctors and patients had evacuated less than three days ago. The disaster that had befallen Khostok was visible here only in small ways -- a glass syringe shattered on the tile floor, a gurney left at an angle in one hallway, the shriveled and dead potted plants beside the exam room doors.

Alexei and Nikita walked in silence, scanning ahead with their flashlights. Alexei was near-positive that his ears were playing tricks on him, but if they weren't then the humming noise he'd noticed was getting louder. And it wasn't a hum, either -- as the volume increased it sounded more like the gurgle of rushing water, splashing and bubbling away someplace unseen. Water in the pipes, maybe? but that couldn't be -- the public water in Khostok had been turned off weeks ago.

It almost sounded like -- but then he'd have to admit that he was really losing his marbles, and faster than he'd suspected. Because under the liquid noises there was an undercurrent that almost reminded him of voices, human voices. The sound of their footsteps kept him from focusing on it, but Alexei didn't want to ask Nikita to stop in the middle of the hallway so he could listen to something that probably wasn't even there.

Would Alexei recognize one of the blight hallucinations when he had one? Because that spot under his ribs had begun to itch, prickling and tingling the way his foot did when it fell asleep. The notion that he was actually going insane -- not just feeling crazy, but legitimately losing touch with reality -- sank like a stone in his gut. Now that he'd caught the blight it was only a matter of time; even if if this wasn't a hallucination now, he'd certainly be having them later.

But that noise sounded so much like human voices that Alexei could almost make out the words. If he just listened a little harder...

" -- for a second," Nikita was saying.

Alexei came to a halt. "Huh?"

"I said, let's stop here for a second." Nikita jerked his head toward the door of one of the exam rooms.

"Uh, okay." Alexei followed as Nikita pushed open the unlocked door and stepped into the room. It was a conventional doctor's office with a metal examination table, a rolling chair for the doctor and rows of white cabinets. A quick sweep of the flashlights confirmed the room was empty and free of inkweed.

Nikita shucked off his backpack and Alexei did the same. "I wanted to talk to you without Elena around," Nikita explained. He drew in a deep breath and faced Alexei. "What's the chances of curing her?"

So that's why Nikita had opted to pair off with him. "Oh. Um...honestly...I don't know."

Alexei squirmed a little. "Really. I don't exactly understand what's happened to Veronika, but she went into 'remission' right after we gave her the thiopental. Theoretically that's what triggered it, but that's only my theory -- I didn't get the same result from Tatyana when I gave her the same thing, but there could be a million reasons for that."

Nikita listened with folded arms. The flashlights were hardly enough to illuminate the entire room, and the half-light threw black shadows onto his face, blotting out his eyes. "What did Yura think about Veronika?"

"...uh, Yura?...he wasn't sure either," Alexei said lamely.

"But he was studying the blight with you, wasn't he?"

"Yeah."

"Is that how he died?"

Alexei's mouth went dry.

"He caught the blight, didn't he?" Nikita's tone was calm and even. "That's what killed him."

"How -- who told you?" Alexei squeaked.

Nikita said nothing for a long, long time. "I knew it," he grated.

Alexei realized too late that he'd been tricked into the confession. The room was shrinking around him, squeezing all the air out of his lungs. He backed up and bumped into the exam room cabinets, pushing aside the rolling chair and sending a jar of cotton balls spilling across the countertop.

"So one of the women knew about him, too." Nikita didn't sound so calm anymore. "Which one? The soldier?"

"I...I..." Alexei turned for the door. A firearm seemed to materialize in Nikita's hand -- one of the ones Mikhail had given them for self-defense -- and he took aim at Alexei's chest. "Sit. Down," said Nikita, and in that moment Alexei was positive the man was going to kill him.

On boneless legs Alexei wobbled back to the rolling chair and sank into it.

"Who else knew about him?"

"...both of them," Alexei said.

Nikita seemed surprised, but it was hard to get a good look at his face -- the flashlight beam was jittering back and forth, making the shadows in the room seem to dance. Dimly Alexei realized that this was because his hands were shaking. Nikita was shining his own flashlight full into Alexei's face, spotlighting him as if he were under interrogation. Which, in a way, he was.

"You idiots don't know my brother like I do," Nikita said. "I knew he would never -- never -- send someone else to save Elena in his place. And if you could get out of the Labs, so could he."

Nikita's flashlight was blinding him, making it hard for Alexei to think. Not that he was much for thinking right about now. That rushing sound he'd noticed earlier was rising, swelling in volume, drowning out whatever attempts at rational thought he might have made.

"So you might have lied about knowing him; that's what I thought at first. But you had Elena's photo. And even if you'd stolen that from Yura, I couldn't figure out your motivation. If you just wanted out of Khostok, you went way out of your way to get Elena and me."

The irony of being held at gunpoint by someone he was rescuing did not escape Alexei. Dazzled by the light, he shut his eyes.

"So your story only makes sense if you really *did* know Yura, and he died before he could escape." Nikita's voice came cutting like a razor through the self-imposed darkness. "And you were just too much of a coward to tell me so."

There was no sense in denying it.

"So tell me. How did he die?"

Alexei opened his eyes. "...you really want to know?"

Nikita nodded.

"Well...he did catch the blight. He got it from a patient at the Labs." Veronika had been kind enough to keep Alexei's lie a secret, and he saw no reason to implicate her in Yuri's death.

"Is that how he died? from the blight?"

Alexei shook his head. "He was -- " Much to his horror, his voice cracked, and Alexei swallowed hard. His eyes were burning. "The CSF were keeping him in quarantine, at the Labs. I -- I brought him -- " Oh, he couldn't do this. He turned away from the blinding glare of the flashlight, shutting his eyes again.

The click of the hammer cocking back echoed in the exam room.

" -- I brought him the thiopental to use on himself," Alexei said quickly, eyes still closed. "He took the whole bottle."

And he waited, in agonizing silence, for the roar of gunfire. Nikita wasn't speaking -- didn't even seem to be breathing, in fact -- and at last the suspense was too much for him. Alexei slitted open one eye. Nikita was still holding him at gunpoint, but the hand holding the firearm had begun to tremble.

"You're lying," Nikita whispered. "He'd never do a thing like that."

Alexei wished he was. "Why would I lie about that?"

"Because you're the one killed him."

Alexei went for Nikita's throat. The rolling chair went sailing across the floor and crashed into the wall, unnoticed.

"Get back! dammit, get back!" Nikita yelled. Alexei had his shirt collar in both hands -- he'd thrown the older man against the far wall of the exam room and was shaking him.

"Why would I kill him?!" Alexei shrieked. "Why?!"

There was a cold ring of metal pressing against Alexei's side. "I *will* shoot you if you don't get off me," Nikita hissed at him.

"Go ahead!" Alexei's eyes were wild. "Shoot me! do it! I've already been shot once, maybe your aim is better than the last guy's."

Nikita thought he was insane -- it was written plainly on his face. "Get *off* -- " he repeated, and shoved Alexei back. The young man lost his grip on Nikita's collar and went stumbling backwards across the exam room. The flashlight clattered to the floor and Nikita bent to retrieve it, never taking his eyes from Alexei.

"You don't understand," Alexei said brokenly. "He saved my life. Look -- " He undid his buttons with fumbling movements and dropped his shirt to the floor. "Look," he said, turning to show Nikita his scarred shoulder. "The CSF shot me when the quarantine started. If Yura hadn't rescued me I'd have bled to death. How the hell could I kill him after that?"

But Nikita wasn't interested in his shoulder. "Sweet mother of God..." Nikita flattened himself back against the wall. "You've got the blight."

Alexei glanced down at the splotch of black across his ribs. It had definitely grown larger since that morning; the palm of his hand no longer covered it. "Yeah, I do."

" -- How?"

"Last night." Alexei picked his shirt back up and slipped into it again. "One of those faceless things got into the room. That's why I was screaming."

"It -- it infected you?" Nikita's tone was purest horror.

Alexei nodded. "So you can shoot me if you want," he offered, "once we're all out of the city, I won't mind. But you have to let me help you and Elena to get out. I promised Yura I would."

He took a step towards him and Nikita recoiled. "You stay away from me."

"Please."

Nikita was shaking his head. "You lied to us," he said, edging toward the door, firearm still trained on Alexei's chest. "I don't care why you did it -- I deserved to know that my brother was dead." His eyes glittered. "You can find your own way out of Khostok. If I see you again, I swear I'll kill you."

Alexei's expression was unbearable and Nikita had to turn away. He darted out of the exam room and slammed the door after him, grabbing one of the gurneys and forcing it up against the door. He knew that wouldn't hold Alexei longer than a few seconds, but that would be long enough.

Reholstering his gun, Nikita broke into a sprint, charging back the way they'd come. He had to get Lena away from that woman -- if all three of them had lied about Yuri, he couldn't trust any of them anymore.

And he *could* find his own way out of the city. He didn't need any help with that, and certainly not the help of this blight-infected troop of madmen. He'd get his niece to Byatin all on his own.

And then he could tell her. He'd wait until then. There was no point in upsetting her during the trip; not when there were so many things that could go wrong between here and safety. He could even adopt Lena once this was all over. Yura would have wanted --

Nikita cut off the thought and killed it, swallowing back the lump in his throat. Later. There would be time for that later.

The pool of light cast by the flashlight bounced ahead of him like a will o' the wisp, guiding his way. Nikita glanced up as he streaked past a window. He was positive -- or nearly positive -- that it was the same one they'd entered through. He knew they hadn't taken too many turns since they'd split off into groups. He at least was certain that Veronika and that soldier woman had taken the right-hand fork, and he plunged off in this direction.

But thirty paces later Nikita skidded to a halt, dust billowing up around his feet. The hallway had split again -- according to the overhead signs you went right for the BURN WARD, left for the INTENSIVE CARE UNIT. Panting, he scanned the dusty floor with his flashlight, looking for prints. Someone had spilled a folder full of x-rays in the hall, spreading a fan of transparencies across the tile, and Nikita bent down to see if any of them were marked by bootprints.

He'd only been hunting for half a minute when he heard someone shout. Instantly he was on the alert, snapping upright, his gun already out of its holster. Nikita assumed that Alexei was chasing him down, so when the report of distant gunfire came echoing down the halls it shocked him. Why would Alexei be firing his gun? had he come across another one of those faceless things?

Or maybe he hadn't. Nikita had seen his face before he'd left the young man in the exam room. The sudden certainty was terrible -- if Alexei had used his firearm, if would have been on himself.

Nikita hovered in indecision for a moment. Should he go back? Did he really *want* to go back and see what had happened, knowing that it was at least partly his fault? Couldn't he just pretend not to have heard anything and continue searching for his niece? Nobody would have blamed him. After all, Lena was depending on him, and if he --

He'd just turned back around when someone shrieked, the cry rolling in waves down the hall. None of these sounds were coming from Alexei's direction, Nikita realized: they all came from ahead of him, in the direction he was headed. And that cry had been unmistakably Elena's voice.

Nikita nearly slipped on the spilled x-rays in his haste. He dove into the right-hand fork and went pelting down the hall toward the Burn Ward, gun in one hand and flashlight in the other, frantic prayers racing through his head.

Fortunately most of the doors in the hallway were closed, leaving only a few rooms for Nikita to check. He ducked into each one, thrusting his flashlight into the room, sweeping it back and forth for a moment before hurrying on. He was desperate to find the girl, but at the same time he almost dreaded it. If the inkweed -- or one of those faceless things -- or any of the other nightmares in this building had gotten hold of her...

Room 506 was just like all the others in the Burn Ward, nondescript and sterile-looking. Nikita was just stepping back out of the room when something seized his ankle, and he screamed loudly enough for the entire building to hear.

But when he looked down he received an even greater shock. The thing that had grabbed him turned out to be Tatyana, lying stretched out on her side on the floor. Blood was pooling on the tiles beneath her.

"Shit!" Nikita dropped to his knees beside Tatyana, turning the woman over onto her back. Her face was ashen, eyes glassy. One hand was clamped onto her side, and the blood welling up through her fingers glinted blackly in the faint glow of the flashlight.

"Oh god. Are you -- " Nikita had no medical experience but this looked bad, very bad. "I mean, what -- "

"The old man," Tatyana whispered. "He's got your girl."

The bottom fell out of Nikita's stomach. "He -- why?"

"My fault." Tatyana closed her eyes for a moment. "Veronika...heard something. Left. I found some medical stuff in here. I was changing Elena's bandage, and the old man saw us. Saw her." She opened her eyes again. "He shot me and took her."

Nikita didn't need any further explanation. If Mikhail had seen his niece without the bandage on her chin he would have known she was infected. And he had already made it abundantly clear what he thought of those who'd caught the blight.

"Go find her," Tatyana said.

"But -- what about you?"

Tatyana squinted up at him. Picking up her head, she gingerly lifted her hand away from her side for a moment, looking at her injuries. With a sigh she relaxed again. "Didn't hit anything vital." She winced. "...I think."

"I can't leave you here," Nikita protested. Nevermind that he needed to pursue Mikhail right away, or that the soldier woman had also lied to him about Yuri's death. It wouldn't have been right.

"I'll be fine. There's...bandages on the counter. And morphine too, I think. Give it to me."

Quaking with adrenaline, Nikita rose to find the gauze and painkillers scattered across the countertop. He was bending down to administer these when Tatyana took them from his hand. "I've got it," she said. "Go. Go now."

Nikita got back to his feet. "I'll come back for you," he promised. "We'll get you some proper medical attention. I swear."

Tatyana nodded, squeezing her eyes shut. "Go."

Nikita went.

If he'd been alarmed before, Nikita was in a panic now. The doors blurred past him as he raced down the hallway. Over and over the same six words thundered in his head: what did the old man want? He'd been explicit about his desire to rid the city of the blight-infected -- he'd gotten it into his head that they were marked by the Devil, or some such raving nonsense -- but if that was his thinking, why kidnap Elena?

A thousand horrible possibilities paraded through his brain. He pushed them away. He couldn't think about it now; it'd drive him crazy if he did. He just had to find her. Tatyana hadn't mentioned anything about Mikhail hurting the girl, just that he'd taken her away. He wouldn't have bothered to nab her if he only meant to shoot her later, would he?

Finding Tatyana had been difficult enough; if Mikhail didn't want to be found, Nikita realized, the building was big enough to hide in for days. He could spend weeks searching the place and still never find them. And there was always the chance that the crazy old man would stumble into a nest of that black weed, vanishing under the surface, and drag Lena into the devouring jungle after him. He could just about hear her screams...

" -- uncle!!"

The shriek came from behind him, and Nikita whipped around. As it turned out, there had been no need for him to find the old man: Mikhail had found *him*.

"Easy, easy," the old man crooned. He came shuffling up the hallway toward Nikita, squat and ridiculous in his tactical gear. A flashlight had been clipped to the strap of his backpack, leaving one hand free to grasp Elena's shoulder and the other one free to hold a gun to her head. From the girl's colorless face Nikita could see that she was frightened well past the point of tears. The blight stood out like a splash of ink on her chin.

"No," Nikita breathed.

"You know what to do." Mikhail jerked his head upward. "Go ahead and toss your gun over here, then get yer hands in the air...slowly, now."

Like a man sleepwalking Nikita cast his gun onto the tiles and lifted his hands up over his head. "Don't hurt her."

"Hah!" Mikhail laughed shortly. "You need yer eyes checked! Take a good look -- Satan's put his mark on the girl now." He dragged the muzzle of the gun over Elena's chin and Nikita realized that he'd be fully capable of killing the man with his bare hands, just ripping his throat right out with nothing but his fingers.

"She's just sick," Nikita said, trying to keep the tremor out of his voice. "It's not anything unholy."

"Lies! what about those things -- the things without faces?!" Mikhail's eyes were starting out of his head. "Yer tellin' me that those things are the Lord's creation?!"

"I don't know anything about them," Nikita said. "I'm telling you that Elena's not possessed by the Devil or anything like that. She's just a little girl, and I just want to get her out of the city."

He could tell from the man's expression that Mikhail didn't believe him. "Numerous are his lies," Mikhail said, wagging his head. "Don't think I don't know what yer doing -- I know the Dark One's sent the lot of you to get me, to infect me and my home with the soul-rot, to keep me from cleansin' the city of your filth."

"Oh, for the love of -- *you* picked *us* up!" Nikita shouted at him. "We haven't been sent by anyone! we're just trying to get out of the city before everything goes to hell."

"Hell's exactly where the city'd be headed, if I wasn't here to stop it." He bared his teeth, pressing the gun's muzzle against Elena's temple. "Yea, for He hath placed into mine hands a flaming sword..."

"You don't know what you're doing," Nikita told him, and now he couldn't stop his voice from trembling. He knew that Elena could see him panicking, could see that her uncle was helpless to save her, and it took everything he had not to look her in the eyes.

" -- to be wielded in the name of righteousness and swift justice -- "

"Please!" Nikita dropped to his knees on the floor. "I'm begging you -- just listen to me for a second! You don't understand -- "

Mikhail's voice was building up to a crescendo, reverberating from the walls of the empty hallway. " -- to smite the wicked and drive them back into the fiery pit!"

"Elena!!" Nikita shrieked.

"*Amen*!!"

The report of the gun was deafening. Nikita and Elena both screamed, but the sound was drowned out by the absolutely unearthly bellow that came tearing out of Mikhail. Stunned, Nikita watched him go staggering away from Elena, colliding with the wall. His mouth hanging open, the old man reached around to his back and brought his hand up to his face. The fingertips were streaked with blood.

Nikita realized what had happened a moment before he spotted Alexei. The young man was standing at the far end of the hallway, wisps of smoke curling from the gun he held in both hands. He'd crept up from behind while Mikhail was preaching and shot him in the back.

"Run, Elena!" Alexei shouted.

Elena crossed the floor in two quick bounds, leaping into her uncle's arms. Holding her close, Nikita snatched his gun from the floor, but he needn't have worried -- Mikhail wasn't interested in the two of them anymore. Roaring like a wounded bear, he turned and charged toward Alexei.

Five more gunshots shattered the air as Alexei and Mikhail exchanged fire, but none of them seemed to make contact. When the old man was no more than two yards away Alexei broke and ran, sprinting back toward the exam rooms again. Mikhail was close on his heels as they swung around a bend in the hallway and out of sight.

Nikita dragged his niece into one of the rooms, shutting the door after them. He was weak all over with relief. "Are you hurt? are you hurt?" he demanded, checking her face, her neck, her arms and legs.

Elena was obviously quite shaken but she insisted that she was fine. "The soldier lady got shot," she said, her face crinkling up.

"I know Lena -- I saw her. But she's fine, she's fine." Nikita hoped he wasn't lying to her. "She's safe in one of the rooms."

Elena looked into her uncle's eyes. "Then we've gotta go help Lyosha."

"Okay, we will." The enormity of what they'd just avoided was dawning on Nikita, bit by bit. "Of course we will."

~~~~~

Alexei flew.

He could hear the crazy old man stampeding through the hallway just behind him, grunting and panting like a beast. Alexei knew that Mikhail had taken at least one bullet but wasn't positive where he'd been hit. Apparently that wasn't enough to slow him down very much; his insanity seemed to have lent him strength.

Sailing around another bend in the hallway, Alexei threw himself against the wall and took aim. When Mikhail came flying into view Alexei took three more shots, aiming for his head. Mikhail ducked down behind a gurney and two shots went wild, and on the third pull of the trigger the gun went *chk*. Out of ammo.

Alexei bolted again. Mikhail toppled the gurney with a crash and resumed the chase.

As he ran Alexei grabbed anything within reach, throwing it down behind him: potted plants, carts full of medical supplies, more gurneys. In spite of his age Mikhail dodged these obstacles without much difficulty, though he did stumble on one of the potted plants.

Once there came a resounding crash from behind him and Alexei looked back, hoping against hope that Mikhail had fallen on his face. Then he saw that the old man had thrown the hallway doors closed and was shoving a metal crutch in through the door handles, barring it from the inside.

His heart sank. Even if Yura's brother was coming to rescue him -- and at this point Alexei was not so certain he would -- now Nikita wouldn't be able to reach him. He was trapped in this hallway with the madman.

"Nothin' can save you from the wrath of the Lord, boy!" Mikhail howled.

Alexei's lungs felt like they would burst. He swung a sharp ninety-degree turn into another hallway and -- too late -- saw the overturned wastebasket directly in his path. His foot plunged in through its plastic side and wrenched to right. Pain exploded in Alexei's ankle and a scream tore out of him, his vision whitening for a moment. When it cleared again Alexei found himself on his hands and knees, scrambling instinctively across the tile towards the open doorway of the employee lunchroom on his right.

The darkness within was almost welcome. Alexei had dropped his flashlight and spent firearm in the hallway but there was no time to retrieve them. Biting back further screams he dragged himself deeper into the lunchroom, looking for someplace to conceal himself.

If Mikhail hadn't seen him duck into the room -- if he thought that Alexei had just run on -- he might have a chance. He had no better ideas than hiding in a cabinet until Nikita found him or Mikhail got himself eaten by the inkweed, but this desperate plan was better than no plan at all.

The scent of burnt coffee and old cigarettes lingered in the air. Alexei could barely see his hand in front of his face, but he could just make out some low-lying shapes ahead of him that looked like supply cabinets, perhaps big enough for him to hide in. Hissing through his teeth, ignoring the tingling in his side and the invisible hammer pounding on his ankle, he pulled himself forward, reaching out to feel for the smooth surface of the cabinet door.

His fingers grasped something soft and flexible, a thin tube that bent easily under his fingers. String? Electrical wiring? He felt along the strand and encountered leaves. Was he grabbing one of those withered office plants?

But then those little lights began to flicker to life, one after the other, and Alexei understood. He'd grabbed an inkweed vine.

Stifling a scream, Alexei jerked away from the plant. But his touch had stirred something in the growth, and now there were ten lights -- twenty -- fifty -- two hundred -- innumerable little gems of light, glowing in all the colors of the rainbow, filling the walls of the room with a map of stars. The lunchroom was choked with the stuff. It was all around him, covering the walls on all sides. Stiff with fright. he watched the gems expand and unfold into glowing petals, like a time-lapse of a blooming flower.

Alexei smelled honey. His left side was on fire.

The young man was just starting to crawl away from the inkweed when Mikhail came bursting through the door, kicking a wastebasket across the room. Alexei nearly swallowed his tongue. He made a split-second decision and dove headfirst into the inkweed, burrowing into the tangle.

"I know yer in here!" Mikhail raged, waving his flashlight back and forth. He'd exchanged his handgun for a shotgun, tucked into the crook of one arm. At this kind of range the shockwave from the blast would kill instantly, Alexei imagined. That was probably the best he could hope for. With his left side still itching and burning he shimmied backwards into the black growth, away from the old man, praying that the vines and leaves would hide him from the flashlight. Or even that Mikhail would be too spooked by the inkweed to explore the room further.

"Dropped yer gun outside the door, you did," Mikhail gloated as he stalked around the room's perimeter, letting the flashlight beam play over the lunch tables. He stopped short when he spotted the first tendrils of inkweed -- Alexei held his breath and prayed -- but the old man only snorted and went on searching, giving the black stuff a wide berth. "Might've figured you'd go to hide in someplace like this."

A feathery touch tickled across the nape of Alexei's neck, and he clapped a hand over his mouth before he yelped aloud. He wanted it to be anything else: a cobweb, a piece of paper, even an actual spider. But he knew better than that. Still he sat there, every nerve alight, feeling it as the little tendrils played across his arms, his face, slipping under his shirt, wrapping around his legs, his throat.

But he was as good as dead if he panicked now. These vines were small ones, Alexei reasoned, and the inkweed wasn't doing anything other than tickling him at this point. There were no little chewing mouths, no skin-dissolving acids, no poisons he could detect. Just those black vines, the soft black leaves, and the innumerable little flowers that crowded in closer and closer to his face...

A flicker of movement caught Alexei's attention. One of the glowing blossoms was close enough for him to see that there was something stirring inside it, something right at the heart of the flower. At the center of the petals was a luminous green gem, smooth as a marble, and a little black dot was dancing back and forth across the marble's surface. It darted left, right, down, up, and then centered itself on the green gem just in time for Alexei to realize what he was looking at.

An eye. The green marble was an eye. There was an eye inside that glowing flower. *All* of the flowers, Alexei realized suddenly, had similar gems hidden in their petals.

The inkweed had eyes, hundreds of them. And it was looking right at him.

To his credit, when Alexei burst shrieking out of the inkweed it did startle Mikhail quite a lot. It gave the young man enough time to take three steps toward the door before his twisted ankle gave out and he dropped to the floor.

"Gotcha!"

Alexei rolled over onto his side, clutching at his ankle and groaning. Mikhail's flashlight beam spotlighted him where he lay. Beyond the glow he could just make out the old man's crookedly triumphant grin, and the twin black holes that were the barrels of his shotgun.

"The armies of darkness can never prevail against the host of the Lord." Mikhail radiated smug satisfaction. "Should've known that."

It gave Alexei a little consolation to think that Mikhail's gunshot wounds would be difficult for him to treat, especially since he was going around shooting at anyone who could have patched him up. Maybe he'd die of infection in a few weeks. That would be nice.

"I'd use you as bait," Mikhail told him, "Same way I used the girl. But you're a dangerous little serpent -- best to stamp you out right here."

(*I'm sorry,*) Alexei told the ceiling overhead. (*I'm so sorry, Yura. At least I tried.*)

"Look at me," Mikhail said, annoyed at being ignored. "Want you to see who's endin' yer sin-cursed life. You'll wanna tell yer infernal master all about me."

Alexei looked at him. His eyes widened.

"Yeah, that's better. I'd be frightened if I was in your shoes." Looking gleeful, Mikhail pumped his shotgun once and took aim at Alexei's head. "Ashes to ashes, and dust to dust."

"...look behind you," Alexei whispered.

"Eh?" Mikhail blinked. "What's that?"

Alexei pointed.

Mikhail turned and found himself looking at a bulging, distorted human face. Then he realized what he was seeing -- it was his own warped reflection, mirrored on the face of one of those faceless nightmare beasts.

The old man dropped his flashlight. It struck the floor and went out.

What happened next was unclear to Alexei -- the only light came from the glowing flowers, giving the whole lunchroom an dim, undersea quality. He distinctly heard Mikhail give a gurgling scream.

Then the faceless thing's tentacles shot forward, wrapping about the old man's body like so many pythons, and then releasing him with a snap that flung him like a ragdoll against the wall of the lunchroom. Alexei heard the crack as his skull struck the wall. Mikhail dropped to the floor and scrambled back to his feet, spitting curses, reaching to grab the dropped shotgun. Points of light slid over the thing's skin as it went after the old man.

Mikhail took aim with the shotgun and fired, once. Alexei saw the faceless thing knocked backward from the force of the blast. Mikhail gave a scream that ended in manic laughter. A shadow passed between Alexei and the lights as the thing came back towards the old man, and a tentacle whistled through the air to yank the shotgun from Mikhail's hands, smashing it into the wall.

The old man was shouting at the top of his lungs, but either the fright or the concussion seemed to have robbed him of the ability to speak coherently. Tentacles flashed through the air again, coiling around Mikhail's neck, his torso, his arms and legs. The faceless thing took a firmer stance and lifted -- lifted -- the old man into the air, with him squirming and writhing like a hooked worm. Then it hurtled him forward and smashed him up against the lunchroom wall. Still gripping him in its black tentacles, the thing drew Mikhail back and smashed him into the wall again.

And again. And again. And again.

Delirious with horror, Alexei crawled under one of the lunchroom tables and curled up into a ball. He buried his face in his hands. Over and over, the wall-shaking impact rocked the little room. Five times. Ten. Fifteen.

When the faceless thing finally released its prey, the misshapen bundle that had been Mikhail hit the floor with a wet slap. Alexei risked opening his eyes and saw that the faceless thing was looking directly at him. It took a step towards him, faltered, and collapsed. It twitched once or twice, made a weak effort to rise, and then the thing lay still.

Seconds stretched into minutes and still neither of them moved. Alexei expected it to come awake at any second, choke him with its ropy tentacles, bash him into an unrecognizable pulp. But the thing lay motionless there until Alexei finally summoned up enough courage to move out from under the table, reaching for Mikhail's flashlight with nerveless fingers.

He switched it on and shone the light on the faceless thing. The first thing Alexei noticed was that it was *breathing*. He hadn't thought of the faceless things needing to do something as mundane as breathing the air, but the uneven rising and falling of its side was unmistakably familiar.

And then he noticed its hand. One arm was bent toward Alexei, and he could see that the thing's hand was not perfectly black. The inky skin had faded near the wrist, revealing flesh that was pink and almost...almost human-looking.

Alexei couldn't resist. With one hand on the lunchroom table to balance himself he hobbled towards the faceless thing, ready to flee at any moment. As he got closer he could see that more of its glossy black skin had disappeared, as if melting away like ice.

In fact it *was* melting away. The process was incrementally slow but the edges of the black patches were dissolving, shrinking back to reveal the flesh-tone underneath. When he swept the flashlight up to the thing's head and realized that he was looking at hair -- human hair -- that the inky stuff no longer concealed, Alexei almost turned away. He wasn't sure if he wanted to see this, to know something he wasn't going to be able to forget. But the burning in his side drove him on, and he stepped around the prone body of the faceless thing to shine his flashlight into its face.

But the thing on the floor was no longer faceless. It wasn't even really a "thing" anymore -- now it had begun to resemble a human, a wounded human being lying naked in a puddle of rapidly dissolving black goo. And not just any human being.

It was Veronika.

Alexei must have made some kind of sound, for Veronika turned her head. With effort she focused on his face. She tried to smile. "Hullo, Alexei."

He couldn't speak. This *was* Veronika, and yet it wasn't -- her pupils were the size of quarters, eclipsing the irises and almost covering the whites of her eyes. Her midsection was a gory mess of black and red. Alexei remembered that the faceless thing had taken a shotgun blast to the stomach. Had that thing really been Veronika? What had she become?

Veronika attempted to rise again but her strength seemed to be fading. Alexei knelt down next to her, afraid to touch her.

"I...talked to them," Veronika said. Black liquid bubbled out through her lips.

Alexei still couldn't speak, but he must have looked puzzled enough. "...the things," Veronika said. She was, quite irrationally, still smiling at him. "...with no faces."

"...you did?" he managed to say.

Veronika nodded.

"What did they say?"

"...you wouldn't understand," Veronika wheezed. "Not yet."

Alexei felt like his brain was coming apart. He had a million questions and no way of asking any of them. "You need medical help," he said weakly, looking away from those polished-obsidian gems that were her eyes. Swallowing back his nausea Alexei grabbed Veronika's shoulder and tried to pull her into his arms. Twisted ankle or no, he would figure out a way to get her back to the others. Maybe if he could get her onto one of the gurneys...

Something tugged Veronika out of Alexei's hands. He looked and saw that the inkweed growth along the wall had put out several long vines -- these runners were coiling around Veronika's feet, working their way up her legs even as he watched.

"Oh god," Alexei muttered. He reached over to grab the inkweed and pry it from her ankles. It resisted him with a very un-plant-like strength, the tendrils squirming like snakes in his grip, and before he'd untangled one vine there were already three more taking its place.

Not only was the stuff wrapping around Veronika's body like a constrictor, but it was pulling her as well, dragging her inch by inch towards the dense tangle of inkweed growth along the wall. And Alexei, like a fool, had left his lighter along with his backpack in that exam room.

He ripped another vine away and was rewarded with a slap on one cheek, the tendril lashing out like a tiny whip. Another one fell onto his shoulder and began to curl under his arm, and Alexei struck at it to drive it away. "Shit, shit..."

"It's okay," Veronika said. A half-stained hand came down on Alexei's own. "Don't bother."

He looked dumbly at her. "...it's only trying to help," she whispered, as if that explained anything. She slid another inch closer to the inkweed and Alexei yanked her back again. He could feel in his arms that he was going to lose this tug-of-war -- the combined strength in those little vines was immense. Even if he hadn't twisted his ankle he still wouldn't have stood a chance.

"I'll bring the others here," Alexei told her, still trying to drag her away. "It's afraid of fire -- if we had torches -- "

"It's really okay," Veronika insisted. Now the black patches on her skin were no longer melting; in fact, several had begun to grow again. Down below her knees, where the inkweed had its firmest hold on her, the inky goo was spreading. It was covering her legs and flowing back up toward her hips, smoothing out across her skin into a familiar black shine. In a dazed sort of way Alexei was fascinated by it; he'd never seen anything move like that. If only it hadn't been eating his friend --

Alexei was still fighting the vines when Veronika seized his hand. He looked at her.

"Tell Tanya I'm sorry," she said.

Alexei shook his head.

"You have to." She released him and lifted a hand into the air. One of the inkweed tendrils fell into her open palm and Veronika closed her hand around it. The vine went taut, pulling, and she let herself be dragged across the tile floor into the knotted jungle of black vines and shining, luminous little flowers.

Alexei crawled after her, scarcely aware what he was doing, but Veronika waved him away before he could grab her again. The inkweed vines were falling on her thick and fast now, bundling her up like a grub in a cocoon, pulling her deeper into the heart of the growth. Veronika's black eyes sparkled out at him from within the inkweed, two dark gems amidst a sea of glowing ones.

"I'll see you at the river," she promised.

"No," Alexei whimpered. Then a loop of vine dropped in between them, and even her eyes were lost from sight. Alexei plunged both hands into the weed but couldn't reach her; he could feel the inkweed tendrils tightening around his arms, his wrists, and in the end he had to jerk himself free once more.

A half-dozen vines came snaking through the air toward him and he scooted backward on his hands and knees, making sobbing noises in the back of his throat. One of the vines latched onto his wrenched ankle and Alexei squealed out loud, grabbing onto the leg of the lunchroom table to yank himself out of its grasp.

The vines retreated. Alexei saw other inkweed tendrils descending on Mikhail's corpse and he turned away before he was sick. The old man's supplies had probably been destroyed by the pounding his body had taken; and besides, it wasn't like Alexei would have been able to bring himself to steal Mikhail's pack or his weapons.

With his head still reeling from the overpowering scent of honey Alexei dragged himself out of the overgrown lunchroom, back into the hallway. He didn't look back.

~~~~~

It had taken everything Nikita had in him to lift the steel filing cabinet up onto the gurney, but the effort had been worthwhile. Dragging the cart up the hallway to get enough space for a running start, he set off at a brisk jog, pushing the gurney ahead of him. At three yards from the double doors he let go, covering his ears as the makeshift battering ram smashed into the double doors that Mikhail had barred from the inside.

After enduring five attacks of a similar sort the doors were beginning to show signs of weakening. They were dented inward where the bed was hitting them, and the bolts on one of the door hinges had started to come loose. Nikita pushed the gurney away and tried shaking the door, but in spite of the loose screws it still held.

The only thing to do was keep at it. Nikita had dragged the gurney halfway up the hall again when he heard something scraping along the other side of the door. He paused, listening, then reached for his gun as the door began to swing open.

"Alexei?!"

Nikita ran to greet him and stopped before he got there. It *was* Alexei, but the young man looked like he'd been through hell in the past fifteen minutes. His shirt was blotched with inky patches and bloodstains and he was leaning on a metal crutch he'd found in one of the hospital rooms.

"Wh -- where's the old man?"

"Dead." Alexei's tone was hollow.

Nikita took a second look at Alexei's soiled shirt. He retreated a step.

"I didn't kill him," Alexei said. "Veronika did."

"*She* killed Mikhail?!" Nikita didn't believe it. He looked over Alexei's shoulder. "Then where's she?"

"...the inkweed got her."

Nikita's blood froze over. Those clutching black ropes sprang readily into his mind's eye and for a second he thought he could feel the squeeze of the tendrils around his legs again, dragging him down into darkness. Would it suffocate you first? Crush the life out of you like a python with a mouse? or did the inkweed start to -- to "utilize" you while you were still conscious, still --

"...are you sure?" was all Nikita could think to say, and the words sounded stupid even to his own ears. "We -- we might still be able to get her." He made a move towards the doors. "If we hurry, we might -- if she's not -- "

Alexei didn't move to stop him, but his expression said it all. That icy prickle of fear became the cold weight of defeat, pressing down on Nikita's chest like an anvil. "Oh God," he said quietly, putting a hand over his eyes. "We've got to get out of this place."

Alexei nodded. "Where's the others?"

"...they're safe," Nikita said. "I left Elena with Tatyana. They're in one of the rooms in the Burn Ward."

Alexei began hobbling down the hall. When Nikita recovered enough to reach out to him Alexei flinched, twisting away.

"Hey -- " Nikita grabbed both of his shoulders. "Listen -- I'm sorry, I really am. If I hadn't picked a fight with you -- "

"It's fine." Alexei was staring at a blank spot on the wall.

"No it's not." Nikita shook him a little. "Honestly -- I didn't -- I mean, I'm really sorry."

Alexei shrugged. It was like trying to hold a conversation with a sack of flour.

"Listen, I take back what I said. You can come with us if you still want."

Finally Alexei met his eyes. "You sure?"

"You saved Lena's life. I can't thank you enough for that." Nikita swallowed. "Besides...I don't know if we'll make it out on our own. Either of us." Not after what had happened to Veronika.

When Alexei said nothing Nikita stepped up beside him, pulling Alexei's arm across his shoulders. The young man only resisted for a moment before he gave in, slumping against Nikita.

"Come on -- let's get everyone out of here."

Alexei didn't disagree.

~~~~~

Finding his way back to the two women was easier than Nikita had anticipated. The sound of upbeat chatter and bursts of giggling were loud in the otherwise noiseless halls, and the two men followed them right to Room 506.

"Hey there!" Tatyana greeted them as Alexei and Nikita appeared in the doorway. She was sitting propped against the wall, shirt hiked up and stomach swathed in what looked like several rolls' worth of gauze. Elena was sitting beside her. "Come in, come in," she said brightly, "we're just having a little chat, right Lena?"

"Auntie's been telling me some funny stories," Elena said, smiling.

Alexei hesitated as he took in Tatyana's bandages. "Um, are you okay?"

"Jus' fine, completely fine." Tatyana reassured him. "Got a little bit shot, you see, but I'm feeling quite alright now." She patted her stomach. "Lenuchka's an excellent nurse, she got me fixed up in no time...I was telling her she ought to be a medic, the Forces can always use more medics, 'specially women. Men aren't really cut out for those kinds of things...you know, when I was in boot camp, the camp medic was a guy who fainted at the sight of blood! it's true...he had his assistant take care of you if you came in with anything worse than a bug bite, and we all thought he was just lazy, but then this one guy..."

Alexei glanced sideways at Nikita. "Morphine," Nikita whispered.

"Oh." Alexei turned back to Tatyana. "Uh, how much morphine did you take?"

"Enough," Tatyana sniffed. "I know what I'm doing -- we went over emergency aid in training, you know. You science types think nobody else knows how to tie their own shoes, but let me tell you -- "

"That's not what I meant," Alexei said quickly. "Can you walk?"

Tatyana reflected for a moment. She braced her hands against the wall, pushing herself up off the floor, then winced and sank back down again. "Maybe not," she admitted.

"I'll help you up," Nikita offered. "We're heading back to the hotel now; we can spend the night there."

"You're kidding! what about the old man?" Loopy as she was, Tatyana didn't miss the look that passed between Alexei and Nikita. "Oh. You got him, eh?" She half-smiled. "Hope you gave 'im one for me."

Nikita was holding her under the arms, trying to coax the soldier onto her feet. "Let's just go," he said.

"We can't go just yet -- we gotta wait for Nika," Tatyana pointed out.

Another look passed between the two men. Tatyana's half-smile slipped off her face, and all at once she seemed entirely sober. "...where is she?"

Elena tugged on one of Tatyana's belt loops and the woman looked down at her. "Remember what I told you, auntie? She's gonna wait for us at the river."

A pair of inhuman eyes, dark as polished obsidian, flashed into Alexei's thoughts. Goosebumps broke out over the nape of his neck and he rubbed them away.

"...the river?" Tatyana repeated. Nikita looked anxiously at his niece, and Alexei couldn't blame him for it -- if the girl was having another blight episode, now there was no way to bring her out of it. But Alexei knew that this wasn't the case.

Tatyana muttered something. A moment later her knees buckled and Nikita caught her before she was back on the floor again.

"Let's just go." Nikita was all but begging them. "We need to get out of this building -- I can explain everything later."

~~~~~

"Glukhovsky here."

"Comrade Regional Secretary -- this is Colonel Akimov."

"Ah, yes, yes. How are you, Aleksandr?"

"Fine, thank you."

"Good to hear it. Ready to give your report?"

"Yes, sir."

"Then let's have it -- I'm listening."

Akimov cleared his throat. "Yes sir. At present, one hundred percent of the uninfected citizens have been evacuated to Byatin. Reports from the capitol and the surrounding cities indicate that the quarantine has been maintained, and no blight cases have turned up in any of the state hospitals."

"Good, good. What about the infected?"

Here Akimov hesitated. "Two thousand, four hundred and seventy-three Khostok citizens have been quarantined in the city due to contamination with UEC-571. Until two days ago we had the Lubukov Agricultural Labs working to develop a cure for the blight syndrome."

"What happened two days ago?"

"...we lost the Labs two days ago, Comrade Secretary."

"You lost them, eh?" Glukhovsky sounded thoughtful. "How? mutiny? sabotage?"

He could hear Akimov hunting for the right words. "Well, as you know, the failure of the ventilation system in the Labs caused UEC-571 to be dispersed throughout the building."

"Yes, I remember."

"Ah, we believe this failure of the ventilation system lead to near hundred-percent infection of the Labs' civilian staff, though their infections remained dormant for longer than the general population."

Glukhovsky hrm'ed into the receiver. "So they all came down with the blight? but there were only a couple hundred employees there -- how did we lose the whole building, Aleksandr?"

Glukhovsky had known Akimov for some time -- had taken the young Colonel under his wing at one point, you might have said -- and knew how rare it was to hear someone like Akimov fumbling to explain himself.

"Sir -- confidentially -- it is my belief that some people who contract the blight don't die from it. It seems like -- we haven't been able to observe this process in action, but -- they appear to be...mutating."

"...'mutating'," Glukhovsky echoed.

Akimov swallowed audibly. "Yes sir. These victims are coated with a compound very similar to pure UEC-571 that seems to make them much stronger and faster than a normal human being, and quite a lot more resistant to damage. It was these altered victims that overran the Lubukov Agricultural Labs two days ago, overwhelming an entire squad of my best men. The soldiers were only able to bring down two of these entities, but from the corpses we were able to conclude that they had once been...human." Akimov paused before continuing. "Since the quarantine began, I have lost greater than ten percent of my soldiers."

"I see," murmured the regional secretary. Akimov could hear him drumming his beringed fingers on the desktop. "Has the research data from the Labs been lost?"

"No, comrade secretary -- we have all the files in our possession."

"Ahh, well then, that's excellent news." Glukhovsky sounded heartened. "Aleksandr, we'll be needing you to pull your men out of Khostok as soon as possible -- no less than forty-eight hours. I'll want you to make it a top priority to bring the research data safely out of the city. You'll deliver it to me personally," he added.

"Yes, sir." Akimov said.. "...permission to speak freely?"

Glukhovsky was expecting this. "Fire away."

"With all due respect -- I was originally given three months to accomplish my mission here," Akimov said, with just the barest hint of panic in his voice. "The Labs haven't produced a cure yet; we will be able to retake the building, but we will need more researchers and more men...in forty-eight hours, we can't possibly -- "

"Calm down, Sasha, calm down." Akimov sounded calm enough, but Glukhovsky knew him better than that. "I'm updating your mission parameters. Clearing Khostok of the blight -- through whatever means necessary -- will be your primary objective now. Your secondary objective will be to bring me that data."

"Yes, sir."

"I know this contradicts your earlier orders," Glukhovsky explained, "but I've been getting more and more pressure from Moscow to see this affair terminated and to produce some conclusive reports on the situation."

"Yes, sir."

"Don't sound so low -- this won't go against you."

"Understood, sir." Akimov took a deep breath. When he spoke again the steel had come back into his voice. "If I may, comrade Secretary, I would like to formally request that you authorize Operation Starlight."

That was what Glukhovsky had been waiting for. "Of course I'll authorize it," he said. "You'll have the cans delivered to you by nightfall."

"Thank you sir."

"You'll come by for a drink once this is all over, won't you?"

"Of course, sir."

"You're a fine commander, Sasha," Glukhovsky reassured him. "I'll look forward to seeing you in a few days."

Akimov thanked his superior again and disconnected the call. It was kind of Glukhovsky to make an effort to reassure his protégé, especially when they both knew Akimov had failed in his duties. For Glukhovsky to go out of his way to change the mission parameters just went to show how fond the secretary was of the young colonel.

Still, Akimov had failed, and he was not too weak to admit it to himself. In his initial conversation with the secretary he had been tasked with two very simple objectives. One: to maintain the quarantine of Khostok. And two: to clear the contamination from the city. As the Labs had never developed a cure for the remaining infected citizenry he'd been unable to bring the second task to hundred-percent completion, and now had to resort to such hideous methods as this. To call for Starlight was a tacit admission of his own failure.

Succeeding at one of his two objectives was not good enough -- fifty percent completion equaled one hundred percent failure. A washing machine that only washed half of one's clothing was still considered a broken machine. And there was no place for a broken machine but the landfill.

But Akimov was getting ahead of himself -- he still had other duties remaining. There were announcements to be made, first of all, and orders given to enact Starlight. There would be a mad rush to carry out the operation and clear all remaining personnel from Khostok, and Akimov would be needed for that.

He still had his obligations, after all. Broken or not, this machine would still complete the rest of his assignment.

~~~~~

As it turned out there was no need for Nikita to explain anything. Back at the hotel they found that Elena had accepted Veronika's disappearance with a distinctly unchildlike calmness, and she filled the silence over their dinner with more remarks about this river. Elena unpacked and repacked her gas mask bag as the three adults ate their baked beans in stony silence.

The little blue flame of the camping stove flickered and danced in the darkened penthouse, throwing light and shadow onto everyone's faces.

Finally Elena drifted off into sleep, bundled up in quilts with her bag tucked in beside her.

At Tatyana's suggestion Nikita had Tatyana's gas mask on the floor and was tinkering with it, teasing little wires out of the built-in radio and twisting them together with some electrical components he'd scrounged from elsewhere in the hotel. The vacant eyepieces of the mask flashed with light from the stove. Alexei was staring out through the glass patio door again, watching as purple dusk descended on the lightless city.

From the sheen of sweat Tatyana's face they could see that the morphine was wearing off. She lay on her good side on the blankets, staring into the flame of the camping stove, brooding. They'd brought some extra drugs with them from the hospital -- Alexei had even found more thiopental in the pharmacy, as if it would do them any good. But after they'd all gotten back to the hotel Tatyana had refused any additional narcotics.

Alexei had more medical knowledge than the rest of them and had done for Tatyana as Yuri had done for him, swabbing the gunshot wound with rubbing alcohol and bandaging it again. There had been some black streaks in her blood, like ink swirled into the red, but mentioning it would have been pointless and so Alexei said nothing. He'd elected to leave the bullet in place for the present; he wasn't sure he could get the instruments sterile enough, and there was always a risk of causing further harm by poking around in there without proper training.

Both Alexei and Nikita had reassured Tatyana that they'd get her to an actual doctor as soon as they could, but none of them seemed to believe it. As her chattiness wore off Tatyana had grown more and more withdrawn. When she finally spoke again it was the question they both knew she would ask:

"She's dead, isn't she?"

Nikita glanced up at her. Alexei nodded.

Tatyana swore like a shipyard worker. "It wasn't Mikhail," Alexei murmured, seeing her face. "It was the inkweed."

Tatyana rolled over onto her back and threw an arm across her face, hiding her eyes in the crook of her elbow. Looking pained, Nikita focused all his attention on the radio.

Alexei left his place beside the window and limped across the room, favoring his sprained ankle. He sat down beside Tatyana. "She really did like you," he said.

Tatyana made a noise that might have been a laugh.

"She did." Alexei was fiddling with a piece of carpet lint. "She told me...to tell you that she was sorry."

This time Tatyana was silent. Alexei was still hunting for something else to say when a loud crackle of static interrupted his thoughts.

"Got it!" Nikita whispered, adjusting the volume. He'd cannibalized an old wood-paneled desktop radio from one of the nicer hotel rooms, wiring it up to the concealed radio mounted inside Tatyana's gas mask. It was a crude surgery, but with everything connected properly it allowed the old desktop radio to function as an external speaker.

"It's working?" Tatyana asked hoarsely. "Good." When she went to sit up she gasped, the color draining out of her face, and Alexei helped her as she eased herself back down onto the blankets again. Her cheeks gleamed wetly in the low light.

"I'm alright, I'm alright." She waved. "Turn it up -- Akimov makes a general address to his troops just about every night. I wanna hear what he says."

Garbled voices began to mingle with the static, and Alexei leaned in closer. Nikita tweaked and twisted the wires, trying to get clearer audio. All at once a voice burst onto the channel:

"Pigeon, this is Sparrow. Repeat, this is Sparrow. You'd better bring me back my boots or you're going to wake up with a dead rat inside one of yours. Over."

Alexei almost laughed.

"It *does* work," Nikita said, amazed. "Not bad for a rush job without any real tools, eh?"

"Not bad at all," Alexei agreed.

Nikita poked at the wiring a final time. "And my dad said I'd never amount to anything."

"...Yura said the same thing," Alexei remarked.

"Yeah; our dad used to tell us things like that." Nikita looked almost nostalgic. "He was a genuine bastard sometimes."

"At least you had one."

"Mm? what happened to yours?"

Alexei gave the question a long consideration. "...ran off with some woman when I was twelve," he concluded.

"Attention all soldiers," the radio interrupted, and they turned towards it. "Attention all soldiers. This is Colonel Akimov speaking."

" -- that's him," Tatyana said. "Listen."

"To begin, I would like to personally thank each and every one of you for your tireless work during the quarantine," the voice stated. "I know many of you have lost comrades in the course of this assignment, and rest assured that I am as deeply affected by these losses as you are. But tonight I have good news for you.

"As of 1500 hours today I received approval from Regional Secretary Glukhovsky to proceed with Operation Starlight. Repeat -- we will move forward with Operation Starlight. The deadline is twenty-four hours from now, and that means that all military personnel will be out of Khostok at this time. Please proceed to your commanding officers immediately for directions."

Tatyana groaned aloud. Alexei started to ask a question but she hushed him with a gesture, pointing at the radio.

Akimov went on. "Personnel responsible for maintaining order at Camps Two through Five, and those stationed to guard the Volgin River or the Volgin River Bridge, will maintain their positions. All other manpower will be diverted towards setup for the initiation of Starlight in twenty-four hours' time.

"Moreover, comrades, I ask that you all remain on highest alert until you are evacuated." Akimov's voice grew softer and the listeners leaned towards the radio. "The incident at the Agricultural Labs should serve as an example to us all that even the most highly-trained soldiers may be overwhelmed by the as-yet unclassified threats we face here. I personally do not want to lose any more men.

"That is all. Your commanding officers will explain your duties to you. Again, I thank you all. Colonel Akimov out."

Static rose in the silence following the announcement. A minute later the radio channel came to life again, soldiers calling back and forth to each other for clarification on the message, but Nikita turned the volume down.

"The colonel's insane," Tatyana said dully. Both men turned to her. "What's Operation Starlight?" Alexei asked.

Tatyana's blue eyes glowed in the light of the camping stove. "You remember the gym, right?"

Nikita started to his feet. "They're gonna -- " He glanced over at Elena and lowered his voice. " -- they're gonna gas the rest of the camps?!"

But Tatyana was shaking her head. "They'll gas *everything*," she intoned, her voice a hoarse whisper. "They don't want anything getting through the nets -- Operation Starlight is meant to sterilize the city."

Alexei began to regret the dinner he'd eaten earlier. Nikita put both hands over his mouth. "They wouldn't."

"Oh yes they would." Tatyana bared her teeth. "I know the Colonel, and he'd do something like this without looking back. It'll clear out the blight -- at least they think it will -- and mop up anyone who might live to spread rumors about the quarantine." She closed her eyes. "We went over this before we came into the city; Starlight was Akimov's backup plan, his last resort."

"But -- to kill all those -- there's women and children and -- it doesn't make any sense!" Nikita stammered. "Why kill them? why not just -- I don't know -- lock them away somewhere and keep trying to cure them?"

"Secretary Glukhovsky must think they're dangerous," Tatyana said shortly. "He was the one who ordered Khostok sanitized in the first place. And Starlight wouldn't be happening if he hadn't approved it."

"Dangerous? how? Both of you've got the blight, and you're not dangerous at all!"

Tatyana blinked, and with difficulty she craned her neck to look at Alexei. "*You've* got it too?"

Alexei lifted the hem of his shirt a few inches, then let it drop. Tatyana sank back onto her blanket with weak chuckle. "We're all doomed."

"...I think the blight is...well, I don't know if you'd say it's 'not dangerous'," Alexei said. "Certainly it's not worth killing thousands of people over, but...we really don't understand it."

Nikita still wasn't sitting down. "What do you mean?"

"Well..." Alexei bit his lip. "You remember when I told you that...that Veronika was the one who killed Mikhail, right?"

"Wait -- *Veronika* killed the old man?" Tatyana rolled over onto her good side so she could see Alexei.

Alexei nodded. "Yeah, she did. She saved my life, too; he was this close to shooting me when she arrived. But she wasn't -- I mean, I didn't recognize her right away. Veronika was...she looked like...one of those things." He held up his hands in front of his face, illustrating. "One of those faceless things."

Tatyana and Nikita gaped at Alexei, unblinking. Slowly Nikita sank back onto the carpet. "...how did you know it was her?" he asked.

Alexei didn't want to remember it, but he owed it to them to finish explaining. "She was wounded during the fight with Mikhail," he said. "She took a shotgun blast right in the stomach."

Tatyana made a little noise deep in her throat, rolling over onto her back again. "That's how I recognized her," Alexei hurried on. "Because when she got shot, the black stuff -- those things are coated in this black sort of liquid -- it started to melt." He shivered mentally. "When it melted, I saw her face."

The silence in the room was an almost tangible thing. Alexei wouldn't have blamed the others for doubting his story -- he certainly did. His memories of the ordeal had all the qualities of an old nightmare: the darkness down in the barrel of Mikhail's shotgun, the sudden materialization of the faceless thing, the old man's brutal end, the dying creature in the puddle of ink that looked so much like his friend.

And the inkweed, lest he forget, the inkweed with its snakelike coils and those terrible lizard eyes darting back and forth inside the blossoms. If God were merciful all of this madness would have been nothing more than an extended and particularly vivid blight hallucination. Alexei would have been grateful to believe that, though it would've meant he'd slipped much further than he'd thought.

But if he'd dreamed it all, then what had happened to Mikhail and Veronika?

"I tried to save her," Alexei protested, though nobody had accused him of anything.

"She was hurt, but I thought she still had a chance."

He knew without looking up that Tatyana and Nikita were staring at him. "But she didn't want me to save her. She wouldn't let me, and I don't know why. The inkweed was dragging her away and she didn't -- I don't even think she was scared." He put his head in his hands. "She said she'd meet me at the river," he finished.

Someone's hand touched the small of his back. Alexei glanced over his shoulder -- it was Tatyana, petting him through his shirt.

"I keep hearing about that river," Nikita said softly. "You remember how Elena kept talking about it over dinner."

Alexei remembered. "They wrote something about a river on the doors in the gym, too." Tatyana's voice came floating up out of the darkness in the room. "What's it mean?"

"No idea." Alexei lifted a shoulder. "Maybe the blight victims have a common auditory hallucination that sounds like running water. That could explain why they all think they're hearing a river."

Nikita looked back at his niece, asleep in her cocoon of quilts and blankets.

"...I was...hearing something like that today," Alexei admitted. "At the hospital. Sounded like running water, but...I'm pretty sure all the water in Khostok's been turned off for awhile." He scratched absently at the stain on his left side, which had begun itching again.

"Waterfall," Tatyana murmured.

"Huh?"

"...I thought it sounded like a waterfall." Her face was turned up toward the ceiling but Tatyana's gaze was fixed on something much further away. "I heard it in the hospital too...glad I'm not the only one."

Nikita looked back and forth between the two of them. "It's possible," Alexei said. "If the disease causes lesions on the brain, or distortions in ear structure, it might produce similar hallucinations in many different people."

"Well, I didn't hear anything, but I'm not surprised you guys did." Nikita hugged his arms closer to his body. "That building is awful. Should be burned to the ground, if you ask me."

Tatyana made an amused sound. "Probably will be, after Starlight's over. It's full of evidence."

"But we've still gotta go back there -- you know heard what the Colonel said." Alexei turned to look through the patio door again, at the black silhouettes of unlit buildings just visible against a night-blue sky. "The bridge and the Volgin River are both gonna be crawling with guards...and we'll die of exposure if we try to go over the mountains. Getting into those warrens is our only hope for getting out of Khostok."

"We're not even sure if the shelters are *real*," Nikita pointed out. "All we have is some scribbling on a cereal box and that old bastard's word that there's an entrance under the hospital. We could be looking for something that doesn't exist."

"Oh, they exist alright." Tatyana murmured. "The only question's whether the entrance is under the hospital or not." Her eyes flicked open again. "Listen -- I want you to leave me here," she said suddenly. "You can't -- "

" -- no," said Alexei.

"We're not leaving you," Nikita chimed in.

"Both of you -- just shut up for a second." Tatyana rolled herself over onto her good side. "I'm not going anywhere like this, and you'll die if you're still in Khostok when they enact Starlight. They're gassing the whole city, remember, not just the camps. You've got to get into the warrens first thing tomorrow."

Alexei looked down at her. "We'll go tomorrow, but we're bringing you with us."

"How?" Tatyana shot him a defiant look.

"We got you out of the hospital, didn't we?"

She snorted. "That took hours -- *and* you had the truck. How d'you suggest we get a truck into the tunnels? or are you gonna carry me the whole way, with your ankle like that?"

Alexei glared back at her.

"If we have to," Nikita said.

Tatyana was clearly too tired to argue, but she wouldn't budge. "I'm gonna slow you down too much," she said, rolling onto her back again. Her eyes flickered shut. "If you get killed trying to escape, it's not gonna be my fault."

"We can't leave you." Alexei reached over and squeezed her shoulder. "You helped us rescuing Elena and Nikita from that camp, remember? And I'd never have gotten out of the Labs if it wasn't for you."

One of Tatyana's blue eyes slitted open. "...after what I did to you, that makes us just about even."

"We're not leaving you." Nikita repeated. He sat forward to blow out the little blue flame of the camping stove, and a deeper darkness flooded into the room. "Let's get some sleep -- we all need to be rested if we're getting into those tunnels tomorrow."

Alexei could see the wisdom in that suggestion. He pressed Tatyana's shoulder one last time. "We'll talk about it tomorrow, okay?" he whispered.

Tatyana grunted something like 'alright', and that was good enough for him. Alexei crawled back to his own blankets, careful not to bump his sprained ankle. He pulled the quilts over his body and up over his head, shutting out the rest of the world.

She'd change her mind tomorrow; Alexei was sure of it. They wouldn't have to lose anyone else. Tatyana had said it was alright; if she'd said that she couldn't have been completely determined on dying here in the city.

Or maybe Alexei had misheard her. Instead of 'alright', maybe what she'd actually said was 'sorry'.

Alexei pulled the covers down again. "...Tatyana?" he whispered. "Tatyana?"

But there was no reply.

# CHAPTER FOURTEEN

"Hey! *Hey*! Careful with those!!"

Owl and Stork both looked up at the officer who was waving them down. Distracted, Owl's hand slipped from the corner of the large wooden crate they were carrying and it lurched to one side. Their superior gave a yelp of alarm, leaping backward. "*Careful*! you idiots!"

"I got it, I got it." Owl grabbed the box again and steadied it.

"You drop that box and it'll be the last thing you do." The officer was retreating again, stabbing a finger at the crate.

"We've got it, sir." Stork sounded exactly like a man who'd been awakened at 2 a.m. and dragged from a soft, warm bed in order to stack wooden boxes in a quarantine camp. "Can we go now?"

The officer waved them away and the two soldiers started lugging the crate down the hall again.

At least there was one advantage in doing this grunt-work in the middle of the night: peace and quiet. The soldiers' footfalls and the faraway burbling of a forgotten aquarium might have been the only noises in the entire building. Red Camp Two had once been an elementary school: bright mosaic tiles covered the floor and colorful children's drawings stared down at the two soldiers from the dim-lit walls. Owl couldn't decide if all the finger-painted decorations made the building more or less creepy.

"What's *his* problem?"

The wooden crate blocked his view of his companion, but Owl could hear the exasperation in Stork's voice. "That's Falcon...he came over from Camp One." Owl's hands were slipping again -- the gloves on his protective suit were a bit too loose -- and he tightened his grip. "You heard about what happened, right?"

"Yeah?" Stork grunted. "Yeah, I heard about it -- he was there?"

"Yeah."

Stork gave a low chuckle. "No wonder he's so twitchy."

"Yeah. I'd be the same way if I was in his shoes," Owl said.

Stork was in the lead, walking in reverse, and he pushed himself backwards against the double-doors that led into the cafeteria. The two guards stationed at the cafeteria doors nodded to them as they passed through the doorway. "Back corner, by the trashcans," one of the guards whispered.

"Got it," Owl said.

The cafeteria was as ill-lit as the hallway -- it was, after all, the middle of the night. The CSF occupiers had cleared the school's cafeteria of tables and chairs, replacing these with row after row of nondescript folding cots. Almost all of the several hundred inmates were sleeping; a clandestine supplement added to the inmates' dinnertime soup ration had guaranteed that.

Adorable woodland creatures cavorted through the mural that ran along the walls of the cafeteria -- painted by the school's "best" student artist, from the looks of it -- and the little chipmunks and deer and bunnies watched over the sleepers with unblinking eyes. Up on the far wall framed portraits of Chorma's glorious leaders looked down on the cafeteria, faces radiating godlike health and benevolence, their eyes silently condoning what Owl and Stork were doing with their wooden crate.

Or would they have condoned it?

With a little flush of guilt Owl banished the thought. Akimov had ordered it and the Regional Secretary had authorized it, and that was all he needed to know.

There were already two other crates in the corner beside the trashcans, plain unlabeled wooden boxes like the one Owl and Stork had brought. They bent to deposit their cargo beside the other two, careful not to jostle any of the contents.

"Is that the last of 'em?" Stork asked.

"For this area. But Falcon says -- "

The sound of splintering wood interrupted Owl, and the two soldiers lifted their heads. When they heard it a second time there was no mistaking it: something was behind the other two crates.

Stork flicked on his flashlight and shone it into the shadows behind the boxes. His shout of alarm was near loud enough to wake the entire cafeteria, drugged or not.

"It's that thing! one of those things!" Stork came stumbling backwards out from behind the crate, grabbing for his rifle. "It's getting into the crates! Shoot it, shoot it!"

Owl hadn't seen it yet, but Stork's panic was infectious. He unslung his own rifle as he backed away from the corner. "What it is?" he asked.

Stork only gibbered and pointed. Then a blob of shadow detached itself from the darkness behind the boxes, rising up over the top of the crates.

At first glance the thing looked like a runaway shadow, separated from a physical body. It was only when the light hit it and the skin gleamed that they could see it was three-dimensional. It perched catlike on top of the stack of crates, looking back and forth between the two soldiers, its tentacles rearing overhead like the branches of a tree. The thing had a bundle of wires and broken circuit boards clenched in one black fist -- the electronic guts from one of the Stardust devices.

Stork moaned. Owl was still hunting for the safety on his rifle when someone snatched his AKS-47 away.

The thief was a skinny little boy, his skin half-blackened with the blight. When Owl turned he found the boy holding him at gunpoint with his own rifle, which looked comically large in the kid's hands.

"Stay back!" The boy growled, a puppy imitating a wolf. "It's just trying to help!"

"...how are you awake?" Owl asked.

But when he looked, he realized that the little boy wasn't the only one. Underneath his protective suit Owl broke out in goosebumps: better than half of the inmates were sitting up in their cots, faces turned towards the corner, silently observing. One or two had risen to their feet and were shuffling over toward the crates. The inmates' eyes were black marbles, without whites or irises.

"Not enough sedative," Owl remarked to himself, feeling his mental screws starting to loosen.

"*Get back*!!" Stork screamed. "*Everyone get back*!!"

Owl jerked awake to find his comrade brandishing his gun at the crowd, driving them away from the boxes. Even the little boy darted backwards a couple paces, though he didn't relinquish Owl's rifle.

"You don't understand!" a female voice cried. Owl and Stork turned back to the crates. A young woman in a ragged blue dress had gotten herself in between the faceless thing and the soldiers, arms out, shielding the thing with her body.

"It's trying to save us," she explained. Her eyes were black and depthless, but her face held a look of strangely glacial calm, almost serenity.

(*Could they all be sleepwalking*?), Owl wondered.

The faceless thing laid one of its glossy hands on the woman's shoulder. She took no notice. "It knows you're trying to kill us," the woman went on. "It just wants to help us...to help *all* of us." She reached out to Stork. "If you would -- "

The rattle of gunfire echoed from the cheerfully-painted walls. Owl gasped, and squeals of dismay came from the crowd of inmates behind him. The young woman swayed on her feet and folded backwards, red flowers blooming on the blue cotton of her dress. As she fell the faceless thing bent to catch her.

Owl should have acted -- tried to get his gun back, at least -- but somehow he couldn't. Stork was shouting something unintelligible and now the black nightmare was kneeling down on the floor, cradling the woman in its arms, looking into her face. The gesture was so uncannily human that Owl hesitated, staring at the scene before him, not understanding.

Then the thing began to melt.

There was no better word for it. The shiny black of its skin turned liquid and began to run, like melting wax, flowing down the faceless thing's chest and arms and onto the woman's body. It swept over her in an inky wave, spreading out across her skin, obliterating her dress, covering her face --

When Owl looked up Stork was already dashing back across the cafeteria floor, swinging his rifle left and right to shove the inmates out of his path. The guards at the cafeteria doors were gone. Owl wailed and took off after his comrade, leaping clear over one of the cots on his way to the door.

"Wait! wait!"

Owl was only halfway to the doors when the murals on the wall began to move. In the dim half-light the painted woodland creatures seemed to squirm, slipping through the grassy landscape towards them. Owl glanced back in mid-stride and realized what he was seeing: not painted animals but more of those nightmare beasts, dropping down from the ventilation grates along the walls, swarming into shadows along the cafeteria walls.

In that glance he saw five -- ten -- twenty of the things flooding into the cafeteria, some of them coming after him, others moving toward the crowd of blight-afflicted inmates that were rising from their beds to greet them. The inmates were smiling, some of them laughing, and if his eyes didn't deceive him there were little children running toward the monsters with shouts of joy --

And then Owl's boot snagged on someone's backpack strap and he went sprawling on the cafeteria floor, the respirator of his gas mask pinging off the tiles. With his ears still ringing from the impact he rolled over, looking up just in time to see one of the entities looming over him with its tentacles outspread.

Stork flinched at the sound of Owl's screams, but he didn't look back. When he struck the cafeteria doors they shuddered in their hinges. Stork grabbed the door handle, twisted it, and threw his shoulder against the door.

"Let me out! Let me out! Let me out!"

On the other side of the locked doors, the former cafeteria guards exchanged looks. A dull booming echoed up and down the hall as Stork threw himself against the doors again and again and again.

"Comrades! Let me out! I'm begging you! Dammit, open up!"

Boom, boom, boom. Plaster drifted down from the ceiling as the doors shivered under each impact.

"What's going on here?"

The guards turned to find Falcon standing behind them. One of them cleared his throat. "There's...those, uh...humanoids, sir. They got into the cafeteria."

"Please!!" Stork begged, rattling the door handle. "Open up!"

Falcon lifted his chin. "...who's in there?" he asked, almost whispering.

"Stork and Owl," replied one of the guards. The other was fidgeting with his rifle.

Falcon looked the quaking double-doors with a sort of distant curiosity. "Were the crates already in place?"

"I, uh -- I think so, sir."

"Well, in that case -- "

Stork gave a single, earsplitting scream. One of the guards clapped his hands over the sides of his mask, but the shriek had already been clipped off. Something thumped heavily against the inside of the doors, and then there came a soft scraping like a heavy sack being dragged away.

Both guards backed away from the doors. The three stood staring at the locked double-doors before them, not speaking, listening.

"...how secure are these locks?" Falcon asked.

"Very."

"Good." From the tone of his voice, Falcon was holding himself together only through tremendous effort. "We'll have to get word to the Colonel right away."

The guards nodded. "Where d'you want the rest of the crates, sir?"

Falcon did not reply.

"Sir?" The guards glanced at each other, then at their superior again. "Um...sir?"

Falcon wasn't even looking at them anymore. "How did the entities get into the cafeteria?"

"Ah, well...through the ventilation system, I think." The guard was nervously flicking the safety toggle on his rifle.

"Makes sense," Falcon remarked. "You know, the ventilation system runs through the entire building, not just the cafeteria."

Both guards stiffened. " -- We'll need to board up the ventilation ducts!" one of them exclaimed.

"Don't bother." Falcon said faintly. "They're here already."

The two guards turned in the direction their superior was facing. Some fifteen paces away stood one of the entities, waiting patiently for them to finish talking. The open mouth of a ventilation duct yawned in the wall overhead.

One of the soldiers lifted his rifle, putting the faceless thing in his sights.

"I wouldn't bother with that either." Falcon had started to retreat, shuffling backwards down the hall.. "Won't do any good."

"Huh? why?"

"This -- " Falcon waved at the thing with a trembling hand, "this is divine punishment. It's retribution for our sins."

The two guards exchanged another look.

"But if you want to stay here and try to stop the wrath of God with a handful of manmade bullets, you go right ahead." Falcon crossed himself. "Lord have mercy on us all."

The thing at the end of the hallway extended its eight tentacles, the black ropes unfurling into the air like the limbs of a monstrous spider.

All three soldiers turned and ran.

~~~~~

A shrill electronic whine broke into Akimov's sleep. He blinked up at the ceiling overhead, trying to remember what the noise meant. Pushing himself upright, he swung his legs over the edge of the bed and stared down at the carpet, waiting for his head to clear.

Against the darkness of the bedroom his arms and legs were white and bony-looking. Akimov passed a hand over his face, over the smooth patch of scar tissue that covered the left-hand side of his jaw. Organic creatures were just so hard to repair. Not like machines.

That noise; what *was* it?

Thirty seconds later the colonel was reaching for the radio on his bedside table. He disabled the keening alarm and spoke into the receiver. "Akimov here."

"Colonel sir -- this is Falcon, at Camp Two. Sorry to wake you."

"It's alright." Akimov squinted at the unlit dial of the room's clock. "Something to report?"

"Yes, sir." Falcon paused. "We've lost Camp Two."

Akimov suddenly felt a lot more awake. "Camp Two, you said? It's been entirely lost?"

"Yes, sir."

" -- how?"

"Those humanoid things. They came in through the ducts and overran the camp." Falcon's tone was calm, even conversational. "They got to the inmates first, but they took the entire building before we could react. We got about half the crates in place before they came."

Gears were already turning in Akimov's mind, conveyor belts whirring, levers marching up and down. "Were any soldiers lost?"

"Oh yes," Falcon murmured.

"...Well? how many, comrade?"

"Oh. All of them, sir."

Akimov took the radio from his ear, blinked at it a couple times, then put it back up to his ear again. "Say again?"

"We've all been lost, sir."

The colonel rose to his feet. "Get ahold of yourself, Falcon. Say again -- how many soldiers remaining at the camp? or have you abandoned the building already?"

The radio hissed with static for a moment. "As far as I'm aware, I'm the only one left here, Colonel." Falcon was sounding more and more distant, almost dreamy. "Those faceless things -- they move so *fast*, sir. You have no idea. They've got octopus arms coming out of their backs -- at least that's what it looks like -- and once they get hold of you, that's it. 'Least it seems like a quick way to go -- there's not too much screaming after they grab you. I think they -- "

"Falcon!" Akimov cut him off. "Where are you right now?"

"Uh?" Akimov could hear the soldier shuffling around on the other end of the line. "I think I'm in a storage closet, sir."

"A storage closet."

"Yes, sir -- I see brooms and mops, so I think it's a storage closet. I'm sitting on a mop bucket right now." Falcon gave a rather uncharacteristic giggle. "I ran in here when the things started attacking. There was a bit of screaming earlier, but now it's very quiet. I tried to take a headcount before I contacted you, sir, but I couldn't get anyone on the radio. Near as I can tell...I'm the only one left."

Akimov put a hand on his bedside table to steady himself. Starfall. He was going to have to call the regional secretary again; this time, he'd need to ask Glukhovsky to call for the tactical strike codenamed Starfall. Crates or no crates, Starfall would take care of the blighted and those black mutants to boot. Starfall would wipe the city's slate entirely clean.

"Comrade Falcon," Akimov said, putting on his sternest tone. "When you can, I want you to -- "

A small explosion went off in his ear, and Akimov snatched the radio away from his head. "Falcon?" he called. "Falcon?! Come in, comrade! What was that?"

Splintering, crunching noises. A sound like broken bits of lumber clattering onto a tile floor. And then only the quiet hissing of feedback.

"Falcon!!"

"...it's here, sir," Falcon's whisper was barely audible. "I guess it heard us talking. It's taken the closet door off its hinges."

Akimov sank back onto his bed again.

"I've enjoyed serving under you, Colonel," Falcon said. "I always thought you were a fine commander. I apologize that I wasn't a better soldier."

"You were an excellent soldier, comrade."

"Thank you." Falcon sounded like he meant it. "I don't blame you for what happened at Camp One, sir -- not my place to say if it was right or wrong. In the end, only God can judge us."

"Amen," Akimov said. He placed the radio onto the bedside table. It continued to hiss for another minute before the line went dead and he switched it off.

Five minutes later Akimov was zipping up his protective suit and cinching his gas mask tightly into place. His plans had already been revised and re-revised several times over, and he'd settled on what he felt was the correct course of action. There were dozens of little details to be hammered out, but the bulk of his new strategy could be summarized by a single word:

Starfall.

~~~~~

"Wake up, Alexei, wake up!"

Alexei floated back up into consciousness. He was lying on the floor in a darkened room, covered in blankets. Yuri was kneeling beside him and shaking him awake.

"Mmmhh?" Alexei inquired. Yuri pulled him up into a sitting position and Alexei rubbed at his eyes, squinting at the unfamiliar surroundings. Even Yuri looked strange this morning -- his glasses were missing, and his hair was shorter and much darker than Alexei remembered.

...because this wasn't Yuri. As Alexei's vision sharpened the younger brother morphed into the older one. "You awake?" Nikita asked.

"Mrf," Alexei replied. It felt like his head was full of cotton, and his left side was burning fiercely. "What's wrong?"

"She's gone."

"Uh?" The details of the penthouse were clearer now, but Alexei's memories were still catching up with him. "Who?"

"That soldier woman, Tatyana." Nikita said hoarsely. "She's disappeared. She was gone when I woke up this morning. The door's still locked -- she couldn't have gone out that way -- but the patio door was open."

Alexei's stomach gave a lurch. He wasn't too groggy to understand what Nikita was implying -- if Tatyana's had exited the room from the seventh-floor balcony, there was only one direction she could have headed.

"I didn't hear her leave," Nikita went on, glancing back towards the patio door. "She must have -- oh! *Elena*!"

Alexei jumped. Nikita left his side and dashed out onto the patio, snatching his ten-year-old niece away from the railing. "What are you doing out here?! It's dangerous!"

Alexei got to his feet and limped out onto the patio, eyes narrowing at the chill morning breeze. A watery sun was peeking through fragments of pearl-grey clouds. He had to steel himself before he could peek over the railing, but the view from the seventh floor was anticlimactic. There was nothing on the street below them -- no corpse, no red stains, not even so much as a boot. Neither were there any footholds or handholds within reach of the balcony.

Unless someone had locked the door after Tatyana had left -- which seemed very unlikely -- she must have gone over the railing. But to do so without leaving any evidence?

"You need to stay away from the balcony," Nikita scolded, pulling Elena back into the room. Alexei turned back to them.

"...Lena," he said softly, "did you see where Tatyana went?"

Elena's round face was still puffy from sleep. She clutched her little survival pack against her chest and nodded.

"You did?" Alexei crouched down in front of the girl. "Where did she go?"

"She went with the shiny people last night." Elena said matter-of-factly.

Nikita hesitated before kneeling down beside Alexei. "Which people, Lenuchka?"

"The ones that're all black and shiny. They said they were gonna help her."

"...those things again." Nikita groaned. Alexei was shaking his head. "...but how? How'd they get her out of the room?"

Elena pointed to the patio door. "They picked her up and flew out the window."

Nikita chuckled weakly. "...they can *fly*?" Alexei asked, dumbstruck.

" 'Course they can fly." Elena gave both adults a look of immense pity. "They've got wings."

~~~~~

It was a damned easy job, being the Police Chief's secretary. All you had to do was take messages, screen phone calls, keep the calendar updated and look nice when visitors came in. That was all. It was an easy job *and* a prestigious one; far preferable than being some piddling bureaucrat's coffee-fetcher, for instance.

And Police Chief Petrenko had always treated his secretary so well. Never forgotten her birthday, always gotten her a small something for the holidays -- a painted mug or a hairbrush or some other little gift. And he'd never been indecent with her, never implied that she could earn a little bonus by staying late at the office. Of course the Chief was a married man, but he knew several such married men who'd never have hesitated to stoop to --

An avalanche of paperwork cascaded down from the stack atop the filing cabinet, spilling over the chief's head. He muttered a string of words that might have been a prayer or perhaps a very long oath. And after all the kindness he'd shown her that thoughtless secretary of his had up and evacuated to Byatin with the rest of the police force, leaving Petrenko with his skeleton crew and a whole office's worth of critical paperwork to pack up before the impending evacuation. Leaving this sensitive information behind in the building was out of the question, but with nobody else remaining in Khostok it fell to poor Petrenko to try to collect it all.

The chief had gotten together four boxes' worth of absolutely invaluable, under-no-circumstances disposable paperwork from the poorly-organized filing cabinets. He came across a dust-filled coffee mug emblazoned with a patriotically decorated fir tree -- a New Year's gift for that ungrateful woman -- and flung it into the wastebasket with another curse. He was still knee-deep in snowdrifts of paper, swearing and mumbling to himself, when the door of his office swung open.

Petrenko's head bobbed up. Colonel Akimov stood in the doorway, flanked by two high-ranking CSF soldiers.

"Ahh, Chief Petrenko," Akimov said. "Good to see you here." He held open the door. "We're evacuating the city now; please proceed to the ground floor. An armored personnel carrier is waiting for us."

A sheaf of papers slithered from the folder in Petrenko's hands and scattered across the floor. " -- *now*?!" he squeaked.

"Yes, now."

"Butbut -- that's -- I can't go now!" Petrenko clutched the now-empty folder in both hands. "You said it'd be next week! All of this paperwork needs to be shipped to Byatin, or put into storage at least -- if we just leave it in the building -- "

The colonel sighed. He gestured to his men and the two soldiers stepped forward, each grabbing one of Petrenko's arms. Chief Petrenko's shoes scarcely touched the floor as the CSF escorted him from his office, down the hall and into the elevator.

Once they were inside the elevator Petrenko squirmed free of his captors. "I can walk, I can walk." He straightened his shirt and tie with a little huff. "What's the meaning of this?"

Akimov stared straight ahead at the elevator doors. The colonel was carrying a thick folder of his own, tucked under one arm. "The CSF is leaving Khostok today," Akimov said. "There's been a change of plans."

"Well, that's no reason to drag me out of my office. *You* can leave the city, but I have responsibilities of my own, you know."

Akimov was nodding. "And I do apologize for the short notice. However I highly advise you to come with us. After the CSF is out, nobody will be leaving Khostok."

"I have my own car," Petrenko reminded him, eyeing the elevator buttons. "I can just drive myself out tomorrow, once I'm through packing. I still don't see -- "

" -- there won't be a bridge to drive on tomorrow, Chief Petrenko."

Petrenko opened and closed his mouth a few times, rather like a goldfish. He was still trying to wrap his brain around the idea when the elevator doors slid open. His escorts didn't try to pick him up again, but the hands on Petrenko's shoulders told him that returning to his office was out of the question.

The rest of the skeleton crew had already left the building, it seemed, and the lobby of the Khostok Police Department HQ was empty of employees. An armored personnel carrier sat idling on the street in front of the main entrance stairs. Akimov waited patiently as Petrenko locked the front door of the building, then followed him down the steps to the waiting car.

Inside the vehicle were a double handful of CSF soldiers and the four remaining policemen who'd stayed behind at HQ. They looked about as bewildered as their chief felt. Petrenko realized he was probably wearing the exact same expression.

Akimov pulled a folding chair down from the inner wall of the vehicle and seated himself, balancing his folder on his lap. "It would be a good idea to buckle up," he said.

It struck Petrenko that he ought to be a little grateful -- at least the Colonel hadn't forced him onto the carrier at gunpoint. It was considerate of him not to humiliate the chief in front of his crew.

He'd never been inside a personnel carrier before, and it took a few seconds before Petrenko had puzzled out the catch that released the folding seat. A minute after he'd strapped himself in the vehicle lurched alarmingly, the roar of the engine setting the walls and floor to quivering.

"We have the chief and are on the move," Akimov said aloud. He had one hand against the radio controls on the side of his gas mask. "Repeat, we are on the move. Estimate one hour to rendezvous point Green."

Petrenko was quick to discover that he didn't care very much for the personnel carrier. It was essentially a giant metal box, like a great black refrigerator on wheels. And the "ride" was felt less like they were in motion and more like the giant refrigerator was being violently shaken from side to side. Petrenko resorted to bracing his hands on the wall behind him to avoid bashing his head against the metal. How the colonel was able to carry on a conversation through all this was beyond him.

"Comrade Egret -- Colonel Akimov here. Have you reached anyone from Camp Three yet?" Pause. "Understood. Proceed with the evacuation orders as planned, but keep trying to contact them. Akimov out." Another pause, and Akimov pressed a few buttons on his mask radio. "Comrade Gander -- Akimov again. What's your status? ...fine, seventy-five percent is fine. Lock the doors and get your men onto that carrier. Remember, I want everyone at point Green by 1300 hours." Akimov paused again, listening. "It doesn't matter if they are destroying the crates. Starfall will take care of that. Just get everyone out and -- "

A tremendous jolt shook the carrier. Petrenko's skull thumped against the side of the vehicle and he bit down on his tongue to stop from cursing. Moments later a series of blows rained down on the sides and roof of the carrier. It sounded like nothing so much as a hailstorm, and the noise inside the vehicle was deafening. The CSF soldiers and policemen all cowered away from the walls, covering their heads like students during a bombing drill. Petrenko doubled over in his chair, hands on his ears, looking to Akimov for an explanation.

" -- and get to the rendezvous point," the colonel shouted into his radio. "Akimov out." He lifted his head, turning towards the driver. "What's wrong?"

The soldier in the driver's seat turned back over his shoulder. "Inkweed, sir. It's grown over the bridge."

" -- and the noise?"

"...Also the inkweed, sir." The driver hollered. "It's, uh, hitting the carrier."

Faces turned upward. The straps that dangled down from the ceiling were dancing with the rhythm of the pounding.

"Are we making progress?"

"Yes, sir."

"And the carrier's holding up?"

"Yes, sir."

"Good. Keep going."

"Roger that."

Akimov sat back in his seat. Petrenko threw his dignity to the wind and pressed his face against his knees, wrapping both arms around his head. The hailstorm had graduated into a team of thugs with baseball bats, all of them whacking away at the carrier like children going after a stuffed punching bag. Petrenko had no clue what the 'inkweed' was, or how it could have been responsible for the thrashing the carrier was undergoing, but he had no opportunity to ask.

An aeon went by before the noise started to taper off, diminishing until it sounded like an overzealous automated car-wash, and then back to a pattering of small hailstones. And then sweet, blessed, sanity-restoring silence.

Trembling, Petrenko lifted his head. His subordinates lowered their hands from their ears, all looking similarly pale and frightened. The scent of honey wafted through the cabin.

"Are we through?" Akimov called up to the driver.

"Yes, sir -- we're over the bridge now."

Everyone in the vehicle, CSF included, gave a sigh of relief. "Remind me to commend you for your driving, comrade," Akimov said.

"Thank you, sir." The driver's voice was shaking.

Petrenko licked his lips. "What's...what's inkweed?"

"That's classified, Chief Petrenko." Akimov turned to him. "But it's the reason you wouldn't have been able to cross the bridge in any civilian vehicle."

Ice filled Petrenko's bowels. "That was the Volgin River Bridge?"

Akimov nodded. There were no windows in back of the personnel carrier and suddenly Petrenko was grateful for that. He wasn't entirely positive he wanted to see the classified thing that had given the armored car such a beating.

"So, we're just...leaving it there?" He couldn't resist asking. "Can't...can't the, uh, the 'ink-weed' get across the bridge too?"

"Probably," Akimov said. "That's why we're going to blow it up."

Petrenko imitated a goldfish once more. Akimov lifted a hand to his mask radio.

"Attention all soldiers. Attention all soldiers. This is Colonel Akimov speaking."

~~~~~

"Comrades, I know the past few hours have been a challenge for us all. Your continued bravery and loyalty is a great gift to your nation, and a testament to the strength of the Special Forces.

"At the present time we are still moving forward with Operation Starlight. In light of the recent skirmishes at Red Camps Two through Five the deadline for complete CSF withdrawal from Khostok has been set at 1300 hours today. At that time all personnel must be evacuated from the city and gathered at rendezvous point Green.

"Placement of the Stardust devices, containing the camp populations, or combating hostiles should all be considered secondary objectives -- complete evacuation of all military personnel takes priority. If we are unable to place enough Stardust devices to ensure even coverage of the city, a backup plan is in place to deal with that outcome.

"We will have carriers standing by to pickup those soldiers who were not able to evacuate with their unit. Send out a distress call via the open channel if you need pickup.

"Once again, comrades, I thank you for your tireless service. Colonel Akimov out."

Nikita swallowed his mouthful of stale bread. "Thirteen hundred hours?"

"That's one p.m.," Alexei muttered. Both of them stared at Tatyana's gas mask where it lay on the carpet, still wired up to the external speakers.

"I know. That only gives us...oh, crap. That means we have like four hours before this Starlight thing happens." Nikita dropped the remainder of his bread onto the carpet and climbed to his feet, grabbing his backpack. "Lena, get into your jacket -- we've got to go."

Alexei got up as well, testing his sprained ankle. The binding he'd wrapped around it seemed to be giving it some support, though it still ached whenever there was weight on it. At least he had the tingling under his ribs to distract him -- the blight had grown to cover his entire side now, reaching down nearly to his hip.

Sighing, Alexei hefted his backpack onto his shoulders. "'Stardust devices'," he echoed. "That's what Tatyana called the black can we found."

Nikita was helping his niece into her jacket, and he shot Alexei a look of undiluted terror. Neither of them had really doubted Tatyana's predictions about Operation Starlight, but hearing it confirmed was especially chilling.

"I can't believe it," Nikita whispered. "All those women and children...for them to just leave them to..."

Elena glanced up at him and Nikita cut himself off, biting his lip.

There was a tense silence in the penthouse as the two men went around the room hunting for anything they have forgotten to bring. In their backpacks they had food, water, first aid, blankets, spare flashlights, plenty of batteries, fuel for camping stoves, and Alexei's own handmade innovation: wooden chair legs with oil-soaked rags tied around the end of each one. Alexei hoped they wouldn't have to use these last ones.

"We've got everything?" Nikita asked. Alexei stooped to retrieve Tatyana's gas mask from the floor, disconnecting it from the wires.

Nikita was shaking his head. "That's too heavy -- leave it behind."

"No, we might need it." Alexei inspected the respirator filter. "It should still be working...we can put it on Elena if we need to."

From his expression Alexei could tell that Nikita understood. "Let's hope we don't need to."

Alexei nodded. He turned the mask this way and that, early-morning sunlight gleaming golden in the mirrored eyepieces.

"She was so proud to be in the CSF, you know," Alexei said softly. "Her father was a lieutenant."

"Yeah?" Nikita wedged another flashlight into his backpack. "No wonder she got into the 'Forces."

"No, her dad didn't want her to join. He disowned her when she signed up."

Nikita oh'ed. "That...explains a lot. When did she tell you about her father?"

"Uh...she didn't."

"Then who told you?"

Alexei looked up from the gas mask. "Well...nobody did," he said, with a look of dawning confusion. "I just...maybe I...I don't know." He buckled the mask around a strap on his backpack. "Maybe I made it all up. It sounds right, though."

Nikita shrugged. "How's your ankle?"

Alexei leaned on his foot and winced. "It'll hold up."

"Good." Nikita squeezed Elena's hand, looking down at her. "Ready?"

"Yeah!" Elena chirped. "Let's go to the river!"

~~~~~

"Comrade Secretary, this is Colonel Akimov."

"Ahh, Aleksandr. Good to hear from you. Tell me, tell me -- how are things going down there?"

Colonel Akimov glanced around the interior of the otherwise-empty personnel carrier. After reaching their rendezvous point the soldiers had been kind enough to clear out of the vehicle, leaving Akimov to make his report to the Regional Secretary in private. They would assume he needed the privacy because his report would contain classified information. And that was fine with Akimov; let them assume that.

"We've reached rendezvous point Green. Sixty percent of my remaining soldiers are here with me; the rest are en route as we speak. I anticipate all military personnel to be clear of Khostok by 1300 hours."

"Sound good. And the data?"

"We have all of it, sir." Akimov patted the stack of files in the folding seat beside him, careful not to disturb the small piece of machinery that served as a paperweight. At least he'd been able to accomplish *that* part of his mission. "Both the old and new findings from the Lubukov Agricultural Labs on UEC-571 have been collected and compiled, along with a report summarizing the data."

"Excellent!" Glukhovsky's cheeriness contrasted with Akimov's somber tone. "And how goes Starlight, Aleksandr?

"Truthfully...it's not going as planned, comrade secretary." Akimov was acutely aware of his own ineptitude. His failure in Khostok had been spectacular, and no amount of careful phrasing on his part could change that. "Do you recall the...'mutated' blight victims I mentioned earlier? The ones that overtook the Labs?"

Glukhovsky recalled them, yes.

"Since we spoke, these victims have...well, they've launched a coordinated counterattack on all the red camps." Akimov couldn't keep the defeat out of his voice. "At my last tally there are no more than seventy-five percent of my original forces remaining. We had no warning...and we just weren't equipped to put down an organized rebellion."

"Understood. How many Stardust devices are in place?"

"Perhaps half of what we received was successfully placed before the camps were overrun. Also, comrade Secretary, these mutated victims seem to be...my men report that they're destroying the devices after they're in place. Deliberately, it seems. I have to assume more than half of what was placed has been disabled."

The secretary hrm'ed thoughtfully, and Akimov shut his eyes. Subconsciously he had begun stroking the paperweight atop the files, as if it were a cat -- the smoothness of the metal and the preciseness of the little machine's dimensions were soothing to him. Unlike Akimov, this machine was flawless.

"That's not good, Aleksandr."

"My sincerest apologies, comrade Secretary."

"Well, what are we going to do?"

Akimov opened his eyes, drawing himself up in his chair. "Sir, my plan is to detonate the Volgin River Bridge once the last of my men have cleared it. We have the explosive charges in place already. This measure will seal off Khostok's only exit and hold back both the regular infected civilians as well as the mutants...and anything else that may have sprung up in the city."

"A sound idea. And then what?"

"And then...I would like to request that you call for a Starfall strike on Khostok."

Glukhovsky caught his breath.

"I know the difficulty in approving such a strike," Akimov went on, "and it pains me that my incompetence makes such an act necessary. But it is my conclusion that Starfall will accomplish what Starlight can not. It will eradicate Khostok as a source of potential leaks -- chemical *or* informational."

"...A persuasive argument."

Persuasive or not, Akimov knew that Glukhovsky's authority only went so far. It was already somewhat arrogant of him to ask directly for Starfall; he couldn't even be certain that Glukhovsky had the clearance to approve such a strike, even if he was willing.

"I take full responsibility for my failings, comrade Secretary."

"Ah, no need for all that, Aleksandr. I'll approve it; sounds like there's no better way to put an end to this experiment."

Calling the Khostok disaster an 'experiment' was an interesting choice of words, but Akimov would not have dared to make such an observation. "Thank you, sir."

"Of course." The Secretary gave an expansive sigh, and Akimov could just about see him settling back into his velvet-cushioned, hand-carved desk chair. "You said you'll have all your men clear of the city by 1300 hours?"

"That is my estimate, yes."

"Then I'll take care of the preliminaries for Starfall while I'm waiting," Glukhovsky said. "I'll have the pilots stand by until I get word from you."

"Thank you, sir." Akimov couldn't resist the urge to bow, though he knew the secretary couldn't see him doing so. "It has been my deepest regret that I was not more competent as a colonel."

"Ahh, that's you, Aleksandr -- always with the formalities." Glukhovsky didn't seem bothered in the slightest. "I'll wait to hear from you."

Akimov thanked the regional secretary twice more before releasing the call. It had gone better than he'd hoped -- he might have been worthless as a commander, a tool unfit for such a task, but at least he could maintain himself with dignity until the end. At least he could do that.

The colonel checked the clock inside the carrier. He expected it to take another few hours before the rest of his men were clear of the city; then he could make the call to initiate Starlight. And then he just had to find someone to carry the lab data to Glukhovsky. Akimov would not be able to bring it himself; he couldn't bear the final humiliation of confronting his old mentor with his failure. The engineer would blame himself for the machine's flaws, even though the fault here lay with the machine itself.

And speaking of machines. Akimov lifted his paperweight again, marveling at its perfection. It rested heavily in his hand, smooth and cold and gleaming. Flawless.

Akimov smiled inside his mask. Then, pulling a cloth out of his pocket, he started to polish the gun.

~~~~~

Alexei had only been in the Gurlukovich Memorial Hospital for five minutes when he started to lose his mind.

After climbing back in through the second-floor window Nikita had elected to lead the way down the hall, the beam of his flashlight stabbing ahead into the darkness, holding Elena's hand. Alexei was following close behind. As far as Nikita was concerned the building was utterly quiet; even with the dust muffling their footfalls it seemed like their progress could be heard throughout the hospital.

He strained his senses trying to hear. Nikita knew, with the kind of intuition that pricked up the hairs along the back of his neck, that they weren't alone in the building. The inhuman things that walked these halls could hear *them*, no doubt, and that made the silence all the more oppressive.

When Alexei blundered into the wall the thump nearly launched Nikita out of his shoes. He spun around to find Alexei sliding down toward the floor. "Alexei!"

From Alexei's point of view the hospital was anything but silent. The rushing murmur he'd heard on their earlier visit was back again, ten times louder and more insistent. But it wasn't correct to say that there were human voices in the torrent -- the voices *were* the torrent. That's what he was hearing: millions upon millions of people, all talking at once, laughing and weeping and cheering and crying and singing, the chorus building in volume with each passing second.

It was like all the phone lines in the world were suddenly plugged into Alexei's brain, and he knew with utter conviction that if he hadn't already lost his sanity he would be losing it momentarily. He was swimming in the cacophony, waves of sound surging over his head, washing him off his feet, pounding him into senselessness, building to an intolerable crescendo that would leave him --

Nikita had already slapped him twice and was preparing for a third when Alexei came around again. He gasped, clutching at Nikita's arms like a drowning man.

"Alexei!" Nikita shook him. "What's wrong?"

He couldn't remember how to speak. Nikita dragged him to his feet -- Alexei realized he must have fallen to the floor at some point -- and peered into his face by the unsteady glow of the flashlight. "What's wrong?!"

"It's the river," Elena whispered. Alexei looked past her uncle and found the little girl standing in the middle of the darkened hallway, watching him with an ink-stained smile. "Alexei's hearing the river. Aren't you?"

"I hear it," Alexei croaked.

Nikita blinked at him. "...You hear what?"

"The river." He pointed at Elena. "Like she said...I think I can...hear the river."

Nikita looked back and forth between his niece and the younger man. "Alexei...she didn't say anything."

Alexei let his hand drop. "I need you to stay with me," Nikita said urgently, squeezing his shoulders. "You've got to keep it together."

"...okay."

"Can you still walk?"

When Alexei nodded Nikita released him, and he steadied himself with his hand on the wall. His ankle was throbbing but it still held.

"Let's keep going," Nikita said. He took Elena's hand and headed off again, checking over his shoulder to make sure Alexei was following.

Alexei limped off after them. His left side was pulsing with fire and he put a hand under his shirt, pressing the palm of his hand against the feverish skin.

It was starting, and it was more overwhelming than Alexei had ever anticipated. Even now those voices were still lingering in his head, faded but not vanished, chuckling and murmuring like an underground spring. Or like a river.

This was the start of the auditory hallucinations. Soon to follow would be the delusions, visual hallucinations and finally complete psychosis. Insomnia was another symptom, but of course it had been weeks since Alexei had slept normally.

And then there was death. Their research had shown that death came to all of the blight victims, sooner or later. The only exception had been Veronika, but Alexei had no clue what had happened to her, or what she had become in the end. Maybe death would have been preferable to becoming...becoming what?

The yellow circle cast by Nikita's flashlight floated ahead of them, throwing sharp shadows behind the debris that littered the hospital's halls. Alexei hobbled after it. He had to keep his sanity until they were through the warrens. Once they were through he could let himself go to pieces. It would almost be a relief -- he'd been headed in that direction for a while. But not yet. Not just yet. He'd made a promise to Yura, and he was going to fulfill it or die in the attempt.

When the voices suddenly peaked in volume Alexei flinched away, reflexively covering his ears. It was only when Nikita tugged on his wrist that Alexei realized he was talking to him.

" -- in case there's a fire!" Nikita said.

"Uhh?" Alexei lowered his hands.

"I said, we've got to find the stairs and get down to the ground floor. This place's got nothing but elevators, and without power they're worthless. But there's got to be stairs too -- they have to have them in case there's a fire."

Alexei could see the logic in that. "Have you seen any?"

"No." Nikita shook his head. "I thought there might be some towards the front of the building, but -- "

" -- I know where the stairs are," Elena put in.

Alexei looked at her. "I do," she insisted, smiling. A sort of dull shock ran through Alexei when he realized that her lips weren't moving when she spoke. "You just have to follow me."

"...more than one staircase," Nikita was saying, oblivious to the exchange.

"Follow me," whispered the little-girl voice from somewhere inside Alexei's head. "This way." Without further ado Elena turned and began walking down the hall.

"...but we can't -- Lena!" Nikita went after her. "Get back here! where d'you think -- "

Alexei put a hand on Nikita's shoulder. "Uh -- let's try going this way."

Nikita gave him a searching look. "...alright," he said at last. He caught up with Elena and took her hand, but the girl remained at the head of the group, leading the two men off down another hallway.

Fifty paces later Alexei was stumbling again. His lame foot hit the ground at the wrong angle and Nikita caught his arm before he went down.

"Your ankle?"

"'s fine," Alexei said.

"I can tell." Nikita drew Alexei's arm across his shoulders. "Here."

"I'm fine -- I can walk." Alexei tried to pull away, but Nikita was holding onto his wrist. "You're doing an awful job of it. Just lean on me for a bit -- you can walk later."

Alexei mumbled a thank-you, letting his weight fall against the older man.

"It's all this dust," Nikita said, sweeping his flashlight across the floor in a broad arc. "Makes everything slippery. They oughta fire their janitor -- he must be dead-drunk all the time, letting the place go like this."

Alexei cracked a smile.

"In fact -- hey, Lena, stop, stop." Nikita came to a halt at a juncture in the hallway. "Look, we're going in circles."

Alexei looked at the circle of floor spotlighted by the flashlight. Sure enough, there were several sets of footprints marching on ahead of them. "We must have circled back around somewhere."

"We haven't gone far enough for that," Alexei pointed out.

"Or doubled back, maybe..."

Elena was tugging on her uncle's hand. "It's this way," she insisted, and to Alexei's great relief her voice was no longer inside his head. "I know it is!"

"Hush, Lena."

"Wait, wait -- some of these aren't our footprints." Alexei pointed his own flashlight at the floor. "Look there -- those are from someone's boots."

A quick comparison of their shoes proved Alexei right. "Maybe it's from the CSF, before they abandoned the place." Nikita had unconsciously lowered his voice to a near-whisper. "Or one of the camp inmates?"

But Alexei had found two additional sets of prints, one small and one large, and all at once he understood. "They're from the other day," he whispered back. "The boots are Tatyana's...see, those ones over there are Veronika's. The big ones are the old man's."

Goosebumps pricked at Nikita's skin. Finding the footprints of their dead comrades wasn't the same thing as seeing a ghost, but it was close enough. "Seems like we've been over the whole damn building," he murmured. "I'm not surprised." He pointed his flashlight at the ceiling and found the signs overhead pointing them towards the Atrium, the Gymnasium, the Pediatric Ward and the Maternity Ward. The stairwell that descended to the atrium was a black void at the end of the hallway.

"The atrium!" Nikita took a step back. "That's where we are! That was the first place -- "

Elena chose this moment to yank herself free of her uncle's grasp. Without looking back she darted down the hall and plunged headlong into the stairwell, the metal staircase clanging under her feet.

Nikita yelped and took off after her, nearly pitching Alexei onto the floor before he caught himself against the wall.

"Lena! Lena, come back! *Lena*!!"

Alexei righted himself just as Nikita disappeared into the blackness after his niece. He stared after them for a moment, then dropped his backpack onto the floor and dug into it, coming up with a lighter and one of the broken chair-legs. Pulling the backpack onto his shoulders again Alexei charged off down the hall as fast as he could limp.

The darkness in the stairwell was so thick it was almost solid. Nikita's pitiful cries echoed up from further down the stairs. When Alexei caught up to him Nikita had reached the inkweed already and was half-buried in the foliage, thrashing and fighting as the inky vines looped themselves around his arms and legs. He was still shouting Elena's name.

Alexei stopped and flicked the lighter on, holding it up to oily rag they'd tied around the chair leg. With a soft *whoomph* the homemade torch caught fire and the stairwell flared with orange light.

"Nikita!" Alexei stepped forward, swinging the torch like a club. He struck at the inkweed and a shower of sparks rained down onto the stairs. After weathering half a dozen blows from the torch the inkweed shrank away, recoiling like a living thing. Nikita fell backwards onto the stairs.

"Lena!!" Alexei caught his collar before Nikita went diving back into the jungle again. He whirled on Alexei, grabbing his arms. "It's got her! it's got her!!"

"Calm down!" Alexei shoved the older man up against the wall, away from the inkweed. "Get your torch! we'll go after her!"

For a moment Alexei thought Nikita was too panicked to understand him -- then Nikita's eyes cleared and he reached back, grabbing the wooden stake out of his backpack. Alexei touched his flame against it and Nikita's torch caught fire as well.

They turned towards the inkweed again. Nikita was first down the stairs, sweeping his torch in flaming arcs ahead of him like a man trying to fend off a wild animal. Several steps down they found the inkweed was once more blocking off the stairwell in a solid knotted mass. Nikita held the railing with one hand and jabbed forward with the torch. The little vines shrank away from that searing heat, the flowers shrinking back into closed buds.

"It's working!" Nikita shouted back. Step by step the two of them advanced on the inkweed, forcing it back. The stairwell seemed to descend forever, dark and narrow, and in the torchlight the inkweed cast hideous shadows on the walls. The aroma of burnt sugar filled the air.

Alexei glanced over his shoulder and his heart sank. The black growth had closed in behind them, blocking the way back up the stairs. Nothing to do but keep pushing forward and hope that their torches held out until they were through the worst of it. The thought that the entire downstairs might be filled with inkweed flashed into Alexei's brain, but he dismissed the idea.

"Lena!" Nikita called out, swinging his torch. "*Lena*!!"

Alexei stumbled, pain shooting through his ankle. They were no longer descending the stairs -- the ground underfoot had leveled out. Glancing around Alexei realized that the narrow walls of the staircase had vanished as well: now there was only inkweed, crowding close on all sides, hanging low overhead. They were surrounded by the stuff, trapped in a cave of black vines.

"*Lena*!!"

And all at once the inkweed began to move. Nikita and Alexei had been driving it back a step at a time, the growth never more than a yard ahead, just out of reach of their torches. Now it was lifting away from them, retreating in every direction. In moments the two men were standing in a sudden clearing in a black forest, with nothing more than a fuzzy black moss underfoot.

Ten feet ahead of them, sitting placidly on the carpet of moss, was Elena. One of the inkweed flowers had sprouted up from the ground before her and she was holding its stem, looking into the blossom with intense interest.

Nikita made a choking sound and ran to her. She squealed in surprise as her uncle snatched her up from the ground.

"You bad girl! How could you -- do you know how dangerous that was?! You need to stay with us!! You could have...you..."

Elena seemed not to realize the risk she had taken. "I'm fine!" she protested, squirming. "I'm fine! put me down."

Alexei limped slowly over to them, holding up his torch, looking in all directions. The circular clearing in the foliage was only about ten feet wide by eight feet tall -- above and beyond that was a matted wall of inkweed -- but it was a relief after the claustrophobia of the stairwell. "...where *are* we?" he breathed.

Nikita relaxed his hold on his niece, though he didn't release her. He lifted his head, gazing up at the black jungle that hemmed them in. "...I have no idea."

"This is the a-tri-um," Elena told them. She broke free of Nikita's arms and picked up her survival pack from the ground. "C'mon, we need to go this way."

Nikita grabbed her shoulder before Elena could take a step. "Oh, no you're not. You're going to stay right here."

"Look!" Alexei pointed with his torch. "Over there!"

They looked. A dent was forming in the wall of inkweed that encircled them, deepening until it was an alcove, then a hollow. It was as if an invisible wedge was being driven into the tangle, causing it to rise and separate until it had opened a channel in the black growth, just wide and tall enough for a man to walk into.

Wide-eyed, the three of them crept over to the mouth of the opening. Nikita pushed his torch into the gap but it was too deep for them to see where it ended. As they stood staring an inkweed bud emerged from the low-hanging growth that formed the ceiling of the channel. With a faint pop the bud burst into full flower, shedding a burgundy light on the ground below. Several feet further down the channel another bud dropped out of the ceiling and bloomed, glowing greenly. And further down there was a third flower, then a fourth, and a fifth.

Elena pointed down into the hallway that had opened in the inkweed. "We go this way," she said.

Nikita and Alexei looked at each other. "...what *is* this stuff?" Nikita whispered.

"How would I know?"

"Weren't you studying it?"

Alexei shrugged. "We...never found out what it was."

Nikita looked back down the channel again, at the inkweed blossoms dangling down from the ceiling like multicolored glass lamps. "Is it...is it from this planet?"

"...I have no idea," Alexei confessed. Holding his torch aloft, he stepped into the channel. Nikita hesitated, then took a firmer grip on Elena's hand and lifted his own torch, creeping in after Alexei.

The path through the inkweed twisted left and right, doubling back on itself, occasionally so narrow they had to stoop to pass through it. The claustrophobic feeling from the staircase would come back to Alexei at these times, a tightening in his chest. Overhead the inkweed flowers bloomed as they crossed beneath them, then dimmed once they had gone past. Alexei remembered all too vividly what he'd seen inside those petals in the exam room and he fought back the urge to look up.

Alexei was starting to doubt that they were still inside the Gurlukovich Memorial Hospital anymore when they emerged into another circular clearing, much smaller than the first. A large white blossom drooped down from overhead, glaringly white, spotlighting something huge that lay at the center of the clearing. It was a giant circle of rusted metal like the world's largest manhole cover, balanced on one hinged edge on the ink-furred ground. Mounted into the center of the circle was a wheel covered in flaking red paint, and above that were stenciled the letters B 2 0.

Nobody spoke for a long moment.

"Well I'll be damned," Nikita exclaimed. "He was *right*!"

Alexei sidled around to the other side of the cover. It had been lifted away from a metal-rimmed hole that plunged down into the ground. By torchlight they could just make out the ladder, as rusted as the shelter door, descending into the well of darkness.

Nikita came up beside him, looking around at the tangled foliage that bordered the clearing. "Where are we now?"

"Still in the atrium, I think. The hospital had an indoor garden." Alexei cocked his head to one side. "They probably had this entrance buried under a flowerbed or something. Pretty good way to hide it." He leaned forward. "Look...someone's written something here."

They brought their torches closer. On the underside of the upraised door three words had been spelled out in broad strokes of black paint:

TO THE RIVER

Below the words was an arrow, pointing down into the hole.

"That river again." Nikita was holding Elena close against his side. "You remember what it said on the doors in the gym?"

Alexei nodded. "D'you think this is where they all went?"

"Who?"

"The people they were holding here."

Nikita wasn't sure. "Well, they weren't in the gym...maybe they did come this way." His brow furrowed up. "But how'd they know there was a shelter entrance here?"

"Well *some*one was here before us." Alexei ran his hand over the inside of the door. The lettering was dry.

"The old man?"

"Nah, he said he hadn't found this entrance yet." Leaning forward, Alexei dropped his torch into the hole. It sailed down for several yards before hitting the unpainted concrete floor of the shelter, scattering sparks. What looked like a tangle of black wires on the floor began to squirm, edging away from the torch, and Nikita cursed under his breath. "It's gotten into the warrens!"

Alexei frowned. "We've got extra torches," he said. "We just need to make it through the shelters. I haven't seen the inkweed growing outdoors anywhere...I don't think it likes the sunlight."

Nikita nodded soberly and handed his torch over to Alexei. The ladder gritted underfoot when he stepped onto it. Alexei and Elena held their breath as he went down, but the ladder stayed intact and Nikita reached the bottom safely. He picked up the fallen torch at once, swinging it in a half-circle as he checked the room.

"Looks okay," Nikita called up to them. "Lena, you come down next."

Elena made the descent without incident, and Alexei tossed his torch down into the shelter before climbing down himself, trying not to put too much weight on his bad ankle.

Looking up from the shelter floor Alexei could see just how deep underground the warrens were. The entrance was nothing more than a bright circle overhead, scarcely bigger than the palm of his hand. The white inkweed blossom that hung overhead shone down at him through the entrance and Alexei turned away from it with a shudder.

Nikita was still in awe. "This place really exists," he said softly. "I don't believe it."

"I guess Tatyana was right -- they probably built lots of these during the Great War." Alexei retrieved his torch and straightened up to take a look at their surroundings.

The shelter was clearly a wartime project, and bore all the marks of hasty construction: bare concrete walls and floors, unlit bulbs in wire cages, hand-lettered signs, buckets of paint and rusted masonry tools lying abandoned on the floor. A webbing of inkweed clung to the corners of the hallway, small buds twinkling in the dim light. The corridor they'd arrived in was undecorated save for a large map glued to one wall, its paper yellowed and fragile with age.

"Look at this..." Nikita squinted at the map. "Cafeteria, theater, library, school, greenhouse, sickbay...there's a whole city down here."

"It smells funny," Elena complained.

"This place is older than you are, Lena."

Alexei half-smiled. "Probably older than I am," he murmured.

At the end of the corridor lay a large oblong room with hallways branching off from it on all sides. The dust-frosted chairs and tables said this space might have once been a meeting hall or perhaps the cafeteria. Ancient cans of beer were scattered across the floor. Tacked to the walls were a scattering of propaganda posters, their bold reds and greens faded into shades of brown. The inkweed was here too, growing like mold along the borders of the walls, creeping from the edges of the floor towards its center.

"'The...nation...of...Chorma...lives...on'," Elena read aloud. "'We...are the...future...of the Motherland'." She looked at another poster. "'Comrades live together...in peace and tran-...tran-...'"

"Tranquility," Nikita finished. "This place oughta be a museum."

There was a large patch on the wall where the cement was darker, and on the floor below it was a square of heavy cardboard in roughly the same shape as the patch. Alexei bent and lifted the square by one corner, turning it over, then instinctively took a step backward.

"Oh wow," Nikita remarked. Right-side up, the poster showed the ample and beaming face of Chorma's Glorious Leader, larger than life and glowing with health. "Hope the DIO doesn't catch whoever took that down."

Alexei swallowed. "The back of the poster wasn't dusty," he said. "Someone did this recently."

"Yeah...probably this guy." Nikita lowered his torch closer to the floor. A series of blurred footprints stood out clearly on the dusty concrete. "Looks like they were barefoot, too."

"Could be one of the camp inmates," Alexei suggested. "They might have lost their shoes when they escaped from the gym."

Straightening again, Nikita cupped a hand beside his mouth. "Hello!" he shouted. "Anyone hear me? Hello!"

"They could be hiding," Alexei whispered.

"Hellooo!" Nikita called again, then added "We're not the Special Forces! we're just civilians! We won't hurt you!"

Nikita's own voice came echoing back to him, and when the echoes trailed off there was nothing. "They might not even hear us," Nikita said, lowering his arm. "This place looks like it's pretty big."

Alexei had to admit the warrens seemed like a vacation paradise compared to the horrors of the gymnasium. If someone had been trying to hide out from the CSF and their poison-gas weapons they couldn't have picked a better spot for it. The only problem with the shelters was the inkweed -- though the growth along the walls was scanty Alexei knew it could flourish in a matter of hours. Being trapped underground in an unlit bomb shelter with the stuff blooming in the darkness all around you sounded like a special sort of Hell.

Elena tugged on her uncle's arm. "I wanna see the library."

"No, Lena -- you could get lost down here."

Alexei looked up. "Speaking of getting lost...do we know where the exit is?"

"The map said it was somewhere in that direction." Nikita pointed with his torch to the corridor with 'HALL A' stenciled above the doorway. Alexei could see that the flaming rag was almost consumed, burning down to the wooden stake underneath. "And it looks like our comrades were searching for the exit too."

Running in and out of Hall A were innumerable trails of footprints, dark streaks against the lighter dust. None of the strangers appeared to be wearing any shoes. "Let's hope they found it," Alexei said, and limped off in the indicated direction. Nikita was right behind him with Elena in tow.

The monotony of the cement corridor was broken here and there by more patriotic fliers, telling the explorers that 'THE HARDER WE WORK, THE FASTER WE RISE' and advising them to 'REPORT ALL IDLE TALK TO THE HARMONY SUPERVISOR.' One poster in particular showed an oak tree with its roots in a stylized bomb shelter and red foliage emblazoned with the Chorman flag; the text read 'EVEN THE MIGHTY OAK SPRINGS UP FROM UNDER THE EARTH.'

"They were serious about this," Nikita muttered, reading one of the posters. "They thought we could live underground, like moles. Unbelievable."

"They're still serious about it."

Nikita glanced sideways at Alexei. "You don't think we'll actually go to war with America, do you?"

"I don't know." Alexei was chewing on his lower lip. "But we weren't researching fertilizers at the Labs, I can tell you that."

Nikita nodded. "I know. Yura told me."

There was an awkward silence.

"...I really am sorry," Alexei said at last, wincing at how pathetic he sounded. "I just wasn't sure how to tell you, and later on..."

"It's okay," Nikita said quickly. "Let's talk about it some other time. I don't want her to..."

Both men realized Elena was missing at the exact same moment. Nikita gasped and spun around, looking back the way they'd come. The hallway was empty of everything but footprints and posters.

"Lena! Oh, damn it all..."

"She was right there!" Alexei said. "She can't have gone very far -- come on!"

The two of them rushed back to the cafeteria, Nikita in the lead and Alexei hobbling along behind. He had the beginnings of a headache and someone had upped the volume on his auditory hallucinations, but now was not the time to mention it.

"When I catch her she's going to be sorry," Nikita snarled.

"Take it easy -- she's just a kid."

Elena wasn't in the cafeteria. No fewer than ten doorways opened onto the oblong room, not counting Hall A, and Nikita started to panic. "She could be anywhere down here! We could be searching for hours!"

Alexei was scanning the stenciled letters above each of the doors. Suddenly his heart leapt. "The library!" he exclaimed, pointing to one of the exits. "I'll bet she's in there!"

Nikita was first into the room, with Alexei a close second. The library was bigger than the cafeteria, its walls and ceiling barely touched by the torchlight, full of the musty smell of mildew and decaying paper. Rows of bookshelves filled the room, and beyond them was a cluster of inexpensive study desks.

"Lena? Are you in here?"

There came a high-pitched giggle from somewhere in back of the room. "Lena!" Nikita shouted, disappearing into the rows of shelves. Alexei heard him gasp in surprise, but it wasn't until he'd caught up with Nikita that he understood why.

They had found Elena again. She was kneeling on the cement floor beside one of the study desks, her survival pack open beside her. She'd taken a chocolate bar out of her pack and was reaching out to offer it to the indistinct shadow that cowered under the desk.

When Nikita and Alexei came stampeding up the shadow turned to them and a gleam of torchlight fell on its glossy head. Alexei's heart stilled.

"Here, take it," Elena whispered, offering the candy. The faceless thing turned back to her -- it was a small one, they saw, no bigger than Elena herself -- and crept forward another few inches. A black rope sprouted from the thing's back and extended towards the offering.

What happened next was a blur to Alexei. Nikita swore and grabbed the Tokarev pistol from his side holster, racking the slide back. The thing jumped in between Elena and her uncle and she shrieked for them not to shoot it. And then it looked as if all the shadows along the wall were leaping into the room, filling it with darkness.

But all this was nothing but noise and motion to Alexei, for all at once his head exploded.

Or at least that's what it felt like. Something came unplugged in his brain and the murmuring undercurrent of voices was suddenly a waterfall, and he was caught beneath the downpour. A billion sensations rushed into him too quickly for Alexei to fight or even comprehend all that was rocketing through his skull -- he was burning and freezing, in agonizing pain and overwhelmed with ecstasy. The lives of a thousand strangers flashed simultaneously before his eyes.  Everyone in the world was shouting at him at once.

It seemed to take millennia before the torrent of sensations died down enough for Alexei to think again. When he came back to himself he was curled in a fetal position on the library floor, clutching his head and screaming at the top of his lungs.

"*Alexei*!" Nikita was kneeling beside him on the floor, shaking him. "*Alexei*!!"

Alexei coughed and gasped for air. As the room around him drifted back into focus he was genuinely shocked to realize they were still in the underground library in the shelters. His torch lay beside him where it had fallen, guttering against the cement. He couldn't have been out for longer than a minute.

Now that he'd partly recovered his sanity Alexei could see what had caused the room to fill with shadows. No fewer than a hundred of those faceless humanoids had materialized in the library, gathering around them on all sides, their eyeless heads pointed towards the two men. They must have been hiding out of sight and had shown themselves when Nikita had drawn his gun. Elena was hidden back behind a double row of the humanoids, barely visible.

"Alexei!" Nikita hissed. He was still holding the Tokarev, aiming at nothing, glancing back and forth between the crowd of faceless things and the young man on the floor. Under the orange glow of the torch his face was chalky-white. "What's wrong?!"

Alexei just whimpered. It felt like the skin along his left side was literally searing, burning down to the bone. The whispering voices began to swell in volume again and he wailed, squeezing his eyes shut. "No no no -- "

The tide of voices checked itself and receded, a wave drawing away from the shore.

"Alexei?"

The next thing Alexei heard sounded like a thousand-person choir. [*PEACE*,] the voices thundered in unison. [*PEACE. PEACE. NO VIOLENCE.*]

His brain still reeling, Alexei opened his eyes again. The humanoids stood waiting, unmoving. Several of them were holding up their hands, palm-out, towards the humans.

[*NO VIOLENCE.*]

Alexei groaned. "...I think...I can hear them."

"What?" Nikita blinked at him. "You...you can hear these things? how?"

"...in my head..."

Nikita seemed to accept this without question, though given all that they had been through this was not so surprising. "What are they saying?"

Alexei pushed himself up into a sitting position, pressing one hand against his temple. "They don't want any violence."

Nikita looked wildly around the room. He didn't lower his gun, and Alexei could understand why: being surrounded by a multitude of these things was frightening enough, but when they were all so utterly quiet the scene became something out of a nightmare.

[*PEACE. PEACE. PEACE.*] The chorus rolled around in Alexei's skull.

"...tell them to give me back my niece," Nikita quavered.

[*WE HEAR YOU,*] the chorus replied. [*WE WANT TO HELP YOU.*]

"They understand you," Alexei said. He lifted his head. "If you want to help us, give Elena back. Please."

[*WE CAN NOT.*]

"Why?!"

"What? what are they saying?" Nikita demanded.

[*YOU WILL GO; YOU WILL DIE. YOU MUST STAY.*]

"...they want us to stay here."

"Like hell we will." Nikita rose to his full height, aiming his gun into the black assembly.

[*NO VIOLENCE!*] Now the chorus was pleading. [*WE WANT TO HELP. OUTSIDE YOU WILL DIE. STAY HERE. HERE IS SAFE. HERE IS THE RIVER.*]

"Wait, Nikita, wait." Alexei struggled to his feet again, grimacing at the soreness in his ankle. Both torches were flickering their last and he retrieved a fresh stake from his backpack, lighting the new from the old one. "They're...they think they're helping us. They're saying that we'll die if we leave the shelters."

"...well, where else are we supposed to go?"

[*STAY HERE,*] the voices replied. [*STAY WITH US. STAY WITH US. STAY WITH US.*]

Alexei shook his head. "Oh, no. No we can't."

"What? what?"

"They want us to stay here with them."

"Why?!"

[*STAY WITH US. BECOME US.*]

Alexei's mouth went dry. He turned to Nikita, but it took a couple tries before he could get the words out. "...they want...they want us to become one of them."

Nikita grew even paler.

[*YES. BECOME US. BECOME US.*]

"We can't! you have to let us go!" Alexei faced the crowd again. "Listen -- all of you were human once, weren't you? You came down here from the gym inside the hospital, right?"

For the first time the faceless things seemed uncertain. One or two of them looked at their comrades or scratched at their heads as if trying to recall.

[*YES,*] they concluded at last. [*SOME OF US.*]

"...I knew it."

"Oh god." Nikita was shaking his head.

"They're the same as Veronika," Alexei murmured. "They've just been...I don't know. Changed." He dropped his torch to the floor and took a step towards the things. "If you still remember what it's like to be human, you have to understand -- we want to *stay* human. Nikita, Elena and myself. Please...we don't want to hurt you, but you have to let us all go."

[*YOU CAN NOT STAY HUMAN,*] the chorus reassured them. [*TWO OF YOU ARE ALREADY BECOMING US. YOU WILL ALL BECOME US.*]

Alexei knew exactly what they meant, and a lump of ice sank into his stomach. The burning along his left side had spread up as far as his shoulder and was creeping down his arm. His head was still throbbing from the episode he'd endured earlier.

"We don't want to hurt you, but we'll do it if you force us." Nikita gripped the Tokarev in both hands. "Human or not, you can't be bulletproof."

[*YOU WILL NOT SHOOT.*]

"Nikita," Alexei said. "They're not buying it."

"Yeah?" He cocked back the hammer on his gun.

The humanoids shifted, some of them drawing to one side. From out of the crowd Elena emerged, her pale skin and blond hair standing out brightly against the dark gleaming bodies around her. She was holding hands with the small humanoid she'd found earlier. Elena's candy bar was in its other hand.

"Uncle Nikita, don't hurt the shiny people." She sounded perfectly calm and reasonable, if a little worried. "They're just trying to help us."

Nikita made a strangled noise.

[YOU WILL NOT SHOOT WHILE THE YOUNG ONE IS HERE. WE KNOW YOUR MIND.]

Alexei swore. "They're psychic."

"Huh?"

"They -- they're reading our thoughts." Alexei closed his eyes for a moment. "They know you're not gonna shoot them with Elena right there."

At last Nikita lowered his firearm. "Well damn," he said weakly, and there was genuine despair in his voice. "That's not really fair, is it?"

Alexei couldn't reply. The library shifted and wavered around them in the uneven glow of Alexei's fallen torch, yellow light playing over the humanoids' skin. It really wasn't fair. They couldn't have come so far and lost so many of their comrades only to end up like this, trapped underground with these distorted, faceless things until they forgot what it was like to be human.

Alexei knew there was a way to escape this; he just couldn't think of it right now. In fact he couldn't think too well at all...the throbbing in his temples had become a pounding, hammering away at his thoughts, chiseling into his brain...

It was Nikita who finally ended the standoff, clearing his throat. "I want to propose a trade," he announced. "I'll give you my gun if you give Elena back."

"But they don't want your gun," Alexei muttered. "They want *us*."

Nikita ignored him. "How about it?" he asked the crowd, lifting his chin a little. "If you can read my mind you'll know I'm not trying to cheat you, right?"

Across the room the faceless things were stirring, looking at each other. In Alexei's head the whispering voices grew a little louder -- he cringed in anticipation -- but not loud enough for him to make out the words. It almost looked as if the humanoids were considering the offer, though Alexei couldn't imagine why they would care about Nikita's gun.

"So? how about it?"

The faceless things turned back to them. [WE ACCEPT THE OFFER.]

Alexei blinked.

"Good," said Nikita. "I'll hand it to you...let me come over there." He crossed the room without looking back, hesitating only for a second before stepping into the midst of the humanoids. Alexei watched as he knelt down next to his niece.

"Lena -- are you alright? are you hurt?" Nikita held her shoulders and turned her this way and that, inspecting. Elena shook her head. Nikita looked her full in the face for a moment, then pulled the girl forward into a hug.

"You're a good kid," he said as he released her. "Go with Alexei now, okay?"

Elena stepped back from her uncle, wide-eyed, then turned and darted back across the room. Alexei caught her outstretched hand in a kind of daze.

Then the crowd of humanoids drew together around Nikita and Alexei finally understood. When they'd read Nikita's mind they had realized he wasn't actually offering them his gun.

"No," said Alexei. "No, no, *no*!!"

"Get out of here!!" Nikita was waving frantically. "I asked them to give you ten minutes!"

"*NO!*" Alexei screamed, and he heard his voice breaking. "Take me instead! *Take me instead*!"

"Dammit, just *go*!!"

The crowd was drawing tighter around Nikita, the mass of black bodies all but hiding him from view. Their tentacles uncoiled and reared up over the tops of their heads, a nest of cobras all preparing to strike. One of the humanoids turned its blind face in Alexei's direction.

[*WE HAVE YOU ALREADY,*] the chorus boomed. [*OUR BLOOD IS YOUR BLOOD. YOU WILL BECOME US SOON.*]

The tentacles flashed downward and Nikita screamed. He was still shrieking when Alexei snatched up his torch and bolted from the room, dragging Elena after him.

The two of them plunged through the cafeteria and into Hall A without breaking stride. They were several yards down the hall when the echoes of Nikita's cries finally faded. They kept running.

Hall A seemed to go on forever, miles and miles of featureless cement corridor, and at last Alexei could go no further. He dropped the torch and slumped against the cement wall, his vision blurring. His ankle was a pulsing knot of agony.

"Dammit..." Alexei slammed his fist against the wall. A sob escaped him. "Dammit!" He punched the cement wall a half-dozen times more, bloodying his knuckles, then sank down to the floor. "Dammit, dammit..."

A pair of little arms wound around his waist, squeezing him. "Don't cry Lyosha." Elena's voice was muffled against his shirt. "It's gonna be okay."

Alexei looked down at the top of her head. "'m not crying," he snuffled, wiping his eyes with the back of one bloody hand. It was never going to be okay -- in fact it had never been less okay -- but if Elena wanted to believe that was the case then Alexei wasn't going to contradict her.

"It's gonna be okay," Elena repeated, looking up into his face. Her blue eyes shone with youthful conviction. "We're almost there."

"We are?"

She nodded, pointing to his fallen torch. Alexei saw that the flame was flickering as if in an unseen breeze.

Fresh air!

Alexei looked around. They'd reached a four-way juncture in Hall A, and two other corridors branched off to the left and right of them. When Alexei lifted his torch the flame leaned to the left, brightening and dimming.

"The exit must be that way," he said huskily, pointing to the right. Elena nodded. "Let's go," she said, and took his hand.

Their progress was much slower now. It felt as if he'd torn the ligaments in his ankle even further during their escape from the library; Alexei was limping badly. Elena stayed by his side, leading him onward as if he were the child.

Ten minutes, Alexei reminded himself. Nikita had bought them ten minutes. Ten minutes before a horde of nightmare beasts came boiling out of the library to run them down. If the mental assault he'd suffered in the library had been caused by the faceless things -- and Alexei had every reason to believe it had been -- they wouldn't even need to lay a finger on him. And who said they had to physically catch up to him to obliterate his sanity like that? For all he knew they could make those kind of attacks remotely, bringing him down no matter where he was.

Alexei found that he didn't care. He would keep going. He had no alternatives, and nothing else was important to him anymore except this girl.

When they turned a corner and encountered a glowing crescent moon end of the hallway, Alexei thought he was hallucinating again. He blinked rapidly but the crescent remained brighter than ever.

Elena tugged on his hand. "There it is!" she said.

"It is?" Alexei limped along after her. The moon grew larger as they came closer, and as his eyes adjusted Alexei finally saw what they were approaching. It was the red wheel mounted in the circular steel door that gave it away: they'd found the exit. That luminous crescent was daylight, seeping in around the edge of the half-open door.

In spite of his ankle Alexei started to run. Elena loped along with him, cheering.

The door was only a few inches ajar, and the rusted hinges squalled as they pushed it the rest of the way open. After the dim obscurity of the tunnels Alexei stumbled into the daylight and was promptly blinded. He dropped his torch and heard it expire with a sizzle. Breathing hard, Alexei sank down into the grass just outside the exit and waited for the dazzling glare to become more endurable. The sound of Elena's laughter receded as she bounded away.

"Lena!" he called after her. "Don't go too far!"

By degrees Alexei's sight came back. His first thought was to wonder what time it was -- they'd entered the warrens by midmorning, noon at the latest, but the outdoor world seemed to be in twilight. Somewhere nearby a stream was gurgling, and Alexei was almost certain it was not an illusion this time. The breeze blowing across his face brought a scent that was somehow eerily familiar.

Honey.

And then his vision cleared at last. Now he could see that the shelter exit opened out of a hillside, the ground sloping down into a valley some feet below. He spotted the river he'd heard at the bottom of the valley, glinting in the weak sunlight.

It was then that Alexei realized he was no longer on Earth.

Everything that grew around him -- grass, shrubs, trees -- was alien, with colors and geometry unknown to this planet. The grass he was seated in was soft and black, more like animal fur than anything. Within arms' reach was a cluster of flowers big as hibiscus blossoms, their stems black as ink, petals phosphorescing orange and greenish-yellow.

Vines like tangled utility cords sprawled across the furry ground, their slender black leaves tipped with indigo. Further on down the riverbank the black plants grew larger, some of them taller than an adult human. The biggest ones had the appearance of young willow saplings, though with luminous blue berries like clusters of sapphires dangling among the black foliage.

Elena was dancing up and down the riverbank, knee-deep in a patch of flowers like glowing white crocuses. "We made it!!" she called up to Alexei, cheeks flushed with delight. "We found the river!!"

In speechless amazement Alexei rose to his feet and made his way down the slope to the riverside. Elena grabbed him in a tight hug. "Isn't it so pretty?!"

There were no words. Alexei looked out across the water, then up at the sky. High overhead hung a curtain of pearly mist like a blanket laid against the black treetops, reducing the sun to a bright blur and keeping the ground below in dusky twilight. It was like he'd told Nikita: the growth didn't like the sunlight.

"Inkweed," Alexei said. "This...all of this is inkweed, isn't it?"

But Elena was too busy picking flowers on the riverbank to answer him. Alexei took another good look at the rippling water, noticing the fishlike shapes that flashed in the depths. The river was easily twenty feet across, and from its color it was quite deep.

"That's where the contamination started." Alexei was really speaking to himself, as Elena was hardly paying attention. "The Volgin River. We're at the Volgin River. That's where the exit was leading us." He cast another glance at the alien trees and bizarre flowers littering both of the sloping banks. The inkweed had conquered the area completely.

Even on the further shore Alexei could see that the black foliage had taken hold there, spreading up until the top of the valley disappeared into the low-hanging mist clouds. There was no way of knowing how far the inkweed had crept. If he was correct about it not liking the sunlight then it was limited to indoor areas, or outdoor ones protected by a layer of fog. But if he was wrong...

"Elena...can you swim?"

"Mmm?" Elena looked up from the luminescent daisy chain she was making. "A little bit."

"I see." The stabbing in Alexei's ankle told him that he wasn't going to be doing any swimming anytime soon, let alone with a heavy backpack on. Clearly both of them would sink like rocks before they'd gotten halfway across. Alexei had thought they'd be fine once they'd gotten out of the city limits; he was a fool not to have considered that the Volgin River might be too deep to ford in some places.

He looked up and down the banks, but the width and color of the stream was unchanged. Alexei knew the river *was* shallow enough at some points to wade across it, but which direction would take him to the shallows? would they reach it before nightfall? he had only the vaguest idea how much daylight was left, and what would it mean to be stuck out here in this eldritch jungle after dark?

Under better circumstances they might have been able to retreat back into the shelters for the night, or even for long enough to cobble together a raft. Hell, they might have been able to wait in the shelters until Alexei's ankle mended and they were better prepared to hike to Byatin -- they'd be out of the elements in there, and the shelter was likely to be stocked with food and water and fuel.

But all that was a pipe dream. The humanoids were in there, doing god-knew-what to Yuri's brother and waiting to give the same treatment to Alexei and Elena.

Right on cue, a twig snapped behind them. Alexei knew what it was before he even turned around.

Making its way down from the shelter exit along the sloping hillside was one of those faceless things. Alexei had thought there'd be more pursuers than that, but even a single one was probably quite capable of taking down a little girl and an injured young man. The thing came slowly, pushing aside the drooping branches of those willowlike trees, carefully treading around the flowers. It looked quite at home among the inkweed; an unearthly Adam in an alien Paradise.

Alexei drew his Tokarev pistol from his holster and racked the slide to put a cartridge in the chamber, stepping in between the thing and Elena. He was too exhausted to feel very afraid anymore; hell, he was too wrung out to feel much of anything at all. He only knew that he'd failed.

The humanoid stopped when it was only a few yards away. It looked at the two humans -- as much as it could be said to "look", not having eyes -- and put both hands in the air.

[*No violence,*] whispered the voice in Alexei's skull. There was no more thousand-man chorus; this time it sounded like a single person.

Alexei took aim. "There's gonna be violence if you don't get back." A part of him wanted to laugh at his own false bravado, but he was too weary to do that either.

The thing lowered its hands. [*You are tired,*] it said, and it was not a question.

"Yeah." It made sense -- if the thing could read his thoughts it probably knew his feelings as well. "I'm tired."

[*Then come with us.*] The thing gestured back at the shelter exit.

"No," Alexei said.

[*Why not?*]

Alexei snorted. "Because I don't want to."

[*Then where will you go?*] it asked.

"I'm going to Byatin, and I'm taking this girl with me." Alexei had already realized that he was never going to make it to Byatin -- wasn't even going to make it out of Khostok, in fact -- but that didn't mean he was just going to surrender here.

The faceless thing canted its head to one side. That movement stirred something in

Alexei's memory, something he could just about recall, perhaps if he hadn't been so very exhausted.

[...*why*?]

"...huh? 'Why'?" Alexei echoed. He wasn't prepared for this -- was it trying to reason with him? was it trying to understand him? He glanced at Elena, who was standing beside him and apparently listening to the one-sided conversation. She had donned the crown she'd braided from the inkweed flowers, and it burned as brilliantly as a halo against her golden hair.

"She's my best friend's daughter," he said wearily, looking back at the faceless thing. "I promised him I'd get her out of the city."

[*We can keep her here*,] the thing offered, indicating the shelter exit. [*We can keep you both here*.]

"No," said Alexei. He took aim at the humanoid, though he didn't hold much hope that bullets would stop it. "If you want her you'll have to kill me first."

For half a minute the thing didn't respond. Then, unmistakably, the sound of laughter shimmered through Alexei's head. [*Oh Lyosha*,] it said. [*You've changed a lot*.]

Alexei's heart stopped.

The humanoid's skin rippled and changed, growing duller. Then it began to dissolve. The process started at the top of the head, inky skin melting away like candle wax, revealing caramel-colored hair under the black shell. Human features emerged on the thing's face, mere suggestions of nose and eyes and mouth at first, becoming more defined as the ink trickled away.

It was exactly like what had happened to Veronika, though this humanoid wasn't wounded. But seeing that the thing was human underneath wasn't what shocked Alexei, held him rooted to that spot, unmoving, scarcely daring to breathe. For as the black skin slid away and the human being beneath it took shape, Alexei realized that he *knew* this person. If it had been two decades rather than two months since he'd last seen them, Alexei would still have remembered that face.

It was Yuri.

His hair was longer and his glasses were gone, and under the ink he turned out to be wearing jeans and a ragged tee-shirt, but there was no mistaking who it was. It took a matter of minutes for the ink to vanish completely, and once it was gone Yuri beamed at Alexei as if he'd just done a particularly clever trick.

"Hello again, Lyosha."

For an instant Alexei thought he would faint, though in the end he simply dropped the gun. "Papa!" Elena squealed, bounding across the black grass towards him.

Yuri swept her up into his arms. "Lenuchka! Your papa's missed you so much, did you know that? have you been a good girl?"

"I've been good! I brought everyone here, like you asked me!"

"Yes, yes, you did indeed! Excellent job!" Yuri kissed his daughter on both cheeks and plopped her back down on her feet. "You've had a long trip though -- how are you feeling?"

Elena was grinning and grinning. "I'm hungry," she said.

"Ahh, well, that's fine, we can get you a nice big dinner tonight." Yuri patted Elena's shoulder, then glanced back up. "...Lyosha? you alright?"

Alexei couldn't answer. When Yuri took a step towards him Alexei jerked backwards, stepping down on his bad ankle. Pain lanced up through his leg and Yuri lunged out and caught his wrist to stop him from falling. Something like electricity flashed through Alexei at that contact -- whatever this thing was, it was too warm to be a ghost.

"Lyosha, Lyosha, it's alright." Yuri was holding him by both shoulders, shaking him. "It's okay. It's me, it's really me."

Alexei shook his head. He was pushing against Yuri's chest, trying to get away, but he wasn't fighting very hard.

"Calm down, just calm down. Everything's okay now."

At last Alexei stopped struggling, letting his hands fall by his sides. It took a moment for him to recall how to speak. "...how?"

"Oh, that's a long story, a very long story. Ah...let me see..." Still holding onto Alexei, Yuri glanced around at the inkweed blooming in the river valley. "All of this...I don't know how else to say it, but it's an alien. It's from another planet."

Alexei was ready to believe just about anything at this point, but that didn't mean he understood. "...these are aliens?"

"No -- an alien, in the singular sense. Only one. But a very big one." Yuri gave a sheepish half-smile, as if he knew how silly this all was sounding. "It's trying to help us. Doesn't quite know what it's doing, but it's learning. It saved my life when that overdose should have killed me...and it's done the same for all your friends too."

"...who?"

"Don't you know who your friends are?" Yuri chuckled. "Veronika, and the tall one --

Hawk, right?"

Alexei was reeling. "They're alive?"

"Of course they're alive. We saw to it they got treated. This...this alien, it's helpful like that."

No dream could possibly have been this perfect, or have made so little sense. "...Nikita?" Alexei asked.

"Well, of course! I wouldn't have anything happen to my brother." Yuri looked up at the misty sky. "Listen...I can explain everything, I really can, but we've got about a half-hour before military aircraft come by and start dropping nerve gas canisters on the city. We really need to be back in the shelters before that happens." He looked into Alexei's eyes. "Just trust me, okay?"

Alexei was beyond trying to comprehend all that was happening. Leaning on Yuri for support, he limped up the hill towards the shelter exit, with Elena skipping along beside them and humming a little song. The three of them squeezed past the metal door and into the warrens again. Once they were inside Yuri grabbed the red wheel mounted on the door and leaned backwards, dragging it shut with a loud shriek of its hinges. He spun the wheel to lock the bolts in place.

"There."

Though Alexei had dropped the torch and forgotten about his flashlight, it was no longer quite so dark inside the shelters. Elena still had her crown of flowers, the blossoms blazing with a white radiance that lit the corridor for yards in all direction.

Yuri smiled fondly at his daughter. "...thank you for bringing Lena here," he said, putting an arm around Alexei's shoulders.

"You're welcome," Alexei replied. Or at least he meant to say that. What came out instead was a wordless sob, and he spun around to grab Yuri in a sudden embrace.

"Ah, you're okay." Yuri hugged him back. "You're okay now."

Elena made an attempt to hug the both of them. "Don't cry, Lyosha!"

"Oh, he's fine, don't worry." Yuri was stroking Alexei's hair, smiling faintly to himself. "Guess you haven't changed that much after all," he murmured.

# CHAPTER FIFTEEN

"Comrade Regional Secretary...this is Colonel Akimov. I am calling to report that one-hundred percent of my forces are clear of the city, and the Volgin River Bridge has been detonated."

"Ahh, excellent," came the response from Regional Secretary Glukhovsky. "I'll let the pilots know. We can expect their 'deliveries' to begin landing in the city in about twenty minutes."

"Yes, sir."

"And you, Aleksandr -- let me just say that you've done a fine job. I've discussed you and your mission with some of my associates and they all agree."

Akimov winced. He was glad that none of his soldiers could see him like this. All of his remaining men were waiting outside, relaxing on the grassy hill where they'd parked the carrier, some ten miles south of Khostok.

"Sir..." Akimov rubbed his polishing cloth over the barrel of the Tokarev, making the metal gleam in the artificial lighting. "Permission to speak freely?"

"Go ahead -- what's on your mind?"

Akimov drew back on the slide -- quietly, so the secretary couldn't hear it -- and made sure there was ammunition in the chamber. There was. "...Sir, I really appreciate your kindness, but...you can tell me that I've failed. I'm not a child."

There was a creak as the secretary settled back into his desk chair. "Ahh, Sasha, Sasha. That's very like you."

For nearly a full minute there was silence on the line, and then Glukhovsky cleared his throat. "Well...since the mission is technically complete, it won't do any harm to tell you. All of this is confidential, you understand?"

"...of course."

"Sasha...you were never told the full purpose of this mission." Glukhovsky lowered his voice. "The approach you took -- commandeering the Labs, setting up quarantine camps, pursuing a cure -- were as we predicted. But nobody expected you to succeed; in fact, we anticipated the experiment to end with a Starfall strike from the very beginning."

The gun slipped from Akimov's fingers and clattered to the floor. "...then what was the point of all this?" he demanded, and this was one of the rare times that he couldn't keep the heat out of his voice. "'If I was being sent out here to fail, then -- "

He checked himself before he went too far. If his failure was planned...he had heard of such missions. Usually they were ways of getting rid of a high-ranking officer who'd grown too wealthy or too 'unpatriotic' for the higher-ups to control. But Akimov wasn't one of those! He'd aspired to nothing except serving the Motherland, and for those in power to --

"Calm down, calm down!" Glukovsky said. "We needed to send in someone who would make every effort to save the city and its inhabitants. That was you, Sasha, and you performed as well as I expected. The *point* of this mission was not to save the city, though -- the point was to gather data.

"That's that data you're carrying. Our projections showed that, in the event of public water contamination with UEC-571, no more than 90% of the citizenry of a mid-size city could be expected to survive -- even with an immediate disaster response. This experiment showed that our calculations were correct, and the data you're bringing back to me will be invaluable in advancing our understanding of this bioweapon."

Akimov had quite forgotten about the Tokarev that lay on the floor of the personnel carrier. "...the release of UEC-571 was planned."

"Yes, of course. UEC-571 is a weapon, Sasha -- and until a weapon is tested and its capabilities understood...it is not very useful." Glukhovsky chuckled warmly. "In a way, that makes it a bit like you."

~~~~~

Police Chief Petrenko was not drunk just yet, but he making swift progress in that direction.

After disembarking from the armored car to stretch their legs on the hillside the CSF had changed from military personnel back into regular men. Their relief at seeing an end to this mission was palpable. Several of them had unbuckled their gas masks and a few had even shucked off their protective suits, lying about half-naked in the sunny grass.

And it seemed like every other man had a hip-flask hidden under his protective suit somewhere; it could almost have been a standard-issue part of their field equipment. Some kind soul had lent Petrenko his flask and the chief was seated on a patch of grass under a shady tree, embarking on a much-deserved and long-awaited vacation. All around him were the sounds of relaxed conversation, snatches of songs or arguments over card games, and quite a bit of snoring.

The world had begun to look much friendlier by the time someone came to join Petrenko. He turned and offered a boozy smile to the young soldier settling down beside him in the grass. This young man had close-cropped blond hair and strikingly pale blue eyes, and in profile he was almost attractive. Then he turned, and Petrenko saw that the left-hand side of his jaw had been burnt at some point, a shiny blotch of scar tissue pulling his mouth into a perpetual half-smile. But the young soldier was still decent-looking in spite of that, though perhaps Petrenko was just drunker than he realized.

"Have a drink, comrade," Petrenko suggested, feeling sorry for the boy. He watched as the young soldier took a swig from the offered flask, made a face, and handed it back to the chief. "Rather have tea," he said.

Well, Petrenko wasn't one to judge. "Tea doesn't make you forget your troubles," he pointed out. "And I could use some forgetting." He waved his flask toward the distant city of Khostok. "I was the police chief, did you know that? In charge of the whole damn city. And now who am I? Just a drunk old man. Got no home, got no job, and nobody can tell me when they're gonna start resettling th' city. A month? a year? ten years?"

"Probably ten years," the young soldier mused. Petrenko looked at him, then took another swig from his flask. "But I say to myself -- " Petrenko belched suddenly. "Eh, sorry. I was saying, I say to myself, 'least I'm not your colonel. Right?" He jerked his chin towards the personnel carrier that had brought them. "Least I'm not that one. All that's happened in Khostok durin' the quarantine, you know they're gonna hang it all on the colonel. Those old dinosaurs up in the Kremlin always do. He'll be lucky to get himself a position sweeping floors -- unless it's in the gulag."

The young soldier gave Petrenko the strangest look. Then he sighed. "Well, I thought so too." The soldier looked off toward the silhouette of Khostok, just visible on the horizon. "But I just got off the wire with the Regional Secretary; he wants to recommend me for a promotion to Major-General. I'll be heading to Moscow next week."

Petrenko dropped his flask. It bounced in the grass and lay there, spilling a stream of vodka that vanished into the dirt.

"I should have known you wouldn't recognize me without my mask." The right side of the young soldier's mouth turned up in an apologetic smile.

The men of the Special Forces were exhausted by all they'd been through in the past months -- to say nothing of the madness they'd endured in escaping Khostok -- and it took a lot to rouse them from their naps. Nonetheless several of them had started to sit up, looking around for the source of the sudden commotion. Under a nearby tree they could see their colonel, seated on the ground with his gas mask off. A portly middle-aged man was kneeling in the grass beside him, tugging on his sleeve and filling the air with the sound of loud, drunken crying.

"Comrade Colonel, forgive me! I'm just a stupid old man, I don't mean half the things I say, and besides -- "

"It's alright, it's quite alright."

" -- always respected you military types, you know, protectors of our fair nation -- you have to know I wasn't serious, I was only joking...perhaps I've had a bit too much to drink, but still I'd never dare to speak badly of someone of in your position -- "

"Please, comrade, it's really alright." Akimov was trying to hush the police chief but Petrenko was having none of it. "Y-you don't understand, I just can't go to the gulag!" Petrenko bawled, clinging to Akimov's arm. "I have a wife and two children! my eldest daughter just had a baby! can you picture that young one growing up in this cold world, not knowing her grandfather? for mercy's sake..."

"Calm down, you aren't going to be sent -- "

" -- and with my arthritis and my fallen arches, how d'you think I'd fare in Siberia?! why, I'd be dead inside a week! you'd be sending me to my death! do you really want to murder an old man who's only ever served his country with -- "

Soldiers were turning around to look at the two of them, some of them laughing and pointing. Akimov waved them away. "Petrenko," he muttered, "so help me, if you don't shut up I *will* have you sent to Siberia."

This threat had the desired effect. Akimov was able to pull his shirt from Petrenko's grasp but the police chief stayed kneeling in the grass beside him, hands clasped together, silently beseeching him.

Akimov sighed. "I'm not reporting you to the DIO or anyone else. Now, pull yourself together."

Petrenko hiccupped and nodded. "Thank you, comrade Colonel," he said meekly, and kissed Akimov's sleeve before the colonel could stop him.

A thin whistling distracted Akimov. He looked up. High overhead were two unmarked military planes, drawing parallel lines of exhaust as they sped towards Khostok. It was, he reflected, quite convenient that the disaster was officially reported as a "pesticide" leak from the "agricultural" Labs...there was no need to invent an additional story to explain the casualties.

And how many of the two-and-a-half thousand dead would be acknowledged? one hundred? fifty? Certainly no more than two hundred. But those lucky few would be honored martyrs for the sake of Chorma's progress. Posthumous medals for 'Service to the Motherland' would be awarded, and what had happened in Khostok would be all but forgotten.

Petrenko had been too busy hunting for his dropped flask to pay much attention to the planes. When he recovered it and found it empty he pouted like a child. "Should stick to tea instead," Akimov told him. "Tea wouldn't put you in such a state, I assure you."

"Ahh, won't be able to afford tea *or* vodka anymore," Petrenko replied glumly. "It's going to be water from here on out."

Akimov regarded the chief with a thoughtful air. "You know, comrade...as rare as it is to find a human being of good quality, finding people who are good judges of quality is even more problematic."

Petrenko had been shaking the upended flask over his mouth, but he lowered it when he realized Akimov was speaking to him. "...quite right!" he said, after a pause.

"Take me, for example. I don't find my own performance at all satisfactory, but it seems that the powers that be have been impressed enough to offer me a promotion." He rubbed at the smooth spot along the left side of his jaw. "What does that say about their quality standards?"

"...I think your quality is fine, comrade Colonel!"

Akimov shrugged. "But then again, who am I to argue with Moscow?"

Petrenko began to answer him and stopped, unsure if this was a trick question. "Regardless," Akimov went on, "I find myself to be a decent judge of others' quality. It's a necessary skill for a commander to have."

"Quite right!" Petrenko had no clue what he was agreeing to, but enthusiastic support seemed the safest approach to take.

"Which is why I'd like to offer you a position as my secretary," Akimov concluded. "I find you to be both motivated and honest, two attributes not found in abundance in the general population. And as you're presently unemployed..."

"Quite ri -- ah, what?" Petrenko had the feeling he'd missed something important. He squinted at Akimov. "Ah, comrade Colonel, forgive me, but...did you say you wanted me to work for you?"

"I did," Akimov said patiently. "As Major-General I'll need a secretary to handle important matters. Would you be interested?"

Petrenko blinked, then blinked again. Then he threw himself against Akimov's boots, clasping his arms around them. "Oh, comrade Colonel! you've saved me! for you to show such pity on a poor old man like myself -- "

The idling soldiers began turning around again, and laughter rippled through the crowd. Akimov was still trying to extricate his boots from Petrenko's grasp when the first explosion came. A gust of wind struck them first, whipping through the trees and sending the soldiers' playing cards flying. Moments later the crackle of detonation came rolling across the hills. Looking out towards the Khostok skyline one could see a cloud of yellowish smoke blooming up from among the buildings, like a sickly flower.

" -- what was that?" Petrenko whimpered.

"Starfall." Akimov finally wrestled his boots out of Petrenko's grip. "As I was saying, my job offer to you is on one condition."

" -- anything!"

"You must give up vodka." Akimov's half-smile turned into a full one for a second. "And you must start drinking tea. As my secretary, I insist."

Petrenko gulped. Well, he had said 'anything'. "Of course, comrade Colonel."

"It's settled then." Akimov patted Petrenko's shoulder. "I'll send word to you as soon as my promotion is official."

Nodding, the police chief rolled over and lay back in the grass of the hillside. To the north of them, where Khostok lay, the yellow cloud had dispersed into a smoggy haze, sinking down into the buildings until it was lost from sight.

It could have been worse, Petrenko reminded himself. It could have been much worse. Digging ditches in the frozen ground for eighteen hours a day, or drinking brackish water in a position of relative safety and luxury. Between the two of these, one was clearly the logical choice.

~~~~~

Alexei felt like he had slept for years, though he knew this could not have been true. But he also felt that he had had a thousand dreams, each of them different, and somehow he felt that this had actually been the case. For Alexei could remember every one of those dreams: he had been old and young, male and female, Chorman and foreign. In his dreams he'd seen things, done things, *been* things he had never before imagined. And nowhere in these dreams had he encountered his mother crying over his father.

For someone who'd had so many dreams he nonetheless awoke feeling fresh and alert. The first thing he found upon opening his eyes was a faded poster beside the bed, telling him in bold red letters that 'EACH WORKER IS A GEAR IN THE GREAT MACHINE OF OUR NATION.'

Alexei smirked and looked around. The room was unfamiliar to him, but not threateningly so -- though cement-walled and windowless the place was still somehow cozy. It was warm and dry in here, his blankets were soft and clean, and the air smelled pleasantly of honey.

Honey...

Alexei glanced down. Clinging to the cement wall and the foot of the bed, dominating an entire corner of the little room, was a giant mass of inkweed. Glowing blossoms in blue and turquoise hung over the bed, shedding an undersea light. And several black tendrils of the stuff had snaked their way up under his blanket.

Gasping, Alexei tried to jerk his feet away. A spike of pain shot through his left ankle and something that was wrapped around it yanked it back in the opposite direction.

The inkweed had him.

That was bad enough already, but when Alexei whipped the blankets away he discovered that his left leg below the knee was entirely bound up in inkweed, the visible skin a shiny black in color. He was still screaming two minutes later when Yuri burst into the room.

Alexei's first hysterical impulse was to think that this was another dream. Yuri ran to the bed and grabbed his shoulders. "Lyosha, it's okay! calm down!"

Alexei squeaked and pointed. Yuri held him back before he could tear the vines off of his leg. "It's okay!" Yuri repeated. "It's helping you! don't fight it!"

Slowly the words started to sink in. Breathing hard, Alexei looked back and forth between his old friend and the black tangle that appeared to be eating his foot. "It's *what*?!"

"It's helping you," Yuri said again. He smiled as he settled down beside Alexei on the bed. "It's fixing the tendons in your ankle, actually. You did a number on them, running around on that sprain."

Alexei put a hand over his heart. "...it can do that?"

Yuri nodded.

"...how?"

"Ah, well, that's a complicated question." And Yuri sounded delighted to answer it. "You see, the organism -- what the military calls 'inkweed' -- seems to be able to manipulate organic and non-organic matter near the molecular level. It can do this because it can manipulate its *own* molecules, you see -- this also lets it synthesize certain chemicals and do a whole lot of other neat tricks too." He reached out and patted one of the vines, as if it were a puppy. "You have no idea how fascinating this stuff is. We're just now finding out everything it can do."

Alexei only stared at him. This *was* Yuri, no doubt about it, though his hair had grown out and his glasses were gone. His enthusiasm for discovery was not one bit reduced, and when he was explaining something interesting his eyes still shone in the way that Alexei remembered.

"Oh, yes -- it also fixed my eyesight!" Yuri pointed at his face, beaming. "You noticed I'm not wearing my glasses, right?"

Alexei nodded. "This organism could revolutionize medicine as we know it," Yuri declared. "You remember the woman in Storage Room 8 -- your friend Veronika, right? remember how badly she looked when she came into the Labs? and then she recovered, and we couldn't say how or why?"

Alexei kept on nodding. "It was this organism; it patched her up automatically. And it did it again when...when she got shot. Likewise for that soldier, Hawk -- what was her real name? Tatyana, right? -- it healed her, too. That's what it's doing for your ankle right now."

His instincts were still telling him to panic but Alexei had to admit that the explanation made sense. He glanced down at the black foliage coiled around his leg.

"Is that how you survived?"

Yuri's smile faded. He looked away, suddenly distracted by the poster on the wall.

"...sorry," Alexei said quickly.

"Not as sorry as I am." Yuri shot him a guilty look. "I know...it was stupid of me, I know. I'm really sorry. I never thought I'd seriously consider..." He broke off again, running a hand through his hair.

"It's okay."

"No, it isn't. It was cowardly of me." Yuri took a deep breath and let it out slowly. "Your blight was pretty advanced...were you getting those, uh, episodes? where you can't think straight and can't move and it goes on for hours?"

Alexei almost smiled. "The ones where it feels like your brain is melting?"

"That's the one." Yuri nodded. "I just...I couldn't stand it any longer."

Alexei remembered the library, and his soul recoiled from the memory of that mental anguish. If that had been a recurring event, day after day, with the little gaps of sanity in-between the fits of madness growing shorter and shorter...then he could understand why Yuri had done what he'd done. Alexei felt sure that he would've done the same himself.

"But we found out what was causing that, and we've cured it." The energy had come back into Yuri's voice. "And we're doing the same for you, so don't worry."

Alexei looked closely at his friend. "So you...you're cured? you don't have the blight anymore?" Yuri appeared to be clean as far as he could tell, but there was no forgetting what he had seen that day, watching that faceless monstrosity dissolving and Yuri emerging from beneath its skin.

"Well...yes and no." Yuri paused thoughtfully. "We've all still got the blight, but...it's adapted to us. Or maybe we're adapted to it. It's nothing like you'd expect," he said, seeing the look on Alexei's face. "It only makes people sick like that during...I guess you'd say it's a transitional stage of the blight. Being stuck in transition is what was killing people."

Most of this was too much for Alexei to take in all at once, and the bits that he did understand hardly put him at ease. Suddenly he wanted the black vines off of his leg, wanted to be clear of the stuff completely. "A 'transitional stage'?" he echoed. "Transitioning to what?"

Yuri laced his fingers together. "Being integrated with...with the organism. Once you're integrated with it, everything changes."

Oh, Alexei definitely wanted to get away from the inkweed now. He made the mistake of looking up and saw that one of the blue flowers had descended toward his face, petals rolled back to reveal a luminous marble at its center. A spasm of cold horror went through him and he shrank away.

"I don't want to integrate with anything." Alexei's voice had gone up several octaves. He tried again to pull his leg away from the vines but the inkweed held him fast. "Why would anyone do that?!"

Yuri was squeezing his shoulder, trying to reassure him. "You won't really understand until you're there," he said. "But you can say it opens your mind. That's the best way I can explain it." He chuckled. "Really, the organism explains it a lot better than I do."

"Wait, what?" Alexei tore his eyes away from the unearthly flower. "This thing -- you can talk to it?!"

"Of course we can. That's how we knew it was an alien." Yuri tilted his head towards the blossom. "It told us it was."

"It's...it's sentient?" Alexei boggled at the thing.

Yuri laughed out loud. "It's much, much smarter than we are." He reached out toward the inkweed and a small tendril crept out of the larger mass, drooping into the palm of its hand. "Here," he said, offering it to Alexei.

"I don't want it." Alexei hugged his arms close to his body. "I'm not integrating with anything."

Yuri canted his head to one side in that disarming way of his. "You don't want to be one of the first humans on the planet to make contact with alien life? Think about it, Lyosha!"

Alexei *was* thinking about it, and that was the problem. Still, his scientific curiosity was piqued. Or maybe Yuri's enthusiasm was infectious; it usually was.

"Just talk to it," Yuri urged. "Let it explain itself, at least."

Alexei eyed the little vine with suspicion. "I don't have to...'integrate' with it if I don't want to?"

"I'm sure it's not going to force itself on you." Yuri laid the vine into Alexei's hand. It twitched and began to slither up his arm, rather like a snake, and Alexei suppressed a shudder. "But you know...everyone it's spoken to has wanted to integrate."

The vine was creeping over his shoulder, up his neck. Alexei clenched his teeth, fighting the urge to slap it away. "And I'll be right here." Yuri grasped Alexei's hand. "So don't worry."

Alexei was certainly worrying. When the little vine started to slide into his ear he jerked reflexively, and would have yanked it out if Yuri hadn't been holding his hand. He opened his mouth to protest, but at that moment a soundless explosion went off behind his eyes, and it took his consciousness with it.

~~~~~

There was nothing. Only darkness, deep and without form, without shape or boundaries. Alexei swam in it, lost to the world and to himself. He might have been there for an eternity without realizing it.

And then there were stars.

They flared into existence all around him, one after the other, blazing like living diamonds suspended in the abyss. Presently -- Alexei had no idea how long it took -- the vast space around him was filled with scintillating pinpricks of light. It was like the birth of the universe. He hung in the void, watching the stars come alive, neither wondering nor caring why he wasn't cold or suffocating.

And then he felt it. Something unfathomably immense was somewhere in this airless space, along with him. Alexei thought of someone swimming in a deep ocean whose toes were brushing against a passing whale. It was just the vaguest impression of something there, but if that thing were even a hundredth the size it seemed to be...

But where was it? he saw nothing but stars, glittering and stationary. He looked in all directions and found the same thing -- nothing.

Then the vast thing stirred again, and Alexei knew. He was looking at it already. He was *inside* it.

A white sun burst into existence nearby, showering Alexei with light. He turned and witnessed the sun stretching and expanding, turning itself into a vertical line, then into a symbol. Several more suns exploded to life beside the first, shaping themselves in turn. The row of symbols turned out to be letters half a mile high, written in white fire against the blackness.

Together they spelled out a single word:

*HELLO*

Alexei blinked. "...um...hello?"

His voice sounded tiny in the vastness of this space. Just as he was wondering how he could speak without air, the letters vanished. Swiftly a handful of other suns sprang into existence, arranging themselves in order as they morphed into letters and and then into words:

*HOW ARE YOU?*

Alexei felt like laughing. "Fine," he said. "How are you?"

*I AM FINE.*

The blazing letters hung in space for several seconds, then winked out. No more communications were forthcoming, though Alexei waited patiently for more to appear. When it seemed that the intangible entity wasn't going to offer anything further he finally took the initiative.

"Um...can I ask a question?" It only seemed appropriate to be polite.

*YES*, the letters replied.

"...what are you?"

The response nearly annihilated his mind. It was like that time in the library, only multiplied a thousandfold. Information -- a veritable geyser of information blasted Alexei's consciousness into fragments, overwhelming whatever defenses he might have had. Trying to take it all in would have been like trying to collect a waterfall in an eggshell.

It felt like aeons before the flow of data was finally cut off, though in reality it could only have been a few milliseconds; Alexei's mind wouldn't have survived any more than that. He found himself floating in the void again and screamed belatedly, reaching up to clutch at his head before he realized that he had neither head nor hands anymore.

Light washed over him as more white suns came into being, shaping themselves hurriedly into letters.

*SORRY*

"...it's quite alright," said Alexei. If he'd still had a body he felt sure he would have been trembling.

The 'SORRY' flickered away into blackness. He had asked the wrong question, he realized, or he wasn't prepared for the answer. Summoning up his courage, he opted to ask something that could be answered with a simple yes or no.

"Um...are you...are you...God?"

There was a definite hesitation before the reply came. A sound like the tinkling of hundreds of bells swept through the vacuum. All of a sudden Alexei felt amusement, mirth -- but not his own, someone else's. Some*thing* else's.

The intangible thing was laughing.

More white suns flared up to answer him. *NO*, the thing said. *I AM NOT GOD.*

Alexei wasn't sure whether to be reassured or worried by that response. He didn't dare repeat his initial question, not after what had happened the first time. But it seemed that the thing wanted to clarify, for as soon as the last sentence winked out there were more suns already taking shape.

*I AM NOT YOU.*

This seemed so painfully self-evident that it left Alexei puzzled. By paying attention he could sense that the thing felt this statement to be terribly important, was almost in awe of...of what? of Alexei? but why? It'd already been made quite clear that the thing was incalculably powerful, so much so that it could annihilate a mere human being with something as simple as a careless thought. Why, then, was it broadcasting this sense of wonder?

More suns. This time they spelled out an even simpler sentence:

*I AM ALONE.*

It was such a pitiful statement that Alexei immediately felt sorry for the thing. And yet he still couldn't understand. How could it be alone? It had to have parents, or a creator at least. If it had been a god then maybe it could have sprung up out of nothingness, self-created, but Yuri had said it was an alien. Was it the last of its species, maybe? an exile?

"I don't understand," Alexei said.

This time there were more suns than ever before. As they resolved into words a sort of stillness came over him.

*DO YOU WANT TO SEE?*

He did. He *had* to see. He knew he might be opening himself to another brain-melting blast of data, but it didn't matter -- he had come this far and he desperately wanted to understand this thing.

"Yes. Show me."

Something invisible reached out of the void and nudged Alexei, tugging him down. The stars slipped past him in bright smears of light as he sailed downward, picking up speed, a comet rocketing into a black hole. The darkness closed in around him.

[*Open your eyes,*] prompted a voice.

When Alexei did so he found himself back in the cement-walled room again, with the faded poster on the wall. Yuri was still sitting on the bed and -- Alexei gave a start -- his own body lay there on the pillow, eyes closed and with a black vine trailing out of his ear. If he'd still had a skeleton he would have been chilled right down to his marrow.

" -- am I dead?" he asked nobody in particular.

[*No,*] replied the voice, and this time Alexei recognized it as Yuri's. [*Now, really* open *your eyes.*]

He obeyed. And this time he gasped in wonder.

He could see into eternity.

It was as if he'd come unstuck in time, and was everywhere and nowhere simultaneously. He was in the B-20 shelters, watching a crowd of refugees making their beds on the floor. He was in abandoned warehouses, in empty schools, in deserted streets, in vacant restaurants. He was in the atrium of the Gurlukovich Memorial Hospital, in the now-uninhabited Lubukov Agricultural Laboratories. And he was in the Volgin River valley, watching with thousands of eyes as a dirty yellow fog settled down over that surreal garden of Eden.

He was all over Khostok at once; Alexei had become the city.

No, not the city.

He had become the inkweed.

His eyes looked out of every inkweed blossom; the stems and vines and leaves were his new body. A sense of pulsing, boundless energy thrilled through him, limitless in its potential. Alexei knew in that moment what the inkweed was made of: billions upon billions of microorganisms, invisible to the naked eye. He could feel each and every one of them, alive and awaiting his command.

Some of these microorganisms were devoted to physical functions, growing new inkweed and healing the damaged sections. Others lived only to build more microorganisms, innovating new designs and refining the existing ones. Still others were dedicated to thought processes, gathering and evaluating and storing data. Individually these tiny creatures were simple, primitive, performing only one or two basic functions. Together, they were the brain and body of the inkweed, giving it full consciousness of itself.

He dove deeper in the teeming darkness, exhilarated by his own abilities. By tapping into the inkweed's data-storage microorganisms Alexei could see its homeworld: an ocean planet, where the only safety from violent storms lay at the bottom of the ocean. Here the inkweed had begun its existence as something resembling a coral or jellyfish, an amalgamation of tiny creatures that bonded together for protection.

Over millennia the ocean creature had increased in complexity, adding new microorganisms with new functions as it went. The happy accident that had gifted it with sentience had taken place many eons ago -- and only that once. The creature had been the only self-aware entity on its planet; it had no comrades, no others of its "species", no sapient organisms to interact with. It was completely alone.

So it had sent out pieces of itself, in organic ships crafted by its own microorganisms, to search the galaxy for -- what else? -- sentient life.

One of these ships had arrived on a particular blue-green planet with high hopes; Alexei laughed to see that the ship had bypassed the Soyuz rocket shortly before entering the atmosphere. After all of those aeons under that distant ocean, developing, evolving, always alone, the ocean creature was going to discover intelligent life on another planet.

Alexei saw what the creature had seen, and shared its dismay when it encountered no sentience on the planet he recognized as Earth. Though it had reshaped its body according to the planet's ecosystem -- imitating a harmless plant, with glowing lights and pleasant smells to lure more complex creatures towards it -- it encountered only animals. Herbivorous ones, carnivorous ones, near-hairless bipedal tool-using ones. But nothing with a higher consciousness.

Where was the sentient entity who had built those fantastic geometric structures in space, the one who had shaped the planet's environment to its whim? where was the inkweed's future companion? after having traveled so far, was it doomed to discover that it was alone in the universe?

It was then that the inkweed began the second phase of its exploration, sending out specialized microorganisms that inserted themselves in the nervous systems of those animals, intercepting and decoding the electrical signals. And it was then that the inkweed realized its error.

Those bipedal tool-using animals...they were communicating! they had a pitifully primitive means of doing so, dependent on crude auditory and visual symbols, but they were able to transfer the more basic sorts of abstract information from one animal to another. The geometric structures the inkweed had seen in space were suddenly explicable: linking their minds together using this clumsy means of communication, the bipedals were able to form a superorganism of massive power.

This was the entity the inkweed had been seeking! This was consciousness!

But oh, how young and fragile this superorganism was. The communication between the individual animals was feeble at best, and data became corrupted almost as soon as it left the source. There were a thousand errors, a thousand miscommunications, before the superorganism could accomplish the smallest of tasks. These bipedal animals were carrying out the same functions as the inkweed's own microorganisms, but how inefficiently, and how laboriously!

Naturally the inkweed understood what it had to do. This poor superorganism -- diseased, vulnerable, obviously still in its infancy -- needed to be helped. A specialized but very simple microorganism was necessary: one that would receive electrical signals from other animals and transmit these into the brain of its host animal. This simple improvement would open near-lossless communication between these bipedal creatures. The superorganism native to this planet would evolve at a lightning speed! And it would look to the inkweed as its mentor, its savior, its friend.

Alexei saw the inkweed crafting the first of these specialized microorganisms, releasing them in the form of honey-flavored berries, gathered and consumed by unwitting peasants. Through the inkweed's eyes he saw the black patches blooming on the peasants' skin as the inkweed's microorganisms multiplied within their bodies; saw them receiving the first of the signals from the brains of their fellow humans; saw them driven insane by the overwhelming flood of data they could neither understand nor control.

Alexei saw, and at last he understood.

It had taken the inkweed much longer to understand, and scores of blight victims had given their lives to educate it in human biology. The first lessons were the peasants who had stumbled upon the inkweed, dying from exhaustion after weeks of sleepless insanity. Then came the government officials, cultivating samples of inkweed and destroying whatever else they found growing wild. These samples were fed to "volunteers" at the Agricultural Labs, back before Alexei's time, and they too raved and suffered and finally expired while the inkweed observed them in puzzlement.

Some kind of immune response was being triggered in the superorganism, it theorized. This was not a major setback -- the inkweed's own microorganisms died very frequently, and it viewed these bipedal animals as essentially the same sort of component. The inkweed would persist. As long as the superorganism itself survived there was still hope of healing it, of coaxing it into full consciousness.

Eventually the administrators at the Lubukov Agricultural Labs ruled the blight too dangerous and unpredictable to weaponize. So their researchers isolated a concentrate of the inkweed's specialized microorganisms, labeled it Unknown Experimental Compound 571, and locked this away in Storage Room 5. And there it stayed until a young lab assistant named Dmitri

Fyodorovich decided to steal it.

Alexei recognized the young man. All in a blur he saw his theft of the UEC-571 and attempted flight, the crash, and the dispersal of the compound into the Volgin River, starting the whole process over again. Thousands were sickened; the city thrown into chaos.

And then the inkweed made its discovery.

Alexei's multifaceted sight began to dim, the many views of Khostok fading away into darkness. He made an abortive effort to hold onto the vision before he realized that something else was flickering into view. Not multiple images anymore, but a single one: a human brain. It lay alive and defenseless in his mind's eye, detailed as a textbook picture.

There were no suns this time, but the words flamed in Alexei's mind just as clearly. The same question again:

DO YOU WANT TO SEE?

"Yes," Alexei whispered.

Veins of black shot into the gray matter. The inkweed was changing it, shaping it like an artist with a lump of clay, sending signals to its microorganisms to reformat the internal structures after its own design. But Alexei hardly took notice of the changes, for suddenly it felt like an icepick had been driven into his skull.

Too late he realized whose brain they had been viewing. Far too late; he had told the inkweed that he wanted to see, and it was going to let him *see*.

The pain only lasted for an instant. When it vanished Alexei hung there in the nothingness, gasping with his nonexistent lungs, wondering what it had done to his head.

And then the dam burst open, and the flood took him.

He was with everyone and they were with him; there was no other way of describing it. Voices rushed to greet him -- not the torrent of nonsense he'd experienced earlier, but human voices, overlapping and yet each one clear and distinct. And they were all welcoming him, embracing him, calling his name.

"Alexei!"

"You're here! you made it!"

"Welcome!"

"Another one! welcome, comrade!"

"Join us!"

"Come in, come in!"

He could have wept. It was too much to take in at one time; there was no physical body remaining to defend his soul, nothing to hide Alexei from the deluge of love and acceptance. It washed through him and left him shivering in its wake, naked, defenseless.

The inkweed watched from above, satisfied, as Alexei was carried along by the waves. Allowing these communications to flow freely was only the first step on a long journey, it knew. The inkweed was looking ahead to the glorious future of this infant superorganism, as a unified and harmonious Mind, almost identical to the concept that Alexei knew as 'God'.

The inkweed would link the minds of the bipedals together with even stronger chains, blending their thoughts and memories together until they were all one and the same, each one seeing what the others saw and feeling what the others felt, until there could be no more conflict and no more misunderstanding. It would elevate them until they had reached true, perfect, eternal awareness, forever to be --

" -- wait," Alexei cried.

All at once the voices stopped. He regretted it for an instant, but then understanding came: he hadn't silenced them. He had merely closed his "ears", switching off his ability to hear them. The voices were still there, below the threshold of his hearing, the comforting murmur of an underground river.

A dazed Alexei allowed himself to drift upward, his mind still quivering with all it had just experienced. Presently he found himself back into the cosmic abyss, revolving slowly among the stars.

A single white sun was already flaring into existence, shaping itself into one symbol:

?

Alexei wondered if it were possible to insult this alien. He hoped it wasn't. "Sorry..." he murmured.

Two more suns:

???

"We...I mean, I..." It felt like he hadn't spoken in years. Who was he, anyway? could he even remember correctly? He seemed to recall that his name was Alexei Nikolaevich Raikov, but that might have just been a character in a book he had once read.

And now that the voices had been hushed there was nobody he could ask; he was alone again. It was just him and the stars and this massive alien intelligence, the consciousness that spanned the inkweed and the blight and also a black gelatinous blob inhabiting an alien ocean. If it wasn't God it might as well have been.

Alexei tried again. "We...I mean, I'm grateful to you, very grateful, for what you've done for me...and for everybody, but...I mean, I don't want to...have everyone melt into the same thing."

The question marks vanished. In their place there came a single word:

*WHY?*

Well, it was a valid question. And Alexei knew why he didn't want to fuse with the rest of humanity...he just couldn't quite put it into words. He was starting to see that it was less a fear of losing his identity, and more a fear of losing his friends. Or of losing whatever had made them his friends in the first place.

Yuri had been the only one at the Lubukov Agricultural Labs who had ever really talked to him; but if humanity had all shared the same mind, Alexei would have spoken to everyone. Yuri would have been...well, what? the same as everyone else, most likely, with the same thoughts and desires and memories.

But how to explain this to the inkweed? It thought of humans the way Alexei thought of his fingers and toes -- as part of something greater, useless without their connection to that higher consciousness. It was the group-mind of humanity that the inkweed was trying to contact, reaching out across the galaxy for that single spark of higher awareness, the only one it had found in all of its travels.

"I am not you," it had said, and marveled over that fact. Because the only other intelligent thing the inkweed had ever known was itself. It *was* alone, in a way he couldn't possibly fathom, and had journeyed across the galaxy to find something other than itself.

And then clarity struck him.

"Because we'd become *you*," Alexei told the alien.

There was no reply. But Alexei felt he had the right idea and so he went on, his voice growing louder in the empty reaches between the stars. "If we melt into each other and everyone's thoughts are the same, we'd turn into you. Or something a lot like you. Maybe not right away, but eventually. And you don't want that, do you? a mirror-image of yourself?

"...You can duplicate yourself already, but you didn't, because that's not what you want. You want someone different than you, someone you can talk to. And we can do that -- we can talk to you -- but not if you put us all together in the same brain. Because then we'd just be a duplicate of you, and then...you'll be alone again."

It struck him as funny and perhaps a little ridiculous that he was telling this unfathomably powerful alien what it wanted, daydreaming that he could even begin to psychoanalyze something so inhuman. He mentally crossed his fingers that he'd given the right answer, or at least that he hadn't doomed his species to annihilation by insulting this extraplanetary consciousness.

The reply was a long time in coming. *I CAN WAIT*, the blazing suns told him. *I HAVE TIME.*

Alexei was still puzzling over the alien's response when the stars began to go out. They winked out of existence one at a time, slowly at first, then accelerating until it seemed like a wave of darkness was rushing across the face of the universe.

Alexei panicked, but before he could scream a sudden pressure descended on his back and chest. It felt like he was being squeezed, and the sensation alarmed him until he remembered what it was.

The thing pressing down on him was gravity; that was what it felt like. And his arms and legs felt so heavy because they were *his* again, reattached to his mind after a long absence. And if he was back in his body now, that meant he could --

Alexei opened his eyes.

Yuri was still there, sitting next to him on the bed, watching his face. He grinned broadly when Alexei looked up at him.

"Congratulations, Lyosha."

Alexei gurgled something incoherent and tried to push himself up from the bed. "Whoa, whoa, careful there." Yuri held him down. "You've been out for a while; take it easy."

Having to draw oxygen into his lungs again was a novelty to him, and Alexei lay there just breathing and collecting his scattered marbles for a good minute. The room around him began to look more familiar -- there was the old poster, the clean blankets, the cement walls. He was still where Yura had brought him, down in the shelters below Khostok.

"...how long?" he croaked.

"Oh, about fifteen minutes, give or take." Yuri paused, then burst into laughter at Alexei's expression. "Really! It just feels like forever while you're in there."

'Forever' was not quite adequate. Alexei looked up and saw the inkweed hovering over the bed, its blossom open, the eye at the center regarding him steadily.

"Did I...make it mad?"

"Hardly!" Yuri glanced up at the flower. "It doesn't really get 'mad', I don't think." He chuckled. "Besides...I told it the same thing, and I don't think it got 'mad' at me, either. It just keeps saying it's going to wait."

"Huh? you told it what?"

"Oh, that I didn't want to become part of a collective consciousness. I think most people said the same thing...though I haven't heard anyone explain it as well as you did." Yuri was still smiling.

Alexei blinked at him. "You were...listening?"

"Ah, yeah, you could say that."

"...how?"

"Hmm..." Yuri scratched his chin, thinking. [*Well,*] he said, and all at once his voice was in Alexei's head, whispering. [*I think the organism wanted us to keep our 'presents'. I think it's still expecting us to merge into a collective at some point.*]

Alexei blinked again. " -- how are you doing that?!"

[*You can do it too, Lyosha. You're integrated now.*] Alexei felt something give him a mental nudge. [*Go ahead and try it.*]

Alexei clapped both hands over his skull. [*ARE YOU INSIDE MY HEAD?!!*]

Yuri winced. [*Yes! but no need to shout; I can hear you just fine.*]

And Alexei could hear him too. He touched his mouth, trying to grasp that he was talking without moving his lips.

[*Like I said...it still wants to help us, even if we're not going to merge. It's been helping us all along.*] He gave the inkweed a bemused look. [*I think it's just glad to find something it can communicate with, even if we're not as 'sentient' as it is.*]

Alexei remembered the starry void and the loneliness he'd sensed from the thing.

[*We'd never have been able to save so many people without its help,*] Yuri went on. [*But once the blight victims got past that 'transitional' stage and became integrated with the organism, they could hear us -- that's how we were able to send out the messages for people to get to the river.*]

[ *-- the river!*] This time Alexei managed to sit up in bed. He was weak and a bit dizzy but otherwise felt fine. [*Were* you *the one telling people about the river? because we kept hearing about --* ]

[*That was me* and *the others,*] Yuri clarified, steadying Alexei with a hand on his shoulder. [*When the first CSF soldier became integrated we found out about Operation Starlight. That was why needed everyone in the city to get down to the river valley -- we had to pull them all into the shelters before Starlight hit. Luckily a lot of people integrated spontaneously when* their blight got severe and their microorganism count went high enough; that's what happened to me and to Veronika. The others, well...we had to help them integrate.]

Perhaps it was some side-effect of linking minds, but Alexei knew what Yuri meant when he said that they were 'helping' people. [*That was* you!] he said, bristling a little.

[*When?*]

[*In the penthouse!*] Alexei cringed at the memory. [*You -- you were one of those things! you stabbed me!*]

Yuri looked adequately ashamed of himself. [*Yeah.*]

[*Why?!*]

[*I wanted to make sure you got here,*] he explained with a little shrug. [*Giving you the blight meant we could track you, and you'd start hearing our broadcasts eventually. Besides...if you got wounded, or if you'd still been aboveground when the bombs came down, the blight might have saved your life...like it saved mine.*]

Alexei shook his head. [*You still didn't have to do that.*] he said heatedly. [*You could have just...I don't know, told me what was happening.*]

[*Would you have believed me?*]

Alexei thought about it before he answered. [*...maybe not,*] he admitted.

Yuri was smiling again. [*And I did tell you, Lyosha...remember your dream?*]

Alexei remembered. [*Besides,*] Yuri added, [*I told Lena too. I thought you might listen to her.*]

[*Maybe if you hadn't looked like a monster I'd have listened to you, too.*] Alexei was still sulking.

[*A monster!*] Yuri sounded amused. [*Oh, that wasn't intentional!*]

[*What was it, then?*]

[*Another one of the organism's presents.*] Yuri lifted one arm. [*Watch.*]

Alexei watched. He had a sense of what was coming, but when the glossy blackness flowed down out of Yuri's sleeve and across his arm he still jerked away.

[*It's okay!*] Yuri waved the black arm back and forth in front of Alexei's face, wiggling his fingers. [*It's just a second skin -- like a suit of armor, but very thin. It's made of those microorganisms, of course, so you can control it -- and it heals itself.*]

[*How nice.*] Alexei stayed out of reach.

Laughing mentally, Yuri retracted the armor back into his sleeve. [*It's not* just *protective,*] he said, [*it also boosts all your senses -- you can hear for miles while you're wearing this stuff. And of course it speeds up your reflexes.*] He showed Alexei his arm once more, letting him see that the inky skin was gone. [*And it keeps you warm!*]

[*Not interested.*]

[*Yeah, I know it looks creepy until you're used to it.*] Yuri shrugged. [*We didn't have much of a choice -- even if people could hear us telling them to get to the river, most of them were still locked in the Red Camps and had no way of getting here. We had to go get them -- and if you knew you'd be going up against the Special Forces, you'd want something to protect you when they started shooting at you.*]

This Alexei could understand. [*How many people did you save?*]

Yuri thought about it for a moment. [*There's two and a half thousand people down here, last I checked. Most of the infected made it, including the majority of Red Camp One. We didn't sleep for a few days, but we cleared almost the whole city before the bombs fell.*]

Alexei glanced up at the ceiling, suddenly worried. [*It's okay,*] Yuri reassured him. [*There's air filters built into this place. We're safe down here.*]

[*For how long?*]

[*As long as we need.*] Yuri looked around at the cement walls. [*We're not sure how long it takes for the gas to disperse -- some people say a couple days, others say it might take weeks. But we've got food and water and space enough for a while yet...at least until we decide what to do with ourselves.*]

[*This place can keep that many people for weeks?*]

[*We've got enough food for* months, *if we need it -- you're forgetting who built the place.*]

Alexei hadn't forgotten. [*And won't someone come looking for us?*]

[*Already did. We saw their helicopters.*] Yuri looked smug. [*They used thermal imaging to look for survivors, since most of the dead should've been indoors. No heat signatures, no survivors. I don't think they'll be back until they feel like rebuilding the Volgin River Bridge, and that probably won't be for a while. Remember, they think the city's contaminated.*]

[*Contaminated.*] Alexei snuck another glance at the inkweed, watching them through its inscrutable alien eyes. [*That's kind of true.*]

[*But it's a good kind of contamination.*] Yuri rose to his feet. [*Can you stand?*]

Alexei drew his legs up and swung them over the edge of the bed, the inkweed sliding away from his ankle. The black stains had faded from his leg and from his side as well -- he looked as if he'd never caught the blight at all. All that had changed lay within him now, felt but not seen.

He stood. The left ankle was as strong as the right. "Whoa," he said aloud.

[*Excellent*.] Yuri looked away. [*Thank you*.]

[*YOU ARE WELCOME*.]

Alexei turned sharply towards the inkweed, but Yuri was already leading him out of the room. [*C'mon, Lyosha*,] he said. [*Let's go meet the others*.]

They were halfway down the corridor when it started. Suddenly it was like walking into an ocean of voices, warm waves of laughter breaking over their heads, washing through them. Alexei gave Yuri a look and the older man squeezed his hand.

[*It's okay*,] Yuri said. [*They're expecting you*.]

And surely enough they were. [*Lyosha*!] cried a high-pitched voice, and an instinct stronger than any premonition told him exactly who it was.

[*Lena*?] asked Alexei. [...*is that you*?]

[*Yeah*!] Elena replied. Alexei could feel her presence cuddle up beside him and it was more unmistakably Elena-like than her own face. It was like he'd only ever seen photographs of the girl, mere pictures, and now they were standing face-to-face for the first time.

[*You made it*!] someone else called out.

[*Nikita*!] Alexei was recognizing them more quickly now, learning to trust his new senses. [*You're okay*!]

['*Course I'm okay. The others are here too -- did Yura tell you*?]

Before Alexei could answer another presence surged out of the ocean of voices, cresting the waves like a mermaid. As it reached him it gave Alexei something like a kiss -- a quick touch of intimate contact, just enough to make him physically blush.

[*V-veronika*?]

[*Call me Nika*,] she said, and her laughter was like sunlight flashing from the water. [*Tanya's here too! come say hi*!]

[*I'm already here*,] Tatyana said gruffly. Now that they were connected Alexei could sense the warmth behind her aloofness. It seemed so obvious; he must have been blind never to have noticed it before.

[*Now everyone's here!*] Yuri could barely contain his delight.

[*Wherever 'here' is,*] Tatyana remarked.

But Alexei knew; they all knew. 'Here' was the river, and it was their home.

**- THE END -**

## EPILOGUE

It was a bright sunny day, cloudless and blue, and perfect weather for a picnic.

Alexei lay stretched out on his side on the blanket. He'd eaten two of their roast beef sandwiches and was feeling fine and lazy. Yuri had eaten three and had promptly rolled over to take a nap, his arm thrown across his face to block out the sunlight.

The view from the mountains was magnificent on such a clear day. They'd chosen a place high up on a mountain ridge for their picnic blanket, just inches from the edge of the cliff, and from this vantage point the entire city of Khostok was spread out below them like a handcrafted scale model of a town.

All the old landmarks were there -- the Labs, the hospital, the amphitheater. Far away to the south the remnants of the old Volgin River Bridge lay like broken matchsticks in the river valley, with the thin silver line of the new temporary bridge perched perilously over the water. To one side of the bridge Alexei could just make out Dmitri's crashed car half-sunk in the water, corroded orange with rust and time.

"They still there?" Yuri asked sleepily. Must not have been napping after all.

"Let me see." Alexei squinted down at the city. He swept his gaze up and down the city blocks until it landed on the little pink ants they'd seen earlier. There were two of them down there, poking around in the overgrown streets, wending their way around chest-high weeds and the cracks in the broken asphalt. Even at this distance he could still pick out the colorful clothes and expensive shoes that marked the two explorers as Americans.

"Yeah, but they're headed back to their car now."

"Still think they're tourists?"

"They didn't bring anything but cameras," Alexei replied. "Tourists or journalists."

Yuri chuckled. "One's bad as the other."

The ants hopped back into the green beetle that had brought them. Not a military vehicle; that meant they'd entered the exclusion zone around Khostok without an escort and therefore without the consent of the Chorman government. In theory it was possible to obtain permission to venture into Khostok, but in practice Alexei knew just how likely the administration was to grant that permission to capitalist foreigners.

Alexei watched the little green vehicle roll back across the bridge, headed south to Byatin. The American thrill-seekers hadn't gone more than a mile inside the city limits; certainly not far enough to reach the northern edge of the city where the mountains lay, and nowhere near the forests that blanketed the feet of that mountain range.

Still Alexei was uneasy. Yuri could tell, and with a yawn he rolled over onto his stomach.

"Don't worry."

"I'm not worried," Alexei told him.

"'Course you're not." He shaded his eyes as he peered down at the city. "Look, they're gone already."

"But they'll be back. Or someone else will."

"Naturally." Yuri smiled at him. "But we'll deal with that when it happens, right?"

"Right."

Yuri climbed back to his feet again, stretching luxuriously, and bent to retrieve their picnic basket. Alexei got up as well, rolling their blanket into a long bundle and slinging it over his shoulder. Both of them paused for a moment, basking in the sunlight.

And then they began to change.

Something like black ink began to flow down out of their sleeves, up from the collars of their shirts, soaking through their clothes. Alexei held his breath as it crept up over his face -- it was unnecessary, as they could breathe quite easily through the armor, but he had never gotten over that habit. In moments the shiny stuff had coated the two of them from head to toe in a glossy second skin.

Two black triangles jutted out from Alexei's shoulderblades. His wings unfurled with a snapping sound, catching a gust of wind that sent him stumbling back from the cliffside and nearly made him drop the blanket. Each wing had narrow reinforcing ribs running through it, like the wings of a bat, and the black skin between the ribs was thin to the point of translucency.

Standing side-by-side on the edge of the cliff, wings outspread, the two creatures exchanged looks.

[*Ready*?] asked Yuri.

[*Ready*,] Alexei replied.

They leapt from the cliff at the same time, twin shadows streaking across the face of the mountainside as they made their spiraling descent. The trees at the foot of the mountains concealed the little village of hand-built houses from aerial view but the two of them knew by instinct where they were. They could feel the pull of the others in the village, reaching out across the open space, calling them home.

Folding their wings close to their bodies, Alexei and Yuri plunged in between the treetops and let the forest swallow them up.

~~~~~

17572340R00226